CW01501027

Glory Beckons

The fans of Rifleman Sharpe will love this story. Where a heroic French Marshal, an idiosyncratic English General and a disgraced Etonian playboy are fated to meet and meet again during the Napoleonic Wars. The searing heat of the Peninsula, the frozen wastes of Eastern Europe and the boudoirs of France come to life in this historical adventure. Thoroughly researched, based on the real lives of its heroes. Ney, Wilson and Bruce are the bravest of the brave, in the bedroom and on the battlefield.

—*Major General Julian Thompson CB OBE*

THREE MEN IN A WAR

BOOK I

Glory
Beckons

With Best wishes

Jean Baveystock

JEAN BAVEYSTOCK

Troubador Publishing Ltd
Unit E2 Airfield Business Park,
Harrison Road, Market Harborough,
Leicestershire LE16 7UL
Tel: 0116 279 2299
Email: books@troubador.co.uk
Web: www.troubador.co.uk

ISBN 9781836282112

British Library Cataloguing in Publication Data.
A catalogue record for this book is available from the British Library.

The manufacturer's authorised representative in the EU for product safety
is Authorised Rep Compliance Ltd, 71 Lower Baggot Street, Dublin D02
P593 Ireland (www.arccompliance.com).

Printed and bound in Great Britain by 4edge Limited
Typeset in 11pt Minion Pro by Troubador Publishing Ltd, Leicester, UK

Cover design by Rob Page

The entire world, for eleven momentous years,
was under the influence of one man.
David Chandler

This novel is dedicated to the memory of
Dr. David Chandler
&
Professor Richard Holmes,
who between them ignited my passion for the
Napoleonic Era and introduced me to
Sir Robert Wilson,
Marshal Ney
& Mr. Michael Bruce.

CONTENTS

Glory is fleeting but obscurity is for ever
Napoleon Bonaparte

FROM THE AUTHOR

History is often too good to be true. Especially when it is true.

Nearly three decades ago over a lunch table, I discussed Napoleon's Marshals with the late Dr. David Chandler, at the time one of the world's leading experts on the Napoleonic era. Marshal Ney, with his glittering career and subsequent downfall, as well as sex appeal and obvious red hair, with temper to go with it, sounded very appealing.

On further research I discovered he had met up several times, on opposing sides obviously, with an idiosyncratic English General, Sir Robert Wilson. Reading Wilson's journal, he mentioned bumping into a young dissolute Etonian, Michael Bruce, in Stockholm and becoming friends. I found Bruce to be another intriguing personality.

So, I began to write a novel about my three heroes, based on their lives and times. Fortunately for me, there is a huge amount of contemporary material: letters, journals, despatches, autobiographies, books. Wilson himself kept an almost daily diary. All the characters lived, including their named servants.

The novel started as one but has since become two. "Glory Beckons" begins with the Emperor's Coronation in 1804 and ends just before the Invasion into Russia in 1812. The sequel, "Fleeting Glory" covers the disastrous Russian Campaign, Napoleon's first abdication, and onto the aftermath of Waterloo, 1815. The eleven most incident packed years of the Napoleonic era.

As a Vintner, I travelled extensively all over Europe including Russia, and the Waterloo battlefield. Visiting many of the Napoleonic sites described in the novels.

Now retired, I live in Hampshire with my three working Golden Retrievers and my extensive Napoleonic library.

The French Revolution shattered the European order. Emperors and kings whose dynasties had ruled for centuries suddenly feared for their thrones. When a host of neighbouring nations allied against France, intending to restore the old regime and the deposed French King, Louis XVIII, the resulting war united the new Republic and galvanised its fighting spirit.

Following the execution of the former King, Louis XVI, came the Reign of Terror, a spasm of anarchy, massacres and public executions that ended when a military triumvirate, including the dashing Napoleon Bonaparte, emerged to restore order and competency.

A bloodless coup d'état first made Napoleon effectively a dictator for life. Worries about him needing an heir led ultimately to his self-coronation as Emperor, an absolutely stunning act of political theatre and hubris.

And so began the Napoleonic Era, the fourth and final stage of the French Revolution, a time of war, a time of glory.

PROLOGUE

BOULOGNE, FRENCH CHANNEL COAST

MARCH 15TH 1812

He made love to her with insatiable frenzy, on a lumpy mattress in a chilly billet, while rain and spray dashed against the window panes. Trying to forget in his passion the Emperor's disfavour, the fiasco of his marriage, the likely end of his career.

The house was a far cry from his accepted lifestyle. The grand château at Coudreaux he owned, or his magnificent town houses, one for her, in the best Parisian quarter. Bought and paid for with the rewards of his glittering career. He had always been welcomed in splendid European palaces too.

The last time he had been in Boulogne, six years earlier, he'd been poised to lead the invasion force that would crush the English once and for all, march on London. Then he had lived far better than this. A splendid château by the sea. Sometimes a glimpse of the famous white cliffs of Dover.

Not now. Not here. Here, some miles inland, the candles guttered in the breeze that whistled through the open cracks. Brown stains on the ceiling, as intricate as plans of battle, betrayed the positions of hidden leaks in the roof. The chimney blew back smoke and soot into the room when the wind was from the south. The rugs and curtains were faded and dirty.

A life of service to France and *this* was his reward. Once, the people had called his name in the street, louder even than they called the Emperor's. Remember the Coronation.

For the first time, it occurred to him this adulation was what might have been festering at the back of the Emperor's mind all these years. These feelings directed the great man's mood, when he had to decide what to do with his errant Marshal. A national hero, who had had the temerity to outshine the chosen appointments made for him. Prove his, the Emperor's, decisions wrong – and then, even worse, bring it all to the Imperial personal attention. What do you do with such a man? You give him a job that once would have guaranteed that man all the glory he could ask for – command of the invasion of England.

Only, no one now believed the invasion would happen. French troops were never going to cross the Channel. Too much time had passed, too many opportunities been wasted...

...By the Emperor, amongst others.

Boulogne was a forgotten back-water.

But she didn't seem to mind being here, unlike his wife. Not even the lumpy mattress. It allowed her to straddle him and push and hold and take her time, grip him inside her, slowly work down the way she knew he liked it. Candlelight flickered on the sweat under her breasts as she rode him. Yes, he liked it. *No, he loved it*; how he had missed her. Her oriental perfume. The loud ecstatic noises she was making. The thrusts. He teased her nipples with his teeth.

Three times later, he lay back exhausted. And she fell beside him, snuggling up against his shoulder, drawing the covers over them both.

'So, where the devil have you been?' he spoke at last, trying to put a gruff tone in his voice but hardly succeeding.

'Vienna.'

'And who is in Vienna?'

'The man who sold me the dress you've just ripped off. You've probably ruined it.'

'I have been writing letters to you.'

She pursed her lips. 'And I came post-haste when I did receive them. My lazy major-domo, he failed to send them on. He will be dismissed immediately on my return to Paris. I told him before Vienna, I would be taking the waters in Baden, then I went to visit friends in the south. As I said, I came as soon as I received them. Anyway, I thought you were still in sunny Spain.'

'Bloody Spain, more like it.'

'So, did you lose your rag again, my impetuous Marshal?'

He drew in a breath, ready to protest. Let it out again. He never lost his rag, despite his flaming red hair. He had always known exactly what he was saying.

But not everyone saw it that way, especially his fellow Marshals, and it was probably not a point worth making to her.

'Is that why you are languishing in this godforsaken place?' she went on, with a perplexed frown. 'I could hardly believe it when I heard you were back here. I just had to come to see for myself. It certainly can't be described as a rich command.'

Her voice went up slightly at the end, turning her statement into a question. He cocked an eye sideways at her, smothered a grim smile. Of course. She did love him, in her own way, but she also wanted to know. *Was he on his way up, or was it all down from here?*

If the latter, he wondered what alternative plans she might have made.

'It is still a command, and it will pass. I am being punished for telling the Emperor the truth. The war in Spain. There can never be a French victory.'

'I know, my Marshal. You have said so, many times.' She caressed his thigh. 'I'm back now. I truly want only you in my bed. I was worried, with all this weight on your mind, that you would have forgotten all about me. The little things I need to keep myself always ready for your love.'

'You mean, a house, a carriage, a wardrobe, new jewels; that would make my wife insane with jealousy if she happened to see your Parisian lifestyle?'

'Oh! She knows about us.'

'I know. You must have been indiscreet.'

'She gave me that look in the street when I saw her recently. While you were here, far from the Emperor's affections. And she's obviously pregnant again. I hope it's yours, seeing as you are going to have to pay to feed and clothe it as well as me.'

'It *is* mine. She made sure of that.'

'Please don't forget about me, my Marshal.' She rolled over, giggled. 'I am ever so devoted to you and would be broken hearted if anything happened to you.'

He smirked. 'Not to worry, I will do something brave to make the Emperor love me again. Keep you in furs.' He kissed her, a lover's kiss, not a passionate one. Her lips were swollen and oh so soft.

She had been with him three days, and nights. Unrestrained sex like he'd never imagined, even with her. It was early evening. They were tightly locked on the lumpy mattress. He was teasing her, bringing her almost to climax then pulling away. Never fully intent – a soldier could not afford to be – he thought he heard a pounding of hooves outside.

He put it out of his mind, turned his attentions back to her – until he heard the footsteps on the creaky stairs. She heard them too. He felt the immediate tension in her body.

Shortly, there was a quiet knock on the door. They glanced at each other, and she nodded, resigned. She knew where even she stood in the scheme of things.

It was his steward with a document pouch. He dismissed the man, closed the door, tore it open. Read it.

Read it again.

She rolled on to her front and pouted up at him, chin resting on her hands.

'Well?'

He raised his eyes to meet hers, and slowly smiled.

PART 1

NOTRE-DAME

Accept First Consul General, the Imperial Crown.
People of Paris

PART I

NOTRE-DAME

CHAPTER 1

As Napoleon picked up the laurel-shaped gold crown, his hands trembled.

Marshal Ney had been looking out for that tremble, the shake of those hands. It was more than the freezing air of the cathedral. He hoped against hope that for once Napoleon was simply tense, overawed. That there would be no repeat of the scene he had witnessed in Napoleon's office in the Tuileries two months ago. Everyone else might associate Napoleon with victory, or power, or France, but based on his recent meeting with the great man, Ney associated him with seizures.

From his place high up on an elevated wooden stand, Ney's eyes had been fixed on Napoleon's hands as he stood at the foot of the steps in front of the altar. The thousand onlookers and well-wishers, anyone who was anyone in France, held their breath, all waiting for the Pope to crown the Emperor and, after that, the Empress. The whole congregation stood. The silence in the vast cathedral was absolute.

Ney, though, could not stop thinking about those nervous hands. How a mild tremor might become a shiver across the shoulders, then a shake of the head Napoleon would not be able to hide, a full-blown fit under the eyes of France, the eyes of the world. Ney's concern was making

3

him anxious. He was stood alongside the rest of the newly created Marshals and their wives. He just couldn't keep his feet still, his shifting boots causing the board they all stood on to vibrate. His wife, Aglaé, at least had noticed. She attempted to gain his attention by tugging at his sleeve, looking up at him with a worried frown.

Napoleon's hands were definitely shaking. Shaking like Ney had seen them shake before. They shook all the while he stood in front of the high altar. It was as if Napoleon was paused, hesitant, suspended until a seizure would overwhelm him.

Finally, though, with his mantle of purple velvet peppered with golden bees thrown over one shoulder and his toga billowing, he strode up the steps, completely ignored the startled Pope and swept past him, up to the altar.

Ney breathed a huge sigh of relief, then tried not to gasp when he realised what was about to happen. The Pope was supposed to crown Napoleon Emperor. His Holiness had been summoned here all the way from Rome to make the whole ceremony proper in the eyes of God.

Under the eyes of God, Napoleon lifted the golden wreath high above his head.

He turned to face the freezing congregation jammed into Notre-Dame.

Gradually, gently, Napoleon lowered the wreath onto his own head.

Ney's gasp was now so loud he feared he might be embarrassing himself in front of his peers. Surely this shockwave would now sweep out to the crowds surrounding the cathedral and across snowy Paris, then over all of Europe. Aglaé, though, was gasping as well and so too was Marshal Soult, one of the biggest – if not *the* biggest – arseholes in Europe, who, somehow, with his Prussian bitch of a wife, had ended up seated next to the Neys. All the other Marshals gasped, Masséna with a particular hiss. The Marshals' wives too. Berthier, two rows down, was not only gasping but was so upright and rigid it looked like he'd just been drenched with ice water.

Everything had changed. Everything. A Corsican nobody, just as humble in origin as Ney himself, was now Emperor. Not only this, but he had insulted the Pope and all he stood for, when he'd had the audacity to crown himself Napoleon I, Emperor of the French.

Napoleon turned then, back to the altar, to collect the little crown intended for Josephine. Ney felt Aglaé touch his hand as Josephine now approached the altar steps. With almost regal grace, she knelt in front of the Emperor. She raised her arms and pressed her hands together in prayer. Aglaé sighed.

Tears fell on Josephine's hands as she looked up at her husband. Casually, almost wearily, as if he had done it a thousand times before, Napoleon slipped the crown behind her diamond diadem and gave it a little pat to keep it in place.

'Such an angel,' whispered Aglaé, 'his angel and ours.'

Aglaé was one of Josephine's ladies-in-waiting. They were friends, too. In fact, it was down to this friendship that Ney had been first introduced to Aglaé. If it were not for Josephine and her matchmaking, Ney would never have entered the now-Emperor's inner circle. He would probably at this moment be leading some doomed expedition to capture a far-distant Caribbean island.

The crowning ceremony was over. Only the secular part of the ceremony remained. Ney was amused to see the disbelief and affront on the faces of the Pope and his cardinals. Cardinal Fesch, Napoleon's half-uncle, looked flabbergasted. The night before, he had married Napoleon and Josephine. The Pope had been in complete shock when he learnt their first ceremony was only civil, thus not recognised by the Church.

Earlier that morning, Fesch had led Napoleon up the cathedral aisle, all the while prodded in the back by the impatient Corsican's sceptre. The look on his face at this moment suggested that Napoleon, with his dismissive behaviour, had shown exactly what the new Emperor thought of the Church.

Napoleon's brother-in-law, Marshal Murat, was standing absolutely still. Almost as tall as Ney and with hair that was as dark as Ney's was red, he was head of the Emperor's cavalry and had carried the golden laurel wreath up the aisle on a cushion. He looked somewhat puzzled. His eyes flicked from side to side, as if he were checking everything was real. Probably trying to let it sink in, that the moment they had just witnessed was likely to never again be repeated in the history of the world. It also had to be said that the ludicrousness of Murat's vast ermine cloak and feathered hat was only matched by the theatrical costume worn by Napoleon himself.

The triumphant music from the organ, trumpets and

the massed choirs rang out. The Emperor and Empress, holding hands, processed towards the western end of the great cathedral. Here, the new Emperor would take his non-spiritual vows and make public the promise of his future intentions; how he would lead and govern France and the French people.

The heavy, embroidered velvet train of Josephine's mantle was carried by the three Bonaparte sisters, Caroline, Pauline and Elisa, all of them minxes, according to Aglaé. They had kicked up a big fuss about having to carry Josephine's train today; this was a task for page boys, not the Imperial Sisters. Hortense, Josephine's daughter, and a great friend of Aglaé's since school, made up the quartet. She was hanging on to the back edge, looking so pale that Aglaé turned to Ney, saying she feared the poor lady might faint.

The price of marrying into this family of Corsicans was the rivalry within the clan. Letizia, Napoleon's mother, was absent. Ney wondered if she had failed to realise the importance of the occasion, but surely that could not be true.

But then, she had always disapproved of Josephine, calling her a whore and a Creole upstart to her face. She was too free with her immoral favours when her son was absent, too profligate with the spoils from Napoleon's campaigns.

Lucien, one of the brothers, was not here either. He was still out of favour after marrying someone of whom Napoleon hadn't approved. This didn't seem very revolutionary to Ney. People should marry those best suited to them. It was no one's business otherwise. Then again, who was he to comment on such matters? After all, hadn't his own been a political marriage?

Aglaé held tightly onto Ney's hand as they followed the others, stepping down off their stand. It was such a relief to be moving again, after sitting and standing still for hours and hours in the cold, all through the interminable masses and hymns. Ney relaxed his shoulders, kicked his feet, longed for this to be finally over, so he could take off his tight-fitting dress uniform.

'Whatever was the matter with you, Michel?' Aglaé whispered. 'Is it too much to ask for you to stand without fidgeting, during an Imperial coronation?'

'My uniform collar's too tight, and it itches like buggery.'

The uniform didn't itch. He just couldn't tell her his fears, let alone that he had once seen Napoleon have a seizure. If this became common knowledge, it would without any doubt destroy his reputation. No one would want a potentially sick Emperor in control of France, let alone in command on a battlefield. But as far as he understood, only he, Berthier and Josephine knew of this. If he confided in Aglaé, she would gossip; she just couldn't keep a secret. Everyone in the court would know by supper, all of Paris by morning. And now Napoleon was Emperor, who knew what the ramifications of that sort of prattle would be.

'Would you prefer to wear a smock?'

It was the sort of wifely remark that he was well used to tolerating. 'I have never worn a smock,' he replied. 'Even you know that.'

Aglaé sniffed in disapproval.

The other Marshals and their wives were positioning themselves directly behind the Imperial couple as they moved down the aisle. Other people were leaving their pews and filing out into the nave, to follow the procession towards the last part of the ceremony. Packed together, everyone crept forwards with birdlike steps.

Taller than most, Ney could just about make out Napoleon's golden wreath receding into the further gloom of the cathedral. It was almost unbelievable. Napoleon was now Emperor. Hopefully this meant some advantages for him and Aglaé and their two young sons, one only a few months old.

But it seemed the Revolution to which Ney owed everything, including his patriotic loyalty, was over, finally. The Revolution was supposed to have put the old lifestyle aside, all the court rituals, toadying and rivalries, the French Royal Family, the aristocrats, all the priests. It was never meant to be replaced by another monarchy. The new Emperor's rule, he suspected, whatever was promised, would be nothing less than autocratic.

How strange the swing of time… without the Revolution, he would be overseeing his father's barrel-making factory in Saarlouis, Prussia, if he hadn't already drunk himself to death from boredom. His father had planned for him a safe, dull, dreary, small-town life, arranging employment for him with a local lawyer friend. Eventually, on his father's retirement, he would be allowed to take over the factory.

Just to escape this tedious fate, the young Ney had

realised that he had to join the cavalry, and the French Cavalry at that, not the Prussian. He had risen through the ranks of the Army of the Rhine, from Sous-Lieutenant to Marshal, by courage and cunning in warfare. The accumulation of glory at Mannheim, Winterthur and Hohenlinden. He had come this far entirely by his own merit.

He feared merit was now done. Napoleon had just crowned himself Emperor. He could now demand unquestioning obedience.

The Emperor had been merely First Consul when, some three years ago, he'd summoned Ney for the first time to Paris, to the Tuileries Palace.

Ney hated the thought of Paris, even though he had never been there. Paris was for politicians when he was a soldier. He, of course, knew Napoleon by reputation as the conqueror of Italy, the victor of Rivoli and Marengo. And that he had come to power following the bloody upheavals of the Revolution; he had proved to be the right man to take control of the new France.

He knew very well what Napoleon was up to, lobbying him. Typical Parisian intrigue. It was pretty obvious that Napoleon, nothing to do with soldiering, was intent on breaking up the coterie of the leaders of the Army of the Rhine. He was afraid of men conspiring against him, like Ney's mentor, General Moreau.

Moreau, even if an admirer of Bonaparte's triumphs, was no admirer of his acquired pomp and power. So wanted nothing to do with the group of self-seekers and opportunists from the Army of Italy, who now surrounded the new First Consul – commanders like his brother-in-law, Murat, with his outrageous costumes and feathers.

Ney guessed Napoleon was going to offer him some advantageous promotion to become the First Consul's man on the Rhine. Anyway, a chat with his father before he left had convinced him not to give Napoleon the brush-off. His father hastened to point out that if he made an enemy of Napoleon, now certainly foremost man in France, he might well be dismissed from the army and end up running the barrel-making factory after all. Much better to show his face in Paris then.

He was ushered into Napoleon's office by his Minister for War, Berthier.

The First Consul sat on an ornate chair placed in front of a paper-strewn writing desk, but did not stop dictating to a secretary. It was true what they said of him. He had fat legs and a sallow complexion, as if he never went outdoors. His green velvet coat was overly fine.

As he waited for him to acknowledge his presence, Ney became even more exasperated and fretted about just how much he didn't want to be there. How he preferred being on horseback, in the company of his soldiers, not getting involved with Parisian politics. He liked being known as an original republican and hussar of the old tradition, wearing his hair in a pigtail with a tricoloured sash over his shoulder.

At last, Napoleon stood up. He had to crane his neck to look Ney – at least a foot taller – in the eye.

'Welcome, Citizen General, to Paris, to the Tuileries,' Napoleon said, and then paused. His thumb at his side twitched as if to collect his thoughts. He then strode over to a table where maps were unrolled. No small talk. The First Consul didn't do small talk and very seldom shook hands.

'Let's discuss the Rhine, Ney. What else can we do there?'

Ney stayed put. He realised Napoleon was merely trying to win him over by showing concern for Ney's priorities. For a moment, Napoleon almost seemed to be having a conversation with the papers and maps spread out on the desk. Then there was a rustle of silk behind him.

Just in time, Ney thought afterwards, imagining this awkward pause could have gone on forever. A ravishing dark-haired woman rushed into the room, made it halfway to Napoleon, realised there was someone else there and pulled up short on her heels.

'Oh my, do forgive me,' she giggled, 'I hoped we were alone.'

'Clearly not,' said Napoleon, raising an eyebrow.

'And who is this fine-looking gentleman?'

'This is General Ney, one of the Rhine wonders. Ney, make the acquaintance of my wife, Josephine.'

'*Enchanté*,' said Ney, kissing her hand, suddenly not feeling quite as tense and awkward. She was obviously used to making people relax.

'So, you are one of the Generals keeping our borders in the east safe?'

'*Chérie*,' Napoleon told her, 'Ney is the man who single-handedly took Mannheim for France.'

'Single-handedly?' She sounded impressed.

'Not quite,' Ney said.

'Almost, then?'

'More than almost. He entered the town on his own to see just how easily it could be captured,' said Napoleon.

'Sir, you exaggerate!' Ney said, but he was both surprised and pleased that Napoleon appeared to remember all those details. But then, he was famous for his memory, for facts and faces; he was able to recognise many of the ordinary troops who had served under him and call them by name. Little wonder they were dazzled by him.

Napoleon seemed to vanish into the background, as Josephine took over and Ney experienced a barrage of questions from her. About his family, his opinions on the new Paris, whether he had ever been to the opera, which of the arts he most favoured, the name of his horse and, pryingly, coquettishly, whether he was married, engaged, in love?

Whatever the First Consul had summoned him to Paris to discuss was completely forgotten as Josephine hustled him out, then took him for a tour of the Tuileries gardens. Here she never stopped talking of her love and admiration, almost hero worship, for Napoleon. Ney was beginning to see at first-hand how the Corsican inspired such loyalty, from not just soldiers under his command, but anyone he encountered. Even this enchanting woman. There had to be something extra-special about him.

'You know,' she said, 'you may well be the only person he has ever met who has not wanted something from him. But, for my part, there is something I want from you. I want you to become acquainted with a dear beautiful young friend of mine. I think you might make a splendid pair.

'But before I do, you need to update yourself. No one in Paris has a queue anymore, so you must have that splendid red hair cut and your moustache shaved off as well. And that sash, so old fashioned. Smarten yourself up, then I will arrange the meeting.'

That friend was Aglaé, one of Josephine's ladies-in-waiting. She turned out to be beautiful and refined. A petite brunette with wide-eyes and flawless skin. A curvaceous body to worship.

Almost immediately, they became betrothed. At their wedding at Grignon, her father's château, he'd loved her in her simple white dress and bridal veil, as he in his uniform walked alongside her, under eaves festooned with garlands and chandeliers hung with flowers. The army band struck up in the garden and everyone danced. At Ney's side, at the top table, his new wife fingered the jewelled Egyptian sabre Napoleon had given him as a wedding gift.

In the trees, transparencies had suddenly glowed that spelled out the names of the battles that had made Ney's name: Neuwied, Mannheim, Winterthur and Hohenlinden. Aglaé had squealed in delight. He had kissed her passionately on her lips. The guests had clapped their approval. Ney told himself that he would love her like he loved her today, forever.

Not to be, sadly for them both. He had discovered all too soon that she wanted to spend her life at court, while he wanted to be there as little as possible. She was a sociable animal; he was a solitary one. Of course, divorce was quite out of the question; they would just have to rub along together as best they could. At least there were their two little sons.

The crowd in the nave that followed the retinues of the Emperor and Empress, now stopped inching forwards. Ney and Aglaé paused too, to witness the rest of the ceremony. Two other thrones had been placed on a raised platform over Notre-Dame's great entrance door. There were twenty or so steps for Napoleon and Josephine to climb. Much as Aglaé had anticipated, Josephine tottered her way up, encumbered by her heavy mantle. Then the Bonaparte sisters carrying her train dropped it, in what appeared to be a wilful ploy to ruin the occasion. The weight pulled Josephine back sharply. She could have fallen, or the mantle could have snapped her neck. Napoleon turned his head and barked something. The sisters collected the train, while Hortense almost fell, too. Onwards and upwards, the Imperial couple trudged to their thrones.

The Pope and his clergy, at the far end of the cathedral, went about their lengthy business of replacing mitres, filling thuribles with incense, washing their hands interminably, kissing rings, hems, books, and anything else that could be kissed, before the Pope said yet another Mass.

Ney looked closely. Was Napoleon stifling a yawn? Was he not even bothering to stifle it? He *was* yawning. Yes, he really was. Yawning during High Mass. An example to us all when dealing with officials. That's all the Pope was now: just another bothersome official.

Finally, the Emperor got up to speak, to make oaths to the people and to the soldiers of the new Empire.

'I swear to maintain the integrity of France: to uphold liberty, equality, justice, freedom of worship, and to govern only in the interest of the well-being and the glory of the French people and Empire.'

That unique, inspiring voice, the ring of it, the promises, here in the echoing and greatest church in France, with the assembled celebrated talent of France and all the world listening; despite his reservations, it did send an emotional quiver through Ney.

'*Oh glory,*' he had to whisper. Oh, what glory was to come now Napoleon was Emperor and France was an Empire?

'*Vive l'Empereur!*' the congregation started to chant. '*Vive l'Empereur!*'

The new bell the Emperor had given the Cathedral of Notre-Dame was certainly making itself heard by the time the Neys reached the vestibule of the cathedral and found themselves part of a queue waiting for carriages. Aglaé had been complaining that her feet were freezing. Her thin high-heeled kid slippers had no insulation against the chilly flagstones, when the next wait was clearly going to be a long one.

Everyone who was anyone in the new Empire was milling about, discussing the completely unexpected turn of events. Ney stood to his full height and tried to look aloof, so no one bothered him, only half-listening to Aglaé, who had caught sight of Hortense. Aglaé, dragging Ney behind her by the elbow, went over to talk to her.

'How are you?' she asked, giving her a hug. 'I was so worried about you during the ever-so-long service. And carrying that heavy train. And what a surprise, Napoleon crowning himself! Certainly no one expected that.'

'Well, I knew. Mama told me this morning when we were getting dressed. But I was sworn to secrecy. Napoleon had to tell her his intention so she could be ready when it was time for her to be crowned. The Pope was supposed to do that, too.'

It came as no surprise to Ney to learn it had been preplanned – not a spur of the moment decision. One had to admire the self-belief of the man. Maybe he was right. With Napoleon as Emperor, France could rule Europe.

'How is baby Louis?' asked Aglaé.

Named after his father, Napoleon's brother, Louis was only six weeks old. No wonder Hortense looked so white-faced.

'Louis is not thriving,' she replied. 'I'm really worried about him. And I have one of my headaches. But thank God, I just about managed to stay the course. Mama would not have been very pleased if I had fainted and caused a distraction.'

It crossed Ney's mind, made him smile, that he could imagine if *someone else* had collapsed at the wrong moment and frothed at the mouth, that *would* have caused Josephine the greatest consternation. As well, show the world the new Emperor was only human after all.

'Anyway,' Hortense went on. 'I was determined to show the crass sisters of the Emperor how to behave.'

Aglaé glanced round and sighed. Ney gave her a look and a smile, hoping to reassure her. No one else had overheard and he certainly wouldn't repeat anything said.

'We too have another very young son, as you know,' Aglaé said.

'Yes, when they are older, they can be playmates. And thank you for the loan of this lovely cashmere shawl, it was an absolute godsend. The Cathedral was like an icebox. I see our carriage is ready, so have it back. I am going to try to slip away to be with the baby and take some laudanum.'

As Hortense walked away, Aglaé pointed out that there was breast milk on the shawl. 'And did you see the bodice of her satin dress was stained too?'

Ney grunted. *It would take another mother's eye to notice that*, he thought. Then again, he always avoided studying the busts of other men's wives, especially the wives married to Napoleon's brothers.

He knew Aglaé was such a creature of the court. It came naturally to her, her own mother being a lady-in-waiting to Marie Antoinette – she had thrown herself out of a window on hearing the news of the Queen's beheading.

Then Josephine had stepped in, taken motherless Aglaé under her wing.

Here she was, enjoying looking around at all the notables and celebrities of the new Empire, crowded around the great cathedral's door. Noticing what they were wearing, who they were with: Eugene de Beauharnais, Josephine's son, Hortense's brother - already a capable commander of men himself; Joseph Bonaparte and his wife Julie; Berthier, alone because Napoleon hated his lover, Giuseppa; Masséna, the little monster; Soult and his detestable wife – even Napoleon called her the Prussian Dragon.

With her personal history, it was understandable that Aglaé loved this world. It was just not a world where Ney wanted to belong.

The slightly undignified village-fête atmosphere that had been in evidence this morning when the Neys arrived, was now back, noisy hawkers selling their wares, flogging mulled wine and hot pies. Outside, all of Paris was singing and cheering, with cannons perpetually firing salutes, that to Ney sounded like the din of a battle fought between armies of incompetents.

Napoleon and Josephine had left some time ago but, given the roar that had erupted outside and its duration, it had taken them some time to get away. Knowing Napoleon, he would have made a speech on the steps, promising service and reward, glory and victory in the new war.

For a fair few in the congregation, the Coronation had been an unwanted distraction from the war, now declared against England. Ney himself preferred living in camp, planning the invasion, memorising maps, drilling his men, to standing about in an uncomfortable dress uniform, clapping and muttering pleasantries in the company of courtiers. He could not wait to leave Paris.

A hearty slap on his shoulder brought Ney back to the present moment. Not many men would have the nerve or were stupid enough to lay a finger on Marshal Ney and not expect some sort of reaction.

'Good Lord, what a show, eh?' It was Murat.

His wife, Caroline, Napoleon's sister, had no doubt left with the Imperial couple, leaving him on his own to return to the palace.

'It was something of a display,' Ney answered. Now it was over, the last thing he wanted to do was talk about it. He'd get enough of that at home.

'The hilarious thing was that just as they arrived, I heard Napoleon say to Joseph, "If our father could only see us now."'

'What would yours have said if he'd witnessed you crowning yourself Emperor?'

'Get back in the inn. And yours?'

'Get back in the workshop.'

They laughed together. For all his inadequacies, Murat was always enjoyable company. They were both cavalrymen. Though Murat had come up with Napoleon's Army of Italy and had been with him on his extraordinary expedition to Egypt. Ney had come up in Moreau's Army of the Rhine.

The Rhine was Revolution. Italy was Napoleon. This

accounted for why Ney dressed always like a proper soldier. Murat like a parrot on a horse. Still, popinjay tendencies aside, his bravery and ability to inspire could not be doubted. They would be needed against England.

For months now, the bulk of the Grande Armée had been camped out around Boulogne, in full view on a decent day of the famous white cliffs. Poised to invade England since the islanders had been stupid enough to declare war, after failing in the short peacetime to have Napoleon murdered. The repeated assassination attempts had a bearing on Napoleon deciding to have himself declared Emperor. He needed an heir to succeed him in case the British and their Royalist friends ever managed to kill him. And First Consuls did not leave heirs.

'So,' said Ney. 'Back to the coast after all the celebrations?'

'Wait for the right tide,' Murat said, 'and we shall be ready to embark.'

'The tide turns twice every day,' Ney pointed out. 'Very few soldiers have crossed the Channel.'

'Very few have crossed the Alps.'

Murat must have sensed someone was coming towards them. He turned his head, just as Ney turned his, and noticed Soult trying to barge in on the conversation. Ney stared hard and stood up even taller until Soult, thinking better of it, disappeared back into the crowd.

'You know he's your commander?' said Murat, amused by Ney's reaction.

'Thinks,' said Ney. 'Thinks he's my commander.' He put his hand on Aglaé's shoulder. 'Looks like we are going to get our carriage before we all die in the snow. Do you want to share with us?'

'Thank you, but no. I have my own. Get ready to meet the people, Ney. You know you love them really.'

Outside Notre-Dame, a huge crowd still packed the square, despite the snow, despite the low hanging pewter-coloured sky. Even though many of them must have run out of booze hours ago. The noise had reached painful proportion. Several bands seemed to be playing the Marseillaise all at different times. Cannons fired in the distance. Fireworks burst and showered Paris with colourful sparks.

Aglaé hesitated and seemed suddenly struck, as if frozen, by the glamour of it all. Ney wondered why the throngs were all still here when Napoleon and Josephine had already left, and some time ago. Who were they waiting to see?

'*Vive l'Empereur! Vive l'Empereur!*' the crowd chanted.

Murat strode forwards and with one hand thrust his Marshal's baton at the sky and with the other doffed his feathered hat, swinging it across his thigh as he bowed. For the love of God, this was not the opera. The man was supposed to be a soldier.

Murat bowed three times and then stepped back and flashed his hand, pointing languidly.

'*Marshal Ney, Marshal Ney.*'

'*Marshal Ney, Marshal Ney.*'

'*Marshal Ney, Marshal Ney.*'

Ney's jaw clenched and his shoulders slumped as he realised it *was* him they had waited to see. He gave the crowd a little wave and tried to seek out his carriage at the side of the steps, see if he and Aglaé could disappear. But she, too, was waving, which seemed only to encourage them.

'*Marshal Ney, Marshal Ney.*'

'*Marshal Ney, Marshal Ney.*'

He waved back with added vigour, hoping this would make them stop.

Fame was terrible, a burden. He only wanted glory. *La Gloire.* He wished he could close his eyes, and picture not being here. Not being here with the mob shouting his name. Not being here standing next to Parrot Murat. Not being here on the steps of Notre-Dame pretending to be a celebrity. But being far away from all this hubbub, explaining just how he felt to the only person who understood him. All hot and fulfilled in her bed, his body entwined with hers. His love, his soulmate, his cherished Ida.

PART 2

CAMPAIGN IN THE EAST

The time of Fable is over. The time of History has begun.

Empress Josephine

CHAPTER 2

It was supposed to be a secret, but Ney knew that keeping anything secret here was impossible. Too many interested eyes. Especially when he knew his visitor would appear riding recklessly, astride a horse so obviously borrowed from the Cavalry, dressed in a Cornet's uniform, tailored, of course, to show her full breasts.

So, he had ordered the soldiers, guarding the driveway in front of the château, to wave her through. They were going to be both amused and extremely grateful to see her. Anything that kept the Marshal's mind from yet another drill exercise was to be welcomed.

He paced around the parlour upstairs. Sometimes he stood at the window overlooking the front drive, to check the sentry post, to see if she were here yet. It had been weeks since he had bedded her, or indeed anyone else.

He had, for once, been given a far better billet than Soult. The previous owners had Royalist sympathies so had been bundled out of their château at a moment's notice. It was close to the sea, elegant, large enough to take his staff and give them plenty of office space. Best of all was the main suite. It faced the Channel, its large windows letting in the breeze on the hot August afternoon. In addition to the parlour, there was also one very large bedchamber with a four-poster, one small one and the necessaire

27

together with a marble bath. He had been living here between short visits to Paris since the summer before the Coronation. Meanwhile, he had trained his men, drilled them, prepared them for invasion, in readiness for the conquest of England.

At last, the parlour door flew open.

There she was, the incomparable Ida, tall and slim with endless legs. How he had missed her. His heart thudded. Sweeping her into his arms, hugging her so tightly she protested, he kicked open the bedroom door and flung her onto the four-poster bed.

'You will have to help me undress, Michel. I can hardly summon my maid.'

'That will be my pleasure, *chérie*. Dealing with all those buttons and ribbons will make me feel like I'm unwrapping a present…'

All too soon they were fully naked, endless kissing with probing tongues and gentle caresses. Pressed against her breasts, he could already feel himself coming and began counting in his head the numbers in his Corps – anything to slow the moment. It didn't work, and she was ready, and he was frantic with desire. Finally, she let him inside so he could let go, which he did with a loud shout, taking her with him on a tidal wave of sensation.

Relaxing on the goose-feather mattress in the afterglow, she played with the red curls of his chest hair. He lay with one hand covering her breast, his fingers rubbing her nipple. How he had missed her and her little tricks in bed. And this time she would be his for three precious nights. These nights he knew he could be himself. These coming nights he could confide in her as he couldn't to anyone else. She understood him. These coming nights, he knew, he would be complete.

They both started to talk at once. So much to catch up on since his last fleeting visit to Paris.

Aglaé had come for a visit too, in March. It had been a complete disaster. Ney had hoped that they could possibly rekindle some of the fairy-tale start to their marriage. But this was not to be.

She'd said she had her monthly problems, so had a convenient excuse to keep herself to herself. He suspected it was just that: a convenient excuse. The first night he had cuddled her and had grown hard for her; she was obviously disgusted, pushed him away and sent him off to sleep in the small room. He had never seen her naked. She was always partly covered. He did not know if she even enjoyed sex. She was compliant but never initiated. The weather had not helped. Every day the rain was pouring down and the waters of the grey Channel churned up into white waves.

Her sole topic of conversation was the court production of an opera, *The Magic Flute*, by some Austrian fellow called Mozart. She was flattered, as she had been promised a part in the chorus. Intrigued by the title, hoping at least to be friendly, Ney picked up his own flute and took Aglaé down to the château's music room.

After a few minutes, she gave up playing from her sheet music, complaining the harpsichord was so out of tune.

'Must be the sea air,' she said. 'This does not happen in Paris.'

'Nothing happens in Paris,' Ney replied.

She huffed, lifting her eyes to the ceiling, no doubt trying to pretend she didn't know what he was talking about. The rain on the windowpanes hammered continuously.

On the only afternoon the sun had briefly shone, he took her for a drive – Aglaé didn't ride – along the seashore. To show her where his men were billeted in their neat rows of semi-permanent wooden huts. They had done their best to make them like home. There were freshly dug vegetable beds outside almost every one, ready to be planted. A few chickens scratched about. There was even a family of ducks, the ducklings hurrying after their mother in an anxious line. Ney told her there were some forbidden pigs hidden behind the buildings, but he had decided to turn a blind eye to this. After all, who knew where these men would be sent one day, but wherever it was, they would have to be resourceful, they would have to be cunning and prepared to break the rules.

As their carriage passed, the men, recognising the occupants, saluted and waved. They briefly stopped to speak to some of the men, sitting outside puffing on their clay pipes. The men were deferential but not at all shy. Aglaé in her turn asked questions about their homes and families. As soon as Ney helped her back into the carriage, her smile slipped.

'What horrid men. They stink. Look at my new boots, Michel, covered in mud, absolutely ruined.'

He ordered the carriage back to the château. They sat in complete silence until they almost reached the front door.

She took his hand and very gently said, 'They really are devoted to you, aren't they?'

At least someone is, he thought but did not say, instead muttering something in agreement.

She went back to Paris early, complaining about the long journey, although, as wife of a Marshal, the best lodgings were found for her, as well as the best horses. Ney just had to let out a huge sigh of relief.

So different now with Ida. Her body was not curvy like Aglaé's. She was slim and fit with attractively pert breasts, brown nipples which hardened when he pinched them, long legs and thighs tight from many hours in the saddle.

He knew the prime reason for her displays of affection – they were not really for him but for his position of Marshal. She could boast that her amour was one of the most important men in France, with wealth and status to match. But that did not matter to him. Just that she was there in his bed, giving him sensations he had only dreamt of. She seemed born for his sexual pleasure.

And before they had met, he too, if he could believe her side of the story, had stirred some romantic dream in Ida. She had been the camp follower of Moreau, the General he had served under, before the Empire, after the Revolution, in the Army of the Rhine. Only sixteen, she had been swept away by the lifestyle Moreau offered. She had confided in Ney later that she had never been in love with him, saving herself, as she put it, for '*my grand passion*'.

She had somehow heard of Ney's exploits, probably by reading official reports. How he had taken Mannheim almost single-handed, infiltrating their defences with only a handful of men. How a ravishing flaxen-haired Prussian girl had offered herself to him, imploring him to take her in exchange for him pulling back his men, preventing them from looting her father's farm. He saw the resentment and the hatred in her eyes. Instead of taking advantage, he had told her that if any of his troops did molest her or her father, they would have Ney to deal with. He had never forced himself on an unwilling woman.

Ida started to write to him.

He suspected she had guessed Moreau was about to commit political suicide, foolishly plotting against the Emperor, and, seeing as she was living in a house with a lifestyle completely paid for by the senior General, she had to look for someone else to foot the bills. She inadvertently caused the final rift; she wrote him an even more passionate letter and a mundane one to Moreau, putting them in the wrong envelopes. This was the end of her time with Moreau. Anyway, Moreau was in exile in New York now and it was Ney who was Napoleon's Marshal.

He was somewhat surprised by the pleasure her letters gave him. His replies were far from romantic and less frequent, but hers! There was warmth and a promise in every one.

As soon as she heard he was back in Paris, she invited him with a note to her modest house, on the Rue de Babylone, for their first meeting. He had no idea she would be quite so beautiful: azure-blue eyes with eye lashes exotically long and dark, red pouting lips just waiting to be kissed, the lustrous hair. And tall, long legs, with a slim figure, the contour of her breasts outlined against the green silk of her dress.

Ida had since told him how nervous she was, prowling around the house all day until he appeared. There had been an instant rapport. She was flirtatious, witty and, unlike Aglaé, obviously knew so much about the proper stuff: current affairs and the army. She had been all around the Rhine region, campaigning with Moreau, after all. Soon he felt so relaxed and contented in her company.

Over a glass of wine, he realised quite how much he missed having someone to really talk to, all his friends seemed to be in the military; he could hardly discuss his marital difficulties with them. Apart from the embarrassment, gossip would soon get back to the Emperor and even Aglaé herself. He was simply no longer in love with her, maybe never had been. What was love anyway?

He found himself starting to tell Ida all about his problems at home.

She listened attentively. 'Many people marry for

reasons other than love. You married most probably to please Josephine, but it hasn't done your career any harm. And at least Aglaé doesn't stray like Napoleon's sisters. Always in and out of different beds. Caroline having an open affair with General Junot. Your wife sounds like the perfect court lady, and she has given you sons.'

She kept him waiting for three more evenings, flirting outrageously but keeping him at a distance, the sexual atmosphere crackling between them, until eventually she did take him by the hand and lead him upstairs.

And now she was back again in his bed. Thankfully he did have more than enough money; the rewards from the Emperor were immense. Promotion to Marshal came with it an extra 40,000 francs a year. As well, every so often an appreciative admirer or ally would send him a valuable gift. After Ney's successful diplomatic mission last year in the Helvetian Republic, a Swiss leader had sent him a gold snuffbox studded with diamonds. He could pay all of her extravagant expenses, but she was worth every franc.

The next morning, she asked if she could go for a ride on the beach while he undertook his inspections to assess the readiness of his men before Soult arrived. He lent her his favourite horse, a brown mare called Noisette, a handful for a less-than-able rider. When he came back from his tour of the camp, he hurried up to their room to find Ida struggling to pull down her wet breeches.

'Do give me a hand. It was such a hot day, I took Noisette for a swim and now I can't get my breeches off.'

'Well, there's a first time for everything!'

Between them, they managed to slide the breeches off. It was a struggle, and they collapsed onto the bed laughing. She pulled up his shirt and ran her lips down the thick red hair on his chest, then she went further down, to the curly red hair, taking him in her mouth, worked until he groaned and came.

She sat back on her heels. 'Now it's your turn.'

'You taste so salty,' he said, raising his head.

'Next time I'll sit on an ice cream.'

Later, Ney poured a couple of glasses of wine, and they sat close together on the edge of the bed.

'How was Soult?' she asked.

Ney grimaced. 'Envious of this château. His billet is smaller and further from the sea. He did say he couldn't find any fault at all in the readiness of my Corps, though. He even complimented me on my cavalry. He doesn't really understand cavalry, only infantry. He should never have been given overall command. I know he's busy plotting behind my back, reporting straight back to the Emperor, in no doubt derogatory terms. I don't think he knows you are here, otherwise you would have been mentioned. He still hasn't forgiven me for stealing that girl I told you about in Bonn all those years ago.' Ney laughed. 'It really wasn't my fault she preferred me to his ugly self.'

'I can well understand that. Don't worry, I will never be tempted into his bed,' Ida assured him, joining his laughter and tickling his chest. 'Tell me about Napoleon.

Is he small and stout as the rumour goes and does not look, as you do, good on a horse?'

'He certainly does not look as good on a horse as I do.'

'My Marshal, no one could possibly look as good as you on a horse. But Napoleon, he may not look dashing, but he is one of us, not one of the Bourbons. He will soon lead you into London, even as far north as Edinburgh. How special you must be to be considered a close associate by such a man.'

Ney was silent for a moment. He moved to the window. It was evening now and there were the far-off flickering lights of the massed Army of England. His big secret had weighed heavily on him since the coronation – the horrifying experience he had had in Paris before the event. He had even felt so burdened by it, his great secret, that he considered telling Aglaé. But he knew if he did, it would have been all round Paris, the game would be up, and he might not be stationed here preparing to invade England. Ida, though, would keep it to herself. And she was right there, on the bed, ready and waiting for him to tell all.

He turned back and began to speak.

Knowing how much Ney had researched the best way of shipping horses across the Channel, Napoleon had wanted some sort of update. He had recalled Ney back to Paris. At the Tuileries, Meneval, the Emperor's secretary had ushered

Ney into the Emperor's Cabinet Interior Office. The same office where they'd first met three years before. The same office where the ice between them was given an unexpected, though pleasant, thaw by the incoming and playful swish of Josephine. The room was hot, over-hot, sweaty. Napoleon certainly didn't like the cold. Little wonder the Emperor had enjoyed campaigning in Egypt and Italy. Ney was, of course, in full dress uniform, very uncomfortable, the gold braid round his collar sticking to his neck.

'Ah, Ney,' he said. He looked a little fatter, even more unhealthy.

As usual, they had plunged straight into business. Napoleon never offered any kind of refreshment.

'I am extremely occupied with all the arrangements for the Coronation, but you and I cannot lose sight of next year's objective. Bringing England to her knees. Here, look at these.'

Napoleon strode over to his violin-shaped desk and unrolled two maps, spreading them across the tabletop. As Ney approached, Napoleon reached across the desk to pick up a pair of brass dividers. As he lent forwards, he stopped, his arm suspended in mid-air. He let off a long sigh, then a grunt. Clutching his stomach, his eyes rolled upwards, and he fell to the floor with a thunk, dragging maps and papers down with him. He began to froth at the mouth, his body in spasms, his feet drumming.

Ney stood aghast. Was he was just going to stand there, frozen on the spot, while he watched the greatest military genius since Alexander the Great die. Fitting in front of him. He simply had no idea what to do.

The door was flung open. Josephine was suddenly in the room. She rushed to push a cushion under Napoleon's head, a move that seemed to calm him instantly. His head fell to one side as if he were merely asleep. On her knees, her heels tucked in behind her like a schoolgirl at prayer, Josephine looked up at Ney.

'These seizures return when the Emperor is especially stressed. I hope they will be a thing of the past once the Coronation is over; but, as well, there is this business of the invasion, Michel. He needs to be aware of every detail. He imagines every impossibility. He plans strategies. He has never known failure.'

'Seizures?' Ney exclaimed. 'This has happened before?'

'No one must know, Michel. No one.'

'I understand, Empress.'

Ida sat up, her face both surprised and horrified.

'What does this mean for France? Without the Emperor, who would take command of the army?'

'I can guess who would be first in the queue, that fucking Soult. It would certainly not be me.'

'Do you know if it happens often?'

'I haven't heard a whisper from anyone else, so I can only assume it is a very rare occurrence.' He kissed her hard again. 'You must promise that you will keep absolutely quiet about this.'

'Anything you order, my Marshal, I will obey.'

It was their last morning. They lay naked on tangled sheets, sweaty and exhilarated. There was a firm knock on the door. Ida covered herself while Ney slipped on his robe.

'I ordered that I was not to be disturbed.'

'Important message from Marshal Soult, sir.'

Ney prised off the sealing wax.

'Fuck me. The Emperor has had a complete change of plan. The Austrians are marshalling their forces. The whole Armée is to march to the Rhine. No invasion. The men will be so relieved. No waves, only solid earth. This means you must return to Paris immediately. But will you come to me, later on?'

'Try and keep me away.'

CHAPTER 3

Sir Robert Wilson's pocket watch was always set fifteen minutes ahead of time, so he was the first of the British delegation to arrive. Stiff, stern officials of the Prussian Court were dotted around the room, peering morosely into cups of wine. The conversation was muted. It was a glum lunchtime reception in drab Konigsberg Castle, no sign even of Christmas festivities.

Despite the gloom and chill of the room, he did feel a tiny flicker of hope. He was already bored of being a diplomat, but there must be opportunities here for a man who knew how to take them. Intelligence could be gathered on what the Prussian Government was planning out here. Beaten by Bonaparte at Jena in October, forced into exile on its far eastern frontier, there were surely options to explore. Like how the British Government could give more aid. There was also the possibility of impressing new connections, who might give him the opportunity to get back to proper fighting.

He'd crept in ahead of Hutchinson, his superior officer. Wilson already knew what Hutchinson thought. His report to the Prime Minister could have been written before they left London. Prussia was doomed.

Wilson adjusted his medal, making sure it hung correctly on its red and white ribbon, and gave it another tug. He looked around the room to see who was there. You could not miss the Queen. She was the only lady present who looked like a queen. She was Louise, Queen of Prussia, and as sensationally beautiful as the reports in the British press had led him to believe. Dressed in gold silk, a little older than him and close to his height, her skin was pale and smooth, her hair a rich mahogany brown. She was standing at the window that overlooked the city, the roofs swirling with eddying snow. The Baltic was the colour of pewter in the distance. The clump of grey-coated, elderly courtiers surrounding her seemed like outsized mice, an image that made him smile. He imagined how he would look to her in this company: twenty-nine years old, tall, lithe, brown somewhat-unruly curly hair, his crimson uniform coat a perfect fit, that red and white medal on display.

Wind gusted down the chimney, causing the fire in the grate to flare. She looked up as if to blink away a bright light and her gaze settled on him. Suddenly her attention was not on whatever tale or complaint the little man in front of her was insisting she listen to. She could not take her eyes off of him, that was clear.

Wilson certainly felt more than a spark of interest. He really did want to converse with her. Would she approach him? He was used to court life and knew he had to wait. He did not, however, feel at all out of place in this royal society. And though his German was rudimentary, he had excelled in French at school, the universal court language. He had been brought up in the London court of George III.

His father had been a court painter and thus his playmates had been young princesses and princelings; he was on first name terms with their elder brothers, George, now the Prince Regent, and Freddie, the Duke of York. His father had been the latter's favourite painter, and this connection, to some degree, accounted for why he was standing here now, in Konigsberg Castle, a soldier-diplomat on His Majesty's service. How he'd come to win the medal that hung around his neck, eleven years before. He was under no illusion that it was the medal that drew the Queen's eye.

She was no dove of peace. Wilson knew as much as this. Her husband, King William Frederick, was a ditherer, always vacillating, and tactically inept. Regrettably, although he was his grandson, he was no Frederick the Great; under *him*, the Prussian Army had been invincible.

She was the most vocal member of the Prussian political group in Berlin that had strongly urged the King to ally with the Austrians and the Russians, when they had mobilised that summer against Bonaparte. He'd initially sat on the fence, but after the French at Austerlitz had knocked the Austrians off the board, against all advice, he did declare war on the French. Not waiting until the Russian Army could join them. Well, the Prussian Army had not been defeated for nearly a century and the Prussian Army was far larger than the French. The result? The catastrophic Battle of Jena.

Before the battle, Queen Louise, trying to inspire the men, had paraded in front of them, wearing full armour. They obviously needed more than her inspiration though.

On the day, after a premature and seemingly mad cavalry charge led by Marshal Ney, who started the battle early, the Prussian Army was smashed. Bonaparte rolled into Berlin and his army occupied every western Prussian fortress. The Prussian countryside had been ravaged, all the wheat from the harvest, all the livestock stolen. Leaving the people to starve.

The Court fled in terror to their far East Prussian outpost in Konigsberg. Their last chance for protection from the Corsican ogre was the Russian army, still in the field, had not yet been defeated - the Prussian army being scattered. The rumour was the Russian main force was in winter quarters, not far from Konigsberg. But would *they* be able to stand up to Bonaparte?

Everyone here was just waiting in trepidation. Everyone seemed resigned that Bonaparte, once the weather improved, was going to sweep through East Prussia, defeat the Russians, force the King and Queen into exile, or worse, order their execution. Oppress and partition Prussia according to his whims, then return his attention to thrashing England.

This was defeatist nonsense, of course. Wilson tried to persuade anyone who would listen. While there was a Russian army ready to fight, there was every chance Bonaparte would be sent packing back to Paris, the whole flimsy edifice of his new Europe would start to crumble.

That's what they were supposed to be here for, Hutchinson's party sent from London: to assess how the Prussians were faring; see how the millions of gold Prime

Minister Pitt had been pouring into the war, was actually being spent. There could be no promise of British troops, of course – they were all needed in Spain. It was a dreary, mealy-mouthed mission. He yearned for the war to be his war. He longed to fight again.

Queen Louise rustled through her mousy grey courtiers and made a beeline for Wilson, a more than welcoming smile on her face.

'Your Majesty,' he said, making an elegant bow.

When he straightened up, she fixed him with her lustrous blue eyes, reaching out to hold the decoration hanging under his chin. It was the Austrian Medal of the Order of Maria Theresa, a gilt red and white enamelled cross upon which sat the coat of arms surrounded by the motto *Fortitudini – For Courage.*

'You must be very naughty,' she said.

'Naughty?'

'Wayward then. These are only awarded for disobeying orders.'

'Initiative, Your Majesty. They are awarded for showing initiative on the field of battle.'

'Disobeying orders, I'm sure. Not doing what you're told but getting away with it.'

'It's the outcome that matters most, surely.'

'I know the Emperor Francis of Austria,' the Queen assured. 'He is quite stingy with honours, especially this one. Then again, he is also quite sentimental. Which orders did you disobey to impress him so highly?'

'It's quite a long story, Your Majesty.'

'And who are you? Your red coat tells me you are in

the British Army. But I have never seen this medal worn by a British officer. They are rare enough.'

'Sir Robert Wilson, at your service, Your Majesty.' He bowed again.

'Ah! Sir Robert Wilson, *that* Sir Robert Wilson?'

'You've heard of me already?'

'Your disobedience? No, you sent me your book.'

He had been in Egypt with the British Army during Napoleon's campaign. The book he wrote afterwards recounted in great detail the evil acts the tyrant had committed there. How he had ordered hundreds of Turkish prisoners to be stabbed then drowned; shot was not to be wasted. How he had left his own fevered men to die, callously abandoning them without any food, water, or medical help. Many would no doubt have recovered.

He remembered now that he had sent her a copy. He had sent so many; it was easy to forget where they had ended up. He'd sent one to the Prince Regent and another to Admiral Nelson. He'd even sent one to the Czar of Russia. A brief resume must even have reached Napoleon and recently he had discovered Napoleon wanted him dead.

'And you read it?' he asked, in surprise. He would have thought she would be more interested in gossip than books.

'What else is there to do out here but read?' She frowned, pursed her lips, and tilted her head to the left, all the while keeping her eyes fixed on him. 'Even so, I don't need a book to tell me that Bonaparte is a fiend.'

Just then, she appeared to be staring around Wilson's

shoulder and grimacing at some new arrival. Wilson glanced round too.

'Who is that ghastly looking man?'

'Lord Hutchinson, my commanding officer.'

'Looks as if he's sleepwalking? Appears to me he just doesn't want to be here. Come to the library with me, Sir Robert. It seems we are the only interesting people at this dreary function. I would very much like to hear the long story of how you won your medal, just the two of us.'

'Your Majesty…' He hesitated. It crossed his mind that Hutchinson needed some consideration, reassurance that Wilson was hoping to make an informant of the Queen, not simply recounting his life history.

'Sir Robert, whose orders are you going to disobey, and who is more likely to admire your medal?'

She gestured with her hand. Her footmen opened the door for her. Wilson followed her through, meanwhile trying to give Hutchinson some signal with his eyes, that showed he was still on government business and was not on some solo mission of his own agenda. Hutchinson would assume the latter in any case. He had not wanted Wilson to come to Konigsberg; he had made that perfectly clear on the voyage over.

The library was cold. The Queen immediately had another footman give the fire a vigorous poke and throw on some logs. She sat down on a silk-covered sofa and gestured for Wilson to take the one opposite. She ordered some tea, thankfully not wine.

Now they were face to face, this seemed to have

developed into something of a tête-à-tête and he'd realised that, as well as being a political force in Prussia, she was also bored and restless. Probably looking for fun. He felt himself redden with embarrassment and froze. He might not fear royalty, but he did understand it. Royals expect to get what they want. He was worried that the hot flush he felt in his face was showing, when she got up from her sofa. She sat down next to him and gazed into his eyes. Wilson sat still, even more uncomfortable.

'I need a closer look at your medal, Sir Robert. It looks very heavy. Do you want me to slip it off for you?'

'The room hasn't warmed up yet. Maybe it's not a good idea to start taking things off.'

She put her hand on his knee and squeezed. 'Do you need warming up, Sir Robert?'

He kept his eyes fixed on hers and reached into the inside pocket of his coat. The smaller end of the object in there was cold to touch, but the leather midsection lukewarm. He took it out and extended it to its full length.

'Sir Robert, are you showing me your telescope?'

'It's a very special telescope.'

'It doesn't look like it. Does it have a new kind of lens?'

'I don't think so. My wife gave it to me.'

'Your wife?'

'Just before I left London… She said it would help me see things a long way off.'

'And can it?'

'Your Majesty, it seems cruel and curious that my wife, her name is Jemima, should give me something to help me see, because she, you understand, is losing her sight. Each day her vision becomes more clouded and blurred. Already she cannot really tell if our children are losing their babyish faces and becoming more girlish. She cannot tell if I am the same man she married years ago. When I return from these wars, I will appear the same to her even if my face is scarred. You see, it doesn't matter to me if she can see me or not. She will always be my guiding light. My star. And sometimes when I stare out through this lens…' He put the little telescope to his right eye and blinked his left one shut. 'I imagine I can see Jemima waving on some far-off quay.'

'Oh, your wife is going blind,' the Queen said. 'How tragic for you both.'

'This telescope is already one of my treasured possessions.'

'What else can you see through it? Anything useful?'

'That the major-domo is about to serve us our tea. And I see a chocolate torte.'

The Queen stood up abruptly and hurried to her side of the room.

Tea was served. Torte was cut. Then they were alone again.

She ate a piece of the chocolate torte with a delicate silver fork and took a sip of tea.

Wilson left his cup untouched on the table between them. He waited, pretty certain he would be asked to leave. Then she broke the awkward silence.

'So, come on then, Sir Robert. Now we understand each other better, you can tell me. Whose orders did you disobey?'

Wilson fingered his medal. 'Under whose orders did I display military leadership under fire?'

'If you like.'

'General Otto at Villers-en-Cauchies.'

'You were at Villers-en-Cauchies? That *was* a field of glory. You must have been about twelve.'

'Sixteen, actually. I was a Cornet in the 15th Light Dragoons, my first commission. My first time in Europe. My first time on the field.'

'So, what did you do?'

'I was there. I mean, British cavalry were fighting alongside the Austrians to keep the French out of the Netherlands, a doomed venture considering how the French outnumbered us. Let's be truthful, they were pretty damn near unbeatable in those early years after the Revolution. It was a lost cause.'

'You didn't think it was a lost cause?'

'Oh, I most certainly did. I certainly believed that morning I was going to die. When we scattered a small group of French riders who would no doubt return with force, I knew I was going to die. When we realised we'd ridden ahead by ourselves, we were a mere two squadrons, only three hundred or so horsemen, that had lost the ten other squadrons we were supposed to be leading, I knew I was going to die.

When General Otto, who was an absolute savage, told us that the Austrian Emperor himself was on the field and could well be captured, we knew we had no option but to continue to charge, whatever the odds. All the British and Austrian officers crossed their swords and muttered oaths and prayers. I knew that we were all going to die.'

'Oh dear, Sir Robert. This is such a stirring tale, especially as I can see for myself that you did not die.'

'I so nearly did get into trouble straight away, because General Otto ordered us to take no prisoners. The very first thing I did, during the charge that made our name, was take a prisoner, a French cavalryman, who was wandering about dazed. Another British officer came up to us, shot him point blank through the head, so I didn't get into trouble.'

'He was probably doing you a favour.'

'I told myself when I saw that poor man fall to the ground that I would, in future, not treat any prisoners like that, unless there was a very good reason. In most cases, the defeated are to be trusted, if you show them trust.

'Then we few charged and routed three thousand French infantry, destroying their artillery and their baggage train. We wheeled around in the smoke and the mist, to see that we had succeeded against such odds, I did believe then, that I would live.'

'So, the Emperor awarded you the medal, as he was told you had saved him from certain capture?'

'All eight of the officers were awarded the medal. And we had the honour of being knighted.'

'Such a stroke of luck for one so young at the time.'

'I prefer to think of it as destiny.'

'Our situation here is very grave, Sir Robert.'

'It may seem so, but it is no graver than that of three hundred cavalrymen lost in the mist who, with courage, trounced the best army in the world. We all have that spirit. You, I have heard, Your Majesty, have that spirit.'

Wilson fingered his medal. 'If you regroup, fight alongside the Russians, you will win.'

She didn't look at all convinced. She was frowning. Royalty seldom frowned.

They sat in silence for a few moments.

'Sir Robert', she began, 'trust me, I have met many soldiers, and you do not strike me as the usual type at all, despite the medal and the telescope. The book-writing at such a young age, with such vehemence of argument, makes me think there is something of the lawyer about you.'

'It's strange you should say that. My father wanted me to become a lawyer. He was a painter, painted the people of the English court. In fact, the Duke of York liked my father's work so much that when I met some of the Duke's men on the Ostend packet ship, it was easy to use his name to get an introduction and an army commission. I could not have afforded to buy it, hence...' Wilson brushed his medal again with the back of his hand.

'He stood around all day, my father, at his easel where he painted the portraits of many men who believed themselves to be great. But if you had asked him, he would have said that just wasn't so. Before he died, he gave me three rules to live by. Don't join the army; I would certainly be killed—'

'Which rule you promptly broke and disproved', she interrupted, with a dazzling smile.

'I broke his other two rules.... I married young,

according to him that was a waste of my youth; and I failed to become a lawyer. He so wanted me to make my living using my intellect and education.'

'They are not bad rules, to be fair, for the son of a court painter.'

'My father only portrayed the images of men who pretended to do great things. I always wanted *to do* great things, not just be an onlooker.'

'Like oppose Bonaparte? Oh! Sir Robert, we've heard far too much of that little man getting above his station and crowning himself Emperor. Francis *is* an emperor. Alexander of Russia *is* an emperor. The Ogre is an ill-bred Corsican who has only gained a throne by getting up to his elbows in blood, the very opposite of an emperor. He's going to kill us all if he takes Konigsberg, if he beats the Russians.'

'Your Majesty, I can assure you that will never happen.'

The Queen put her cup back on the table with a loud clink. She raised her hands, palm outwards. She seemed agitated, very worried.

'Sir Robert, in less than two years since his so-called "coronation", the Ogre has subjugated Austria… defeated our armies here in Prussia quite ruthlessly, and in no way looks as if he's going to be satisfied until he has our heads. It is only winter that stands between my husband and the scaffold. Yes, the Russians are holding out, but for how long? Were they not beaten, too, at Austerlitz? And what help is Britain beyond selling us uniform material and muskets for a profit?'

'We destroyed the Ogre's fleet at Trafalgar— that was indeed a victory.'

'What are you going to do, Sir Robert?'

'Your Majesty, I am going to kill or capture Napoleon Bonaparte.'

The Queen's eyes glinted amber in the firelight. She lowered her hands and placed them on the table. She studied him in silence. She looked like she believed him.

Yes, now he had said it, he too believed it. His fate was to kill or even capture Napoleon. He would do this for England, for Prussia, for all of Europe. His name would be written in glory forever afterwards.

'Sir Robert,' the Queen continued. 'It is well known we must decamp very soon even further eastwards, to our fortress at Memel. However, you are not to come with us. You are clearly a man of action, not of the court. I will send you to join someone; I know you will have many common objectives. His name is Hetman Platov of the Don Cossacks.'

In a flash, Wilson's mission had become so much more promising. He bit back a smile. Hutchinson could go to Memel and play the Queen's court games. He would be riding with the Cossacks.

CHAPTER 4

In the courtyard of the Burgomaster's house, Ney was in a furious mood. His blood rose as his axe fell on yet another log. He imagined splitting Soult's face with the blade. In the freezing air, snowflakes the size of a child's fist coiled above the roofs and gables. And, much to the consternation of his staff, guards and his steward, Ney was chopping his own wood.

His guards had tried to stop him. They'd offered to grab a Prussian peasant and have him chop the wood for the fire in the room Ney was using as headquarters. Then they had insisted they would do it for him. A Marshal of France did not chop his own wood. None of the other Marshals would chop their own wood, and some that Ney could mention had probably forgotten how to do so. But who were they to tell Marshal Ney of France what he could or could not do? There was no enemy to fight. The heavy wood would have to take the punishment instead.

Stuck out here, well to the east of Berlin and south of Konigsberg, VI Corps was pretty short of supplies. The common soldiers were half-starved. The land around had already been picked clean before winter arrived. Then men from Soult's Corps had stolen supplies meant for VI Corps. Soult would have ordered them to do so. All to make Ney and his men hungry.

He'd had to send some men out to forage, against the Emperor's direct orders. Maybe, if they found conditions be favourable, VI Corps could also take Konigsberg from the Prussians and load up all that was stored there. If this were to happen, the Emperor would be pleased, surely.

But he'd heard that the Emperor was far from pleased. This was Ney's first campaign under Napoleon's direct command, and he'd already made him enraged. He'd had to send his aide-de-camp, Fezensac, to Warsaw to convince the Emperor that the foraging party was absolutely essential. And no real move had been made against Konigsberg, just reconnaissance.

If all had gone well, Fezensac would be back today. Ney fully expected to be asked to resign his commission, be ignominiously retired. Meanwhile, Soult was having a hell of a good war out here. Soult had the Emperor's ear. There was even a rumour that he might be made ruler of Poland.

Inside now, in the Burgomaster's study, Ney threw some of the wood on the fire. His staff knew better than to accompany him when he was so obviously in a tetchy mood. He poured himself a small tankard of red wine and topped it up with water. The flames in the grate sent a few stray smuts floating up to the air to swoop and curl above the map Ney spread across the table.

East Prussia. It was an old bit of Poland, really, and no more than a network of lakes and pine forest that buffered up against Russia. In the past, it had been a Polish duchy when there had still been a Poland. One of King William

Frederick's ancestors had married into the Duchy of Prussia and conjoined it forever with his principal title, Elector of Brandenburg. Then he'd had to declare himself King *in* Prussia to detach the duchy from the Throne of Poland. It was a short hop from King *in* Prussia to King *of* Prussia, Frederick William.

In the past, the other sovereigns of Europe had laughed at this impertinence; to have used possession of this great frozen puddle to found a kingdom. However, Prussia had now become equal in stature to England or Spain.

Still, a great frozen puddle it might well be, but who held it now would, most probably, win all of Europe. Given that hidden in these pines, somewhere, was the army of Russia under their wily General Bennigsen. The French Emperor's plan had been to wait out the winter in the frosty central towns, then smash the Russians in the spring. VI Corps was supposed to dig in at Niedenburg. Pity there was nothing for VI Corps to eat in Niedenburg. Soult had got there first.

On the map, Niedenburg seemed only an inch from Allenstein. Ney had advanced VI Corps here after Soult's men raided their stores. A gap in the weather then provided an opportunity to send a brigade north to see what they could find. Should they accidentally stray in the direction of Konigsberg, then they might just see how well garrisoned that city was, how likely it could well be taken.

Last year, Magdeburg, that heartland fortress city of Prussia, had surrendered to him without much effort. Frederick William and his interfering Queen had now fled to the town of Memel on the Russian border, their absence providing further encouragement for the garrison of Konigsberg to raise the white flag and surrender.

Still, he was apprehensive, on edge, until Fezensac returned. War was always uncertain. It could go one way or the other, simply because someone mucked up or took some bold brave risk for glory's sake. Random turns of events could have catastrophic effects. Sickness could rip through the ranks. Alliances could collapse. Commanders could die. Heavy snow or rain could fall.

Frederick the Great only survived the Seven Years War because the Empress Elizabeth died, and her army melted back into Russia. Maybe Czar Alexander might die too, then they could all go home, and Napoleon would forget all about Ney's Konigsberg imagined sortie. The Czar was young, popular, new on the scene. Arrogant, too, even for an Emperor. Unfortunately, it seemed he wasn't going to be murdered, as his father had been, anytime soon.

The nub of the matter, it seemed, was the Emperor was holding Ney's few mistakes against him. Allowing them to block out the remarkable feats he had performed on the field, during the last year and a half.

After the combat of Haslach, had he not been vindicated that serving under Murat had been a mistake, that the man had no tactical acumen? *He* had no plan of action. *He* had brushed Ney off when he enquired. 'I make those in the face of the enemy'.

Had Ney not refused to follow his orders, there would have been no victory at Ulm. Murat would have left them criminally exposed. Instead, the Austrians had been trapped against the Danube at Elchingen.

Had he not proved himself when he stormed the bridge there, took the monastery, before personally leading the charge on Michelsberg? Where his infantry overran the defences, so Ulm was laid open.

He knew his VI Corps had done well in the battle. All that drilling they had put in while they waited on the coast at the Camp of Boulogne had paid off. They had even repaired the bridge at Elchingen, before they rode cavalry across it and into glory. All with the Emperor watching, standing on a hill looking down on them.

Undoubted victory at Ulm. General Mack of Austria had surrendered, and with him 26,000 of the enemy, one thousand for each day of the War of the Third Coalition.

Sure, he had not been at Austerlitz, where Napoleon smashed the Austrians, but he had taken the Tyrol and occupied Innsbruck to allow Napoleon a free hand against Vienna.

Most probably it was the impetuous mistake he made at Jena, not waiting for the Emperor's call to advance, that seemed to have left him out of favour. Yes, he *had* disobeyed. Even though the battle had been a decisive victory, afterwards the Emperor had shown his displeasure in no uncertain terms.

That day at Jena.

He often turned it over in his mind, did so again as he put away the map, sitting by the fire with his muddy boots resting on a stool. The mist of that morning. VI Corps lined up against the Prussian centre, waiting for Imperial orders. That Prussian centre had looked soft and unprepared. The advantage was staring him in the face. They were practically inviting VI Corps to have a crack.

So off they charged.

Well, that Prussian centre wasn't quite as soft as it had looked and although it buckled, it did not break. Ney could clearly remember waving his sabre in the air, mounted as he was on Concorde, his horse, screaming for his infantry to hold their square, because from high up he could see they were surrounded.

This sight had forced the Emperor's hand. He had had to order the general attack to begin rather earlier than he intended.

All's well that ends well, and, surely, he had been proved right. If the entire Grand Armée had moved with VI Corps, the battle would have been over before lunchtime instead of after it. Sometimes orders are only there to be disobeyed. Surely the commander in the thick of it has a better eye and ear and intuition.

However, this didn't seem to be the attitude of the Emperor. He had been summoned after the battle and given a good dressing down.

'I shouldn't need to explain to you, Ney, that you all need to follow my orders. Every order. The headless chicken is headless for a reason.'

Ney had to admit that he had kind of shrugged this off at the time. He had been right. Napoleon hadn't seen what he had seen through the mists. Marshal Bernadotte had a far more unsatisfactory battle by not even bothering to turn up. His men hadn't fired a shot. He was lucky not to get a court martial.

When Ney had taken Magdeburg, one of the great citadels of Prussia, Napoleon had seemed impressed again. This was before a clearly beaten Prussia refused to come to terms while Russia was still in the field, wishful thinking. Hence this cat-and-mouse game in the frozen arse-end of the world.

He wondered if he were worrying too much about the Emperor's latest mood. He wondered what Ida would say if he asked for her advice. He began imagining her here, undoing her dress, freeing her breasts. Taking her with him on the fur in front of the fire, as the snow continued to pile on the window ledges.

He was determined too, when he did return to Paris, whether that be in victory or in disgrace, that he should make sure Aglaé became pregnant again, maybe with a daughter this time. He would like that.

A rap on the door bought him abruptly back to the present, away from his dream of soft skin and bare thighs.

'Monsieur Marshal. Lieutenant Fezensac has returned.'

Fezensac: of course, he was expected.

They had met at the camp of Boulogne, fought together in the Tyrol and at Jena. Son of the revolutionary General, Phillipe Fezensac, who Ney had known personally and admired, Raymond Fezensac was becoming more than an aide-de-camp. Able to tell the truth to Ney even if the truth was inconvenient, he was a proper friend. Ney had too few of those. A man who was unable to carry out orders if he thought they would lead to any dishonourable or disadvantageous outcome. Basically, he would have lasted about a week on Marshal Soult's staff.

Fezensac strode into the room, tall, slender, his steel-blue eyes and gently receding hairline adding to his air of intelligence and stoicism, qualities that made him such a useful confidant. Even though his coat was splattered with snow, he was obviously trying to pretend he was not half-frozen to death. Ney called for wine and brandy and urged Fezensac to sit close to the fire.

'This damned country.' Fezensac was cold and tired. 'These roads, Monsieur Marshal, I am surprised the Prussians don't live underground from Halloween to Easter like moles. I have not been on a road for two days that was not waist-deep in mud. Outside of Bartenstein, you won't believe this, my horse loses a shoe, and we must go off the so-called main road to look for a village with a farrier.'

'Did you find one?' Ney asked.

'No, all the villages are deserted. The houses have no roofs.'

'No roofs?'

'Someone has been taking the thatch to use as fodder. Cossacks. It's the way they feed their ponies.'

'It's not what we do,' Ney said.

'Anyway, it's bad for the horses.' Fezensac took off his fur-lined gloves. 'What is happening at Konigsberg?'

'Not under my command, clearly. Otherwise, I would not be sat here waiting for you. How is the Emperor?'

'The Emperor kept me waiting, then finally gave me an interview.'

Ney raised an eyebrow. 'Kept you waiting? Was he not impatient to hear my report? Were you not able to make our position clearer?'

'There is a letter. He gave it to me. Sealed.'

'He didn't want you to read it?'

'I believe this letter contains some words of disapproval designed to remind you of your duty, though written in a way meant not to sound too severe, nor to sound too ungrateful. But I must warn you, the Emperor is absolutely furious with you.'

'And how do you know this?'

'He told me. Personally. He took me to one side, strutted up and down like he was dictating a letter.'

Ney could just imagine the Emperor behaving in such a way, just as he wrote at least three dozen letters a day using his clerks.

'He said, "What is the meaning of these movements that I never ordered, which reconnaissance would weaken the troops and may even endanger them? To obtain supplies? To extend the occupation of the country and enter Konigsberg? It is, apparently, his business alone to direct the movements of the army and determine its requirements on any given day. Who authorised Marshal Ney? Is Marshal Ney now the Emperor and Commander-in-Chief?" This is what he said.'

'And he asked you to return, say all this to me?'

'Yes, sir.'

Ney felt the nape of his neck burn and shame spread over his face; of a sort he used to experience when he'd been at school and caught not learning his Bible.

'And you were not able to make him understand how our lads are struggling out here? Or that men from Soult's Corps took our winter supplies and left us with the thatch?'

'It's obvious Marshal Soult has relished informing the Emperor of every movement made by VI Corps. That Marshal Ney wants Konigsberg because he is bored, that Marshal Ney only wishes to make himself King of Prussia, and capturing the castle will be the first move in that particular endeavour.'

Ney stood up abruptly. 'For the love of God, does the Emperor not know me by now? Does he not know Soult? That snake.'

'If I may suggest, sir,' Fezensac replied. 'I think it's perfectly clear that the Emperor refuses to choose between you. He sees the enmity between you as merely an annoyance. If the Marshals squabble between themselves, then the Emperor can be comfortable on his throne.'

Ney read the letter, grunted, then flipped it into the fire, watched it collapse and fizzle.

'This is a reprimand. Nothing more. We must remind ourselves that nothing *has* happened here. We sent men east to search for food, that is all. We have not menaced Konigsberg. We've not even clapped eyes on the place. Or indeed any Russians.'

'Send a letter saying you understand,' Fezensac advised. 'Hint at a misunderstanding out here. Apologise. Stress your loyalty.'

'It should not need to be stressed; I have proved myself time and time again.'

'You have proved yourself brave in battle, but not wise at court.'

Ney gave Fezensac a hard stare. Not many people

would or could talk to Ney like this and, much as he disliked it, he knew he needed it.

Fezensac took a deep breath. 'You are right, sir, there is no cause for alarm. All the way from Warsaw I saw more bears and lynx than people. As you said, not a single Russian or even Cossack. Everyone is hibernating until spring.'

'We should pull back to Niedenburg?' Ney asked.

'That would be the right move. Then at least we can say we are acting within the Emperor's orders. Our spies report that the larders of Konigsberg are almost bare. So even if we stormed it, we would still not be able to feed our men.'

'We would still have had the glory, though,' Ney muttered. He sat back down. 'Meantime we will not venture far. Send orders to the foraging brigade for their immediate return. And tomorrow the Corps is to march the short route to Niedenburg. Where we will sit tight for a while. More wine?'

They stayed for what seemed a hazy and warm few hours in the orange glow of the fire. There was gossip from the court, stories of the puffed-up buffoonery of Murat and Bernadotte. And that the Emperor had a new Polish mistress, Maria Walewska, who had whiter teeth than the Empress, was much younger, of course, but was otherwise quite stupid. The real reason, therefore, why Napoleon wanted to stay in Warsaw, enjoying Maria Walewska in bed. Rather than join his army in the cold Prussian wastes, chasing the Russian army.

Ney hadn't laughed this much in a long time. Just as he was considering some brandy, there was an impatient knock at the door.

Fezensac hopped up, let in a soldier who Ney recognised. He was a messenger from the foraging brigade, was covered in mud, and looked as if he had been riding hard.

'Monsieur Marshal, I have to report... this afternoon we sighted the vanguard of the Russian Army marching on Heilsberg. Unfortunately, they saw us too. They now know there are French troops near at hand. The Russians are coming. The Cossacks are coming. General Benningsen is coming for us.'

For a moment there was stunned silence. Ney broke it with calculated, confident good humour.

'So, we have poked the wasp nest after all. The Emperor is going to be even more furious with me. Summon my Generals. There are urgent plans to be made.'

CHAPTER 5

EN ROUTE TO EYLAU

FEBRUARY 7TH 1807

The road was uneven, rutted with layers of ice. The open barouche carriage jolted so fiercely that Wilson had long ago given up writing letters and despatches home. He wasn't entirely sure his ink was not frozen in any case. He wasn't entirely sure his blood was not frozen, either.

On both sides, the outlines of thousands of pine trees were softened and thickened by snow. Snow breezed across the barouche. Wilson tightened his thick fur cape across his shoulders and pulled the deep-blue coat of a Prussian officer he now wore, closer to him. Both had been presented to him by Queen Louise before her departure from Konigsberg. Hooves clattered all around him. She'd been concerned for his safety, so had also given him a six-strong escort of Cossacks. Observing their manners and opinions at first hand was proving interesting to say the least.

They had now travelled two days from Konigsberg. Out here somewhere in this forest was the Russian Army headquarters. Somewhere. Wilson didn't even know if his escort was lost. Now he could only hope this road would lead to a settlement of some sort. Someone to ask. It was imperative he find the Russian Army. He had despatches from King Frederick William; he could apprise their Generals of the latest situation as he saw it. Maybe give them strategic advice.

As he'd made ready to leave Konigsberg, the Prussian Royal Family was preparing to retreat even further east, from Konigsberg to Memel on the Russian border, the very last outpost of King Frederick William's kingdom.

In some godawful Russian resort even further up the coast, halfway to St. Petersburg, the real King of France, Louis Bourbon, was living his days as a pauper in a château with a leaking roof where it seemed to rain indoors. As Queen Louise had told him, she feared that would be her fate unless the Russians drove off Bonaparte. That, or the guillotine.

The anticipation of confronting Bonaparte kept Wilson's mind concentrated, his blood pumping. He was so deep in thought that he hadn't realised the barouche had suddenly stopped jolting. The barouche had, in fact, stopped.

Wilson craned his neck out of the carriage to look around the driver's fat lump of a backside. Up ahead, the snow was thick and misty where the white sky met the white ground. He took out Jemima's telescope and, even then, could only just make out two of his escorts trotting off into the distance.

'What's going on?' he asked the driver.

When the man shrugged as if he was too cold to care, Wilson realised he was going to have to go and look for himself. He didn't yet trust these Cossacks; they might well be up to something. If they were just going about some trivial business, stopping for a leak maybe, or had noticed a wild boar or hare or some such. They should have asked his permission to halt first.

'Give me a hand then, man, please.'

Wilson pulled coat and cape around himself, making certain his loaded pistol was in his pocket. The driver opened the door and helped Wilson down, so he didn't lose his footing when his boots hit the ice. His remaining escorts just sat in their saddles, passively waiting. The pelting snow stuck to their astrakhan hats and splattered their red kaftans.

'Petro, what is going on?' Wilson asked the lead rider.

He was already on first name terms with all the escorts. Then again, he was normally on first-name terms with everyone pretty quickly.

Petro looked down and shrugged as if he too didn't care.

'Oh, well, I'll go check myself. You and Bohdan, follow at a discreet distance. Ivan, Stepan, stay with the carriage.'

Wilson trudged into the mist, trying to walk in fresh snow to provide his boots with some grip. Ahead, he could make out one of the red kaftans shaking someone else in the mist.

Cossacks: he'd been very eager to meet up with them, learn more about their traditions, ever since Queen Louise had suggested he meet Hetman Platov of the Don Cossacks. Last night, around the campfire, he had asked his companions about the Hetman. They had explained the Hetman was the 'Hammer of the Turks'; the Hetman was born in the saddle with a blood-stained lance in his fist; the Hetman could kill a man with one stroke of his sabre; the Hetman was implacable, ferocious and stood for Russia; the Hetman regarded Englishmen as girls.

Wilson had laughed this off and offered the vodka bottle again. He liked this Cossack sense of humour. They were horse people, light cavalrymen, like he was, with a fearsome reputation in battle and irrepressible spirit. Men you might need in a fierce fight against Bonaparte. Men he might well need soon.

They did, though, also have something of a reputation for pillage and the slaughter of friend and foe alike. Maybe they had simply inherited some bad habits, that could be controlled with rigorous training and proper leadership. Even so, it was the reputation for unrestrained behaviour that had worried Wilson enough for him to leave his carriage.

As he drew closer, he realised the reason why his carriage had halted was that another carriage had come off the road. Yelelyan, the tallest of his escort, was holding up a man in a fur coat, whose feet could hardly touch the ground.

'What is the meaning of this, Yelelyan?' Wilson demanded. 'Put that man down at once.'

'He's French,' Yelelyan said in a menacing tone.

'Put him down. That's an order.'

Reluctantly, the Cossack did as he was told. The man was broad-shouldered, middle-aged with a bushy moustache. The look of gratitude on his face suggested he was certain Wilson had just saved his life. Crashing his coach, only to be detained by Cossacks during a snowstorm in the middle of East Prussia, must have seemed like having escaped the dark wood only to be threatened by wolves.

Wilson approached the coach. Its two left wheels were lodged in snow at the side of the road, that no doubt concealed some ditch or frozen stream. The driver was slumped, with his back to the front roadside wheel. At first Wilson assumed he was dead, maybe thrown from the carriage, his head smashed on the ice. When Wilson nudged him with his boot, he realised the man was snoring and stank of schnapps. This was certainly the wrong road to be overcome by drink. Little wonder there had been an accident.

Wilson gestured to Yelelyan to pull the driver up on his feet.

As he tried to open the carriage door, check on anyone else inside, the man with the moustache tried to rush him.

Wilson took out his pistol. Yelelyan's hulking colleague, Vasily, grabbed the man from behind and held his sabre to his throat. The man froze.

'Release him, Vasily,' Wilson said. 'He seems to be unarmed and there's obviously someone he cares about in there. We all have protective instincts, do we not?'

Vasily stepped back. The man looked as if he was about to burst into tears.

'I am Lieutenant Colonel Sir Robert Wilson of the British Army. Who are you? And what in God's name are you doing out here, in the middle of a Prussian winter?'

The man was holding up his hands but did not speak.

Still with his pistol pointed at the man's face, Wilson turned and opened the door.

Inside there was a lady bundled up in furs. Straight away she threw her arms around a baby boy about a year old. Her mouth was defiant, her eyes wide. An obviously terrified nursemaid tried to cover a small girl, about the same age as Wilson's youngest, with her cape. Left to their own devices, without his orders, the Cossacks here would rape these ladies, put the men to the sword, loot the coach and leave the children to the snow.

'I see,' Wilson said, turning around. 'You've my word we will not harm you. Who are you?'

The man stepped forward, looked down and prodded his chest with his fingers. 'Monsieur Matthieu de Lesseps.'

'What on earth are you doing out here, Lesseps?'

'A diplomatic mission. I'm France's new Consul General to the Czar. I'm taking my family to St. Petersburg.'

'Well, you're going the wrong way, Lesseps, you're dreadfully lost. You need to turn around and head back to the coast, from which you can find the road to Memel. Then drive up to St. Petersburg that way. This road will only get you all killed or worse.'

'The coach… it is stuck.'

'We'll pull you out… Vasily, Yelelyan, go and get the others, go and get some rope, we're pulling this carriage back onto the road.'

Yelelyan stopped rubbing snow in the driver's face.

'But these are the enemy, Sir, we should—'

'No, we should not. I hate the French as much as you – not you, Lesseps – for them forcing war on Europe and their atrocities I have seen in Egypt and elsewhere; by the blood of Christ, I will kill Bonaparte myself. But I cannot treat *all* of them as enemies. Not women and young children. They are not all the same.'

Lesseps stood speechless on the road. Yelelyan snarled as he passed and sloped back towards the other Cossacks, who were leading their horses towards them.

An hour later, the Lesseps' carriage had been pulled upright, disappearing in the opposite direction. Wilson's barouche was once again travelling through the forest. He wondered if Yelelyan was disappointed he hadn't been allowed to loot their baggage and leave the French to their fate. He hoped Lesseps didn't fall victim to another Cossack band or Prussian patrol between here and the border. Most would not have shown the kindness and compassion he had just shown to that unfortunate family.

Then again, not everyone might one day need the help of a French Consul General when in St. Petersburg. Lesseps had already proved useful in letting slip that the Grand Armée and the Russians were converging on a town called Eylau. That was where the war was heading. And so was he.

CHAPTER 6

EYLAU

FEBRUARY 7TH 1807

When Wilson stepped down from the barouche in the courtyard of the massive barn, the Russians were using as a headquarters, he had never felt such cold. It was late in the evening. The wind had a cutting edge. If the medal at his collar touched his chin, he feared it would stick.

He thanked Yelelyan and the boys. Pulled the Prussian fur cape around his shoulders. Being dressed as a Prussian officer was the best disguise out here, should he be captured. Bonaparte knew of him. The celebrated book on the Egypt campaign was known in Paris. If he was caught by the French, he would be shot. That was a great incentive to avoid capture.

Men stood in loose groups around the yard. Judging by their tattered state and powder-stained faces, some with bloody bandages, there had already been an encounter with the enemy. As he crossed the cobbles in search of a fire, and maybe some soup or a hot potato, it was clear from the chatter that the fighting was over for the first day, but had only recently stopped. It must have gone on late into the evening; no one had emerged the victor.

He also gathered that Bonaparte had now arrived and was sleeping overnight in Eylau town. If Wilson had his opportunity, Eylau would be his grave. He would not be alive after tomorrow.

There was much laughter that the fat Imperial bastard must have been dragged kicking and screaming from the boudoir of the latest silly Polish whore in Warsaw. These were rough veterans in their dark-green coats and ragged fur hats, hunched up against the snow, stamping the ground and laughing, smoking their clay pipes. Wilson tipped his hat to them, and marched into the barn where he suspected, and hoped, the Russian commanders were planning the next day.

The building was dimly lit by dozens of small lanterns and stank of a mixture of straw, sweat, tobacco, vodka and blood. Many exhausted men were lying flat out on the flagstones. Not seeing anyone he recognised, he skirted the great interior of the barn until he found a small room off the main chamber. Its entrance flanked by two huge infantrymen, who gave his medal a glance as he passed through.

A man, he assumed was General Bennigsen, sat on a crate with his white-gloved hands clasped across his knees. The bright, wise eyes he now saw, and short silvery hair had been described by the Queen. Bennigsen was a Hanoverian, not Russian, though he had made his name in the Russian Army during a thirty-year career in which he'd won victories against the Turks and the Persians. He had a reputation as a canny, though cautious, leader, which, along with his not being Russian, could cause friction with other truly Russian commanders.

Big-bearded men in green uniforms sat with him around a meagre fire in which potatoes were roasting. All had glasses of vodka in their hands. Maybe you would die of the cold if you didn't keep knocking back the vodka. The one with the long black sideburns Wilson recognised as Bagration, a wily firebrand General. His tactical nous during the recent Battle of Schongraben, where Marshal Murat had overestimated the size of the Russian force and not attacked, was one of the reasons why there was still a Russian army large enough to oppose the French. All despite the crushing defeat at Austerlitz. Apparently, he had some curious nicknames among his men: 'The Eagle' and 'God of the Army'.

Well, thought Wilson, *among such men it would be hard to lose even against Bonaparte.* He briefly touched his medal, nudging it so it caught the firelight to announce his arrival.

'Good evening, gentlemen,' he said. 'Lieutenant Colonel Sir Robert Wilson of the British Army at your service as liaison officer, with an introduction from Her Majesty Queen Louise of Prussia.'

'Ah,' Bennigsen said, 'we heard they were sending someone.'

'How many divisions does he bring?' Bagration asked, flint-faced, unsmiling.

'He's an observer,' Bennigsen replied. 'And one we—'

'I intend to do more than observe, sir,' Wilson interjected. 'I intend to fight.'

Bagration took no notice. 'They send us one man, only one man.'

Bennigsen handed Wilson a bottle. 'Sir Robert, enjoy our welcome and ignore my ungrateful comrades. Drink up. Many of us here may discover that our next drink will be at the devil's table.'

'With Bonaparte?' Wilson asked.

'He means the real devil, you fool,' said a man who was brooding to one side. He had an aggressive jaw, trimmed beard and drooping moustache, wearing a pale-green coat with a white trimmed collar. He had large watery brown eyes, with strangely long, almost feminine, eyelashes.

Wilson laughed. 'I can't distinguish between the two these days.'

'That is easy,' the man said. 'The devil only looks like a goat. Bonaparte fucks them. He has fucked all the goats in France, all the goats in Austria, now he wants all the goats in Prussia. And if he should come across the devil—'

'Wilson,' Bennigsen interrupted, 'make the acquaintance of Hetman Platov of the—'

'Ah yes, Hetman Platov, your lads who escorted me here spoke—'

'Did they say I'm a wild beast in furs?'

'No.'

'You lie, diplomat.'

'I do.' He laughed and Platov laughed back, not necessarily in a way that made Wilson feel that they were laughing at the same thing.

'Gentlemen, I overheard in the yard that Bonaparte is here.'

'The fat bastard seems to have been in Eylau a few hours,' Platov replied.

'We were unable to drive the French off today?' Wilson asked. 'It would have been easier, than tomorrow with him on the field.'

'Maybe if the English sent more than just you,' Platov

interjected, 'we might all be on our way home now, drowning in Polish gold and virgins.'

'The situation is in the balance,' Bennigsen said, ignoring the interruption. 'And while it is still in the balance, we can afford to be optimistic.'

He went on to describe how, that afternoon, with the armies lined up on either side of the town of Eylau, eyeing each other up, unsure who was going to make the first move, the French baggage train arrived in the town square. When they started to unload as if they already owned the place, the Russian boys caught sight of all that food and stuff; they charged. What started as a skirmish quickly escalated into a full-blown battle for control of the town. There was fierce fighting in the streets and in the graveyard well into the evening.

When Bennigsen finally ordered the troops to retreat from the town, they did so through streets clogged with the dead and the dying, streets smothered by red snow. The carnage must have been horrific. He could see it in General Bennigsen's eyes as he spoke. The man had probably experienced nothing like it in his long fighting career.

'If only you had committed the whole army,' Bagration said with feeling, 'Eylau would be ours and the French on the run.'

'That I very much doubt,' Bennigsen replied. 'At least two of Bonaparte's Corps are not here yet. Davout. Ney. Bonaparte will wait for them. You wanted to be chasing the French across flat land with those crack men still fresh for a fight?'

'Then pray the conditions do continue to keep those so-called Marshals absent, so we'll have even more of the advantage tomorrow. We'll dance in French blood by sunset,' Bagration said. His face grim and determined.

'And they may well have more wounds to lick tonight than we do.' Platov picked a hot potato from the fire and bit into it side-on like an apple.

'It was hell out there, too. Fighting at night with Jack Frost snapping at your balls. You like fighting after nightfall?'

'You feel the cold, Hetman?' Wilson asked.

'I just like to be able to see who I'm killing,' Platov replied. 'In the dark, I could be killing anyone. Murat. Ney. You.'

'It's not about killing, it's about winning.'

'That's a fancy medal. You steal it from an emperor's whore?'

'Hetman,' Bennigsen cut in, 'I suggest you pour Wilson another drink and we'll hear his story of how that medal was won.'

'These people are only here to sell us muskets and leather. The English are not soldiers. They are tailors and cobblers—'

'I'll have you know, Hetman, that when I was a mere youth, I was charging at the French when we were outnumbered ten to one, and still prevailed to carry the day.'

'This I would like to see. I'm sure that, with a medal-with-legs such as you in the saddle, Napoleon will shit his breeches and run back to his whore before a shot is even fired.'

Wilson laughed. 'If you would like to see me in action, Hetman, I would be more than willing to ride with you tomorrow. If only to make sure the Cossacks hold their formation. I'm not sure that has ever happened.'

'You look like a clotheshorse. Not a man for the battlefield.'

Bennigsen got to his feet, brushing dust or something from the seat of his breeches.

'The only way to settle this, Hetman, is to let Wilson ride with you.'

Both Platov and Wilson stood up too. The Cossack was only at shoulder height.

'If he gets himself killed…' Platov declared, stepping backwards and giving Wilson a sideways look that challenged him to make his excuses. 'If he gets himself killed, it's on you, General. If he gets us all killed, it's on you as well.'

All three men knocked back their vodka. The burning sensation hit the back of his throat. Wilson was sure his excitement had flushed his face, though he hoped the rest of the group thought it was the drink or the fire.

'The real problem is, gentlemen, I don't have a horse.'

'Follow me,' Bennigsen said. 'I have just the one for you.'

Outside, a queue now snaked from the inside of the barn to a wagon in the middle of the yard. A sweating blacksmith was sharpening blades on a grindstone he worked with a treadle. Wilson admired the way the man angled a sword against the stone until it sparked.

He followed Bennigsen and Platov into what turned out to be a makeshift stable. Inside, the long room smelled of horse and dung and straw. Grooms milled about, tending to two dozen or so horses.

'Here,' Bennigsen said, leading him to a white stallion at the end of the aisle. 'This is yours for the day. He'll bring you luck.'

'Why? Because he's white?'

'His name is Alexander. He belongs to the Czar. And what belongs to the Czar belongs to God.'

'Oh my,' Wilson exclaimed. 'What an honour.'

'And get this on your duck-shaped head,' Platov said, thrusting a tall, black fur hat into Wilson's hand. 'A blind sniper in Moscow can hit the one you're wearing.'

'Well, it looks very warm anyway.'

'Consider yourself a Russian at war, for tomorrow at least.'

'Now we are all set up,' Bennigsen said, 'let's get back inside before the cold gets to us.'

Platov bumped Wilson's shoulder with his own, almost knocking him over.

'The German is going to gather round all these generals and princes and arseholes. Tell us all about strategy for tomorrow. But we're going to get drunker than drunk because we know we are going to disobey him anyway.'

'Many say this is awarded for disobeying orders.' Wilson tapped his medal.

'Let's see if we can all get one.' Platov slapped Wilson on the shoulder again, ushering him towards the entrance.

Wilson pulled back his cloak and showed Platov the

hilt of his sword. 'I'll catch you up. I need to get this one sharpened.'

Outside the stable, Wilson strode off to the left while the General and the Hetman marched back to the barn. The queue for the blacksmith was long. Wilson had not been put on this earth to queue. The men in line must have realised this too. No one said a word as Wilson marched along the line past them all, then handed his sword to a bald, red-faced man in a leather apron.

'She's a beauty,' the man said, pressing the sword edge to the spinning stone.

It was Turkish, a Mameluke sabre. The steel blade was deadly when properly sharpened. It had been presented to him in Egypt, by the Turkish Grand Vizier. It was one of the honours bestowed on him as an officer in the British army, one that had finally driven the remains of Bonaparte's men out of Egypt.

He stared into the rainbow patterns that flashed across the steel as the blacksmith tilted it this way and that. Egypt had been the last time he'd had the opportunity to do some proper soldiering, to put up a fight against the tyrant. In Egypt, he had seen Bonaparte for what he was, a dictator steeped in blood, a usurper with no ambition to improve the world, only to create his own. It was there he'd learnt of the hideous things Bonaparte had done; the things he had recorded in his book.

In Egypt, he had acquired this splendid sword that tomorrow would seek a reckoning. Tomorrow, Bonaparte would be on the field; so would Sir Robert Wilson, riding one Emperor's horse and wielding his sword against another. He looked up into the drifting snowflakes. He looked forward to morning, for the troops and horses to charge, the guns to fire. Tomorrow, he would strike Bonaparte dead and write his name, Sir Robert Wilson, in the history of glory.

Within minutes, after the first Russian guns boomed, Eylau was ablaze. From the slopes where Bennigsen had deployed his men, with Wilson and Hetman's Cossacks in position on the left flank, flames from the town spiralled into the low white sky. The church spire stood out against the glow like the wick of a giant candle. If it hadn't been lit up by the burning roofs below, it would have probably been invisible.

Snow was blanket-like, the wind driving it at an angle. It was drifting across the battlefield, seemingly thicker the closer it fell to the outskirts of the town.

Wilson reckoned no one could see more than fifteen feet in front of them. If the French came up this hill, no one on the ridge would see them coming. Then again, no one coming up that slope would be able to see where they were going either. The blizzard would be in their faces.

There was fighting on the right flank. You could hear it: shouts, screams, pistol shots. All the while, the Russian cannons roared. When close it was like a soft thump to the ears, further away it sounded like a rumble of thunder. Always, the frozen ground trembled as the cannon balls landed and bounced. The horses whinnied. The horses shivered. No one really knew what was going on. It felt as if no one could possibly be in command. Wilson did not envy General Bennigsen his responsibility on this day, but at the same time admired him greatly.

'Where do you think Bonaparte would be if he could choose anywhere?' Wilson asked Platov.

'If he could choose anywhere, he would be in a goat.'

'I asked for your strategic opinion, Hetman. I did not ask you as a man of the world.'

'Up that tower. Must be the church. It's the only lookout.'

'My thoughts exactly.'

'Fat bastard will never get down, though.'

'Let's hope he doesn't get down quickly.'

'They'll stick some Polish whores at the bottom of it, that'll get him down.'

The sound of cannon fire was beginning to overwhelm them all. Some portion of the battlefield was getting a pounding from both sides. Wilson could see flashes from the French lines, hear the boom from the Russian lines. He retrieved his telescope from his coat.

'The French centre has advanced,' Wilson called. 'Looks like… I can't really see…'

For some time, there was only the clamour in the whiteness and, ahead, the flaming outline of Eylau on the horizon. Restless murmurs spread through the ranks of the horsemen. When Wilson looked over his shoulder, Platov's men, in their big fur hats and lances lofted, were leaning in against each other, as if some whisper was being passed between them. Could they see something he couldn't?

He angled his telescope back towards where the height of the fighting appeared to be. It was as if there was a sheet of paper hanging over the lens it was so white. Then, occasionally, he could make out a rolling billow of smoke. Or an explosion that threw muddy snow up into the air, where it hung like a fountainhead before falling.

But for a few seconds the snow suddenly cleared. The scope of the battlefield became more apparent. Some of the French divisions on the field were running away or trying to, sliding down the slope! With many, many thousands of men seemingly left in the snow, flattened and smashed. Action had paused, apart from a square of infantry engaged on a hillock, way out in the distance

Wilson passed the telescope to Platov.

'The French centre has been blown to bits,' Platov said excitedly.

'The French centre is in retreat. What are we waiting for?'

'Bennigsen's courier, or signal.'

'That is the signal.'

'The sight of French arses?'

'Exactly.'

'And where exactly do you want to go?'

'Eylau.'

'The church tower?'

'The church tower.'

Platov drew his sabre across his body and raised it above his head.

'Men of the Don, Men of the River, the Forest, Cossacks, for the Czar, for Jesus Christ Our Saviour and Lord, for all the Russias, lances ready, forward to the town....

Cossacks... charge!'

Soon Wilson's blood was truly pumping, not with fear but with exhilaration, as with his Mameluke sabre raised, he and Alexander, the white Imperial stallion, were galloping down the slope onto the flatter land where the slaughtered bodies lay already encrusted with snow. Platov to his left, his beard also white with snow, like an icicle-faced troll of legend. He would tell Platov this later. They would share vodka and laugh.

Platov lowered his lance, and the tip sliced through the neck of a staggering French soldier, a man who already seemed to have lost an arm at the elbow. This was the first man Wilson had seen die that day. Seconds later, he slashed a straggler himself. Blood sprayed his knee and Alexander's side as he flew on. The French had taken some beating here. They were dots and ghosts in the mist trudging back towards Eylau, now a curtain of grey and smoke ahead.

The Cossack hoard was at Wilson's back. He killed two more stumbling men and, as he glanced over his shoulder, the Russian infantry had swarmed down the hill, too. A contingent had already surrounded the square on the hillock, some sort of mighty struggle was going on there. Had he set all this in motion? Had he jumped the gun? No point worrying about it now.

He spurred Alexander on. Other horses rolled on the

ground where they had skidded and fallen. In the snow, the ice, it was better to keep moving. Less likely to slip.

Eylau loomed, wreathed in fire and smoke.

Eylau was little more than a large village set in a narrow valley, a few red brick buildings that surrounded the church in a central square. Wilson, still at the head of the Cossacks, Platov swinging his blade at his side, was racing forwards. Still cutting down the retreating men of the field, still not meeting any real resistance. There was a part of him that felt the cannons that had started early that morning, had been sounding all his life. He could not remember them not pounding in his ears, and they would not stop until he and the Cossacks of the Don had driven the French from this crossroads, this town and then this kingdom.

For an instant, as Alexander bore down on the junction ahead, walking across the square was a short stout man in a green coat, hat with cockade. The outline unmistakable from the illustrations in the newspapers and the political cartoons.

My God, thought Wilson, and raised his sabre. *He's here. He's here. It's really going to happen. Close the gap. Close the gap.*

The riders behind Wilson must have seen, too. A great howl went up, a glorious roar as Alexander reached the edge of the square. Under that signature bicorne hat, the man turned, must have seen the horses, the sabres, nemesis. He flinched. He hurried.

Any second now, Wilson knew he could end the whole damn war with a slash of his blade. The Emperor was scurrying away across Eylau's church square, surrounded by only three or four officers. A volley of shots cracked above Wilson's head. Platov was alongside him now, bellowing, sabre high, the tips of lances protruding ahead of him as the Cossack vanguard arrived.

Then suddenly, there was a swarm of blue uniforms, tall fur busbies surrounding the Emperor. His Imperial Guard: best men in the French Army. Bayonets raised. Shots fired.

A musket ball ripped the epaulette from Wilson's left shoulder.

Alexander reared up, almost threw Wilson from the saddle. Platov's horse was on its hind legs too and for a second seemed to be dancing on the cobbles, like a circus pony.

Wilson knew only too well that, although horses could be trained for battle conditions, they were not suicidal; they would not rush headlong into a bristling phalanx of steel and guns. The Guard was forming up in a deep line across the square. The Emperor was striding away, vanishing into the snow. Smoke and snow in his eyes, Wilson was unsure whether the blot in the distance was still a receding Bonaparte or someone else entirely. He sensed the Cossacks being forced back, pulled on Alexander's reins to get him under control, to turn him back up the slope.

All around was that irritating cry, '*Vive l'Empereur! Vive l'Empereur!*'

The Cossacks wheeled about on the field above Eylau, coming together and regrouping in their formations, with Wilson and Platov at their head.

'More men and we'd have done it,' Wilson screamed at Platov, banging his sword on his saddle pommel in frustration. 'More and we'd have taken him.'

But Platov had his arm outstretched, pointing towards Eylau. At first Wilson thought he was pointing at the burning town, at the hubbub and crackle there, to say, look how hard it was, look how hard we tried, be quiet, stop moaning. But when Wilson followed the direction of the Cossack's glove, he saw for himself.

Cavalrymen had lined up above Eylau, opposite the Cossacks. A great many cavalrymen, maybe two hundred at the front, but it was clear that they formed the head of a mighty column, thousands and thousands. At the front, in the middle, their commander. Wilson took out Jemima's telescope to get a closer look, hoping that maybe Bonaparte was taking the field in person.

It wasn't Bonaparte, though. It was Marshal Murat, his brother-in-law, an ostentatious and fantastically fancy dresser. It took some nerve to come dressed for war in a multicoloured frock coat, bright yellow breeches, and a red cap with high white feathers. Then again, Murat had the reputation for bravery and success to go with it.

Outlined against the white horizon, the horsemen on the ridge twitched and stamped. Murat had his baton in the air.

'Shit,' Platov exclaimed, 'they're going to do to us what we just did to them.'

'He's throwing all his horses at us at once.'

Snow sprayed underfoot as the great white mass of the cavalry poured over the lip of the ridge, the rumble of the hooves as deafening as any cannonade. Platov raised his sabre again, urging his men to follow. Retreat. The Cossack party galloped back up the hill; it would be senseless to go anywhere else. Out of the way. The charge appeared to Wilson, as he turned Alexander side on to it, like a gigantic waterfall of horses, an endless river of horse and steel. Wilson almost felt he should pull up Alexander and gape, as he would never see anything so magnificent as this cascading mass again, even if he lived to be a thousand.

The rest of the day provided Wilson with no more moments to stop and stare, to think or wonder. He was constantly in motion, riding ahead to escape other horses, riding in arcs and circles to reconnect with Platov and his men, who he often lost in the snow, or the fray, or when they had been scattered. His right arm felt stiff and swollen by the killing thrusts of his sabre. He'd even lost his hat.

He found himself part way up one of the banks, overlooking the field. He had seen Murat's vast charge divide into two parts, one of which smashed into the Russian centre, the second scattering line after line of infantry, then battering the right flank.

This was where Platov led his Cossacks. Where with a feat of doggedness and strength, the Russians managed to stabilise their line, even though it was pressed to a diagonal angle from where it was meant to be. It was along this diagonal that, for hours, Wilson seemed part of the most butchery and evil slaughter. Cannon after cannon fired over his head, the sounds vibrating deep in his ears.

Dying horses screamed and whinnied. Dying men called for Mother or Emperor. In places, there was not enough room for the dead to fall – they froze upright on the spot. He saw ramparts of corpses, battlements of the dead.

The Cossacks made charge after charge to force the French back away from their line. Blood slid along his sword and drenched his cuff. Rivulets of black blood snaked down the snowy slopes. All the while, every time he looked up in the distance, the town of Eylau burned and, against the white nothing of the sky, looked like a kind of hell portrayed in some medieval painting.

Never for a moment, though, did he believe the day would not turn their way. He knew without doubt that these brave Russian soldiers, who were made of winter, who were robust and heroic and as stubborn as nails, would, before it got too dark, be taking back Eylau.

He still did not believe there would be a retreat as, with Platov alongside him, he watched while another large, fresh-looking French Corps appeared on the right flank. At their head, a tall commander, his coat glittering with medals, mounted on the glossiest and most splendid black stallion.

'That is Ney,' Platov said. 'Marshal Ney is here.'

Bugles sounded.

'Time to go, my friend. You English fight like leopards after all. You did not get us killed, and we did not get you killed. We live to fight another day.'

'Another day?' exclaimed Wilson. 'But the moment is now.'

'The Czar's order is to retreat, unless you want to disobey God's anointed on Earth and take on Ney all by yourself?'

As soon as darkness came, Platov fell asleep with his head on Wilson's thigh. They had withdrawn to a shabby shack on the outskirts of the farm where Bennigsen had used the barn as headquarters. The weight of the Hetman's head was pressurising the left side of Wilson's body, causing a graze he'd picked up on his chest to smart. Still, Platov's upturned shoulder made for a decent enough writing desk. He would report back to Lord Hutchinson in Memel. He would write to Jemima. He would keep his journal, just as long as the ink in his bottle hadn't frozen.

Lights of the Russian campfires flickered and swirled from outside. The soldiers had been beyond brave, it had to be said. Their Generals, though, didn't know what year it was, how to coordinate their forces, how to manoeuvre. Clearly no one had bothered to study how Bonaparte waged war, so *they* could outsmart or predict him.

But that unforgettable action with Murat, the cavalry charge... no one could have anticipated a stroke as bold as that. Despite the horrendous conditions for the horses, the Emperor must have ordered it.

He was alive and uninjured. So miraculously was Platov. But he could still not help feeling a frustration, so deep it felt like grief. They had got so close to Bonaparte by the tower. He could still see the way the Ogre's hat wobbled as he made his hurried way from the Eylau crossroads. Wilson had been so certain of success… *Napoleon should not have escaped him.*

He was about to write this down, when he realised the lights from the fires outside had dimmed. Some sort of low rumble and clatter of hooves could be heard, when before it had been the silence of an army sleeping off its exhaustion. Careful not to let the Hetman's head drop onto the floor, Wilson got up and ventured outside, wrapping his Prussian fur about his shoulders.

The vast number of men who had been camping on the adjacent field had gone, leaving barely glowing ashes and useless junk. On the only road he could glimpse through the trees, columns of horsemen were cantering in the direction away from Eylau. This wasn't right. This was totally wrong. This was absolutely not the moment to act with caution, but to fight on with boldness.

He found Bennigsen dictating a message to a courier in his barn antechamber. Other aides were packing his bags. He looked exhausted, defeated.

'Ah, Sir Robert,' he said. 'I congratulate you on your performance today. You will be praised in my despatches to the Czar.'

'General, what on earth is your army doing?'

'Maybe if the British Government had lent us some men as well as money, maybe the day would have worked out differently. But the British troops would have needed to have arrived yesterday or the day before yesterday, or really the day before Austerlitz, to have been anything more than a waste of life. To save my army I must retreat.'

'But the battle is not lost. Where is General Bagration? We need to gather all your other Generals here too. We've beaten Bonaparte to a standstill. He will not be able to take a punishment like he did today, tomorrow. We have shown this Ogre how we fight.'

'That we have, but we have nothing left to fight with. We have no more ammunition.'

'For the love of God, just give me some men to command. I can turn this battle. I know I can. This battle is still there to be won, and Bonaparte himself captured or killed. It may be Russia's best chance of defeating the French.'

'It is not a matter of spirit. As I said, we have no stocks left, no ammunition, no cannonball, no food, no fodder. We can't run at their guns like Siberian savages—'

'General, I beseech you. Order the men back. The French are certain to be having the same deliberations over there. Whether to stand or run away.'

'Your advice is noted, Sir Robert. If I were you, I would collect my gear together. You can ride with us in the morning.'

'Goodnight, General,' Wilson grunted, and left, his anger making him walk fast, elbowing his way through some Russian officers who were drunk, capering around in the barn, clearly in no hurry to go outside.

Out in the yard, the snow was falling thick again, settling on the cobbles. He would accept Bennigsen's offer to ride with them. Before this, he had letters to write.

Queen Louise and Lord Hutchinson at Memel would have to be informed of the great victory won by the Russian Army.

The British Government in London needed to know that the French had received a battering here. The defeat of Bonaparte was imminent. Eylau was decisive in the fate of Europe. But they must send more money. Send more boots. Send more muskets. Send him thousands of men to command.

Most important. Everyone must be told Sir Robert Wilson had so nearly killed Bonaparte.

CHAPTER 7

EYLAU

FEBRUARY 9TH 1807

'*Vive l'Empereur!*'

Ney pulled Concorde, his great black horse, to a halt. With the flat of his hand, he signalled Fezensac to pull up too. It came again, the cry, this time Ney was even more confused as to whether it was real, or some trick of the breeze; the wind, through some broken barrel in the snow, sounding like a pleading voice.

Even though the snow was light and not the blizzard of yesterday, the cloud was so low it smothered the battlefield and the mounds of the dead, which stretched to the white horizon on either side. Fezensac was alongside Ney now, using a small telescope to survey the carnage. The dead and dismembered lay meshed and smashed together, blue and green uniform alike for as far as the eye could see. The only thing that the cold had going for it, was it suppressed the worst of the smell.

Fezensac was a relatively new officer, despite fighting at Jena and Ulm. Ney knew the sight of death on this scale would be shocking to him. Then again, he'd been in action in the saddle for some twelve years himself, seen nothing like the piles of dead the morning after Eylau.

All across the battlefield, over two leagues at least, were not just the corpses of men and horses, but disintegrated gun carriages, dislodged cannon and the skeletons of burnt-out ammunition wagons. The snow lay scattered with discharged musket balls, semi-buried helmets and abandoned breastplates.

In the distance, a hamlet was on fire; it sent an eerie orange glow to flicker across the snow. And still Ney could hear a man call for his Emperor.

'*Vive l'Empereur.*'

'There,' Fezensac said, pointing.

Ahead, a group of men, grey blurs in the sleet, eased a young officer from a heap of dead men and horses.

'*Vive l'Empereur.*'

He saluted.

He fell down dead.

The men left him to the snow, shuffling off into the mist, presumably to find the wounded they could actually save.

'What a massacre,' Ney muttered, sounding both sad and exasperated, 'all to no purpose.'

He'd arrived late to the battle; his only contribution had been to charge about in the snow until the light finally died, fighting the Russian General Bennigsen's cavalry almost to a standstill. The battle had raged for sixteen hours.

For most of those sixteen hours, VI Corps had been jammed together in the frozen roads around Eylau, the men clearing drifts and freeing wagon wheels from the ice. When they should have been battering the Russians. Still, Marshal Augereau had lost five thousand men in fifteen minutes, just before a Cossack charge had all but captured the Emperor.

Ney could not help but be thankful, though. His Corps was intact and the rest of the Grand Armée was not giving chase to the fleeing Russians. This suggested even the Emperor realised they were exhausted, needed to regroup, sleep if possible in the freezing temperature.

'This was no place to pick for a battlefield,' Fezensac said.

'This was no month to fight a war,' replied Ney. 'I blame Soult. If he hadn't stolen our provisions…'

'Apparently, last night, it was Soult who convinced the Emperor not to concede defeat. Then we woke up to find the Russians had gone. It is no-one's victory, just a bloody draw; so many casualties.'

'He does nothing for anyone but himself and the Emperor still thinks highly of him. His day of reckoning will come, you mark my words.'

'So, the Russians will still be able to snap back, even after this?'

'Wait until Spring. They won't have the weather on their side. We'll be at the fight next time and we will win. Not missing out. Seriously, Fezensac, there can still be glory for the VI Corps.'

Ney could see Fezensac was distracted, staring through his telescope. Picking its way across the field was a piebald horse, upon which sat a slender officer wrapped in a flowing fur cape, face hidden by a hood.

'Who on earth is that?'

'Return and report to the Emperor that the VI Corps is largely unscathed,' Ney said hurriedly in a commanding tone. 'I will see you later.'

He recognised that form ahead, the way it sat in the saddle, the way the delicate gloved hands held the reins. Anger fired in his chest. It was really far too dangerous here: soldiers and murder, looting and war and worse.

'But the Emperor—'

'That's an order, Fezensac. Off you go, now.'

The rider was trotting towards him through the drifting mist. The sound of Fezensac's mount's hooves disappeared behind him. When he'd assessed Fezensac was gone, he urged Concorde forwards towards the approaching horse. When they were side by side, Ida pulled back her hood.

He couldn't quite believe it.

She leant into him, grabbed him.

An impassioned kiss, his heart pounding now with anger and zeal.

This was no place for a woman, among all this death and fire and freezing weather. And desperate men, who had not caught a woman's scent for six months. But oh! If his body felt sluggish this morning, now his heart began to race. He flushed with the need for her.

He reached around her waist, pulled her close to whisper in her ear, 'What the fuck are you doing here?'

Her face was innocent as an angel's as she blithely dismissed the horrors she must have been through. The days on horseback, the cold, the thousands of dead she must have passed to get here.

'Why, to fuck, of course, my Marshal.'

CHAPTER 8

Muffled sounds of merriment drifted out across the water. Captain Charles gave the oars one last heave, and the boat bumped the sandy bank. Charles, Wilson and Platov fell backwards.

The Captain smiled, his eyes above his drooping moustache twinkled as if to say, didn't I promise to get you here in one piece?

For three months now, Charles had been helping keep Wilson in one piece, proving himself already to be a loyal and resourceful valet.

Theirs had been something of a chance meeting. It was some weeks before Friedland. The war was still undecided when Wilson had arrived in the East Prussian town of Heilsberg, to liaise with King Frederick William and to meet the Czar for the first time. It was raining heavily, miserably. A squall had flown in off the Baltic. Everything was sodden; everything drenched.

At The Red Eagle, the inn where he was to lodge, he dismounted Alexander in the courtyard. He imagined he would have to return the horse to the Czar's stables the next day. A small, dripping, water-rat of a man in his mid-twenties with a long drooping moustache and wearing a tattered Prussian uniform came up – the inn's ostler, Wilson assumed.

'My horse has cast a shoe,' Wilson said, in French, without thinking. He flicked the man a groschen. 'Take him to the farrier while I have my lunch.'

The man immediately nodded and took the reins. Wilson had expected the usual peasant shrug or gormless stare, the one you normally encountered in the east when you asked for something to be done. He noticed the man had obviously understood him too, which was another surprise. It was far too cold, though, to hang about speculating. Wilson was very much looking forward to a bowl of thick stew and a hunk of brown bread to help warm him up. A tankard of brown ale as well – he was exceptionally thirsty.

When Wilson returned to the courtyard full of stew and the local brew, the man was waiting. Alexander was nowhere to be seen.

'Sir, I took it upon myself to take your horse into the stable, so he can have some oats and be rubbed down.'

Although impressed by the man's initiative, Wilson could see he was pretty desperate – for a job, a dry coat, something – and now the man had spoken out loud, his was not the accent of a local. He was no Pole. His French had a strong German twinge. The man shivered. He hunched his shoulders and water leaked out of a crack in his boots, where the sole had become separated from the uppers.

It was no good keeping him standing out in the rain like this, whoever he was. Wilson had seen enough men die this year so far. He didn't want to see another perish of cold.

'Here, my man, come inside. I'll buy you something to eat, you can sit by the fire and dry off.'

In the bar, Wilson found the man a stool by the hearth and a blanket to throw over his shoulders. His jacket was hanging over the fire to dry and a bowl of hot stew had been procured. Wilson eventually discovered the man's name was Charles. He was a Lorrainer, hence the accent.

'You have nothing to fear from me, I'm obviously English,' Wilson said, 'but you're a deserter, aren't you?'

'I had no choice but to join Napoleon's forces. I agreed with the Revolution, it was high time someone listened to the people, but Napoleon has gone too far. Squandering lives. For what? The final straw was Eylau.'

'Ah, Eylau, a terrible slaughter. You were there?'

'In the VI Corps of Marshal Ney. I was conscripted and sent to his camp in Boulogne. Rode with him, I was one of his cavalrymen. Now, that *is* a leader to follow. I was promoted to Captain, well, dead man's shoes really. Saw war first hand at Ulm and Jena.'

'Sound victories,' Wilson agreed. 'Ney's men are always said to fight with courage and bravery. At Eylau, you missed the worst of it, though?'

'I saw quite enough of it. The carnage, the dead everywhere, mutilated, something hellish about it. Certainly not my idea of a cause worth dying for. That is why I deserted.

'Stripped this uniform from one of the Prussian dead, probably one of L'Estocq's men. We had been chasing them for days, were supposed to stop them from linking up with the Russian lines. In all the confusion, I joined one of their divisions saying I was from another, had become separated. I speak as they speak, obviously. I liked being with them as much as I liked being with the French. So, one night I left them too.

'Now I am here wondering what to do next. If I go home, I'll be shot, for certain.'

Charles's story encouraged Wilson to think about all these deserters wandering the countryside, not just in East Prussia but everywhere the Ogre's armies had devastated. Not only deserters from the Grande Armée, but deserters from other armies also defeated by France, who might well still be willing to fight against Bonaparte. This Charles here was not a coward. Like all sensible people, he saw through Bonaparte. Realised his seemingly unending desire for absolute power was not in any way good for France.

Over another tankard of brown ale, Charles explained that in Lorraine he was the son of an innkeeper, not just any old innkeeper but the owner of a famous post house, Le Hibou Noir. Until the war, he'd been brought up to one day take over the running of the Hibou. He could cook, launder clothes, sew and even iron. And, of course, as a cavalryman he knew horses, how to ride and look after them.

Suddenly a thought struck Wilson.

'Can you read and write?' he asked. It was important to know.

'Yes, in French but better naturally in German. As well, I can keep records and accounts.'

This Charles could be just the person he had been trying to find. He was tired of making all his own travel arrangements, looking after his clothes, making sure Alexander was properly stabled. He needed more time to write his journal, his letters home, his despatches.

Sure, Charles was technically the enemy, but not morally, and he should be given a second chance, rather than left to an uncertain future out here. If the locals knew him to be French, that would mean instant execution. Wilson had found that if you treated people well, they would treat you well in return. French, Prussian, Turk, it didn't matter. He was about to follow his instinct.

'Would you become my servant?' Wilson asked. 'Well, it will be rather more than that. My valet, that sounds more the ticket. You would? Good. Have a bath then and burn those clothes. And buy some new suitable ones. Proper boots. Here's some money. One thing, you are not to speak French, not here, not anywhere. Stick to German. You'll have to learn English as soon as possible.'

Charles held out his hand, shaking, tears forming in his eyes, quite overcome.

'Sir, I do not even know your name.'

Midway across the fast-flowing River Niemen, the rowboat had drawn level with the elaborate raft and its two astonishing white pavilions. The larger was for the Emperors to conduct their talks à deux. From this angle over the water, Wilson could make out the 'A' painted onto the canvas on this side: 'A' for Alexander, Czar of all the Russias. 'N' for Napoleon would be on the side turned towards the other bank, where the French army was now garrisoned. The smaller pavilion was for the clerks and lawyers. They had been built at speed by Napoleon's famous engineers.

That midday, the Emperors had met on the raft, in the neutral zone in the middle of the river. On the far bank was the Prussian town of Tilsit, though by the end of the week, Tilsit and the bank they had just left, could well belong to some misbegotten new French vassal state. Depending on the earlier negotiations conducted by the Emperors in the main pavilion, rippling in the breeze of a summer's evening.

Wilson seethed at the sight of it. At once sad, angry, vengeful. His mission this evening must be to find out exactly what had been agreed. Somehow, he did not feel very optimistic as to the outcome for Britain.

The war was lost. At the Battle of Friedland, three weeks before, Wilson had been heavily involved in a Russian shambles, yet another hideous slaughter. Russia had lost. Without Russia, Prussia was lost too.

The Emperor of Russia was now forced to come here to Tilsit, treat the Corsican Ogre as an equal. Wilson feared for Prussia, feared it would be partitioned, wiped off the map like Poland had been within his lifetime.

At the start of 1805, just after the Coronation, France

had been sitting in her own borders. Since then, Austria and Prussia had been comprehensively defeated, now Russia. Only the English navy stood between Bonaparte and London and the total mastery of Europe.

Wilson was dressed like a Cossack rather than a Prussian officer this time: grey breeches, a short waistcoat the colour of charcoal, an astrakhan cap and a red caftan. Sporting his new bushy beard, he would have been unnoticed among Genghis Khan's hoards. His medal was safely tucked inside his shirt.

Platov had insisted, however bored and in need of a roll in the hay he himself was, he would not cross the river with Wilson unless he dressed to blend in. Everyone over there knew Wilson had written that book about Bonaparte, the one telling the world of his brutality in Egypt.

It was great to be in the Hetman's company again. Much back slapping had occurred when they were reunited yesterday. But Wilson was disappointed that Platov really didn't know much at all. Rumours were rife, speculation wild. The impressed crowd on both banks had all seen glimpses of the pomp and spectacle. The meeting of the two entourages was like nothing anyone had ever seen before.

The only thing that Platov *did* know for certain was Frederick William, the King of Prussia, had been treated abominably. No tent stamped FW floated on the river. The King had been excluded from the negotiations. Had been left to sulk on the muddy bank. Left to watch as the two Emperors bargained over the fate of his realm.

Rather than be announced in Tilsit town with a gun salute and allotted a fine house as temporary residence like the Czar, Frederick William was given no salute and made to lodge with a local miller. It was Queen Louise who Wilson felt for the most.

During the day before, Wilson and Platov had stared out at the raft and the town over on the other bank. Tots of vodka were swigged despite the warm weather; without the excuse they'd had at Eylau, that only vodka kept the blood in their veins from freezing.

Wilson couldn't help continually going over the defeat at Friedland with Platov, as if the next time he raised it, the outcome might be different.

After Eylau, some cat-and-mouse game had been played across East Prussia, with Bonaparte trying to choose a place to stand and fight, while Bennigsen attempted to lead his army closer to Konigsberg, where it could resupply and reorganise. Ominously, heavily fortified Danzig had fallen, and the part of Sweden with a boundary with Denmark, further back along the coast, had been swallowed up by the French.

Even so, the longer the French were pinned down in the east, the more likely it was that help would come from Britain or new Russian armies. Austria could lose patience, break the conditions of the Treaty of Pressburg. Attack the French army from the rear.

Bennigsen must have known he was unlikely to beat Bonaparte in open battle, yet he had allowed himself to be lured into a trap. Seeing that Marshal Lannes had occupied the town of Friedland, he thought he could damage

Bonaparte's army a little. Maybe Bonaparte could only be defeated piecemeal, with a dozen small engagements rather than a single hammer-blow.

Then the Emperor in person had arrived.

Of course, quite soon it was clear they had been blindingly outmanoeuvred by the master of all Generals. Wilson had watched from a distance, he had to say in wary admiration, as no doubt following Imperial orders, Ney and his elite Corps swept into the town of Friedland, broke the Russian defence. The Marshal, as ever, leading from the front, waving his sword high above his black stallion.

Wilson had implored Bennigsen to retreat, yet the German-born General had insisted on making a stand, with the River Niemen, directly behind the Russian lines, giving the army nowhere to fall back. Wilson had witnessed a slaughter more painful and poignant than Eylau; there at least they had fought the enemy to a standstill and, if their tactics had not been able to win the battle, they had not been led to defeat.

Here was nowhere for the terrified men to run. He saw swathes of Cossacks and cavalry drown in the river; the sound of the screaming so hideous that even now he could still hear it in his sleep. He and Platov had been forced to clear a bridge over the Niemen of dead men and dead horses and smashed carts and wagons, so as many Russian soldiers could scramble across to safety as was possible. All the while with Ney's men bearing down, trying to kill them all.

By the next morning, Wilson had headed for Memel. He had not eaten, changed his clothes, or hardly dismounted Alexander for twenty-four hours, could not remember being so exhausted, not at Eylau, not in Egypt or Flanders.

The question he now asked Platov was, 'Why on earth did Bennigsen back us into the river?'

'War is like this, Brother Wilson. On another day, the German fool would have given different orders. On another day, Bonaparte could have tripped over a rug and drowned in his piss bucket, or not even be there. Decided to stay in bed with his Polish bit of stuff.'

'He might still trip over. That would save many lives.'

'You'd be disappointed, eh? I know you; you want to do it yourself.'

'And you don't?'

'Bennigsen used to be a hero, you know? Murdered the crazy last Czar by throwing a snuffbox at him.'

'We could have used more snuffboxes at Friedland.'

'Not quite on his own, actually. Some other Petersburg princeling arsehole strangled the mad bastard with a scarf.'

Wilson had missed the Hetman's true – though, it had to be said, pithy – insights while he'd been back at the Prussian court. He had been in Memel, dining with the King and Queen, when news arrived that the Czar and Napoleon were to meet on a raft at Tilsit. It hadn't been hard to convince Lord Hutchinson, still his official superior, that he should ride post-haste across country to see what was going on.

Though instructions hadn't included dress up like a Cossack, mingle with the enemy, when there was a high chance he'd get caught and executed. Even so, the world he'd entered when he arrived at the Russian camp on the right bank at Tilsit was not yet the world of peace, but still the world of armistice. He had to have faith that the Czar Alexander would do the right thing and not climb down. He could still withdraw into the vast wilderness of Mother Russia, come back with a new larger army, avenge Friedland, avenge Eylau.

Wilson now counted Czar Alexander not as an important political contact, but a close personal friend. He had first encountered His Imperial Majesty at a dinner at Russian headquarters three months ago. At first sight, he'd been greatly encouraged. The Czar was a tall, elegant and rather angelic-looking man, and given they were around the same age, Wilson felt they could have plenty in common.

On closer acquaintance, however, he had seemed less likeable and shrill at the dinner when they were properly introduced. All he wanted to talk about was how shabby the uniforms of the men around the camp were, what a disgrace they were to Russia. Despite the obvious fact they had been in the field for over a year, in what must have been one of the most exacting and brutal campaigns in the history of war. In any case, Platov liked looking battle-scarred normally. It put the fear of God into the enemy.

A few days later, Wilson had found himself, in the

way that he often did, at the Czar's table at another official dinner. This time he'd been charmed by the man's fluent English and discussion of reforms in Russia. That would bring it more in line in terms of education and freedoms with a country like England. Ideas that agreed with some of Wilson's own opinions. Freedom of the serfs – the majority of Russians still being serfs – seemed to be top of his agenda.

Given that he did have a genuine interest in governing his vast Empire, he more resembled his grandmother Catherine the Great than his father, who was, by all accounts, literally barking mad. This hadn't just been Platov being his usual shameless self. The old Czar Paul, Alexander's father, had been seriously disturbed mentally, feared and loathed by his courtiers.

Later, when they had more of an opportunity to talk face to face, Czar Alexander had obviously been told of Wilson's actions at Eylau and the advice he'd offered to General Bennigsen. Wilson should stay with the Russian army, he insisted, as an official envoy. His help and experience were very much needed. He turned down Wilson's suggestion that Alexander should be returned to the Imperial stable. So Wilson kept his special mount.

Wilson fully realised the young Czar had an exacting job ruling his Empire, especially as Russia had grown so vast in such a short period of time. Now even more of a mosaic of competing factions and interests, as well as a culture that had allowed many of his predecessors to be murdered by members of their court. He seemed grateful when they talked, to have met someone outside of all that, who didn't want anything from him and wouldn't one day want to kill him. He'd even given Wilson another decoration, the Russian Order of St George, for gallantry at Eylau.

Soon they were having water fights in the spring sunshine with a ragtag bunch of officers and Dukes.

Sure, the Czar wanted England to deliver men. Equally Wilson wanted England, as an ally, to send troops to fight alongside the Russians. But London said there were no spare men for East Prussia. Meanwhile, there was war with the Ottomans in Egypt and Turkey again. As well as expeditions sent to found new worldwide colonies. *If they have men and money for adventures in the sun*, Wilson thought, *they have men and money for real war in the east.*

Even so, Wilson believed the Czar would not be intimidated by Bonaparte. He would not betray Prussia and Queen Louise. He would recover, rearm, and fight another day. Wilson had made his own position quite clear. He was sure Alexander was no Bennigsen; he would not talk terms of peace. The Czar would have listened to the advice of one of his personal friends, English, who understood the real Bonaparte, one dedicated to the tyrant's destruction.

'I smell whore,' Platov said, wrinkling his nose while clambering out of the boat. Now on the bank of the Niemen, with Tilsit town looming up above them, they had come ashore, as planned, close to what once would have been a handsome farmhouse, but now in some state of disrepair.

The temporary mess of a division of the Russian Imperial Guard, under the command of Prince Vorontsov, a man who Wilson had met at Bennigsen's headquarters at the beginning of the year. It was at Vorontsov's personal invitation that he and Platov had rowed over to Tilsit. Where they were strictly forbidden to be, neither of them being members of the Russian Imperial Guard protecting the Czar. Wilson knew the Prince had been on the raft earlier. Maybe he knew the outcome of the supposedly secret negotiations. Wilson certainly hoped so.

They trudged up the bank towards the house, Charles at their rear. Inside, they found a great room with long makeshift benches and tables along which sat or slumped men in dark-green uniforms. Some smoking their clay pipes, some playing cards in schools of four or five, others in a stupor with their heads on the tables.

A group of clearly high-ranked officers, given their braid and cuffs, sat around a separate table at the end of the room. Wilson made out the Prince, with his distinctive silhouette. He had a long face and a high forehead, the way his hair seemed to burst over the top of his face always reminded Wilson of a cockatoo. He had never passed this observation on to Hetman Platov in case it became the talk of the Russian army.

Vorontsov must have seen them approach along the aisle, his face at first somewhat puzzled. He squinted, and then, when he realised who was coming towards him, broke into a beaming smile and jumped to his feet.

'Sir Robert Wilson,' he exclaimed. 'For a second, with that beard, I mistook you for some Igor from the Steppes, here to steal our horses. What has our Hetman here put you up to? Can you ride a horse doing a handstand yet? Balance a lance on your heel?'

'Of course he can't,' said Platov. 'He's a jumped-up shopkeeper with a medal. He doesn't even know how to control a horse like a Cossack.'

'Whatever he is, I am glad to see you both made it safely across. Here, join us. We have vodka. We have brandy. We have wine.'

They sat down around the table and were introduced to several other princes, who all then raised their glasses, chinked them together and shouted huzzah. Wilson downed his and enjoyed the way the warm spirit lingered in his throat. Out of the corner of his eye, he was glad to see an orderly had brought Charles a cup of something, too.

Platov was twitchy, he could tell. He wasn't sure if it was because he just didn't like being around these St. Petersburg types with their titles and airs. Or whether the Hetman just wanted to find a brothel. Apparently, there were alluring brothels in Tilsit even though it was hardly a town, more of a glorified village. Wilson didn't want to keep the Hetman from his fun, but before they entered the nightlife, he would just have to wait. Most urgently, he wanted to find out what Vorontsov had seen and heard of the day's Imperial pageant.

Everyone round the table was anxious to be told details of this momentous meeting. Vorontsov spoke in such a quiet voice, they all had to lean forwards to hear him.

That morning Vorontsov had joined the Czar's party in a house on the other side of the river. He said he hadn't seen so many parade uniforms since the funeral of mad Czar Paul, Alexander's father. He knew he ought not to be making these connections and comparisons, but it was hard not to. The Czar was wearing the Preobrazhensky Regiment's uniform, with its fine red tunic and two gold knots embroidered onto the collar. His hair was powdered as white as his pantaloons. His hat was high with a cockade and black plume. With his sword at his side, many medals and sash over his shoulder, handsome, youthful and svelte, he looked like all the glory and honour of Mother Russia.

At mid-morning, someone had shouted, '*Your Imperial Majesty, he's coming.*'

On the opposite bank, Bonaparte was galloping up between two ranks of his Old Guard. Vorontsov estimated there must have been four hundred horses in his entourage. There were shouts and exclamations on either side of the river. Both Emperors clambered aboard their boats with their retinues at the same time, headed for the raft at the same speed.

Vorontsov had wracked his brain to think of another meeting as momentous as this, between two titans; one of the grand old world and one of the sordid gaudy new. They were actually meeting in person. A peace treaty was usually negotiated by ministers, not leaders, certainly never Emperors.

In the Czar's boat, Vorontsov had found himself alongside the Czar's brother, the Grand Duke Constantine,

Bennigsen and sundry ministers. On that boat journey, he had not been able to keep his eyes off the Czar.

Outwardly, the Czar was serene, giving the appearance of being unruffled, unflappable, but every now and again he showed suppressed signs of tension; he clenched his fists, and a shudder would pass through his body. Deep down, he must have known the huge significance of this meeting for Russia.

He was no fool. Bonaparte was the greatest man of the age, a magnificent General and tactical genius, the renowned statesman and builder, a man with dazzling achievements and not yet forty, who had conquered all of Europe in two years. Had now beaten Russia twice – since Friedland, everyone counted Eylau as a defeat too – and today stood with armies poised at the frontier of Russia itself.

The man must have the most extraordinary charisma to lead armies over mountains, to urge men to fight and die for him in the heat of the desert and the icy wildernesses of Poland and Prussia. To command that rabble of Marshals and looters, he must have absolute control over the whole of his army, keep in his head all the logistical details.

The Czar must have known he was going to have to show qualities more than these, if he had any hope of coming out of this summit without being humiliated. He was going to have to command the commander, seduce the seducer, outwit the master. He must have been thinking, too, that any less from him, there might well be men in this very boat who, in six months' time, would be poised behind him with their snuffboxes ready to strike. Ready to murder him. Replace him, even as they had replaced his father with him.

Who could know what Bonaparte wanted? How much power over Europe would be enough?

Wilson recalled – that morning he had just been able to push through the mass of people crowding the banks – glimpsing the two Emperors as their boats drew close to the raft. The French Emperor's contingent included Murat, who Wilson had last seen leading that, it had to be said, phenomenal cavalry charge at Eylau; Ney, of course, tall in his plumed hat; plus a crowd of his hatchet men, aides and courtiers: Berthier, Caulaincourt, that lot.

Bonaparte stood at the prow of his boat ahead of his officials and entourage. Vorontsov said he was so close he could make out the *Legion of Honour* ribbon across the Emperor's shoulder. He wore the dress uniform of the old Imperial Guard, the blue tunic and white breeches, dark blue sleeves. His boat reached the raft a little before the Russian. He hastened across and, with evident enthusiasm, shook the hand of His Imperial Majesty as he climbed aboard the raft. Alexander was nearly a foot taller. They entered the larger pavilion, just the two of them, leaving both entourages to mingle on the raft. What was said inside, though, Vorontsov did not know.

'Any idea how I can find out?' Wilson asked.

'It would be easier for a Cossack to gallop into the Garden of Eden,' replied Vorontsov, with feeling.

'Or we could work on having Brother Wilson disguise himself at the Czar's banquet tonight,' Platov broke in, 'sidle up to His Imperial Highness with a tray of caviar and a notebook.'

'We ought to go,' Wilson said. 'We do have intelligence to gather in the town, Prince Vorontsov. Wonderful to make your acquaintance once again. I'm sure we shall meet on another evening soon.' He gave the Russian officers one more salute with a vodka glass, one more huzzah, before he and the Hetman trailed out into the night, with Charles shadowing behind.

Outside, the town of Tilsit seemed pristine and serene after both the ruin of the farmhouse and the days spent in the rather sordid Russian camp on the opposite bank. Its streets were wide and its houses white, windows reflecting the setting sun. They could hear the burble of chatter in the distance as they strode up a lane. Occasionally, there were cooking smells. The normality of it made it feel eerie to Wilson, as if he were no longer used to living life at walking pace or could not feel comfortable in the every day. For him, ordinary life was now in the hall-of-mirrors world of Emperors and governments, or the battlefield and the heightened anticipation before combat.

'Which one of these buildings looks like a whorehouse?' asked Platov, turning round, moistening his lips, straightening his breeches.

'How the hell should I know?' Wilson replied. 'I'm not an expert in the brothels of Tilsit.'

'What are you actually here for then?'

'Hetman, Sir Robert,' Charles spoke quietly. 'While you were both drinking back there, I anticipated such an eventuality as this, and took the liberty of asking some of the Russian servants. Apparently, there is this high-class place, *The Sign of the Mermaid*, up this street, third lane on the left. Ask for Madam Katze.'

'That was very thoughtful of you, Charles,' Wilson thanked him with a nod.

'What are we waiting for then?' asked Platov. 'We're wasting time.'

'Hey, you've only just found out where it is. You go on without me. I am a married man.'

'So am I.'

'My wife, she's nearly blind. It would not be right.'

'You mean even though your wife can't see the guilt in your eyes when you lie about where you have dipped your wick, you're still not going to enjoy the local hospitality?'

'Run along and play, Hetman. Meet us back at the boat. I need to gather the latest news. I must at least try to find out the terms of the treaty.'

'If I poke a wench who's been with the Fat One, I'll see what I can get out of her.'

With that, he sauntered off until all that was left was the dim outline of his high fur hat and a whistled tune, that hung on the breeze, before being smothered by the surrounding chirrup of grasshoppers.

Further on into the town, Wilson stumbled upon a sight more intriguing to him than anything he might have seen in some tart's boudoir.

Close to what must be Tilsit's central square, the clatter of a great many hooves came up behind him. He and Charles ducked into a doorway, so as not to be seen. Just as Wilson had flattened his back to the door, he was greeted by the sight of Bonaparte himself riding by. He really wasn't as fat as the Hetman continually insisted, though he didn't look especially healthy. His distinctive hat was cocked the way Frederick the Great used to wear his, but Bonaparte simply didn't have his figure and merely looked petulant.

'*So near,*' Wilson couldn't help muttering in frustration, '*and not a damn thing I can do.*'

Next to flash by was Murat, who, this close, not from afar like at Eylau, looked like a May Day chimney sweep. More likely to scare a flock of birds away from a wheat field, rather than hammer the fear of God into Cossacks.

Ney followed. The man was tall and flame-haired, his head back, spine rigid, and long legs, clearly well in control of his magnificent black stallion. Eylau, Friedland: Ney was becoming something of a nemesis. *Someday,* Wilson thought, s*omewhere, we will meet and then he will be on the losing side.*

At his rough estimate, something like one hundred horses passed by, but they had not gone far. Wilson could hear them all circling and clattering a short way up the street.

Once he and Charles walked even closer, they joined the little band of spectators, a mixture of French and Russian officers, standing to gawp at Bonaparte. As he dismounted with some difficulty, Caulaincourt, his Master of Horse, had to help him down. He took some time to collect himself, straightened his hat, then waddled across a torch-lit lawn into a grand house, with troops from the Russian Imperial Guard standing sentry at the portico.

'I wonder what the dickens he's going to do in there,' Wilson said, knowing what Platov's answer would be if the Hetman were here.

'He's dining with the Czar,' Charles answered. 'This is his Imperial Majesty's house while he stays in Tilsit.'

'How do you know that?'

'I just asked him,' Charles said, nodding sideways at a French officer, who was part of the rather overawed crowd standing beside them.

'Well, can you ask him to follow Bonaparte inside and find out what they agreed this afternoon?'

Charles turned and for a second an icy fear prickled the nape of Wilson's neck, as it looked like Charles had taken him seriously. He grabbed Charles by the elbow and started to march back up the street now that Bonaparte had gone inside. The more the pair of them gawped, the more likely it was that someone would recognise him as the author of *A History of the British Expedition to Egypt*. Or Charles as a former soldier of the Grand Armée, who had deserted.

Then suddenly it struck him what he should ask Charles to do.

Concealed in the shadows of a small courtyard at the end of an alley ten minutes' walk from the Czar's residence in Tilsit, Wilson found his purse in his jacket pocket. Took out three coins of tavern money for himself, giving the rest to Charles.

'Now, do exactly as I tell you. Don't bother with the bragging officers dressed as parrots, or approach anyone hell-bent on a good night out. Look for the quiet ones, the clerkish ones, who might be party to the terms. The ones who might work for someone like Berthier. You know who he is?'

'Why, of course.'

'Talk about anything else. Buy plenty of drink. Flatter. Get them to spill the beans. I need as much detail as you can gather of the discussions on the raft today. If needs be, you have money, but only offer it if you already have something from them, so they're already compromised.'

'And then I come back to the boat?'

'Meet me at the boat, yes. Any trouble, you can always hide in the Russian officers' mess. Just say you're with the Hetman.'

'I go,' Charles murmured, and faded into the next alley.

Wilson took a pinch of snuff. It was a good plan he'd concocted. When spying on the French in the camp of the French, why not use one of their defectors as your spy?

After giving Charles a decent head start, Wilson ventured back into Tilsit. He had no clear idea of what he wanted to do, fill in the time while he had to wait for Platov and Charles to conclude their different businesses. He might as well have something to drink himself.

Crossing the main market square, he slipped unrecognised through crowds of French Imperial Guards, milling and laughing. He found a cellar wine shop, a low-ceilinged, smoky basement propped up by stone columns and populated, it would seem, as he descended the stairs, by officers of the Old Guard, Napoleon's "Immortals".

At first, Wilson thought of turning back to the street and finding somewhere else to buy a goblet of wine, or a place where there could at least be a few Russian guardsmen for company as well. Then he thought he might be more conspicuous coming in and then going straight out again. Somewhere down in some far corner, there might be some Russian friends anyway. And on the other hand, he spoke French well, probably with more style and a smarter accent than the majority of these coarse soldiers.

He bought a large jug of red wine, poured a measure into a wooden beaker and stood with his back against a pillar, watching, listening, tuning into the low burble of French voices. These men were Bonaparte's elite. Many would have been with him in Italy when he was making his name, veterans of Marengo. Many would have been to Egypt and more than likely did unspeakable things there. They could have been at Austerlitz and Jena.

No doubt they were at Eylau. He had probably come up against some of them when he and Platov's men so nearly captured Bonaparte at the foot of the tower. This close up, they looked undistinguished, not a gentleman among them. It was hard to swallow that his side had been beaten by this rabble in gingerbread costumes.

'Hey,' said a tall "Immortal", one with a jagged scar down his right cheek. A deep and recent one, the raised skin around the wound was still bright red.

'The Czar of all the Russians has appeared among us.'

He was standing in a group of four men, all clearly a little worse for wear, their movements awkward and fidgety as they shuffled towards him.

'The Czar, the Czar with his furry face and silly hat, how glad we are to make your acquaintance, your Imperial Majesty. Alexander. Nice to see you up off your knees. Must have been an unusual experience, meeting a *real* Emperor with a *real* army today? Maybe there will be peace now, on our terms of course.'

'You're tall for a Cossack,' another remarked.

'My mother fed me on manure.'

The Frenchmen sniggered. Wilson knew not to smile. The Russians never did, unless among people they were really well acquainted with.

He raised his beaker, hoping this would signal he knew the men spoke in jest.

'*Vive l'Empereur!*'

The man with the scar swigged his wine back. He might as well have been drinking from a bucket.

'Speak French?' he asked with a sneer.

'Clearly.'

'Why so glum?' asked one of the others. 'You must be relieved we're all friends together.'

'Mightily.'

The first man fingered his scar. 'Sabre cut from one of your Cossack friends. So, Ivan. You didn't drown at Friedland or freeze at Eylau? We were all there too.'

'No.'

'You don't say much, do you, Mr. One-Word Answer?'

'I am taking in the big occasion,' Wilson replied.

'And what's your story, Ivan the Monosyllabical?'

'Cossack liaison to Prince Vorontsov, Imperial Guard.'

'Ooh, what an achievement. Give this man a medal. We gave you quite a fright at Eylau. Even more of a fright at Friedland. It would be better to remember that, rather than thinking you can insult us. Considering we are all on the same side now.'

'Yes, I certainly don't want to insult any of you, we are all on the same side now.' Wilson repeated.

Sabre Scarface grabbed Wilson's jug, filled his own beaker, then offered the jug around to the others.

'How does it feel now, Ivan, to be allied to the boys who always win?'

'It's a great honour. We look forward to riding with you, wherever the fortunes of war may take us next,' said Wilson, trying to sound star-struck. 'Bonaparte is a magnificent horseman.'

'Pardon!' Sabre Scarface pulled himself up to his full height, with a thunderous look on his face.

'Pardon?' Wilson shrugged, not appreciating quite what he had spoken out loud. All the Guard's officers, with their flushed faces and bloodshot eyes, were suddenly giving him very nasty stares.

'Napoleon. It's Napoleon. Emperor Napoleon. Emperor of the French. King of Italy. Protector of the Confederation of the Rhine—'

'I know, a long list.'

'Have more respect then.'

Wilson tried to think of what an authentic Russian officer like Hetman Platov would have said in this situation, then decided not to say it.

One of the others slapped Sabre Scarface across the arm as if to calm him.

'Hey, he means nothing by it,' he said, 'new to the side.'

'New to the side,' Wilson repeated, trying to sound dumb now.

'He's Emperor Napoleon, right? Get that into your thick head.'

Sabre Scarface wrapped his knuckles on Wilson's skull, quite hard, enough to hurt. 'Just remember that, Ivan, if you're going to play with the boys who always win.'

'Sure,' muttered Wilson. He found himself retreating slowly backwards, rounding the column. Hoping he must have now slipped out of view, he nipped behind another group of standing officers throwing back wine, lengthened his stride until he reached the cellar steps. This was a less than casual exit; he was mildly afraid of hearing the thudding of heavy boots behind him. But they were very drunk so would probably be slow to act or, most likely, not even care that the Russian had vanished.

At the top of the stairs, though, out in what was now a dim moonlit evening in Tilsit market square, he was able to turn into one lane, then another and another, until he was sure he wasn't being followed and could make his way safely back to the boat. He was sweating. The French elite was obviously touchy about the status of the fat usurper.

125

At the corner, where one thoroughfare met a street of shabby artisans' houses, he noticed a well-turned-out carriage standing in the street. Six horses. Someone important must have just arrived. A group of cavalrymen were lining up between it and the entrance of a squat and simple house. A sign above the door was that of a loaf: the house of Tilsit's miller.

The riders were Prussian cavalrymen, given their white coats had dark-green collars and cuffs and their black trousers with a red stripe. It seemed mysterious, baffling even, that they would be lined up outside this humble house so late in the night.

Stepping carefully down from the carriage, came a noticeably pregnant woman, in a black riding habit that gleamed with gold braid. Her black cap was placed at a jaunty angle. Unmistakeably, this was Queen Louise.

It was the talk of the camp that Frederick William, her husband the King, had been treated with utmost disrespect by Bonaparte. This must be the latest of these humiliations. The Czar had been allotted the fine house Wilson had just seen back in Tilsit. The King and Queen of Prussia had been given a suburban miller's house, which suggested just how low they were in Bonaparte's eyes, how right the Queen had been with her fears for the future.

Wilson wished heartily he could follow her into that house, not just to find out what she knew, but to offer his support and sympathy; perhaps even concoct a plan between them to get some help for Prussia, from Russia, from Britain, from somewhere.

He knew all this to be impossible. So he decided to slip away, worried that he might draw the attention of those cavalrymen if he remained a Cossack staring at their Queen. If he caused a brawl in the street, the Imperial Guard was only a few streets away, and, as he had so recently been reminded, the French, Russians and Prussians were all on the same side now. If they found he was English, he wouldn't last the night.

The full moon left a glimmering trail across the now black River Niemen; those pavilions on the raft seemed ghostly in the near darkness. The sound of singing carried from the farmhouse. Vorontsov's boys must be drowning their sorrows.

Wilson was extremely pleased to find the boat still lying on the sand where they'd left it. It had not been washed away or stolen. He was, however, mildly worried that no Platov slouched against the hull or slept across it. And no Charles was waiting for him.

Given how hostile and touchy those Old Guard officers had been back there in the wine shop, he was far more apprehensive for Charles's safety than before. And if anything did happen to Charles, if he were discovered or made a mistake in some way, there wasn't much he could do about it. After all he, himself, wasn't supposed to be here. He could hardly ask Vorontsov to enquire after his missing valet.

Charles, of course, God forbid, might trade a safe passage home and a pardon for the whereabouts of the author of *A History of the British Expedition to Egypt*. He had never had that feeling about his valet before, but still, a different world was opening up. It could prompt even loyal men to perform cowardly uncharacteristic actions.

He was much relieved when, a quarter of an hour later, Charles came padding out of the darkness.

'Charles, my man, how thankful I am to see you.'

'And you, too, Sir Robert. Did you have an enjoyable time tonight?'

'Nothing to report about me, Charles. Did you make any useful contact?'

'Yes. For sure. An underling's underling. A clerk who copies documents.'

'And?'

'It is not good news. As might have been expected, the Emperors have come to terms. There will be no more war. The Czar has agreed to withdraw from a few islands and whatnot.'

'He accepted Bonaparte's terms? They are now allies?'

'It is not just that, Sir Robert. There are secret clauses. If your government does not agree to Russia's demand that Britain too must make peace with France, then Russia will declare war on Britain and block all trade. Russia will move on Finland. Napoleon says they can have it. Napoleon, he already plans to move on Denmark and capture their fleet to attack Britain. That is what is proposed.'

'Oh God.' Wilson gasped. He felt his guts turn to water. This was a worse outcome than anything even he had anticipated. Czar Alexander could not be so utterly feeble. He could not change sides like a common renegade or man without honour.

Wilson was going to have to take this news as quickly as he could to London. He was now in possession of top secrets. His mind was already jumping to the voyage ahead; maybe he could beat the Russian courier to it. The Danish ships must be seized before they could be used against the British fleet. Neutral Denmark saved from occupation by some jumped-up pig of a Marshal. He could not see the Czar changing his path again, he had so obviously fallen under the famous spell of Bonaparte. Russia would be at war with Britain, probably not immediately, but for certain by Christmas.

Before he set out, Charles would have to shave his beard off. He would have to look like an Englishman again.

'Apparently,' Charles finished, 'the first thing his Imperial Majesty said to Napoleon was, "I hate the British more than you do."'

CHAPTER 9

At last, Ney could leave the dull formality of Tilsit and the seemingly endless parades on which the Emperor had insisted. Performances to show the other Emperor quite how militant the French Army could be. Although they were now officially allies, friends even, Napoleon did not miss any chance to rub in just who the strongest friend was.

Tilsit was such a small town, Ney's absence would have been noticed. He was the undoubted hero of Friedland, and the Emperor liked to show him off too, seating him near the Czar at banquets. Being ordered to be in the forefront, when the Czar reviewed the French troops. All to embarrass Alexander.

He had to wait a few hours after Napoleon had finally left for Paris, before he could order his own carriage and escort to follow.

'Make haste,' had been his command.

During the journey back, through Konigsberg to Stettin, from Bremen to Brussels and on to gleaming Paris, all he had thought about, imagined, dreamed, was to be with Ida.

But he also had to face the reality of what Aglaé would want. Everyone would know the Emperor had returned in triumph. His past adversary was now his ally; they were united against the British. Who would now be blockaded, their economy would suffer, there would be no more English gold to finance further hostilities. There would be no more hostilities. Aglaé, basking in reflected glory, would be expecting her husband. Ney was the talk of Paris.

So, his first visit to Ida had to be short – too short, two hours at the most. Then he must reunite with Aglaé and the boys. Let the boys handle his sword, be a proper returning father.

Those two hours, once Ida knew that was all they had, were spent as expected, in frantic lovemaking on her bed. Hardly a word was spoken. Her hair was the first thing he untied. Today, she smelled of jasmine. After Eylau, he remembered she had smelled of horse and wood smoke. They had tumbled on some peasant's abandoned straw bales, and once was all they could manage.

This time he spread her on her bed. This time once would not be enough. This time twice was insufficient too. After the third time, they fell into a kind of daze, as if neither could quite take in that he was really there. Safe, they were together at last.

He had to drag himself away.

Now, two weeks later, here he was, back in her bed, Ida naked and warm. On his return to Paris, he found his life had changed. The Marshal was now the hero. The Marshal was now rich, immensely rich. All the Parisian hostesses wanted him at their social events. More importantly, war was now peace.

In peace, Ney wondered what sort of person he could become. He had led his men into the market square of burning Friedland. He had carried the day against the Russians for the Emperor, for Glory, for his own name, too. He had proved he had the talent for attack. Now he wanted something else, to be someone and somewhere else now that war was over. But he wasn't quite sure what. All he had known since his youth was war, after all. Would he miss the exhilaration, the camaraderie?

Earlier he had stepped down from his carriage and out into the balmy summer's evening. The door of Ida's house seemed to open into a magical world that became real when her haughty butler announced the arrival of Marshal Ney. The grand house and the pompous butler seemed to him rather extravagant. He paid for both and much more besides. Ida had little problem spending his money.

She had flown down the stairs into the marble hallway. She wore a high-waisted white evening gown with white, elbow-length gloves, an azure-coloured shawl, matching her eyes, and the thin gold chain necklace that he'd given her that time they'd met in Pressburg. Her hair was tied up in a bun, much like it was when she wore a boy's cap in the saddle. He lifted her, spun her until she laughed, giggled like a girl. Then led him upstairs.

Sometime later, he found himself totally relaxed, almost floating. There was no one else who could make him so fulfilled. He had made love to Aglaé several times since his return; she wanted another baby. But it was nothing like this. The giving, the taking, the sharing, the ecstasy.

He lay facing her, his hand stroking the curve of her waist. Her feet slid over one another, rolled up in the sheet. The breeze that drifted in through the windows was clean and pure, almost surprisingly so, bringing with it not a trace of the charred dead of Eylau and Friedland.

He remembered when they had made love that time in Eylau – after he'd seen her horse picking its way towards him across that devastated field – when he had learnt she had followed the Grande Armée that far east, he had been extremely angry with her. Anger ignited his passion in the shack festooned with icicles. He'd made a modest fire, and they kept most of their uniforms on. They reached an earth-shattering climax together.

Afterwards, she'd wanted to know everything. He had told her. What it was like, how he had arrived at Eylau at sunset, just as the Russians were disengaging. Murat, at his most dashing, had pulled off some great cavalry charge, ten thousand horses he had been told; ordered by the Emperor, which he would have liked to have seen, or, even better, commanded.

He remembered lying back and looking up at the rafters with relief, he was still alive. So was Ida. But even sex had not helped with the exhaustion and aftermath of the battle, the memories of piles of bodies. Made him long for Paris, love in the warmth. Where it was supposed to be with her, not in some peasant icehouse.

Now in Paris, he tried not to think of the past that was Eylau and drew her even closer into his arms.

'So, Marshal Ney, for weeks, all I have heard as I walked the streets of Paris is *Marshal Ney, Marshal Ney, raise a glass for Marshal Ney, hero of Friedland.*'

'I'm sure it's not been quite like that.'

'Oh, but it has. Not that long ago I stopped at Café Frascati for a glass of wine, where Pierre the waiter said to me, "Have you heard, Mademoiselle? Your Marshal Ney has at last tamed the Russian bear at Friedland. Marshal Ney has won the war for France. Marshal Ney has saved Europe for civilisation."'

'He did not.'

'He did.'

'I had my Corps. My men were magnificent as well as obedient, highly trained. The Emperor had the strategy, the vision.'

'And so, you are back in the good books of the Emperor?'

'Well, I did take the town of Friedland and drive the Russians into the river. Napoleon said I'm a lion.'

'A lion. I'd say more of a tiger.' She buried the fingers of one hand into his red curls. Her nails dragged across his scalp and sent a tingle down his spine. She kissed him. He kissed her back.

'*Lion*,' she said. 'And what of the lion's tail?'

'The lion's tail is going to swish about here for quite some time.'

The image this created in her mind made her giggle. Kiss his ear lobe.

'Even Napoleon seems to have had enough of war, for a while at any rate. He wants to play prime minister now, he promises. You know, pass laws, revitalise the economy, rebuild Paris, encourage the artists and the scientists. All good for France.'

'But you know our Emperor as well as anyone. He likes to add countries to his Empire.'

'There's nowhere left for him to take. Britain will be in decline now Russia and Sweden are on our side. Denmark yielded. Portugal is annoying him, but he won't need to do anything about them. They have nothing. They will kneel, too.'

'I have nothing. I will always have to kneel to you.'

'You have nothing? I give you nothing?' Ney cast his eyes at the vaunted ceiling and the ornate chandelier, felt the fine silk sheets, smiled. He put his finger under her necklace and ran it along her collarbone.

'The Emperor,' Ida asked. 'Did he, you know, have another one of those episodes, like the one you told me about, when you saw him in his office fall to the floor – and Josephine had to pretend to be a nurse?'

Loyalty to the Emperor's wife made him take mild exception to her teasing tone.

'If I were you, I'd keep some sympathy for Josephine. She's always been perfectly decent to me. Napoleon needs an heir, though. All Emperors need a male heir. He knows the problem is with her, not with him. She is just too old. That mistress Eleonore gave him his little bastard son Charles, so now he knows he can be a father; apparently, he's looking around.'

'He's going to divorce Josephine?'

'I suspect so.'

'Poor toothless lady.'

'If you'd ever actually clapped eyes on her, you'd know she isn't toothless. Her teeth are just stained black. She sucked on too much sugar cane. When she was a child in Martinique.'

'She's been sucking on things ever since.'

'I must warn you, seriously. There are some observations you ought to keep to yourself, Ida. She's still the Empress of France, wife of the Emperor.'

'Sometimes it's more fun to be the mistress than the wife, eh?'

'Always.'

'So, who do you think Napoleon is eyeing up to be his second Empress?'

He cocked an eye at her. Was she seriously thinking of herself as…? No, he knew that would never be her style. Cramped. She had no interest in life at that level. She would not be alone in asking that question, though. The whole of Paris was.

'No widowed plantation owner's daughter from Martinique, that's for sure. Someone young, someone ready for babies, someone of Imperial stock. My guess – either a Russian or an Austrian princess. He's Emperor of the world, now he's forced the mighty Russians to heel. When has anyone ever risen so high? Not even Julius Caesar.

'You know, he travelled back from Tilsit in four days by carriage. I guess in a hurry to begin the search for his new bride. He beat even me.'

'Didn't you have to wait for him to leave first?'

'True, but I was determined to let nothing stop me getting back to be with you. I tried to overtake him.'

She burst out laughing and swung a pillow at him, which he easily deflected.

'Flattery, flattery, he is the Marshal of Flattery, flattery, flattery.'

Abruptly she dropped the pillow and fell on her back, her breasts heaving in a way he found most enticing.

'Flatten me.'

Ney chuckled.

'It's quite a bore, really. Being back in Paris... Napoleon being back in Paris. I'd like the victory to be forgotten soon. Just so we can get on with living life in the peace. Every night there is another celebratory ball for Napoleon, more fireworks, more cannons fired over the Seine, banquets, balls, balls, balls, and the need to dance, which I never really enjoy.'

'That all sounds rather splendid, Monsieur Marshal. In future, you should take me. You know I like to dance; you would certainly enjoy it with me. You know I like to sip champagne. Who knows?' She sat up abruptly, hands folded neatly in front of her, her chin tilted imperiously up. 'Maybe Napoleon would make me his Empress.'

Ney narrowed his eyes slightly. Coming so soon after telling himself she did not want to be Empress, the effect was slightly unnerving, even if it was meant as a joke.

'Well, we had him as our guest last night. He didn't ask after you.'

Her mouth made an 'O' of mock outrage.

'You entertained the Emperor, and you didn't invite me? I would have loved the sight of the men, their uniforms, all the braid and the medals, the exotic food and wine. You must have served vintage champagne, surely?'

'It cost a fortune. I'll have to take Friedland again to pay for it.'

'Still, I would have really loved to have come. All the court people. All the famous faces. Think of all the notables I could have talked to?'

Ney laughed and pulled her over so she lay on top of him, and he could stare into her shining blue eyes.

'Don't go turning into my wife, Ida. She loved changing our house into a version of Louis XIV's court for the night. That's all she wants to do now. Accompany the hypocritical and devious court people in their prancing about. Bowing and scraping and dressing up like cockatoos. She seems to enjoy gossiping, tittering behind her hand, who is in bed with who. Not you, of course, she would never mention you.'

'You should take me with you to the next party. As I said, you would enjoy yourself a great deal more.'

'I know it sounds exciting, but you'd really hate it. It all gets stiffer and more formal and more ceremonial by the day. To be honest, I think hobnobbing with the Czar has turned Napoleon's head. He now thinks he must be seen as the equal of the Czar. He needs a wife fit for a Czar. A child who will grow into a Czar. He's even trying to change his voice. He's trying hard to lose his Corsican accent.

'In the end, I'll be honest, it was an utterly miserable

evening. These occasions used to be enjoyable, useful even. He would get all the court crowd together and we could talk, share a few glasses of wine. Talk as men, not just as comrades and soldiers. Share jokes. Now, he sits alone, is surly—'

'More *surly* than even you?'

'Much surlier. Last night, everyone sat around with a gloomy face, waiting for some signal from Napoleon that it was permissible for the entertainment to begin. For the musicians to start playing. He didn't give one, so we just sat there. Sat there with the same people we have to sit with most evenings. They're Aglaé's people, too. I'd much rather be charging at Russians again than make small talk to any of them. I insisted on wearing my uniform, though she begged me to dress up like a court jester in some sort of parrot get-up or harlequin suit, embroidered with flowers. It would have embarrassed even Murat.'

'In all the circuses in all the world, there is no clown's costume that could possibly embarrass Murat.'

'No one played cards, hazard or whist. No one could use the very expensive billiard table Aglaé made me buy. As you know, there are very few to play on in Paris. No one even gossiped about Caroline Bonaparte cuckolding Murat with Junot, the Governor of Paris. Not in front of Napoleon anyway.'

'Everyone knows about that – even Moreau, and he's in America. Though, if you had invited me, Monsieur Marshal, I would not have mentioned anything so personal. If I ever do meet Napoleon, I will be extremely discreet. Only make social chitchat.'

'Anyway, after about two hours, the Emperor suddenly stood up and left the room, while beckoning to a lady guest to follow him – Aglaé hadn't even invited her – leaving Josephine behind in tears.'

'Such scandal!'

'Aglaé was absolutely mortified. The party broke up then, everyone too embarrassed to stay. An enormous effort for an endlessly boring evening. And whatever it is we have between us, Ida, we are never boring. Promise me never to become respectable?'

'I promise you; I don't ever intend to be the least bit respectable.'

'I can believe that.'

'So, Monsieur Marshal, what are you going to do, Monsieur Bored – bored of court, bored of Paris?'

He nudged her off him. He raised his elbows and let his head sink into the pillow. She curled up against his side.

'I think I'll buy an estate, out in the real France, make something of it. Make growing something successful. Maybe produce quality wine. I'd like a slower life. I'd like to be closer to the land. Help the peasants in some way.'

'Well, I hope you come back to see me.'

'Every other Tuesday, yes.'

'Monster.' She poked him in the chest.

'Lion, actually.'

Darkness was falling. The room was getting cooler. Ida pulled the sheets up over her hip. After that season in East Prussia, Ney knew nothing would ever feel really cold at home again. At least all that peace-making was complete for now. Austria beaten. Russia cowed. Prussia carved up like a Sunday chicken. Despite impassable terrain, bad weather and the vicious tenacious enemy.

He'd acquired a great respect for the Russian fighting man. Tough, religious, patriotic. Mostly serfs who had to serve for twenty-five years. Their life was the army. So different from the conscripted French.

He very much doubted Napoleon would ever again ask for his honest plain-speaking opinion, given the way he was treated by him now. He felt that they had been lucky in East Prussia. The Russians had simply run out of ammunition at Eylau. If they hadn't, who knows? From discussing the battle at Tilsit over dinner with a few of their Generals, it sounded like some of their manoeuvres nearly succeeded, and they could well have overrun the French.

At Friedland, Bennigsen might as well have been on their side – he misjudged the course of the battle so badly. Napoleon would have to be reckless to ever take an army east again. Thoughts of the swathes and swathes of the dead turning black in the snow after Eylau, made Ney wince.

Then he had to smile to himself. Soult was still out there, still in charge of Napoleon's new amalgamated country, the Grand Duchy of Warsaw. It was quite extraordinary how Napoleon could create new realms, the very existence of which were bound to aggravate everyone. Soult was still embroiled in all that.

It gave him a great deal of amusement to think of Soult stuck out there for months with no summons yet to return to Paris. He hadn't even managed to appear at Tilsit, trying as usual, to pretend to be a proper officer, not an outrageously over-promoted drill sergeant. As indeed he had been, when Ney first met him in Bonn and stole his girl from under his nose, or, more accurately, out of his bed.

He had just had all his baggage wagons ransacked, too. Cossacks had no doubt looted everything he had looted for himself. What do the philosophers call that? *Poetic justice.* Shame it wasn't men of the VI Corps, given how Soult's pack of thieving troops had pilfered their supplies and, in a roundabout way, provoked the Russians in East Prussia, leading to the pointless slaughter of Eylau.

Ney had sent Soult a pair of trousers to help soften the blow. Soult hadn't said thank you; he was never one to take a joke against him. Ney assumed his knives were being sharpened, rather than his hatchets buried.

Even so, as he planned, he would never have to see Soult again. He would purchase an estate, move Aglaé and the boys out there, enjoy the seasons and the peace. He'd been at war all his life, it seemed.

Napoleon must want to stop campaigning now. Napoleon wanted a new child-bearing wife and had to divorce his old one. That would keep him occupied. Then there would only be the business of running from the arms of one woman into the arms of another, a strategy little different from governing the Empire, really.

CHAPTER 10

Rain lashed at the window of the parlour of Hotel Kungsträdgården. He had been promised the best hotel in Stockholm, but in London it surely would be one of the worst. Dismal, dirty even. Quite possibly bedbugs.

Michael Bruce was already bored after only three nights. At least he had the dreary, low-ceilinged, yellow-stained room to himself. Unlike the Danes of Copenhagen, the Swedes he'd met so far hadn't much entertained him. In fact, they had added to his boredom. Unlike Copenhagen, Stockholm was lacklustre, humdrum. He should have been well on his way to St. Petersburg by now, too. He'd heard the women there were exceptionally attractive and willing, and he'd already had enough of Swedish women and their incomprehensible language.

Bruce smirked and sucked on his tawny-coloured, brand-new and highly fashionable meerschaum pipe, engraved with the image of a wolf, as he continued to picture undressing his next woman. Earlier that afternoon, he had presented his letter of credit to his father's Stockholm contact. It was given to him by his father – the tea merchant and important banker back in London. He had drawn out a substantial sum.

Yes, he'd send his valet Adam out in a while, to brave the wind and the rain and the docksides of Stockholm.

He'd give him a few coins now they had money, have him procure some light-skirt, an enthusiastic blonde lady of the night.

Adam's mother, Jeanne, had been French governess to Bruce's sister Fanny. She had enticed Father into her bed and Adam was the result. Five years older, and taller than Bruce by several inches. The "brother" word was never used, though, and few who did not know, would never have guessed when they saw the two side by side – Adam blond and taller; Bruce with his blue eyes, black curly locks and darker, Italianate skin. Yes, Adam might be here on Father's orders, to keep an eye on him, but that didn't mean Adam couldn't get a little wet in pursuit of a good cause.

It had been squally, on and off all day. Now it was really stormy. Thunder rumbled across Lake Mälaren, so no ships would be leaving Stockholm. They would be stuck here for at least another night. If he and Adam didn't get out of Stockholm, if a ship didn't leave soon, he'd have to go home, to London. But he'd hardly be welcomed there by Father, who wanted him to stay in St. Petersburg until the scandal in Cambridge blew over.

Adam seemed to have spent whole days in the kitchen since they'd arrived. Bruce had hoped there would not be any comely, willing, English-speaking girl in there, that Adam was keeping for himself.

He summoned him to the parlour.

'I'm bored. You know what I expect when I'm bored. I need some female company. Adam, I want you to go out—'

'But, sir, the weather; I will get soaked… and the town is unknown to me.'

The door was pushed open abruptly, the candles guttered, and Bruce heard a most English voice.

'Charles, take the saddle bags up to my room, then off to the kitchen with you, dry my cloak and get some food ordered.'

A tall, elegant man in a red coat, ducked his head at the doorway and came into the room. Gold braid on the shoulders, a rather stunning medal around his neck. He must be a British officer with a uniform coat like that. This must be a change for the better. Someone English to talk to, someone who might know all the latest news of who had invaded whom – of any changes to the state of the war. Napoleon was still looking supreme, to be honest, and the British were not exactly covering themselves in glory. In fact, after what he had recently witnessed, Bruce was ashamed to be British.

'No need for you to go out for a while now, Adam,' Bruce decided. 'Go over, invite him to join me, then run along and order bowls of fish stew and a jug of wine for us. And make sure the gentlemen's servant is looked after.'

Adam went to the doorway and, speaking in English, turned his hand back to point at Bruce, who raised his pipe, meeting the eye of the man with the medal.

He smiled.

Bruce smiled too as he stood up to greet the new man. Adam disappeared out of the room. Up close, the man with the medal, somewhat older than him, had a reassuringly honest-looking face and could be called handsome.

He was not as handsome as Michael Bruce, though, nor as young. Michael Bruce spent every morning admiring himself, as he stared into the mirror while Adam shaved him, and now he considered himself the superior in every way. His eyes brighter, his locks more splendid, his look overall more distinguished.

Bruce didn't have a medal, though. A medal must be an asset when he came to attracting suitable girls to marry. Even unsuitable ones to bed. The new man's medal was even more impressive close-up – a cross of gold, red and white that sparkled in the firelight.

They shook hands.

'Michael Bruce, sir. So pleased to make your acquaintance.'

'Sir Robert Wilson, at your service. Thank you for sending your man over.'

He must have noticed that his medal was being carefully studied. 'It's the Austrian Order of Maria Theresa,' he said. 'Not seen one before?'

'Can't say I have. It's a beauty. How did you win it?'

'Cavalry charge back in '94. Protecting the Emperor of Austria.'

Bruce reached out. Wilson seemed to encourage him to study the inscription more closely.

'*Fortitudini*,' Bruce said. 'For Courage?'

'That's right.'

'It's always an honour to meet a brave man. And, to be honest, I'm so relieved to meet someone who speaks English. The local language here is unlike any I've ever heard. You're still a cavalryman?'

'Not quite,' Wilson replied. 'Envoy to the Czar of Russia, British liaison to the Russian Army. Not that I've forgotten how to ride a horse.'

'What brings you to Stockholm then?'

'On a dash home. Government business. Important news needs to be delivered. What about you? What are you doing sat about here? In what must be the dreariest capital in all Europe?'

'I'm on my way to the newest, St. Petersburg. If the rain and wind ever stop and the sea becomes calmer.'

They sat down. Wilson looked at him strangely. He took a pinch of snuff from a silver tin. And as he waited until he had sneezed, then paused even longer, Bruce began to wonder if he had said something untoward.

'I've just come from St. Petersburg,' Wilson said.

'How did you find it? I am very much looking forward to visiting it.'

'It *is* rather remarkable. The Winter Palace is far more majestic than Versailles even; there is the most amazing statue of Peter the Great, absolutely huge. The whole city is a tribute to his vision for a new Russian capital. When you think about how it was constructed, it's more like the sort of enterprise a pharaoh would have been inspired to build rather than a modern ruler. He used serfs though, rather than slaves. But in Russia there is very little difference. What takes you there?'

'My father is most anxious I broaden my horizons.'

'Well, it really isn't a good idea. Bonaparte has gone back to Paris, but there are still French troops everywhere. It's not safe to be an English traveller. If I were still in St.

Petersburg, it would be different. You'd be safer. I have friends in the Winter Palace, friends in the army there, the French Consul General owes me a million favours, and I've a diplomatic passport.'

'My father is a well-connected man, Wilson. I have letters of introduction in St. Petersburg.'

'Without the world at war, Bruce, they might have been of use to you. But now the Czar has turned frosty, even to me.'

This Wilson is quite the name-dropper, thought Bruce. *Impressive, though, and well-travelled, so might be worth knowing and listening to.*

Steaming bowls of fish stew and a jug of wine, with glasses, were brought in by a long-legged buxom blonde girl. She might do. Adam could find her in the kitchen later, stuff some coins in her apron pocket. She'd come running up those stairs to his room at the top.

He ordered some schnapps so he could watch her carrying a tray back to their table from the sideboard, admiring the wiggle of her pert arse as she went back to the kitchen.

Wilson ate hungrily in silence. Hurriedly, not like a starving man, but a man who thought he had better things to do than eat. He eventually stopped when about a quarter of his stew was left. He raised one eyebrow at Bruce.

'Why do you need to broaden your horizons?'

'Sent down from Cambridge. Sticky situation with my tutor's daughter. Embarrassed my Father. He's a banker, by the way. You know what they're like. Astonishing hypocrites. He's been caught out too, with a bit of stuff, but that's another story. He thought I'd best go abroad until the dust settled.'

'That does sound an unfortunate turn of events.'

'Not the first time, either. Got into a mess at Eton. Frolic with a servant girl. Said she was having my baby.'

'And did she?'

'Don't know. Could have been anyone's. Father paid her off. She was only a servant.'

Bruce regretted it as soon as he'd said it. Wilson clearly wasn't interested in talk like this. He ought to find another topic, maybe one where he could impress the older man.

'I met the King of France the other day.'

'You did? I'd heard he'd left Russia. I believe he's having to seek refuge in England; Russia now being apparently leaning towards an alliance with Bonaparte.'

'We had dinner the other night. In Gothenburg. A most amenable evening. Yes, he's waiting passage to London. I gave him a map of Copenhagen as a gift.'

Wilson sat up, giving Bruce his full attention. Bruce was relieved. Obviously, this was a better choice of conversation.

'Why Copenhagen?' Wilson asked.

'I have just come from Copenhagen,' Bruce replied. 'I was having a rather enjoyable time there, actually. I even ate turtle soup at the court. Quite an experience. They catch it in the tropics and bring it back alive. Ready to cook. Have you tasted it?

'I met some interesting men and pretty girls in town too,' he continued. 'Then the Royal Navy arrived and bombarded the city. Although I don't look it, I'm sure I am still more than a little shaken up by the whole experience.'

'Well, I think you'll find the Danes were offered an armistice first.'

In Copenhagen – where he'd been staying for several weeks – despite Admiral Nelson sinking their fleet in 1801, Bruce had found that the Danes were not at all unfriendly towards the British. They were certainly not going to allow their replacement fleet to be used as an invasion force against England, or indeed join Bonaparte's squeeze on English trade in the Baltic.

Yes, there had been whispers, rumours, idle gossip since Tilsit. He had heard it in taverns and at parties. He himself had been asked several times if he knew if any of it were true. That there were secret clauses in the Treaty of Tilsit that allowed Bonaparte to annex Denmark. Was it true that any day now the Royal Navy would sail into the Kattegat with demands for the surrender of the Danish fleet? How should he know? It all seemed bloody unlikely. And in any case, he was only a visitor for pleasure. He wasn't a spy.

The first night of the barrage had destroyed several houses in the street near his hotel. He and Adam had been forced to flee further inland. They had watched the city burn under a bombardment of rockets; the likes of which Bruce could not even have imagined beforehand. Then Arthur Wellesley's Redcoats had routed the Danish militia: a horrible massacre.

'What have you heard about Copenhagen?' Wilson asked.

'Heard? I was there. Saw the whole damn travesty unfold.'

'Travesty?'

'The bombardment. It was still totally unwarranted. I was nearly killed. So many innocent citizens *were* killed though. Their beautiful city left in ruins.'

'Although very regrettable,' Wilson responded, 'the action in Copenhagen was a strategic necessity.'

'*Really*?' Bruce exclaimed. 'You don't think waiting to see what happened might have been a better idea? Maybe if we'd waited for the French to make an aggressive move first, the Danes might well have become our allies instead. Then we might have had all those ships without shelling the town. Now the Danes are well and truly in the French pocket. Who advises our idiotic and belligerent government?'

Wilson raised his eyebrows as if he was talking to a child.

'For your information, Bruce, I was at Tilsit, where I gathered crucial information, including that of Bonaparte's plan to seize the Danish fleet. I hurried home with that information, just as I am hurrying again now.'

'So, it's all your fault those poor Danes are dead?'

'Hindsight is a wonderful thing, especially in politics. You don't know the power of Bonaparte like I do. The power he now holds over Europe.'

'Was such a force really necessary, though? Those rockets—'

'Mr. Congreve's marvellous rockets—'

'You must have known what rockets can do when they are fired randomly on a sleeping town. Everyone must have known, too, what General Wellesley's men were capable of when they're pursuing an army. One who hasn't fought anyone for years.'

'I assure you, I have seen worse, Bruce. Much, much worse dealt out by the French. If you had been at Eylau and Friedland, as I was, you would not have risked the Danish fleet getting into Bonaparte's hands. Using it to land the Corps of men like Ney and Murat on our shores. To march towards London.'

He rose to his feet, towering above the table as he dabbed his lips with his napkin. For a moment, Bruce thought that maybe he'd expressed his own opinion too forcefully.

'So, what are you going to do now?' Wilson asked. 'The Baltic's freezing over. There's no hope of sailing to St. Petersburg until the Spring.'

'I might wait until tomorrow night, see if the situation alters. You know, weather up here can be extremely changeable.'

Wilson frowned; his eyes suddenly looked very serious. He leant closer, glanced around as if anyone could possibly eavesdrop in the otherwise empty parlour.

'Between you and me, Bruce, the reason I need to travel to London with such speed is that the Russian Empire is about to declare war on Britain. This is despite my best efforts to butter up the Czar, incidentally a great personal friend of mine. It is due to the arm-twisting of Bonaparte since Friedland and Tilsit.

'This is highly sensitive information I heard from an indiscreet diplomat in the Winter Palace, a man called Lesseps. He owed me a favour, but no need to go into that. Even now the Russian courier is on his way to London, too. It is imperative that I get this news to our government as soon as God allows.

'And I strongly advise you to return home immediately, despite how angry your father may be when he sees you. For the foreseeable future, the continent of Europe is simply not a safe place for a young man to travel round on his own. The French Army are everywhere and now, even more, will not hesitate to shoot any Englishman they might happen to meet.'

'Oh,' Bruce said thoughtfully. 'Well, if you put it like that.'

'I most certainly do.'

'You really are the first person with this news for London? You're not joshing me?'

'There's absolutely no doubt I will get to London first. I had Charles, my man, pay the chef who is cooking for the Russian messenger tonight, to serve him some bad fish. He won't be fit to travel anywhere tomorrow. I will be at least a day ahead.'

'That's an extraordinarily clever scheme. I approve!'

'It's just you and your valet? I have a coach booked for tomorrow to take me to Gothenburg to catch the packet home. Why don't you and your man join me and Captain Charles? We will go fast, I warn you.'

'That does sound like the most sensible plan of action. However, I cannot allow you to pay for such a costly carriage if myself and my servant are to be your passengers. Here, I am my father's son, able to use my letter of credit. I can well afford to pay my share.'

He fumbled in his pocket for his purse.

'Put your money away. I am an agent of the King. My expenses are all reimbursed. I am much relieved that you are coming with me, that must be the right decision.'

Wilson yawned. 'I'm off to bed now, haven't slept between sheets for too many nights. See you in the morning. Early breakfast, we leave before first light. Charles will have seen to all the arrangements so they will be tiptop. First light, I say. My coach won't wait. If I were you, Bruce, I'd get an early night, too.'

The next morning, Bruce awoke nauseated by the after-effects of too much wine. His tongue was sticking to the roof of his mouth, dried out by a thirst; the likes of which he couldn't recall ever experiencing before. There was some squawking going on. With the only eye he managed to open, he soon realised that the serving maid with the tight arse from last night had rolled herself up in the sheets. And her friend, he suddenly remembered. Three in a bed – well, there was a first time for everything. They were resisting Adam's attempts to shoo them out of the room. They were probably still naked; he had really enjoyed undressing them. He sat up. Coins were scattered all over the floor. Was that their fee or his change from their fee?

Charles suddenly appeared and threw a jug of water in his face.

So, this is how we say goodbye to Stockholm, Bruce thought as he clambered unsteadily into the coach in the grey dawn, to sit side by side with Wilson. It was so embarrassing. He looked like a man who had just had the best sleep of his life, a deep slumber that had bought colour to his cheeks. He radiated new energy, even smelt of bacon and eggs. *Breakfast*: the very thought made Bruce shudder.

Bruce heard scuffling and thuds as Adam and Charles climbed aboard the back of the coach. The wheels rolled forwards. Bruce's head swam. He must have looked pretty green about the gills as Wilson laughed. He had so obviously heard of last night's shenanigans.

'I wouldn't worry too much about missing St. Petersburg. The ladies there prefer their own men to foreigners and Cambridge is a fine city, as you know. The best place for you to study for your future career.'

The reference to Cambridge was a transparent attempt at encouraging Bruce to return there, so he ignored it.

'I've learnt a lot since I came to Europe,' he answered.

He sunk down into his coat, sat hunched, his cheek rubbing on his cravat. Hoping and praying he wouldn't vomit; the swaying coach was now going at full speed. Yes, his new friend hadn't been lying when he said he liked to travel fast.

He wasn't going back to Cambridge, though. Cambridge was what Father wanted, not what he wanted. Cambridge was simply not for him anymore. He wanted to live, to enjoy. The North had been nothing but damp, death, delays and disappointment. Let the likes of Wilson act the man of the world up there, solve its problems. England was cold, too. England had proved callous. Damn Bonaparte, interfering with his life's plans. Damn him and damn the mad Kings of England, Denmark and Sweden. Maybe that was Bonaparte's appeal. He certainly wasn't mad.

Bruce had decided he wasn't going to stay in England long. He wouldn't tell Wilson this. He wouldn't approve, and, who knew, he might be a valuable contact one day.

Bruce was going south. In his mind's eye, he saw cities on the plain, skies like a blue silk sheet endlessly unfurled. Warm, buxom, graceful women in vibrant shawls dancing barefoot in the sand. Michael Bruce was going to Spain. The King of Spain was also mad, but never mind.

PART 3

THE PENINSULAR WAR

I shall be welcomed as the Liberator of Spain
Napoleon Bonaparte

CHAPTER 11

'Well, send him up,' Ney said. He was in the games room and had just started to explain to Joseph Napoleon, his eldest, the basic principles of billiards when the major-domo announced that a message had arrived from Berthier.

'What will he want?' whispered Joseph, peering up at Ney with his mother's eyes. Ney smiled down at him.

'Who knows?' Ney said. 'If his news is boring, don't worry, we'll send him on his way. If we like it, he can stay.'

'You and boredom, Michel,' Aglaé said, bustling into the room with something of the busy hen about her, their three-week-old baby son, Eugene, cradled in her arms. Ney had not been at the confinement – no place for a husband; he'd spent an enjoyable night with Ida. Louis, their four-year-old, came running noisily into the room after her, waving a wooden sword.

'Maybe we should find something for you to do, Michel?'

'We?' he enquired, aiming his cue at the white ball, and lining it up with the red. He then stood up, put the cue down. He hoped the messenger would hasten up the stairs. Even if it was a summons to another long-winded drill and logistics meeting at the Tuileries Palace, the appearance of a messenger might encourage Aglaé to take the children away. Concentrate on something else. He knew exactly what she meant by finding him something to do.

'Michel,' she went on, 'the ladies at court keep telling me that it's our turn once again to entertain the Emperor— especially now he has created you Duke of Elchingen. What an honour.'

Ney sighed. He knew she was immensely pleased to be a Duchess. All those ladies curtsying to her. He would rather be addressed as Marshal.

'The Emperor has not said anything to me, my sweet.'

'Don't be dense, Michel, you know how these things are; *he* doesn't ask *you*.'

'I know. It's an absolute honour to shell out so much money to have the worst evening imaginable. I'll have to take another Friedland to pay for another party, then hate every minute of it. We did this last year. I don't think I have yet recovered.'

He knew Aglaé had so loved dressing up their Parisian mansion and was desperate to do it again. That was all she wanted to do now. Sashay around grand rooms in the latest fashions, mesmerise court with her beauty and status, attend dreary parties where you met the same dreary people night after night. Be seen. To him, her whole existence seemed pointless. A waste: she was not an unintelligent person.

She'd spent the two years he'd been away before Tilsit following the Empress Josephine around and having gossipy little chats, in the company of the other ladies of the court; sarcastic, catty, always sniggering behind each other's backs, scandal-mongering. All the time making sure her clothes were the finest and her jewels the brightest.

The Empress, of course, kept herself well away from the realities of the Front; the pitiful state of the military hospitals, the bedraggled hungry troops on the march, the defeated starving peasants. She only wanted to be part of the triumph when the Emperor returned to Paris, victorious.

Aglaé kept reminding him of her performances in the court operas and recitals. Yes, Ney had to admit, she had a lovely soprano voice. What he didn't go along with was her constant nagging about his flute. Yes, he was delighted to play in private with a small group of musicians from the Imperial orchestra, but not in public. Where he was known as a Marshal, not a paid piper.

Hosting Napoleon at their homes, as all the Marshals were expected to do in turn, was becoming increasingly an ordeal. In all honesty, being in the Emperor's company now was, more often than not, a tedious experience. He seemed to believe that time at his court should not be enjoyed by anyone, it should be like an Imperial Russian court ritual, or how he imagined it to be.

Ney so missed the days before the Empire, the comradeship, the witty exchanges, the enjoyable company. These days, the Emperor spent his time at any old party, sitting alone on an almost throne-like chair, which his minions had to install in advance. Just looking surly. Ney could only assume he thought he was looking Imperial.

Had she already forgotten quite how gruesome it had been the last time they entertained the Emperor? That time he had described to Ida, just after his return from Tilsit, when no one had been allowed to enjoy themselves. The Emperor had left early with an unidentified lady guest. Both Aglaé and Josephine were in tears as everyone else left too, leaving the extravagant supper buffet entirely untouched.

'We have the money,' Aglaé continued. 'Let's agree to host.' She was not prepared to let the matter drop, apparently.

'Maybe we should take ourselves to Coudreaux. Stay there until some other Marshal puts on a show,' Ney suggested, hopefully.

He had purchased the estate with its magnificent château, only a few miles from Paris, with the new riches he'd received from the Emperor after Tilsit. He so much preferred living there to Paris. He had embraced the country life and the country world, far removed from all this pomp and waste and boredom. He knew his boys loved being there, too.

And Ida was not that far away. Aglaé had long ago turned a blind eye to those visits. Ney suspected she was thankful not to have to have sex with him if it could be avoided. He could take his desires elsewhere.

'Oh Michel, I sometimes think you would rather be at war again than enjoy our good fortune.'

Before he could answer, Berthier's messenger was ushered into the room. He handed Ney a white sealed note. Ney broke the seal, read the note and nodded at the messenger that he understood. Then gave the man a coin for his trouble.

Rather annoyingly, the boys had started to chase each other around the table, making a racket. The baby began to cry, while Aglaé was looking at him with curiosity. As he allowed the ramifications of the message to sink in, it crossed his mind there would not be an opportunity for her to get pregnant again for now. And he would have to trust Ida to behave herself.

'I'm so sorry, *chérie*. VI Corps has been given urgent Imperial orders. Joseph Bonaparte has abandoned his throne and Madrid. The Emperor is sending his veteran Marshals to sort out the mess in Spain. And he is coming with us. Your party will have to wait to be held in celebration of our triumphant return.'

CHAPTER 12

CORUNNA

JANUARY 16TH 1809

This time a mighty blast came from somewhere to the north-west, from the peninsula, the harbour there. Whether it was cannon fire striking a warehouse or rampart, or once again Redcoats blowing up their own munitions, Bruce didn't know. But the explosion shook the floor of La Estrella de Mar Roja, despite the hotel being two miles along the cliff from the town. The impact vibrated in his boots. He almost slipped and, for a second, risked falling down on the floor, where he could be kicked to death by the jostling Redcoats crowding the bar.

It was a strange thought. These self-same officers could have been here, trying to get their tot of rum or tumbler of wine every day for nearly all of the three months that had passed since Bruce had last arrived in La Estrella from Plymouth.

The only hotel in Corunna, the one operating as the unofficial officer's mess.

Then, the town had been a peaceful, busy supply port.

Now, the town was besieged, the Redcoats chased to the sea by Marshal Soult and his II Corps. The campaign was lost. The harbour was packed with desperate men, injured men, men who were waiting for the voyage home. But the Royal Navy transport ships still had not arrived.

All and sundry here, including Michael Bruce, could

die at the hands of the French. The hotel was possibly the safest place to hide for the moment. But the time must come when he would have to make his way down two miles of rutted track, back to the harbour, Adam and the horses. He must not leave it too late. Just pray those naval transports arrived.

The Redcoats, crushing Bruce's shoulders as they surrounded the bar, stank of sweat, wine, snuff and saltpetre. He suspected he too smelt as bad; he couldn't remember when he last changed his clothes. Wedged, he couldn't move forwards or back.

He closed his eyes. Then opened them straight away when he saw in his mind's eye the flames on a church roof, trapped worshippers screaming inside: the blood-splattered nuns, raped by the passing enemy; English soldiers lying sozzled at a village crossroads, sleeping, blissfully unaware they were about to be stabbed by French dragoons.

A great shout went up behind him at the doorway. Instructions he couldn't make out. Threats he couldn't quite understand or hear. The Redcoats knocked back whatever was left in their mugs and turned. Buttoning up their coats, they staggered out of the bar. Must be an urgent call to some sort of action, to man some last line of defence or plug a gap. They pushed on either side of him, left and right.

Thank God, I'm not one of them, he said to himself with feeling.

The only person, apart from him, that remained in the room was the bald, leather-aproned rotund barman behind his counter who seemed frozen in terror – *and with reason*, Bruce thought. He knew there was no such thing as a well-behaved army, especially a French army. Had anyone said how far away they were? Bruce needed to know. He tried to assemble the few phrases his meagre Spanish could stretch onto the tip of his tongue.

Another rumbling boom, far off in the distance, rattled the window frames. Something silvery glinted in the far corner of the room. He wasn't the only occupant left after all. Crouched over a round wooden table was a man in a grey waistcoat and a reddish-brown coat, with pale, fine hair, thin lips and a high forehead. He was probably ten or so more years Bruce's senior. He was writing furiously in a notebook, with one of those new metal nibs. Bruce hadn't seen one in Spain, where they probably weren't even used to quill pens yet. It wouldn't have surprised him if here writing was a skill confined to priests.

Bruce had a hunch the man was English, from one of the better schools. He'd kept himself detached during the recent pandemonium. Looked rather out of place. He certainly wasn't a local and, with no uniform, was obviously not a soldier. Bruce was intrigued.

'Good day to you, sir, that's a different sort of nib. I've only seen those in London.'

'One needs to write quickly these days.'

He *was* English, then. His accent had an East Anglian burr that Bruce had not expected.

'How come you have to note anything under these horrendous circumstances?'

'Henry Crabb Robinson. Correspondent for *The*

Times of London. Extraordinary events are unfolding here that need to be conveyed to my readers at home. You know Sir John Moore is dead?'

'I do. Terrible news. An unlucky shot, which tore his shoulder apart, while he was ordering the remains of a Highland regiment to charge with their bayonets. Just because they had run out of shot there was no excuse to retreat. On the outskirts of a village called Elvina. They are burying him now. No time to take his body away from the battlefield.'

'You are very well informed – exactly how?' Crabb Robinson asked, giving Bruce his full attention at last.

'I was there. With him. All the way from Salamanca.'

'All the way from Salamanca?'

So, he was a reporter, not just any reporter but the Foreign Correspondent of *The Times*, the daily paper with the largest circulation of all. If Bruce could persuade this man to write his story, then he would be the talk of London. The people back home, even his father, would be full of admiration. Fame would open many doors. And the rich girls would be desperate to make his acquaintance.

'I am Michael Bruce.'

'Son of Craufurd Bruce, the banker?'

'Yes, that's me. Do you know my father, then? He seems to have many contacts.'

'Yes, I have come across him. So, what brings you to Spain, young Bruce?'

'Well, I came for a tour in the sunshine. What I didn't expect was to be caught up in a bloody war.'

'Sit down, Mr. Bruce,' Crabb Robinson invited.

'Thank you.' Bruce pulled up a chair and sat down. He found his meerschaum pipe in the pocket of his coat, then his tobacco, filled the pipe's bowl and struck a match.

'I think I need to tell you of all the horrific sights I have seen, so you can report the correct story to the British people from one who has experienced the brave retreat of the British Army, first hand.'

Some three months ago, Bruce had stood on the deck of the Falmouth-Corunna packet. The ship was tacking against the wind as land – the cliffs of Spain – came into view. They had experienced heavy weather, gales and a rough sea in the Bay of Biscay. It was good to be able at last to anticipate the beginning of his new escapade. He felt free, devilishly free.

According to Father, he should be in Cambridge, where it was assumed he would be studying to be a barrister, readying himself for a dreary career. Not sparking new scandal by removing the undergarments of female servants, and to just be busy with his books. According to Mother, if he was not to be in Cambridge studying hard, he should be in London for the season, improving his prospects, looking for a rich, eligible young lady to become his honoured wife. All the while under the gaze of a chaperone (so as not to see what was under the skirts until *after* the wedding). He had no doubt that any girl Mother introduced him to would be most probably an heiress, a simpering and sexless fool, who, after marriage, would be entirely to blame for him removing the undergarments of even more servant girls. To attend to his lusts, if she wasn't prepared. Still her dowry would be useful he supposed, husbands had total control over their wife's money.

That was definitely for the far distant future. He had really needed to get away from London to be himself. A good distance from watchful parents. He was in Spain for adventure, and a certain type of sensual adventure. England sometimes allowed such adventure, but it never allowed you to not get caught. English girls were a marriage trap. But the girls of Spain, they were dusky, big-breasted, flirtatious, barefoot types who he could imagine from the ones he had seen in certain publications that the boys passed around at Eton.

He hadn't thought there was much in the way of war in Spain, either. The threat of it seemed so distant. After his sorties to Copenhagen and Stockholm, he'd felt the need to take the advice of that man Wilson. Go south. Get right away from the looming presence of Bonaparte in Eastern Prussia and the aggression and brutality of his so-called countrymen.

At least Bonaparte liked women. Just as he, himself, liked women. Every Englishman he met didn't seem to like women. Those at home preferred money. Those abroad preferred war.

The small and far from magnificent harbour of Corunna came into sight, the gateway to a Spain that he hoped would be waiting for him – not so much with open arms but with open legs. Bruce reminded himself he had not had the pleasure of a real live woman since Stockholm. Then it had been with two willing girls; the three in a bed had been a revelation. He made a mental list of the sort of woman he would need once the packet dropped anchor: not too tall, not too plump, not too ignorant, not too smart. This last of the list to be emphasised above all else in the instructions he would give to Adam, when he sent him off into the town to look for the right wench.

Most of the time he just wished his parents hadn't insisted his so-called brother travel with him. 'You're not going otherwise; you are too young to be in Europe on your own,' Father had said, before handing him his substantial letter of credit and a purse full of gold. But Adam *did* have his uses; Bruce could hardly go round the back streets looking for light-skirt himself.

The harbour was too shallow for ships to drop anchor close to the shore. Bruce already knew this, hence his insistence that he and Adam travel light. Their few cases were loaded onto the rowboat. He kept the leather knapsack close, made especially for the trip, a thoughtful present from his mother, with his gold and flintlock inside. Adam had a pistol too and they had both been given instruction on how to fire.

As the rowboat approached a jetty, a disgusting reek wafted over from the town. On first contact, Spain stank. Stank of refuse and rot, putrefying fish and death. Adam, ever credulous, tried to make out that maybe the land smelled more pungent after all the days they had spent in the fresh sea air. *More likely*, Bruce thought, *that here they catch netfuls, gut the fish, then leave the innards to the gulls on the docks and quaysides.*

Corunna. The name had a certain ring to it. It sounded like a festive destination, a place that would ring with song and dancing in the evenings after heady days of heat and wine. Yet here it was, swathed in mist and stinking of fish. He soon discovered as he surveyed the town from the back of a cart driven by the most miserable peasant in all of Iberia, how it was also crawling with English Redcoats. What on earth were they doing here? Thousands of miles from Bonaparte. He asked the surly peasant driver what was going on, but the man just shrugged. It was a shame that no one rich and celebrated was here to welcome him to Spain.

The stink only lifted when they reached La Estrella de Mar Roja, high along the cliff. Apparently, the only hotel in town and clearly not even in the league of the Hotel Kungsträdgården in Stockholm.

First impressions did not bode well. Bruce expected there was not even a proper parlour, the place to be full of thieves. Still, all he needed was a room of his own where he could entertain some local tarts. Spend a few days enjoying his first real taste of freedom before deciding where to go next in this big, wide, sandy world. That world would be his pleasure palace. It might even broaden his horizons as Father had instructed!

He paid the surly peasant, then sent Adam back into Corunna on the back of the cart with explicit instructions to bring back somebody willing, in a dress. He needed to experiment with a hot-blooded señorita.

The bar of La Estrella was full of heaving, shouting, singing, and arguing Redcoats, apparently officers, some half in and half out of their uniforms. Someone was playing an accordion, sitting next to him were two barefoot girls who gave him the eye. Neither looked very appealing. Bruce thought he might as well wait to see what Adam turned up with before he settled for any entertainment offered here.

He tested his Spanish by ordering a jug of wine. Casting his eyes around the bar to see if he'd missed any prettier girl, he noticed a man at a round table – the metallic lace epaulette on his right shoulder marked him out as a Captain. One of his sleeves was empty, hung slack at his side.

Bruce took a sip of wine. It struck him whatever had happened to that fellow's arm, he would probably be able to tell him something of why the town was overrun with Redcoats. What exactly was going on in Spain. He needed to know this, not because of his enthusiasm to follow current affairs, but because he really didn't want any more military games to get in the way of his Grand Tour.

He sauntered over. The man's eyes were bloodshot, and he too stank of sweat.

'Michael Bruce, of London, Eton, and Cambridge. Mind if I sit down? Of course you don't. Here, have a top-up.' Wine was poured liberally into the man's mug. 'Whatever has happened to your arm?'

The man drank deeply. Then answered, 'Surgeon had it off me.'

'Oh no, I hope you were engaged in some distinguished struggle, with whatever enemy you face out here.'

'Too much of this,' the man said, poking at his mug with his thumb. 'Next day, couldn't sit straight in the saddle and came off me horse. Fell on a jagged rock. This place is all rock and sand and death. Might as well hand it back to the fucking Moors.'

'Quite,' Bruce agreed. 'I hear they cut out the tongues of wine drinkers. What exactly are you doing here, Captain... er?'

'Gorlick. 'Ere, got any more of that brew? Thank you, I don't mind if I do. Captain Gorlick of the Fifteenth Hussars to you.'

'So, what is next for Captain Gorlick of the Fifteenth?'

'Ten more pints of this, so hopefully I'll sleep till Falmouth. I'm off home on the next packet. I'm mightily relieved to be leaving, I can tell you. I had to ride three hundred miles with only one arm, hurting like the devil, too. I told Old General Moore when I went to say goodbye, even an officer can come off his horse, wine or no wine. I pretended I was sorry to be abandoning him in the struggle to come. He was just about to chase after Marshal Soult, if he could only find where he'd gone.'

'Who is this Old Moore? I thought you wanted to hand Spain over to the Moors?'

'Sir John Moore. He's camped down in Salamanca.'

'Sir John Moore!' exclaimed Bruce excitedly. '*That* Sir John Moore? Stuffy sort of type? No fun, no humour? Doesn't like Christmas? Knows my father?'

Gorlick shrugged. 'Could be the same one.'

'Are there two Sir John Moores in the British Army?'

'Not to my knowledge.'

'Oh my. Salamanca, you say? What on earth is he doing there?'

'We are assisting the Spanish rebellion.'

'What rebellion?'

'Against the fake King Joseph Bonaparte, another of the Emperor's brothers he's stuck on a throne. The Spanish Army and practically all the Spanish people have taken up arms against him. They are calling Bonaparte himself the Antichrist; they are the most fanatical Roman Catholic nation I have encountered. It could be said to be a religious war. Our army has been sent to their aid. As I already told you, Sir John is pursuing Soult.'

'Salamanca, that's where I will be going next, Captain Gorlick. Sir John needs a visit from me, sounds like he might like to see a friendly face from London. Any chance I can beg or buy a map from here to Salamanca?'

'No, but I can sell you something else if you've plenty of gold. Follow me, before we get too sozzled.'

Around the back of the hotel was a small grimy stable where Captain Gorlick introduced him to Hamlet, a big bay, and Ajax, a spectacular dappled grey. Among the finest horses Bruce had seen, despite being around horse-breeding people all his life.

They looked fit, obviously of good temperament, familiar – according to Gorlick – with the roads and the terrain, as well as the heat of Spain. It was no fault of Ajax he had fallen off and landed on the rocks. He was very short of cash now he'd lost his commission as well as his arm, and if Michael Bruce was intending to travel to

Salamanca and beyond, this pair of fine horses were just what he needed.

'Oh yes, I'm sure they will do splendidly.'

He handed over what seemed a hefty amount of his father's gold. Still, it looked like Captain Gorlick deserved some fortune now he had a pretty bleak future to look forward to. Bruce watched him waddle off into the darkness and was left patting the warm flank of the grey horse. Ajax, he had already decided, would be his to ride. Adam could have the bay. And he could keep an eye on them here in the stable after he'd turned up with what should be the first of Michael Bruce's new female companions.

Probably best, though, not to tell Sir John any tales about his fun in bed with local girls when they reached Salamanca. Bruce thought he was a dry old stick and not interested in that sort of entertainment. Still, he would roll out some sort of carpet for Michael Bruce, and no doubt show him around the city and introduce him to the social whirl.

Bruce was still getting into his stride. The wine jug was empty, as were the two bowls of surprisingly tasty stew they had consumed. The British supply boats had arrived; fresh food from England at last.

Crabb Robinson set aside his nib and laid it with his notebook on the table.

'I am not sure,' he interrupted Bruce, 'that the British people are quite yet ready for such a story, fascinating as it is just to hear the way you tell it. You're sure you're not really Lord Byron masquerading under another name?'

'No,' Bruce replied with a grin. 'Personally, I think he writes godawful poetry.'

'You want me to mention your father is also your valet's father, and you use your half-brother to seek out local tarts for you?'

'Happens to be true, but you're right, maybe do not include these details, might upset your feminine readers.'

'To be honest, I think we can merely report to my editor that you arrived in Corunna looking for adventure and discovered your family friend, the great and noble General Sir John Moore, was encamped at Salamanca, and you went there to see if you could aid in the war effort. So, what happened on the road from Corunna to Salamanca?'

'Three hundred miles and no girls, that's what happened.'

'You saw nothing that interested you?'

'I saw absolutely nothing of interest.'

'And in Salamanca?'

'He wasn't there.'

'You mean he wouldn't see you?'

'I mean, I didn't see him. He was out of town, reviewing troops, issuing orders. No one was there to meet us, show us around. It was most disappointing. The place is drab; a university with no undergraduates, too many churches filled with old people praying, no social life at all. The military men's sole topic of conversation was the war. We hung about for four days, or maybe five, mainly just to rest our legs and the horses, of course. Then real boredom began to get at me.'

'You didn't even meet Sir John Moore?'

'Not the first time we were in Salamanca. In between times, I headed for Madrid. Knew my godfather was there and I would have a real welcome.'

'Madrid? And what happened in Madrid?'

'Bonaparte.'

CHAPTER 13

Bonaparte was supposed to have been defeated, of course. Since Bruce had arrived in Madrid, every Spaniard he rubbed shoulders with, insisted that the French had been driven out of Spain. The fake King Joseph had run away with his tail between his legs. Their General Castanos had overwhelmed them at Bailen. Was now preparing to invade France itself and take Paris from under Bonaparte's nose.

It was then with some surprise to Bruce, only three days after he had arrived, as he was lying in bed with God only knows who, after drinking God knows how much of God knows what the night before, that Adam barged in without knocking. Just as if he was allowed to swan in whenever he liked.

'Mr. Bruce. We need to leave urgently. Bonaparte is marching on Madrid.'

'That's nonsense. Bonaparte. I was reliably informed his army had been completely crushed.'

'But, sir, Bonaparte himself has arrived in Spain. He has forced his way over the mountains and won a significant victory at Somosierra. And right now, he's marching towards Madrid.'

'I'm sure he'll leave us be as tourists, we're not exactly spies. Be a good man and fetch me some breakfast, something for the wench.'

'Sir, the rumour is that the French will shoot all Englishmen on sight when the army arrives in town.'

'Poppycock. Sir Charles Stuart is still British Minister here. This house is our safe place.'

They had been staying in Sir Charles's mansion as guests for the last three days. The British Embassy was a veritable fortress.

'Sir, it was Sir Charles who informed me of the urgency of this turn of events. He himself has already left Madrid. He insists we do, too. He did come to collect you, but you could not be roused.'

Bruce got out of bed, wrapped the sheet around his waist, leaving the girl uncovered and still drowsing. She wouldn't mind being seen in the nude; it happened often enough. He staggered over to the nightstand and poured the jug of water over his head. His head throbbed. His eyes were sore. His throat was parched. He threw open the shutters. The sky above Madrid was a bright, clear blue, deep and beautiful.

The harsh light made him blink. Sir Charles was right. Pandemonium down below, people running this way and that. Carts, overladen with household stuff and elderly people clinging on the top, were being hastened out of town, the horses being whipped. Shops were being shuttered up. Windows were being boarded.

Fear stalked the streets again and these streets had already seen massacres, so much blood running in their gutters. He and Adam were going to have to leave smartish. Such a shame! He was just beginning to enjoy himself here and now the damnable Bonaparte was spoiling his party yet again.

Madrid: capital of Spain. He'd expected it to be more like London than Stockholm. It was basically, though, a Stockholm made out of sand, shit and flies. The cathedrals were crumbling. On the outskirts, all the houses were built of mud bricks. The people a miserable lot, dressed in ragged clothes. Their only pastime seemed to be praying. Well, that hadn't done them much good, apparently.

Even the roads were in a terrible condition because the stones had been ripped up to toss at the French. It made getting around by horse rather more arduous than was usual in a city. Still, so far, the two ladies of the night he'd sampled were marginally better-looking and certainly more cheerful and eager to please than in Stockholm, or Corunna for that matter.

When Bruce had arrived in Madrid, as he on Ajax and Adam on Hamlet rode through the desolate streets, he felt exhausted, as if he hadn't slept for days. It was mid-afternoon, late in the year with a certain nip to the breeze despite the sunny climate.

If Father's friend Sir John Moore had proved elusive in Salamanca, hopefully this was not to be the case of Sir Charles Stuart. He was one of his godfathers and had been present at the christening. His, of course, not Adam's. No one had celebrated *that* event.

The horses had trotted wearily into the courtyard of the Stuarts' official residence in the centre of Madrid,

Bruce almost too tired to dismount. A smiling Sir Charles had appeared, flanked by two grooms and two maids bearing beakers of water and damp towels. This was more like it!

'Michael Bruce, what a delight, what a surprise. We are both a long way from home,' Sir Charles welcomed him.

Bruce noticed his hair had receded a little more since they last met in London at some Christmas fete his mother had organised. He kept this observation to himself.

'Should your father see you in such tattered clothing and in dire need of a shave, he might well assume you have been flogged for desertion.'

'I am not enlisted, Uncle Charles.'

'Come, take some refreshments. Let me show you to your quarters. Be our guest. Stay as long as you like. We are short of amusing company here. You must use us as your headquarters to explore Madrid.'

'I think I've already seen it.'

Even so, if he could find adventure in the only hotel in Corunna, he could find it in the only real city in Spain. Three days here and Sir Charles had taken him to one ball and an opera. He and Adam had wandered around the liveliest areas of the city, weaving in and out of tavern courtyards and wine shops, looking for girls, looking for vendors of decent port rather than sellers of the often-wretched local wine.

He'd noticed many of the Spanish men hung around in full dress uniform whatever they were doing, apparently not on a military activity at all. When he'd mentioned this to Sir Charles, he was informed that dressing up was a way for '*the better off*' in Madrid to avoid conscription. They could pretend to be soldiers but dodge the horror of battle. They would pay for their uniforms and equipment, do a bit of conspicuous parading or guard duty, but effectively they had bought an exemption.

Bruce quite understood this instinct to hide from the beastliness of combat, but from his bedchamber window he could see none of the usual popinjay types strutting about. No one was wearing their uniform. There was a strange rushing sound on the breeze, distant crowds, shouting. The city was clearly in ferment.

And then the terror struck: if the French caught up with him, no amount of Father's gold was going to stop them from shooting or hanging him. It was not supposed to be like this. Why couldn't peace continue long enough for him to enjoy his Grand Tour?

'Adam, saddle the horses. We're leaving. Right now.'

He tried to keep the tremor out of his voice; he didn't want Adam to realise he was so frightened.

'What about our luggage, sir?'

'Forget it. We'll pack only what fits in the knapsacks Mother gave me. And take whatever her name is down with you. Quickly, Adam, while I dress.'

When the room was empty, Bruce poured what was left of the jug of water over his head, hoping to shock some of last night's wine and port. The wine in his head stayed put as he tugged on some clothes, stuffed his gold, letters of credit, pipe and pistol into his knapsack. Napoleon was coming. Madrid was over. Spain was over.

Salamanca. He would head back to Salamanca. Sir John might still be there. If he had already left, they would just have to find out which way he'd gone and follow him.

Some two hours later, they were on the road out of Madrid, going back the way they had so recently come. Only this time the wheels of hundreds of carts and wagons, and the hooves of hundreds of horses, mules and donkeys threw up vast clouds of dust that obscured the sky. Making the plain seem even more desert-like. Everyone who wasn't Spanish – and many who were – were fleeing Madrid before Napoleon arrived. The going was slow, their horses plodding in the heat. The roads were too crammed and crowded to make any sort of progress.

What worried Bruce most was not provisions for him and Adam. He was more concerned they would run out of water for the horses. Adam had filled as many skins as he could, back at Sir Charles's, but if they weren't topped up and ran out, eventually the horses would give up the ghost. Then he and Adam would be left stranded, wilted in the dust with an enormous French army creeping up behind them unopposed.

It took two days to reach Toledo. The city was eerie. The arrival of the hordes coming from Madrid didn't seem to worry the locals at all. You wouldn't have thought war was coming, that the Ogre of Corsica was coming, crushing cities and armies, like the locals crushed grapes.

But shops here were open and willing to sell. Markets were thriving. He wasn't going to stay long enough to find out if this tranquillity and normality would continue once the French army stormed through. They found a hostel and beds. Adam slept with the horses in case they were stolen. Their supplies of water were thankfully replenished. They were gone from Toledo at dawn the next day.

The following day, the roads were far less busy. Bruce, at last, had a chance of observing the scenery. The plain here was vast, almost featureless, except for looming far-off mountains, snowy peaks where Bonaparte had already crossed.

Later, they came to a fast-flowing river, which again allowed the horses to drink their fill. Their mounts were exhausted and needed rest and fodder. It was a matter of some discussion whether they should push on and get as far as possible along the road to Salamanca, or camp where they were. Even though they didn't really know exactly where that was.

The river was fordable, so they crossed it, leading the horses on foot. As the short day was beginning to turn to dusk, the riverside pathway opened out into a tiny hamlet, a scattering of hovels little better than hutches. Bruce stayed with the horses at the centre and sent Adam off with a coin to see if someone here would rent them somewhere to sleep for the night. The place alarmed him. He hadn't been convinced before that people actually lived like this. That they had to scratch each day's existence from the dirt. It made him think how people of his class could stay in their own enclosed entitled world, not really knowing what happens beyond. No idea how the majority of people have to exist.

Adam came back seemingly pleased that they could stay in the largest and best household here. This was hardly the stately manor. Any sense of 'best' was relative to the other shacks and houses, better suited for animals than people.

The inside of it stank worse than a stable anyway. One large hall, hay-strewn, was shared by two men, three hideous women, a dozen staring children. As well as cows, that were openly milked, pigs, chickens and ducks, all of which did their business whenever they felt like it. A fire in the middle of the room sent smoke up into the rafters. There was no chimney, so the curling smoke continually trapped in the back of the throat. Bruce soon picked up the same hoarse cough that everyone else had. The stew he gratefully received was grisly fat balls in a thin sauce that tasted vaguely of mud. It might have been better not to have eaten it, despite being famished. When the fire reduced to smouldering embers, the family kicked off their wooden shoes and slid into the straw, fully dressed, to sleep.

Bruce was afforded the luxury befitted to his station by being allowed to sleep on a chest, with his cloak pulled around him and a pillow of straw under his head. Something like sleep followed. It was an uneasy sleep; he had some doubts as to whether he would ever wake up.

Nor would he want anyone at home to find out his Grand Tour had come to this. He had literally ended up in the muck.

It was still dark when he woke with a start. Some vast shadow loomed, something solid, breathing in the gloom, not one of the large peasant women. A cow. A cow had lumbered over and was eating the straw of his pillow. This was the absolute end. His dreams were in tatters. This was not what he had expected when he'd stood on the deck of the packet and seen the harbour of Corunna come into view. Or, for that matter, when their horses had trotted around the courtyard of Sir Charles Stuart's residence and, for three days, all of Madrid seemed to want him.

If Sir John had left Salamanca and they had no idea in which direction he had gone, they would face certain death, either from the French, the locals, or the winter. It seemed a nightmare with only one end. Why, oh why, had Bonaparte come from Paris to spoil Michael Bruce's fun and adventures?

CHAPTER 14

'Keep an eye on her,' Ney told Fezensac as he handed over the reins of the horse he'd borrowed. 'She's a skittish one, not like Concorde.'

The stables at Charmatin were small and squalid, and the local grooms, with their sly glances, made him uneasy. He did not want to turn his back on them. He hadn't wanted to turn his back on any Spaniard since he'd arrived in this damned country four months ago.

He left his aide-de-camp with the six escorting guards. At least they had all made it here from Madrid unscathed, only an hour's journey, unbothered by bandits or pot-shots from the scrub.

He did feel spruce and clean today. His valet had given him a decent shave this morning and he had donned the smarter of his Marshal's uniforms. After all, he was about to have an audience with the Emperor, yet another one he might not survive with all his feathers intact.

Behind him, the men must have thought he was out of earshot.

'Eh, Raymond, remember that horse at Eylau that bit that Russian's face off?'

'This isn't that horse. But I wager she would have your face off as well.'

'My wife tried that on me. That's why I have to approach her always from the rear.'

Ney smirked. It had at least been good to be back with the men of VI Corps. Despite his position, part of him would have preferred to have stayed in the stable with the men, shared a pipe or some snuff, rather than face His Imperial Majesty's fury.

In the main courtyard, the azure skies overhead and the crisp, rather than cold, December weather confused him. Maybe he had preferred it in East Prussia two years ago, when at least you could depend on winter being winter. Inside, the house was grey and hardly furnished. In the hallways and rooms downstairs, aides and couriers milled and chattered, carrying boxes of books, map cases, bottles. Upstairs, a sentry outside the bedchamber saluted, opened the door.

'Marshal Ney, Sire,' he announced.

He gestured with his hand and allowed Ney into the dingy, cramped room. There was a huge fire roaring in the grate with a waist-high pyramid of logs piled next to it. It crossed Ney's mind whether the Emperor felt he needed to keep himself overly warm to ward off seizures.

He was apparently sulking, sitting on the end of the bed kicking his heels. He looked much fatter than the last time Ney had socialised with him in Paris. He did look a little like the big, greedy baby depicted in the cartoons in the London press. Journals that were easily obtained on the streets of Paris. At least Ney could now see where they had got the idea from. It was no laughing matter, though. He must show nothing other than humility and respect, given what he was supposed to have done. He saluted.

Napoleon didn't stand up. He slowly turned his head and opened one eye wider than the other.

'What have you got to say for yourself this time, Ney?'

Ready, but of course unable, to ask His Imperial Majesty the same question, Ney felt his face grimace. With the heels of his boots pressed together and the point of his sword brushing the back of his knee, the light of the fire flickering across the frowning Emperor's cheek, it felt that the last year had not happened.

That the hero of Friedland had not enjoyed his fame and new-found wealth, that he had not had days of joy in Paris and at the estate he had bought at Coudreaux. That there had not been wine and dancing with Aglaé, wine and passion with Ida, and mornings spent teaching his boy, little Joseph, how to ride a pony. All this had seemed to be his new life as a very successful man, until that courier arrived in early August. Napoleon himself was to intervene in the escalating war in Spain. Going to the Peninsula in person. Marshal Ney and VI Corps were accompanying him.

Contrary to Ney's optimistic predictions, after Tilsit, the Portuguese had not closed their ports to the British. For some reason assuming if they couldn't sell their port wine, they'd run out of money. Last year, Napoleon had had enough of the excuses coming from Lisbon and saw Portugal as a soft target, with an unprepared army that was ripe for absorption into the Empire. And the British wouldn't be able to stop him.

Napoleon had sent General Junot to swat the Portuguese fly. His army was allowed to pass through Spain, because by now Spain was allied closely enough with France to have its troops fighting against the Swedes, its ships sunk by the Royal Navy.

Plenty of troops were sent to Spanish towns to back up Junot's invasion. Murat and his cavalry were sent to Madrid for, it was said, totally friendly reasons. Even so, moving men across Spain was much easier in Napoleon's head than it was on the ground. So, it was with a much-reduced force that Junot marched into Lisbon a year ago. The city crumpled like a paper doll under a dragoon's boot.

Enough warning, though, had been given for the Portuguese Royal Family, the Braganzas – probably a sharper bunch than the Spanish Bourbons – to flee to Brazil under British escort. They had taken their treasury and art collections with them. Lisbon's merchants and anyone who was anyone in Portugal had boarded the ships, too. Portugal had been stripped bare of wealth, even before any French Marshal had a chance to set foot there.

For Napoleon, however, it looked like Portugal had folded at the merest display of French arms. The whole of Iberia was now open for him to incorporate into his Empire. Its thrones were available to whoever he wanted to sit on them. At that moment, it must have all looked very easy to him.

Not long after, Lisbon flared up.

Trade had collapsed. The whole economy collapsed. Life in the city was at a standstill. No one was in charge of the rest of the country. Napoleon made Junot really popular by sticking a whopping indemnity on an already bankrupt country. The whole place was in turmoil and Junot was completely unable to cope.

Ney even felt a bit sorry for him. He had been sent into what was, in retrospect, an unpredictable mission in an unstable country, a long way from France. Where he had expected an easy victory and a Marshal's baton. Instead, he had stones thrown at him by peasants. There was no enemy army to come out into the open for him to beat, redeem himself. Meanwhile, in Paris, Napoleon wrote him off as a failure when Junot had followed orders to the dot.

Murat, or some other Marshal, might well have been sent to relieve Junot. But last May, Madrid openly revolted against Murat, while Napoleon was in Bayonne trying to swap Spain's mad King Carlos for his idiot son, Fernando.

Murat's boys probably went a bit far repressing the fighting in Madrid. Napoleon must have concluded that all the Spanish opponents could be dealt with at once and decided the best way to restore order would be to install one of his stumbling, cowardly brothers as King of Spain. None of them were up for it, apart from Joseph, who was already sitting on what was probably the least enticing throne in Europe, Naples. Spain must have seemed like a promotion. So, Joseph was installed as King in Madrid, and with him the promise of order, stability, reform, the Code Napoleon, all that the new Empire could offer.

Were the Spaniards grateful and excited? No, the whole country exploded. Not only did the whole country explode but it encouraged the rest of Portugal to revolt, too. Armies were prowling all over the Peninsula. Savagery that wouldn't even enter the head of the most deranged and ferocious Cossack broke out. Torture and rape and butchery ran amok. It was hardly safe to be a French soldier. To cap it all, some British upstart General called Wellesley, kicked Junot out of Lisbon. Central Portugal became to all intents and purposes a British stockade.

If news of all this hadn't been sufficient to send Napoleon into a day-long incandescent fury, just imagine the outburst in the Tuileries when a courier brought news that General Dupont had been routed at Bailen, in the hot south of Spain. Not by a British General reported to be a bit of an infantry genius, but by a Spanish rabble led by a nobody called Castanos.

In Madrid, the Spanish were proclaiming a great patriotic victory. That the army of Spain would now march on Paris and knock the Emperor off his perch. Suddenly, Madrid was no longer surrounded by a screen of French troops and was open to attack by overwhelming numbers of Spanish. Brother 'King' Joseph Bonaparte had to make a hasty exit.

Ney could almost sense the incredulity following the success at Bailen being felt, not just in London, but in Berlin, Vienna, St. Petersburg, and Stockholm. This was the first ever defeat of the French Empire of Napoleon. France was clearly not invincible.

This Spanish triumph had to be avenged. The Emperor had ordered the cream of the Grand Armée to Spain along with his top Marshals. This is why Ney now found himself stood in a country house on the outskirts of Madrid, being scowled at by Napoleon, when he should have been in Paris, relishing the slow removal of Ida's dress, the softness of her breasts and the squeeze of her thighs against his thighs.

He could see from Napoleon's expression that as far as he was concerned, the reason he was here in a country house on the outskirts of Madrid, instead of gallivanting around Europe looking for a bride fit for the equal of Czars, was that his Marshals were greedy incompetents. *They* had drawn him into this mess. They couldn't win a battle without him holding their hands and telling them what to do.

Napoleon's strategy had been to take Madrid, use it as a stepping stone to oppress all of Spain. Ney's VI Corps had been part of the left-wing of this thrust. The plan was for Marshal Lannes to punish Castanos, for the fluke of Bailen. Once his army was in retreat, in a pincer movement typical of Napoleon, Ney was supposed to take Castanos from behind, wiping what remained of his forces out for good and leaving the prize – Zaragoza – open for Lannes to take before the onward push to Madrid.

VI Corps, though, had stayed where it was, had not moved for two days. Castanos had escaped with much of his force unscathed and was now safely inside the city of Zaragoza. Lannes was forced to lay siege. It was looking like it was going to take months and months for Zaragoza to fall, when Napoleon needed Lannes elsewhere.

Well, Ney had assumed Spain at least was a chance to add to his reputation as a lion, not to his reputation for disobeying orders. The thing is, as far as he was concerned, he hadn't disobeyed orders. He'd been bogged down by the orders being incompatible with the conditions.

'I thought my orders were clear,' Napoleon said, standing up and trying to strut along the length of the cramped room as if it were a parade ground, with his left hand tucked in his jacket. Ney wondered, not for the first time, whether he did this out of fear of losing control, fear of fitting.

'And in Vittoria you said you understood, Ney.'

'I did fully comprehend. My Emperor.'

'Then tell me why did you not close the trap with Lannes? Why is this amateur soldier Castanos still on the loose? These Spaniards are usually no better than Arabs. Running away is their idea of glory. Why do I have to do everything myself?' he shouted.

'Sire, with all due respect. No one could have delivered on those orders. On the ground, the timescale, it proved impossible. Even though I marched my men almost beyond endurance. There were no proper roads. Even in Prussia, in winter, there were roads.'

'Let me remind you, Marshal, that you used roads as an excuse for not arriving on time at Eylau.'

'The roads there were impassable and needed to be cleared for horses, Sire. Here, there are not even roads. Their roads are what we use to herd goats. The maps I was given were clearly so old, they might as well have been of the Garden of Eden. I find now that messages sent to me did not arrive, intercepted by the marauding peasants. And we were sat at the foot of mountains, full of brigands and irregulars, sniping, stealing, sneaking, cutting throats.'

'More excuses, Ney. Look around here. These are roads much better than the ones I used to cross the Alps.'

'Sire, I was told Castanos had defeated Lannes.'

'Lannes, defeated. By Castanos. *Unthinkable.*'

'It was two days before I was informed of the truth. By which time, it was too late.'

'I gave the order, Ney.'

'What would you have me do, squander VI Corps as well as Lannes's in the unlikely event that Lannes had been defeated?'

'Ney, I have seen you overcome greater odds.'

'In other places, where the peasants are not hiding behind every tree, ready to cut our throats. I thought caution amid confusion was prudent, Sire.'

'Well, I suppose you did keep the Corps relatively unharmed. Only a few men lost to the – what do we call them here? – the *guerrilleros*.'

'They revolt me, Sire. They should come out and fight like men.'

Ney said this to conceal his grudging admiration for them. What would he – or indeed Napoleon – have done in their position? If an army that they knew they could not beat in a fair fight, came over the mountains and deposed their King, messed with everything, stole vast sums of French treasure, wouldn't they fight them in any way they could? Wouldn't they cause as much mayhem as possible?

'They will not stand and fight again when they see the Grand Armée in all its glory, eh?'

Napoleon's attempt at standing up to face the much taller Marshal failed, and he sat down with a bump on the end of the bed.

'Relax, Ney, I won't have you shot this time.'

Ney allowed himself to breathe more easily. Perhaps Napoleon had seen his soldier's logic after all. He was not known as the greatest French commander for nothing. However tangled and obscure the situation seemed, Napoleon had always been proved right in the end. Ney hoped this was so, this time, anyway.

'You still like a fire, Sire?' he asked, changing the subject, nodding at the blaze.

'I can't warm up,' Napoleon replied.

'Not even here? Remember after Eylau?'

'It's said it's better to be too warm than too cold.'

'You don't fancy staying in Madrid then, Sire? It would certainly be warmer in the centre. There are several more comfortable places which would make a grand HQ. The abandoned British Embassy for one.'

'No, I'd rather remain here. Away from the stench. They may call it a capital city, but it's a sinkhole, isn't it? It's more like Cairo than Paris or Vienna. Mud huts everywhere, hovels no better than pig sties. Crumbling churches. I hear they have pulled up the stones in their own roads, leaving deep potholes, the oafs. When we're finished here, when Spain is French, we'll leave instructions to build a city the world will never forget.'

'I am sure you will, Sire.'

'We need to show these people Spain is French now. Tomorrow, Ney, I'll come to Madrid, review the troops, including the VI Corps. Show the hovel-dwellers a real army before we make our move.'

'Our move, Sire?'

'There is news from Soult.'

'Soult, Sire? I provided him with a pair of Polish trousers. Do they no longer fit?'

'No ruler on earth could reconcile the pair of you. You all need to be working in concord. It's the way conflicts are won.'

'I assure you that I only want to win, Sire.'

'But for that you all need to cooperate. Soult has lost two brigades of cavalry.'

'To the Spanish?'

'No, to the British.'

'The British?'

'Sir John Moore's force is advancing towards Salamanca. That's where we're heading. Catch them in a trap. Cut off the leopard's tail. Then Spain will fall, and we can all go home. Ready your men, Ney. I will inspect them at dawn tomorrow, then we ride. Across the Sierras.'

On the walk back to the stables, after the relief subsided that he had not witnessed another Imperial shaking fit, came further relief that tomorrow he would be on the way to doing some proper fighting. Taking his cavalry out into the wide-open spaces of the Sierras against an enemy who would at least stand and fight.

But something about Napoleon bothered him. Something about his tone when he'd said "we can all go home" sounded like he wasn't taking this campaign seriously. No, the worry was the result of the campaign seemed to him like a foregone conclusion: a doddle, the country a shambles, its armies a rabble, its allies shopkeepers, who were certain to lose any brush with the Grand Armée. His concentration was elsewhere. He wanted to be back in Paris, pursuing a new bride.

Meanwhile, responsibility for victory was going to land on Ney's shoulders and the shoulders of men like Soult. From what Ney had seen so far, this was not a land, nor a people to underestimate, even when they came at you with paving stones, piss pots and frying pans. At the moment, it really did feel like the Imperial Army risked being beaten by men armed with such inadequate weapons.

Back at the stables, Fezensac told him the skittish mare had bolted. Two men had already been sent after her, but it wasn't certain whether she could ever be caught. Knowing the Spaniards, they would have already given her a home.

'I've acquired one of the Emperor's horses for you,' Fezensac continued.

'Well that certainly won't be skittish,' Ney said, 'you could put a child on anyone of them, they're so placid.'

The Emperor's horses were so over-schooled, no one ever fell from them. No one. To do so would be very bad luck indeed.

CHAPTER 15

'Michael Bruce!' The man sent out to greet them from the Bishop's Palace, which had been commandeered for the British HQ, grinned up at them. 'Haven't seen you since school when you were with the stylish set. Now you look like a child's puppet that's been dragged through the mud.'

'That's a pretty accurate description of my recent exploits,' Bruce agreed.

Slumped against the neck of Ajax, Bruce mustered the strength to smile down at the man. James Stanhope was sporting the smart scarlet jacket and blue trousers of an aide-de-camp. He had always looked a lot scruffier at school. Everyone had wanted to look scruffier at Eton. Stanhope had actually managed it.

Bruce and Adam had ridden up into town exhausted, but mightily relieved to find the army was still at Salamanca. It was more than heart-warming to see Stanhope after such an eventful journey. It was miraculous to have arrived here at all, let alone unscathed and in one piece. They could have been starved to death, or dead from thirst. They could have been strangled in their sleep by crazy peasants.

And they had at last arrived in Salamanca, found both Sir John and his army were still here. Bruce could hardly believe it. He had reported his arrival to the sentries, first making certain they knew he was English, just in case. They had pointed him in the direction of the Bishop's Palace, and it was Stanhope who had been sent out to greet him.

'It's really good to see you, man.'

Man? They were men now?

'How did you end up out here, Stanhope?'

'I could ask you the same question. Me, my sister, Lady Hester, put in a word with Sir John.'

'Sir John is a friend of my father,' Bruce replied.

'I'll take you to him,' said Stanhope. 'But, be brief. It's organised pandemonium here. The army marches tomorrow.'

'Tomorrow?'

'And you can't stay here. No one is staying here. You will just have to join the army!'

'Thank the Lord we arrived before you'd left. I would not have had the least idea what to do if you'd gone.'

'Here, let me help you down.'

Bruce slipped off his horse, brushed himself down and adjusted the straps of his knapsack. Adam had already dismounted. Bruce grabbed Ajax's reins and pulled them around so Adam could take hold of his horse, but as he did, two Spanish grooms unexpectedly appeared and took the reins themselves. To Bruce's further surprise, Stanhope then ushered both him and Adam into the palace.

As they walked through cloisters that heaved with scurrying couriers and aides, Bruce felt simultaneously underwhelmed by the bland light-brown stone of the building, woozy from a combination of sleep deprivation and immense gratitude that he was here unharmed.

Unwashed, unshaven in front of Sir John, he would have normally been concerned with his looks but was far too tired to care.

Almost asleep on his feet for a few moments, he came back to earth with a jolt to find James and Adam were talking quite amiably, like old friends. Stanhope appeared concerned for Adam's well-being, genuinely interested in what he had to say. Not merely interrogating him as a recent arrival for any information that could be useful to the military. It was quite strange to hear Adam talk at length about the sights of Madrid and descriptions of the desolate plain. He never talked like that with Bruce. Stanhope was explaining, as they crossed a courtyard, that as winter was fast arriving, it would obviously grow colder soon. Adam wanted to know how this would alter the army's strategy.

Stanhope flung open an office door; it made an unfortunate bang as it struck the wall.

'Michael Bruce, sir.'

A huddle of red-coated officers all poked their heads up from where they studied a large map laid out on a table. Bruce tried to suppress the thought that, for a second, they had resembled a pack of upright stoats.

The tall, handsome, slightly greying figure of Sir John stood up and pressed his hands to the desk. When Bruce was a child, he'd thought Sir John looked like a white parrot. He would never have dared say this out loud, knowing how well his father respected this Scottish soldier, and noting even at an early age that Sir John was not much fun. Even so, it was well known in London that Sir John was a steadfast friend, brave on the field. A truly gifted General, well respected by his men. Bruce had heard, too, although he trained his men hard, he was always looking out for them; he did not believe in flogging or corporal punishment.

Just now he looked remarkably stern.

'Gentlemen,' Sir John said, 'maybe you can take some refreshment while I attend to this miscreant.'

The officers pushed past, all upright and brisk, none of them so much as making eye contact, let alone smiling.

'Michael Bruce. You have two minutes of my time. What on earth are you doing here? What do you want?'

'I am exploring Spain, sir.'

'It's really not the best of times for a Grand Tour.'

'That has been made abundantly clear to me since I arrived.'

'And you've chosen not to enlist, not to fight for your country? At your age I was across the Atlantic, fighting for our King.'

'You think we'll lose this war, too?' Bruce dared to ask.

Sir John sighed and spread his hand over his map. 'If Bonaparte beats us, we'll be like the rest of the world. If we do beat him, mind you, it will be by ourselves alone. Not in any way thanks to our Spanish allies.'

His eyes sparkled. His expression changed from the exasperated look he had been giving Bruce to one of dogged determination. *This is a man*, Bruce thought, *who really could defeat Bonaparte.*

'Now then, there is to be no cavorting or mess-hall malarkey here for you.'

'So, sir, what exactly is going on?'

'In short, Bruce, we were ordered to come here to assist the Spanish drive out the French. But they are so disunited and disorganised, they cannot help themselves, let alone let us help them. Now Bonaparte is here in person with many of his senior Marshals and Veteran Corps.'

'I know, sir. We had to leave Madrid in a mighty hurry.'

'Tomorrow, we are heading north. We have had some luck. A French courier was intercepted with Imperial orders for Marshal Soult. We know now he is camped on the River Carrion, towards León. I suspect he doesn't realise we are so close. We can strike.

'It will not do to have to report to London that we had to abandon the Spaniards without any struggle at all. And Bonaparte may be tempted to take some of his Corps south, straight to Portugal. However, I am in command of the only British field army, there is not another waiting at home. I cannot risk losing it, so we must proceed with caution—'

'Sir John, if I may,' interrupted Stanhope. 'Bruce has two of the finest horses I have ever seen, horses that have already proved their stamina and have, according to Adam here, been in service before. They have heard plenty of gunfire. Might it not be useful to have these boys join us as messengers on our journey north?'

Bruce whipped his head around, mouth opened to protest. Neither man noticed.

'We could then make use of them as well as escort them to safety,' Stanhope finished.

'Well, I suppose your father would never forgive me if I let the pair of you fall into French hands. Attend to it, Stanhope. These two young men are your responsibility. They liaise with you. And you, Bruce, this is not fun and games. We are at war. Behave.'

Bruce had the sense to close his mouth and smile, weakly, to cover his outrage. Sir John smiled briefly in return, dropped his gaze back to his map, then waved his hand across his chest. They were being dismissed. The interview was over, it would seem. Before Bruce could express his gratitude, or find the right polite words to express his disagreement, he certainly didn't want to have any part in military action, he was being ushered out, back into the courtyard. Being marched to who knew where by Stanhope.

Fury surged inside him, and he dwelt on it because it hid something darker inside him – a feeling to which he was not accustomed.

Those few days gallivanting in Madrid felt so distant that they might as well have happened to someone else. He was now caught up in the war. He was a civilian, now apparently attached to the army, with no idea where they were going nor what they were supposed to do, or how dangerous it would be. Spain seemed suddenly dark and forbidding. For the first time in his life, he was really frightened.

CHAPTER 16

When lightning forked on the grey horizon, the Irish soldiers standing next to Bruce, mounted on Ajax, crossed themselves in awe. From where they all gazed down from a ridge, out on the plain, there was Sahagún, a French-occupied small town somewhere between Valladolid and León.

It had snowed endlessly. Since he'd been part of an army on the march, nine days now, through the wintry terrain, Bruce had almost grown used to shivering in the wet and the cold. Today, he and Adam had been trudging alongside this company of Irish Guards since dawn, but despite Bruce's best attempts to fraternise, they were quiet, surly. Maybe surly was rather unfair. They were most probably scared. He was scared, too. He just thought the odd joke or friendly word would help to pass the time, or make things seem less unreal, less deadly. Still, the ordinary men seemed distant. It had to be admitted that he felt more at home with the staff officers, people like Stanhope.

He was lucky, too, that he and Adam were able to spend their nights in each temporary army HQ, however mean a barn it happened to be. There was hot food, a fire, a chance to thaw out a little. He had not undressed completely since Salamanca. The men were not so lucky; they had to bivouac wherever they could.

And he had suddenly found an unexpected respect for Adam. He never grumbled, however atrocious the conditions were, he was always in a positive frame of mind and appeared to have endless energy. He seemed at his ease talking to everyone, be it Sir John or an uncouth Irish regular. He noticed too that Adam was keeping an almost fraternal eye on him. When he felt absolutely exhausted at the end of the day, it was Adam who, without asking even, found them a corner to sleep and some straw; fetched him a helping of whatever there was in the communal stew pot; unharnessed Ajax when his fingers were just too cold to unfasten the buckles. The only person who knew of their true relationship was James Stanhope. Bruce had asked him to keep it to himself. As far as the world, and even Sir John knew, Adam was his travelling companion. Nothing more.

Since Salamanca, Bruce had ridden through the bleakest landscape he had ever seen. It was so featureless. Hours and hours would pass with nothing to see but snow drifts. It seemed the only people alive were marching in the British Army. There were no Spaniards, no locals, and there was no sight of an enemy. When there was a tree, it looked dead, haunted even. Black ravens were hanging on the boughs. Apart from these, there were no birds. Near silence. Just the muffled sound of horses' hooves, creaking carts, and cursing marching men.

Every day, under Stanhope's instruction, Bruce and Adam had been entrusted with messages up and down the line. Bruce, for the first time in his life, felt really useful; it was quite a satisfying feeling. Even Sir John, when he saw him fleetingly, had said they were doing a good job. It had become necessary to concentrate. Otherwise, it had all become a bad dream, an endless nightmare. It had been hard to stay awake sometimes, to stay in the saddle; to fall off Ajax would have made him look completely incompetent.

When he did have a minute to think, though, it seemed just too sad and ridiculous to be exposed to the snow and elements like this. When, really, as he had imagined his time abroad would be, he should be carousing and circulating in Madrid with Sir Charles urging dignitaries to shake his hand, flirting with exotic señoritas.

On the other hand, looking down at the Irish soldiers, who were stiff-backed with jaws clenched, all of them ready to engage the enemy when ordered to do so, it seemed the London Michael Bruce had vanished. He was just another man on a horse among other men and horses.

Trumpets sounded and Lord Paget's cavalry poured over the lip of the ridge, headed for Sahagún. For all his tiredness, a thrill ran down Bruce's spine. No man could fail to be energised by such a sight. According to Stanhope, taking this shabby collection of huts and hovels was the first step to destroying the nearby army of Marshal Soult.

The following day, at noon, Bruce and Adam stood in the central square of Sahagún, its shacks, roofs and thoroughfares still thick with snow. The whole town was now swathed in a dense fog, which made seeing much further than your outstretched hand a challenge. The shapes rumbling past only close-up revealed themselves to be supply carts, no doubt full of meat and biscuit for the men. Not the grey elephants they had appeared to be when they were further back in the gloom.

The day before, Lord Paget's cavalry had secured a stunning victory, charging the French line at the vineyards adjacent to the town, with such swiftness and ferocity that the French Dragoons had been smashed and fled within a few minutes. The town fell pretty soon afterwards.

The French, in their hurry to leave, had left plenty behind. There was food, ammunition, fodder, horseshoes, even nails; the lack of horseshoe nails for the English farriers had become a huge problem – plenty of shoes, no nails. Bruce believed all this unforeseen manna from heaven almost, could mean Sir John would soon attack the forces of Soult, a mere twenty miles away.

Beyond the outskirts, out there, somewhere in the drifting fogs and snowy wastes was to be a final battle. Whoever was the winner would determine whether Bruce and Adam did manage to get safely back to Corunna, out of this hellhole country.

'Come on, Adam,' Bruce said. 'Let's see if we can find somewhere vaguely warm to burrow in until we thaw out.'

Sometime the next day, the sound of Redcoats cheering drew Bruce, pipe in hand, out of the church where he, Adam and a gaggle of Sir John's aides-de-camp and his clerk were sheltering from the cold. Soldiers were shouting and cheering the cavalry as it trotted out of the town. The army was about to march towards the Frenchies. At last, the fight was on.

Then it all changed. Bugles sounded. The horses were trotting back into town.

Bruce looked to his right as a red blur flew past him towards the church door. Before he'd had time to spin around on his heels, James Stanhope, slightly out of breath, his horse snorting, paused with one hand on the archway.

'Bruce, have Adam saddle your horses. Stick with me. We're leaving within the hour.'

'What's the hurry? Where are we going?'

The look on James's face implied he thought Bruce was being a complete idiot.

'Have you not heard? We have more news: another French courier with orders from Bonaparte to Soult has been captured. All we seem to have achieved so far is to let Bonaparte know exactly where we are. Bonaparte, with Marshal Ney and some twenty thousand men, has crossed the mountains. They have us in their sights. You know his reputation for moving his army fast, even over difficult terrain; remember he crossed the Alps? There is no time to waste. Sir John has given the order to retreat. We are marching towards Corunna as fast as possible.'

'Bonaparte, not again,' Bruce groaned. 'I am starting to think I have upset the Lord, or one of his angels at the very least.'

CHAPTER 17

THE CORUNNA RETREAT

DECEMBER 24TH 1808

It was Christmas Eve, and it was raining. The snow had turned to slush as the army set off westwards, away from the French. It went on raining. The rain made the rivers swell; the fords were deep, dangerous to cross. The black mud on the roads sucked at their boots. The men, having been ready to fight just a few days before, now in full retreat, were gloomy and ill-tempered. Some of them Bruce spoke to, said they would rather die in their boots fighting the French, than wear their soles into holes running away. This would be true dishonour. There were a few carols sung to the accompaniment of an accordion and guitars when they halted; otherwise, no one seemed to have the heart to celebrate.

Bruce remembered a few Christmases ago. Sir John had spent the day with the Bruce family, a loner with nowhere else to go. His mother had made a huge fuss of him. He wasn't the jolliest of guests. Bruce had avoided sitting next to him at the festive feast.

For the first time since he left London, Bruce found himself feeling a little homesick.

He had never been so wet. He and Adam were still with Sir John's staff at the rear of the retreating army. Thankfully with food and some sort of night shelter for them, and oats and fodder for Ajax and Hamlet. At least they were infinitely better off than the ordinary soldier or the stragglers. Women and children, tinkers, artisans, whores; no one waited for them as they fell further behind; the march was relentless.

As yet, there had been no sign of the enemy. Was this large force really chasing after them?

In a churchyard where they had stopped for the night, a huge bonfire was lit, the pews and anything else that could be burnt thrown onto it. Everyone crowded round. Drying out.

Charles Stanhope, James's elder brother, came out of the gloom, his lanky frame unmistakable. He too had been at Eton with Bruce but was a little older. Bruce had caught up with him at Sahagún.

'Here, Bruce, I believe you are going to be in need of this.' He handed Bruce an impressive-looking sabre. 'One of the useful life skills they didn't teach us well enough at Eton. When I have a moment, I'll show you how to parry and thrust.'

Bugger me, Bruce thought. *Do they expect me to fight, or, worse, do they need me to?* He glanced sideways at Adam, running his eyes up and down his half-brother's gangly arms. When Charles wasn't looking, he gave the sabre to Adam.

'You have a longer reach,' was his answer to Adam's surprised reaction.

Then Adam and he were expected to march – yes, really march. Ajax and Hamlet were assigned to various aides taking orders from Sir John to the vanguard. Terrible tales came back. Sir John at the rear had kept his forces tight – they were always readied in case of attack. Strict discipline. No looting. But the men at the front of the column, the men whose only thought was to get safely back to Corunna, had turned into a pack of wild dogs. All discipline had totally disintegrated.

Every village Bruce passed through after them, had streets running with red wine. Casks were split open with men on their hands and knees, scooping up wine into their mouths before it drained away, until they became insensible. In one hamlet, there were dozens and dozens of them, still alive, still snoring. Adam and Bruce scurried around, tried to shake them awake. Then orders came from Sir John that they were not to waste any more time, so they just left them, either to die of cold or by the hand of a Frenchman. He heard that one of the most glorious castles in Spain had been totally trashed, every surface, every picture stabbed by bayonets. They had burnt valuable tapestries, furniture, portraits, just for fun, not for warmth. And heaven only knows what had happened to the servants. The owner had fled to Seville.

A monk had been drowned in a barrel when attempting to shield some nuns from rape.

The officers had given up trying to control the men under their command. Well, they had bought their way into military life, assuming they would stay in England, drilling, strutting about in eye-catching uniforms, but here they were risking their lives. So, if their men misbehaved, well, that is exactly what you would expect from such scum. All they wanted to do was to get home. They just left their men to roam the streets at will.

The rearguard with Bruce reached the small town of Bellevente. There was an advanced army warehouse stocked with thousands of pairs of boots, biscuit, salted meat, shirts, trousers. Musket shot and powder too. They were all told to help themselves and the officers did not bother to take control. Mayhem: so much was just spoilt.

However, the French, they were told, were worse off. Best news, they were running out of ammunition; their supply lines, thanks to the Spanish guerrillas harassing daily, were in complete disarray.

Bruce dismounted behind a tree; he did have the indomitable to Ajax himself for a change. He had drunk too much already that morning and needed to piss. He nearly jumped out of his skin as a dragoon with a drawn sabre charged past.

'The French are crossing the river.'

He rode forwards and found Sir John with his entourage looking across a steep valley. He sat open-mouthed, a short distance behind them, watching the action. There was Lord Paget, twirling his moustache on his magnificent bay.

And there, on the other side of the valley, pouring over the river, was at last his first sight of the enemy. It was an awesome scene. There must have been four or five hundred mounted Imperial Guard Chasseurs. As they reached the nearer bank, they were forming lines, the horses at the front pawing the ground. Bruce began to sweat though the air was cold.

Much to Bruce's surprise, Paget ordered his far

smaller force to retire. Bruce hastily joined them. About a mile from the river was another valley. There Paget halted his men. Some more Hussars joined him from Bellevente town, summoned no doubt by a fast-riding aide-de-camp.

As the French advanced rather cautiously across the open ground, the British suddenly appeared from their hiding place and charged.

Bruce had seen cavalry charges before. On practice manoeuvres. This was his first experience of what happened when they engaged the enemy. The noise! Oaths, clashing blades, thundering hooves.

As the two sides collided and merged in a mêlée, Bruce could only follow by watching the colour of the uniforms. The order had been, 'Hurt the horses.' The heavy British sabres flashed in the air and men tumbled to the ground as their mounts were slaughtered. Steel clashed, men and horses screamed, blood spurted.

Bruce felt his gorge rise as in quick succession he watched a Frenchman's arm cut off like a carved sausage, and another have the top of his head neatly sliced off with one blow. He made himself look away, and his attention was suddenly caught by a group of horsemen on top of a small rise. They seemed to be positioned around a stout man in a green coat, with a sideways hat, on a snow-white horse. His mouth dropped open. Was that… *him*? Had Bruce actually set eyes on the Ogre of Corsica? That *would* be a tale to tell.

At last, the battle was over. The French retreated in chaos, except for their famous General Lefebvre, who was now captured and admitted that Bonaparte himself had indeed watched the action.

Bruce crept away from the triumph as soon as he could, to a place where he could be alone, and vomited.

So, that is what war is about! Just who can kill or injure the most. He realised then what huge responsibility was placed on someone like Sir John, ordering his soldiers to almost certain death, while trying to keep as many men alive as possible so they could get home. Uptight, taciturn, maybe, but what an extraordinary commander. He never took rash decisions, only carefully calculated military ones. Somehow, they were still managing to keep ahead of their pursuers.

After this, the pace of the retreat increased. More and more of the exhausted, injured, or sozzled men were abandoned. Stragglers could be seen stretching for at least a mile behind the rearguard.

It became even colder; snow was falling again. Draft mules and bullocks fell by the wayside. The oxen pulling the army's silver coin keeled over from thirst or frost. The entire contents of the chests were tipped into a ravine.

And then, all along the way, Bruce saw peasants circling and stalking, ready to rob the backpacks of any unfortunate enough to slip on the ice, or succumb to the freezing weather. And then there was the horrible sight of the horses… hundreds of them lying dead on the roadside.

On New Year's Eve, Moore pressed on up the steep icy roads, into the mountains. Corunna was still a hundred miles away. The roads were little more than tracks, winding their way up the mountainside. One slip and you were gone.

Two pieces of really good news had filtered back from Spanish spies. Bruce joined the officers raising their glasses in a thankful toast.

Napoleon had decided the British were running away and would be caught with their backs to the sea. His triumph was complete, the Spanish armies smashed, the British in full cry. His presence was no longer needed; Soult could easily finish the job. He would be returning to Paris where, so the spies said, he was to look for a new bride. Also, Ney apparently was not, despite Imperial orders, sending some of his men to reinforce Soult. He had taken his whole force further north into Galicia. The rumour was Ney and Soult were disinclined to fight together, or even help each other out, no matter who the orders came from.

On 6th January, in the mountains above Lugo, Moore decided to make a stand. Spanish spies reported Soult had arrived and was preparing to attack. He had no indication that the whole British force was in front of him; he was sure it was still only Paget's brave cavalrymen who had been the rearguard ever since Sahagún. There had been stores of ammunition and food from another forwards garrison. The men were fed. Hot food. The atmosphere throughout the straggling column suddenly changed. Orders were obeyed with alacrity. The men cleaned their muskets, sharpened their bayonets.

The advancing French were in for a surprise. Fifteen

guns blazed out from the mountains. When they marched, rather tentatively, uphill, they were intercepted by Moore's infantry. He led from the front, mounted on his striking cream-coloured horse. They fled. The British cheered. And pursued. More than four hundred prisoners were captured.

This time, Bruce had kept well away, almost holding his breath as he watched the whole attack with Adam, from a viewpoint above. It was still scary. He found himself cheering loudly too, as the French scuttled away.

They waited until it was obvious the French were not returning, so they withdrew, grumbling and cursing back up the mountains. It was a fearful night, dark with high winds. The straw put out to mark the withdrawal routes was blown away. Officers got lost and took their almost mutinous men for miles in the wrong direction. Bruce managed to stay on track, leading Ajax and Adam with Hamlet, with a small troop of cavalrymen, who were also leading their tired mounts. Bizarrely, their little group was joined at dawn by an orderly leading a mule with heavy panniers, that were full of medical supplies, strapped to the animal's sides. He produced a very welcome bottle of brandy, which they shared.

There was a time when Bruce hoped the enemy might have retreated; no sign for a day or two. They reached a village called Guitiriz where things seemed calm enough for them to wait for a while, long enough for any stragglers to catch up. When a thunderstorm broke overhead and the hail came down, they knew then they were free from French attack for that night at least. Adam found a stable, somewhere with straw where the horses could sleep in safety.

Surprisingly, Charles Stanhope turned up and ushered them into what had been designated the officers' billet. There was an amazing fire blazing already and they all stood around drying their clothes, trying to thaw out. A red-faced overweight man burst into the room, Sir David Baird, another British General, who was shouting that this was his billet, that this was outrage, that they must all leave now. They took no notice; the man was laughed out back into the darkness. No one was quitting that fire. That fire was keeping them alive.

The mountain paths seemed endless after that; every time they reached the top of a pass, they were expecting to see the glimmer of the sea. Bruce felt more dead than alive. Every step an effort. It was only the promise of safety and food that kept him going.

Once again, Adam was seemingly tireless, always on hand to offer assistance, never complaining, always optimistic. Looking after the welfare of Ajax and Hamlet. He had become more of a friend than a servant. Without him, Bruce was certain he would never make Corunna.

He had even found a pair of boots that fitted Bruce when his had split at the seams. He refused to reveal to Bruce where they had come from, so Bruce suspected they had been removed from a dead soldier. Dry feet were bliss! He'd had to smile. Whatever would Mother say to him, wearing something second-hand, previously owned by a common soldier.

After days of thinking about it, praying for it, there

it was! The sea. Officers with their telescopes could just discern in the distance a forest of masts in the bay with the White Ensigns. Bruce, coming over the last ridge, couldn't believe his eyes. The world was suddenly green, orange trees were in blossom, wildflowers covered entire fields. Somehow in the time they had spent marching from Sahagún, winter had become spring.

The entire world seemed lit up, white, for a second. Then, an ear-shattering thunderous roar. The blast was so loud it smashed all the windows in the bar. Bruce dropped his pipe and ducked under the nearest table as glass splinters flew in all directions. For a second, it felt like the world had finally ended. The cliffs would now collapse, and La Estrella would slide into the sea.

His ears were ringing. For a second, he wondered whether he needed to check that his head was still attached to his body. Finding it still there, he snatched up a napkin and stroked the glass shards off his coat. He twisted around. His ears were still ringing.

The barman was drawing himself back up over the bar with an expression on his face like that of a bewildered baby. 'That's the garrison arsenal gone up,' he said, after a pause. 'The army is detonating any munitions they can't take, so Soult can't get hold of them.'

Now it seemed obvious the bar of La Estrella had not suffered a direct hit by French cannon, Bruce clambered

to his feet and rushed to the window. It was hard to see –
it was now dark, the middle of the night, in fact – but, in
the bright moonlight, it did seem that there could be more
ships on the horizon and more in the harbour. Certainly,
more now than there had been two days ago when he and
Adam had finally left the mountains.

Worryingly, they had found the ships in the harbour
were not transports but supply boats. There had been bad
weather, storms. The rescuing fleet been delayed leaving
Vigo. The supply ships had been welcomed though. As
soon as Bruce and Adam made their way nearer town,
there was fresh food to be had. Chicken, roast potatoes,
no meal had ever tasted so delicious. Then a visit to the
local barber. He had hardly recognised himself looking in
the mirror. A black curly beard! He looked like a pirate. It
was a great feeling to be clean shaven again. Not wanting
to stay in the town, now in a state of turmoil, they had
made their weary way back to La Estrella.

Bruce shuddered as he found his pipe and returned
to his perch on his stool next to the bar. Much as Sir John
had sometimes been a bore of monumental proportion,
he had made sure everyone who wanted to reach Corunna
had made it here. Under him, the rearguard of his army
had fought doggedly, forcefully.

Never before had Bruce known someone who died
while on active service. Whenever, in the past, he'd idly
speculated on his own death – not that he was ever going
to die – he had assumed he'd die duelling, trying to win a
fair maiden's hand. He very much doubted he would die

young for England. Now it seemed a distinct possibility.

From outside, Bruce thought he could still hear volleys of shots. He was not sure if they were from rifle, pistol, or musket – he could tell the difference now – or if he had been hearing shots for so long, he could no longer distinguish between gunfire and silence.

The blast must have jogged Crabb Robinson's hand; the look on his face was as disgruntled as the barman's was terrified. There was a great inky splash across his notebook, though the inkwell remained miraculously upright. The man did have the most fussily neat handwriting and well-maintained notes.

'So, that is my story. More wine?' Bruce asked, nodding in the direction of the bar.

Crabb Robinson tilted the jug in front of him. It sloshed. It was not yet empty. He poured out two measures into the cups on the table.

'Let's maybe make these last, Bruce. Time is short and I must finish my article, ready to catch the London packet. The subscribers of *The Times* will want to be told all the fascinating details from your eyewitness accounts of the glorious events, that are coming to a final act not far from here. Reading it will cause hubbub, I assure you, at many a breakfast table. You know that most people at home will censure Sir John for not standing and fighting Bonaparte?'

'What point would there be in that? This is England's only field army. There are no other troops waiting at home to take their place. Sir John had to preserve it to fight another day.'

'Quite right, Bruce,' someone said from behind him.

Crabb Robinson's eyes looked past him with a questioning gaze. A hand appeared on Bruce's shoulder. When he turned around, he realised the voice belonged to an ashen-faced James Stanhope.

Bruce stood up. It seemed the right thing to do.

'It is so good to see you alive, Bruce, I thought you might be here. I came to check on you. I had feared the worst.'

'Nothing will kill me here, Stanhope, except the wine, which I suggest you partake of, despite its lethal reputation. This is Mr. Henry Crabb Robinson of *The London Times* – don't talk to him; he'll want to hear your story, then probably won't want to pay for it. Anyway, we have been drinking the brew all night and we're—'

'Bruce,' Stanhope interrupted. 'Charles is dead.'

'Charles! Oh my God, Stanhope. That is the most terrible news… I'm so sorry… he was like a brother to me, too.'

Stanhope's legs seemed to fold under him and for a second Bruce thought he was collapsing, but he dropped onto one of the stools, grabbed the wine jug and poured himself a cup.

'Maybe we do need that extra jug of wine,' said Crabb Robinson, scrambling up.

'Perhaps they have something stronger,' Bruce asked. 'Cognac, rum, whisky?'

Stanhope tossed his cup back, swallowed, shuddered, and stared out of the shattered window into the swirling night.

'Before you ask, I do not know the exact details.'

'Then, how, my good fellow, do you know for sure that Charles is dead? It is absolute carnage out there.'

'Messages came. Charles was at the Heights of Santa Margarita. He did not return.'

'I'm so, so sorry,' repeated Bruce.

'I have been searching backwards and forwards across the battlefield, and up and down that ridge, looking for any sign of him or where his body might be.'

Crabb Robinson reappeared and placed three glasses of what smelled something like brandy on the table. The barman followed at his shoulder with another wine jug.

'My God,' Stanhope continued, 'we'd only just buried Sir John, and then this news about Charles arrived. I have been trying so desperately hard to find him, Bruce. The thought of him lying where he fell and left for dead in the mud... he may even still be alive—'

'Excuse me,' Crabb interrupted. 'You say you were at Sir John's funeral?'

'If you can call it a funeral, yes.'

'He's really buried already?'

'Those were his instructions. When he accepted he was dying, he said he wanted to be buried here. Ghastly hurried affair. Just three of his staff officers, the chaplain and myself up on the ridge. No coffin... had to roll him into the trench in just his overcoat. With his Bible. A few words from the Chaplain before it became too dangerous, and we heard cannon close at hand again.'

'Sounds devastating,' said Crabb.

'If you'd been anywhere near the defending army out there, sir, you would know exactly how fearful it all is.'

'Be assured, we have witnessed the most unspeakable things,' Bruce added.

'Do you know what his last words were?' Stanhope went on. '*Hester. Do remember me to your sister.*'

'Hester?' Bruce asked.

'Yes, Hester, my sister. My sister, he was supposed to marry her. Oh dear, this is far more than a tragic day for us; Soult still hunting us, and Sir John buried in indecent haste. First Sir John and then Charles, and now my sister without her intended and the one who loved her so. At least the transport ships are finally here. At least we can be gone from this terrible place. Gentleman, I propose a toast.'

All three stood and raised their brandy glasses.

'To Sir John Moore, hero of Corunna,' Stanhope said.

'Sir John Moore.'

Brandy was downed. Wine was poured.

'To Charles Stanhope, my irreplaceable brother.'

'Charles Stanhope.'

The wine was dry and stuck in the back of Bruce's throat. He went to the window and stared out through the broken glass. Two of the finest men dead, for what? Bonaparte was the killer, the murderer.

Down in the harbour, lights twinkled, ships creaked. There was a great murmuring and a great clamour, many shots of many pistols. And in this moment, all he could really think about was the name of a woman, the name Hester. He had never met Stanhope's sister, but he wondered what she could be like if she could be the very last woman a man such as Sir John could have spoken about. She must be some woman indeed.

Down on the beach an hour later, just as dawn was breaking, Bruce was met with such a scene of calamity and grief and so soon after the almost unbearable news – the death of Charles. Along with James Stanhope and Crabb Robinson, he had scrambled in shocked silence along the clifftop track from La Estrella to the town.

Redcoats and cavalrymen were pouring towards the ships now awaiting them anchored just off the harbour quays. Increasingly it looked like the perimeter was now held by Spanish troops in their white uniforms. He was trying hard to believe that this really was the end of the retreat. His eyes were sore; he needed sleep. He felt the acid burn of nausea in his throat. Yes, Crabb and he had consumed a significant volume of wine and brandy. Dulled the grief, but he was far from drunk. Stanhope then bade his farewells, saying he was joining his company and insisted Bruce make his way out to the nearest ship, just as soon as he found Adam.

Crabb left in search of the Falmouth packet, where he was to lodge his report on the Corunna retreat and the death of Sir John Moore. Bruce had felt somewhat disappointed that the journalist had not even bothered to say a proper goodbye, considering the appalling night they had just lived through together.

And now another sight, as if Spain had one more horror to show him.

The sound was terrible in the way it repeated. A way off, it had been impossible to work out what it was. First a pop, then a sharp whine. Then a horse with blood streaming from its head galloped by.

Once he had made it to the beach, Bruce realised what was going on.

Against the red-streaked dawn sky and the masts of the fleet that encircled the beach, dead horses were piled, one on top of another. Here and there, an upright horse and a soldier beside it with eyes closed, a pistol in hand. This close up, the pop was now a bang. The horses let off a terrible, plaintive scream when they fell. Across the beach, men were found crouched beside their dead equine friends, weeping as if they had lost a wife.

It was clear what was unfolding. Plainly there wasn't enough room on the ships for all of the horses, and to prevent them falling into the hands of Marshal Soult's men, and used to hunt down Spanish and Portuguese allies, they had to die.

Oh God. What had Adam done with Ajax and Hamlet? *Where in heaven's name was Adam?*

He scanned the beach frantically, looking left to right. Trying to see through heaps of dead horses and scrabbling packs of men, some clearly as drunk as he ought to be.

Down by the shore, he picked out a man leading two horses behind him, that must be Adam. He ran across the beach, dodging the blood and the bodies and the terrified neighing. The still live horses were panicked by the smell of blood.

He kept having to move slightly to his left all the time, as Adam was constantly changing direction. Eventually, when he was in shouting distance, he called out. Adam stopped, and Bruce was able at long last to catch up with him.

This close to the shoreline, he could see exactly what was happening. As there was no way to transport horses to the ships by raft or some such – Corunna's harbour was notoriously shallow – some horses were being swum out to the ships and hoisted aboard using a sling-like machine attached to the deck. Some horses were being allowed on board, then. The owners were in the boats urging their steeds along.

Adam looked deadbeat, exhausted.

'My dear man,' Bruce said. 'Why did you not join us for stew and wine at the hotel?'

'The horses, sir. It seemed right to keep them here, not to trek them up there – only to trek them back down again.'

'This,' Bruce exclaimed fervently, as he poked his finger over his shoulder at the pile of horse bodies, 'this will not happen to Ajax and Hamlet. We'll ride back to England ourselves rather than put a ball in their heads.'

'Agreed, sir. I just saw a horse drown, following its rider's boat out to sea. I don't think I shall ever forget it.'

'Ghastly. Look, I have an idea. This way. Follow me.'

They retraced their steps along the shore to where Bruce had just earlier noticed a man organising a steady stream of horses from the beach to a waiting ship. Ten minutes later, Ajax and Hamlet were getting an appreciative pat and a great deal of admiration from a certain Captain Swales of the Dragoons. Who had been immediately convinced that fine horses such as these two should not be destroyed, but sent aboard without delay. A little of Father's gold ensured that the horses would be delivered safe and sound to Father on their arrival in England.

As Bruce trudged back up the beach, with Adam at his shoulder, he felt that amid all this carnage, he had at least ensured the safety of his special horses. Who had proved their endurance and fidelity so many times. He felt it was the best thing he had done in his life so far.

He stopped for a moment; yes, it really was the captured French General Lefebvre being escorted to a jolly boat on his way to imprisonment in London. In full uniform, *Légion d'honneur* sash over his shoulder, he had his head held high, looking straight ahead.

Up on one of the jetties, they ran into Crabb Robinson.

'I thought you'd left,' Bruce said.

'I'm not leaving,' Crabb replied. 'More accurately, I'm not returning to London.'

'Why ever not?'

'I am a war reporter, Bruce, and this war is far from over. Whatever London may think of what Moore has achieved here, most of his army is going home and for the moment he's only stalled the French. Anything can happen now. Lisbon is the place. Lisbon is where the action will unfold. That's where I'm heading. Just thought I'd say goodbye and good luck properly.' He held out his ink-stained hand.

'Lisbon?' Bruce repeated.

'There's a packet from here, just as there's a packet from here to Falmouth.'

'We won't get the packet,' Bruce declared. 'They stink. I'll procure a schooner for us.'

'Us?'

'We're coming, too. Adam, we're going to Lisbon. I feel there could well be things I need to do there.'

'What sort of things, sir?'

'More important matters than before. And as Mr. Crabb Robinson of *The Times* so rightly says, all the action is heading south and so shall we. Lead on, Crabb. There must be an office somewhere in this godforsaken town where we can hire a schooner and crew.'

He spun Crabb around by his shoulder, gave him a light shove and directed him along the jetty. He had a strange sensation that he had come to Spain and found his real self. He realised he had led a pampered, spoilt, selfish life; his school chums would call him a prig. He would now approach Lisbon to look for something other than whores. He seemed to have managed well enough without them since Madrid.

CHAPTER 18

LISBON

APRIL 22ND 1809

The delivery of the new uniform for Charles had been promised within a couple of days. As he stepped out of Santiago the tailor's shop into the sun, Wilson let the beauty of the whitewashed city overwhelm him again. Lisbon *was* beautiful, but only if you kept looking up at the elegant spires and bell towers, and held your nose. Otherwise, it was a waist-high gutter patrolled by crazy priests and missing a government. He must have stared a little too long at the bright dome of the Church of Santa Engrácia as he felt someone lurch into him. Before he could properly recover his balance, he recognised the young fellow who bounced off his shoulder. None other than Michael Bruce.

'Michael Bruce... how on earth... what the devil?'

'Sir Robert Wilson, do be fair, I am not the devil.'

'What on earth are you doing here?'

'What are *you* doing here? No, don't tell me, whatever it is, it'll be boring.'

'Shouldn't you be in Cambridge?'

'Well, obviously I'm not. I came here for the sort of jaunt I was supposed to have in St. Petersburg, except you talked me out of it in Stockholm. I came here instead. So did Bonaparte.'

Wilson laughed. 'You're going to have to wait until

Bonaparte has finally been defeated for the parties to start again, Bruce. Until then, the affairs of our time are a serious business for serious men.'

'I think I've seen enough of your sort of affairs to last a lifetime. War at its very worst. I am an extremely stressed man.' Bruce smiled. He well knew Wilson would not expect him to be stressed by anything; it was not in his nature.

'Anyway, shouldn't you be in London?' he continued.

'London is not for me right now. I've a new appointment, heading up a legion of Portuguese. I've come to Lisbon to arrange supplies, boots, bayonets, whatnot.'

Wilson gestured at the shop behind. 'Ordered a new sort of uniform for Captain Charles. You remember Captain Charles? His breeches were so thin from riding they were chaffing his thighs.'

'Your man? The one who threw a jug of water over my face in Stockholm?'

'If you had not been so hungover, he wouldn't have needed to.'

'That is fair, I suppose.'

'You'll be pleased to know I now have another Mr. Fixit besides Charles. A Portuguese, name of Luis Silva; Portuguese mother, British sailor father. Speaks the language and knows everyone. Like Charles, he's very resourceful. Can get hold of anything if you ask him.'

'Are you saying it would now take two of your minions to get me out of bed?'

Bruce laughed at himself in a way Wilson would have

thought unlikely back in Sweden. Overgrown children rarely, if ever, have the nous to laugh at themselves. The boy had moaned for most of their carriage-ride back to Gothenburg, bleated about his aching head, his thirst, his father, returning to England. Certainly, he was much more mature, still charming though.

'So, have you seen any action?' Wilson asked.

'Dodged Bonaparte. Drove me out of Madrid, then from Salamanca, even Corunna.'

'Corunna?'

'Not you too, Wilson. No one wants to talk to me about anything else besides the retreat. It's quite the door-opener here. Gets you into the best parties. Everyone wants to buy you a jug of wine if you were at Corunna.'

'Look, Bruce, you must tell me all about it. Do you have time for a drink? I want to hear all about Corunna and Madrid.'

'I can always make time for you, Wilson. Walk with me. I know an agreeable spot in the main square.'

They started to make their way down the street. Wilson was desperate to find out if Bruce knew the latest news, where the enemy might be, what exactly was going on. He had been out in the sticks for months; it was maddening for him not to be up with the latest intelligence. Bruce would probably know nothing, of course, only the reputation of certain ladies and which squares and doorways they frequented.

This part of central Lisbon, the Alfama neighbourhood, had not been touched by the earthquake that levelled most of the city sixty years ago. It was still a maze of steep, narrow lanes and small secluded squares. Filthy like the rest of the city, stinking of human and animal waste, rot.

There was bustle though; shops were open. Every market they passed seemed to be doing a roaring trade. There were Redcoats on every corner, traversing every thoroughfare, and they had money to spend. The city had taken them to heart. Last year, the French, like the occupying army they were, had trashed the place, stolen everything and raped many women, until they were driven out by the British.

They crossed back through the largest plaza in Lisbon, the one the locals called the Doors of the Sun. There was a lovely little tavern on the far side with tables outside. Wilson found them a shady place under the lemon and orange trees to sit, out of the relentless sun. Ordered a jug of wine. Even he thought it too early for port. Bruce smoked his pipe.

Bruce, it had to be said, *had* seen some unforgettable sights. Had been with Sir John Moore during that heroic rearguard retreat from Salamanca, where he'd even glimpsed Napoleon himself, observing the French fracas at Bellevente. As well, the last bloody stand outside the port of Corunna, where the pitiful remnants of the British Army waited to be carried home. Although still a glib and somewhat flippant young man, he seemed to have changed for the better.

Another change. Bruce was genuinely interested in Wilson's activities. Back in Stockholm, you could tell he just wasn't listening. Now he seemed captivated, was in no hurry to leave, bought another, more expensive, jug of wine. Tapas and olives. He even suggested Wilson should move in with him while he was in Lisbon.

'It's a very large house, I suppose you could call it a mansion. Plenty of room. It belongs to some member of the Royal Family, sailed off to Brazil. The servants take the rent, but who cares. They look after me terribly well, cooking, laundering and so forth. You can have a proper bath. But best of all, there are no bedbugs. You will find the usual boarding house is crawling with them.'

Wilson accepted with alacrity.

'Tell me again why you left London. I haven't been back for months, what is it like?' asked Bruce, leaning back in his chair, giving Wilson his full attention.

London was the last major city in Europe Bonaparte hadn't occupied. London was still normal. After he'd returned from Russia, for a while he'd been a normal citizen of normal London, a family man living out his normal family life in his normal house. Many months of this and he was climbing the walls with boredom.

Matters had come to some sort of a head last year, when he'd started to find himself leaving home as soon as he could. He'd taken to having his breakfast with his wife in her bedroom each morning. Jemima was fast losing her sight completely. It had obviously deteriorated further while he'd been away.

He would make himself useful in the mornings,

helping her dress and tying her hair. Making sure she did not knock anything off her tray or fail to find her kidneys and eggs. The room was small, stuffy and, even he had to admit, rather smelly. Jemima had problems sometimes using her chamber pot. The new nursemaid was clearly unable to control the children. Charlotte and Georgina danced into the room whenever they liked and made a hullabaloo more appropriate to the corridors of Bedlam.

After just too many of these mornings – the certain ennui setting in whenever he tried to sit down to write at his desk – he'd found himself every morning taking in the air of the normal, busy, untouched London streets. Striding across the Thames, he'd head for Brooks's, his gentlemen's club in St James.

One particular morning, he was alone, sitting morosely upstairs at the bar.

'Good day, Wilson,' a familiar voice said. Turning round, Wilson was delighted to see Granville Proby.

'Your Lordship!' *Well*, he thought, *he is an Earl, although rather tedious, as his whole conversation centres on how he served under Nelson at Trafalgar and won it to boot.*

'Granville will do, Wilson,' said the Earl. 'Have a pink gin?'

'What has been happening in your life?' Wilson asked. 'Mine is completely devoid of any action.'

'I've just come back from Plymouth,' the Earl replied, 'a bit of shore leave while the "*Iris*", my frigate, is undergoing repairs.

'Nothing on, Wilson? Well, I might have the very

thing. I heard in port there are a few hundred Portuguese soldiers encamped in Plymouth, who left Lisbon hurriedly after their King and Queen sailed to Brazil. They are all very dispirited, but they miss their Portugal and are mad keen to return and fight Bonaparte. I'll introduce you to the Portuguese ambassador, de Sousa, a funny little fellow! I also happen to know his embassy is paying their expenses, so I'm sure he will be delighted to see the back of them.'

Wilson had met de Sousa before – rather like himself, a man who did everything with immense gusto. So, he went hot foot to the Portuguese Embassy where, luckily, he had an immediate meeting with the Ambassador. He thought this idea of shipping the expensive miscellaneous men back to Portugal might well solve his problem, so promised to approach Lord Castlereagh, the Secretary of State for War. It's always who you know in life.

The following week, Wilson was appointed to raise a Portuguese Corps of some three hundred men, horse, foot and artillery. He was given the rank of Brigadier-General in the Portuguese service. And pay to match. The new force was grandly called the Loyal Lusitanian Legion.

Wilson could simply not believe his luck and immediately had his tailor create a uniform, suitable for his new rank; green jacket, white breeches and plenty of gold braid. His men were also to be suitably dressed, their uniforms, muskets, horses and cannon all paid for by the British Government.

Thankfully, he had to admit, leaving his domestic problems behind, he, with Charles, set sail to the port of

Oporto with the three hundred or so Portuguese soldiers. While at sea he went below, his excuse being he needed to learn a few necessary words of Portuguese from his men so he could shout commands. In reality, he wanted to fraternise and very soon knew them all by name.

It was here he had first met Luis Silva, an outstanding character. He was the obvious choice for promotion, so Wilson made him Sergeant before they went ashore. His Portuguese mother had been raped repeatedly in front of him; to say he hated the French would be an understatement.

Wilson was proud of his little army. They were all driven by their hatred of Bonaparte. Many of their sisters, wives and mothers had been raped too by the French when they occupied Lisbon. Organising the Legion had confirmed what he already believed; treat the common soldier with respect, feed and clothe him, supply decent equipment, pay him on time, and he will follow orders without question and fight when necessary. Flogging, used as punishment by the British Army, just didn't work. Beating the skin off a man's back, painful blow by blow, did not engender loyalty, just resentment.

It had been quite a journey so far. Initially, he had landed at Oporto, a city in some dire straits and extremely vulnerable to attack. Should any considerable French force make its way along the River Douro from the sea. Just the sort of situation Wilson felt was well suited to his talents.

He and his green-uniformed soldiers were applauded everywhere they went.

He'd also succeeded in his first objective, which was to make sure he didn't have to take orders from anyone. He took no notice of the fact he was, in theory, to report to the British Army, as well as the Portuguese. It also became evident, for some obscure reason, that the Bishop of Porto, head of the local Junta, thought Wilson's independent army should be his own private militia. All these considerations Wilson just shrugged off, ignored. His was a Portuguese unit as far as any interfering British commanders were concerned, a British one to any Portuguese.

After he'd established his own HQ in an especially fine house, he set about recruiting the Legion up to full strength, on the way procuring enough equipment and material. There were many more volunteers than he could clothe, let alone arm, so he, with Silva's aid, selected the best. Then he drilled and trained the force until it was ready to strike. As his men seemed to grow in confidence and commitment, Wilson grew more restless and more impatient to act.

In December, on hearing that Bonaparte himself was in Madrid, he marched his seven hundred men into Spain. In hideous wet and freezing weather, slowed down by rivers glutted with rain, he had eventually reached the city of Ciudad Rodrigo, hoping to join with British forces there. British forces who had already left.

The city was full of buzzing, dreadful anticipation. The French were expected to take the city any day. After having taken command of a larger Spanish levy – his legion now three thousand men strong – he had come face to face with a French army that fled straight away without a fight. Intelligence gathered from locals by Luis Silva suggested the French didn't fancy their chances against the green uniforms they thought were British crack riflemen.

Now with their tails up, the Legion swept down to Salamanca, wreaking havoc with Marshal Soult's lines of communication with Madrid. They harassed and undermined the French division of General Lapisse, taking out his despatch riders and couriers, seizing his supply wagons, distributing leaflets in several languages encouraging French soldiers to desert this barren land. Many did. Many joined the Spanish guerrillas if they could. At least then there was a chance of being fed and surviving.

Even when he received firm orders to turn the Legion back towards Lisbon, he captured a French outpost and then squared up against Lapisse's Infantry division. Their forces were equally matched – he was convinced his men would have had the better of the day, had they not run out of ammunition and had to withdraw. It was to his great regret that, in the meantime, Marshal Soult had taken Oporto in his absence.

'So, here I am in Lisbon,' he told Bruce, 'sorting out supplies for my Legion. Being kind of in-between authorities, I cannot rely on the authorities. I must organise things myself.'

'That sounds awfully wearing.'

'I don't actually have an official commander, and I like it that way…'

The sound of a large clatter of hooves drowned out the rest of Wilson's riposte. A company of two dozen or so red-coated guardsmen had entered the plaza and were trotting across the cobbles. At the front, a tall, straight-backed commander in a magnificent uniform of red and gold, sat back in his saddle, shoulders slightly swaying. With the longest nose Wilson had ever seen. Seriously, it was a miracle that someone hadn't shot or sabred it off during an encounter with the enemy. If he'd had a nose like that, he wouldn't have survived his first action in Flanders, wouldn't have won the medal. This nose, he quickly realised, had inspired the ordinary British soldier in Portugal to nickname its owner Old Nosey.

Obviously, those ministers back in London had, at last, seen what Wellesley could be capable of, had seen the value in the man. He was supposed to have a particular talent in the motivation and deployment of infantry. Sir John Moore was dead, so Wellesley was back. This was Sir Arthur Wellesley himself.

Seeing him trot past, assured, implacable, Wilson knew he would so like to sit down with the man and talk tactics, talk strategy. He was, it was well known, an avid and determined flogger of wayward or sluggish soldiers. Despite it being in Wilson's opinion, a barbaric, medieval and ultimately counter-productive practice that in the end made men hate their commanders. Wilson was sure he could talk Wellesley out of using it. There were many better ways to motivate the fighting man. He had shown this with the Legion.

However, here, riding across this square was a man who had already triumphed over the French at the Battle of Vimiero last year, with a mixed Anglo-Portuguese force. If they combined their forces and put their heads together, they could surely drive the French out of Portugal, then Spain. Back to Paris.

The last of the guardsmen's horses disappeared from the Doors of the Sun. It was almost certain that Wellesley would be at the mess tonight. There was nowhere else for superior officers to socialise in Lisbon. Another of Wilson's chance encounters could be engineered. New schemes could be schemed, strategies discussed. Wilson had a few in mind.

A pincer movement to crush the French before the gates of Madrid; a lightning strike to take the city itself. And should the fake King Joseph Bonaparte be driven out of Madrid, who knows what other fake thrones would topple elsewhere in Bonaparte's new Europe.

Bruce poked his thumb over his shoulder. 'He went to my school. Many years before me, naturally.'

'Who did?' asked Wilson.

'Old Nosey, of course.'

'You know him?'

'Slightly, he's been in Mother's drawing room.'

'What are you doing tonight?'

'Her name is Iolanda.'

'I see you could well be an asset for my Legion, Bruce. Join me in the officers' mess. I need to entertain Wellesley.

I'm fully confident you can bring some youthful brio to the dinner.'

'Right you are,' Bruce said, standing up. 'By the way, here's my address, get Charles to bring your baggage over. Then he and Adam can sort things out. I'll even get them to press my evening clothes.'

Before Wilson had a chance to murmur 'thank you', Bruce was weaving his way across the sun-filled square, tipping his hat to at least two attractive ladies as he passed them by. The whole coincidence made Wilson chuckle. Michael Bruce in Lisbon. Michael Bruce as entertainment, at what could be a very important occasion for his Legion's future, as well as himself.

'I was alongside Plunket as he took the fatal shot,' Bruce said, slamming his wine cup on the table.

For a second, all other chatter round the table ceased. The officers were now at least an hour and a half into their wine and jokes. They froze, then leant across the table with interest at the mention of the famous sniper, Rifleman Plunket.

Bruce smirked and caught Wilson's eye, before turning back to face Wellesley. Wilson was pretty nearly sober, but so was Wellesley. Bruce was well away, unstoppable with his stories.

Wilson tried to keep smiling, not wanting to give away just how frustrated he was that Bruce had monopolised

Wellesley all evening with, no doubt, excessively embellished tales of derring-do. *Embellished*? Made up, more like it.

'Yes, somewhere past Lugo, Plunket and I, we saw coming up behind our rear a contingent of French. Many, many horses. They were fresh and spruce-looking. We knew they would soon close the gap, and we would be done for. From our vantage point, I could see the French General, Colbert, resplendent, upright, haughty. Obvious it was the General, looked like a General, don't you know.'

Wellesley let off another of his braying laughs which were beginning to grate on Wilson. He twiddled his red and white Austrian medal, just in case Wellesley had not yet noticed it and was about to ask him where it had been won. Under what unusual circumstances. Normally, they were the first questions anyone asked when they first met Wilson. He was aggrieved. At least this would be a true story.

It was strange enough that Bruce had known Sir John Moore, plausible given the lad's family connections. But knowing Plunket personally, master of the amazing new rifle and a dead-shot at great distances, was guff. He'd be saying he'd jousted with Bonaparte next.

'I point out General Colbert. Quick as a flash, Plunket lifts his rifle…'

This was clear evidence that Bruce really didn't know what he was talking about. These guns were far too heavy to be lifted like broom handles and lightly tossed about. Luis Silva had taught him how to fire a rifle when they were first in Oporto. It was a devilishly heavy piece of kit. You, if possible, to ensure accuracy, fired it lying prone.

Wellesley was an infantryman. He must realise and get bored of this make-believe soon. No, there he was again, heehawing like the biggest donkey on the farm.

'And he takes aim. He takes a long breath as he looks down the sight. He adjusts. He calculates. I see him in his head steadying himself. He pulls the trigger…' A pause as Bruce predictably once again thumped his tankard onto the tabletop. 'And down in the valley, a good mile away, the General falls from his horse. All the Frenchies look skywards as if Almighty God has struck down their man. Now I look at Plunket; he looks at me. I say to him that was a fluke if ever I saw one. Anyone can knock out a General from a mile away, a piece of cake. At which point he reloads and lifts the rifle to his shoulder again.'

He would be lying down, thought Wilson, disapprovingly.

'He took aim once again and shot right through the head of the General's aide who was clearly trying to rouse his commander, assuming perhaps that the poor man had simply collapsed from exhaustion or over-excitement or something.'

'And that's how he proved the first shot was no fluke?'

'No, that's how we stopped the French from getting to us before we could board the ships at Corunna. One at a time.'

'Bruce, you are a fine storyteller, I'll give you that,' Wellesley said. 'If I ever achieve anything on the field of battle, I expect I will hear later that you were with me, giving me the orders.'

'Oh, I have already shared a field of battle with you.'

'Oh! Have you now?'

'Copenhagen.'

'And what, pray, were you doing in Copenhagen?'

'Watching the Congreve rockets fall, sir.'

Wellesley did now take a small sip of wine, laughing that farmyard laugh again. Wilson so wished he hadn't run into Bruce outside that tailor's shop. The atmosphere round the table had now turned so comical and frivolous that he could hardly keep himself in check. Bloody Etonians, that was it. Wellesley was an Etonian, too. They were unserious people, all of them.

Bruce got up from his chair, waved his arm behind him and trudged off. The men at the table all stood up and clapped. They were clapping, applauding the Etonian as he weaved his way towards the privy.

By the time the port had been passed round, Bruce had been absent for so long, Wilson was starting to worry. Wondered whether he should go and look for him. On the other hand, he was not put on this earth to drag insensible Etonians from wherever they were, even slumped in a Lisbon latrine.

Anyway now he wanted to listen closely to Wellesley. He lent across the table. Some other officer had just asked him what his plans were for the next move against the French.

'Soult is now settled in Oporto,' Wellesley said. 'I understand from my local spies he has no idea we're here. So, we kick him out. Kick him out of Oporto. Kick him out of Portugal, then kick him out of Spain. There's a strong rumour Bonaparte is redirecting some of his Veteran troops from East Prussia to shore up Madrid. If we deal with Soult first, we can take Madrid before they have time to arrive, we'll wrong-foot Bonaparte.

'So, gentlemen, just as soon as we've organised our Portuguese contingents, we march on Oporto.'

A buzz of excitement circled round the table. Many of the officers stood up and toasted Oporto. Wilson could always tell when real soldiers were relishing a real fight. And these men had been idle for a while and were clearly itching to get to grips with the French.

But what part could he play? He was not under Wellesley's command. He knew Oporto, though. He had local knowledge; he had spent five months there last autumn. In his mind's eye, he could see the city and its surrounding terrain, the River Douro.

He might be most useful, offering a little cloak and dagger assistance. He could take a small group of men, a minimal posse, Captain Charles, Luis Silva, a few more trusty members of the Legion, just tag along with Wellesley's men. The regular Portuguese would be in their green uniforms so his men would not stick out.

No one would notice, no one would even care. After all, he would be there to help, not hinder. Perhaps he would be given the chance to lead an important sortie.

The chair next to his scraped; someone jogged his elbow; his drink splashed all over his uniform.

'What did I miss?' Bruce asked. 'Only the bloody port. How am I going to survive all this talk without my port?'

CHAPTER 19

OPORTO

MAY 12TH 1809

The explosion was so ferocious it shook the track. Some of the startled horses reared up and whinnied. It became clear the best thing to do was to call a halt for a few minutes, let them calm down.

The noise disturbed the tranquil morning as it echoed along the steep sides of the river valley. A plume of smoke and dust drifted up into the air and hung like a brown mist above the tops of the trees. Glancing sideways at the river, the Douro, Wilson noticed muck and discolouration on the surface of the water as it headed for the sea. He turned to Luis Silva, who had been trotting alongside him all night prior to the explosion. Usually, he was an astute observer of events.

'The bridge,' they said in unison.

'That makes things a great deal more difficult,' Silva added, almost under his breath.

Wilson urged his men to continue onwards. Along with Silva, the party included fifteen Portuguese riflemen of the Loyal Lusitanian Legion, and Captain Charles, the only one of them wearing a civilian uniform. They rode past houses and cottages on the outskirts of Amarante, the smart suburb on the opposite bank from Oporto. All with orange-tiled roofs but some bearing the scars of recent skirmishes or rearguard actions. The foliage and heavily blossomed trees in the orchards provided excellent cover from any French sentries or snipers on the other side of the river, as well as a high vantage point where they could view the opposite bank.

Where, until a few minutes ago, the Amarante bridge had stood, was now a void. It had been the only strategic crossing left over the wide and fast-flowing Douro, four or five bridges along the river having already been destroyed by one side or the other since early Spring.

Should an army as large as Wellesley's manage to march across it, Oporto would be laid open to a full-frontal assault. Not long ago, when the French had taken Oporto whilst Wilson was in Spain, the Portuguese army, under General Silveira, although soundly beaten in the suburb of Amarante, had been encouraged to stand and fight on the bridge. Soult was forced to stay on his side of the river.

A mine had been lodged under the bridge by the locals, its firing mechanism a musket pointed directly at the explosives, its trigger connected to the far bank by a string. Such an ingenious idea, Wilson had thought. Should the French make a serious attack that looked like succeeding, the Portuguese would have detonated the mine.

However, the French had apparently cleared the bridge by using a mine of their own, one that not only threw the Portuguese soldiers from the bridge into the fast-flowing water, but also frazzled the string that tied the musket to the bank.

Since the French victory here in March, Soult had had the bridge repaired but today had blown it up himself. This was the latest incident where all the British plans could become unstuck. Not unexpected though; past experience had shown Soult was always on the ball. Wilson was well aware any hold-up crossing the river would allow the French to regroup, to fortify, to flood Oporto with reinforcements from Spain.

Too long a delay here, let alone a heavy defeat on this side of the river, would mean not only would Soult hold Oporto, but Lisbon would also be wide open to an attack. From Ney or Lapisse or the fake King Joseph or whoever else was massing around Salamanca.

'This will really give Old Nosey a headache. I cannot believe,' Wilson said, 'even he has ever crossed a fast-flowing river before, without a bridge. Maybe I can provide a solution.

'We need to get a better view,' he went on. 'We need to see exactly what is happening. Wellesley usually identifies very much the same as I do, when it comes to strategic planning. This time, God be thanked, I can be a step or two in front. I have the local knowledge.'

Silva glanced upwards to his left, at what looked like a looming white convent. It was clear that Redcoats were already milling around on the flat roof.

'How about up there, sir?'

From the height of the convent roof, the lush countryside spread out on either side. The river snaked darkly below.

To the west, the sea sparkled behind the hills. To the north rose the pantile roofs, churches and towers of Oporto. Wilson, with Silva close to his shoulder, pushed his way through a pack of men, many who he recognised as Wellesley's aides and staff officers.

Everyone looked serious, hushed, muttering as if trying to puzzle out whatever to do next. They were far too occupied to take any notice of Wilson and Silva's green uniforms. After checking around to see if Old Nosey himself was anywhere to be seen and finding no sign of the Commander, Wilson made his way to the balustrade at the edge of the terrace roof. He took out his telescope, the one that had been such a good friend for so long, scanning the far bank. Trees. The odd abandoned fisherman's hut. The wreckage of a few boats obviously sabotaged by the French. But no sight of any French soldiers. Apparently, no one was watching this part of the river. No one was keeping guard.

'Come on,' Wilson said. 'We won't find anything up here, and if we did, Wellesley would know about it before we do.'

'Is that a problem, sir?' Silva asked.

'Of course it is, if we want to keep ahead of the game and grab some glory for the Legion. Let's scramble down to the bank for a closer look.'

Down by the river, in the coolness there, as they both swiped at the clouds of gnats, that made trudging through the moist, long grass an ordeal, Wilson noticed a huddle of civilians peering intently across the river. A twig or branch or something, must have snapped underfoot as Wilson approached, for a startled man turned around quickly, pointed a pistol.

Oh dear, thought Wilson. He had faced death in the snow and the sands, on land and sea from Flanders to the Cape of Good Hope, but he'd never thought he'd die by the hand of a panicked peasant in a leather apron and wooden shoes. The best reaction, he decided, was not to put up his hands and maintain his *sang-froid*.

Silva barked something, patting his green tunic, the uniform of the Loyal Lusitanian Legion. The man with the pistol smiled apologetically, tucked his weapon back into his belt.

By the time the man was trying to give Silva a hug he'd not been prepared for, one of their number was waving at another man furiously rowing a small skiff across the river. When the boat bumped the shore and the men helped to pull him onto dry land, he started to babble in Portuguese.

Whatever he was saying was unintelligible to Wilson, who, despite his best efforts to learn the language, had so far only mastered sundry instructions for the ordering of food and drink, as well as a selection of commands for the deployment of troops and cannon. Silva didn't need encouraging to translate and was soon, it would seem, urging the man to slow down and start at the beginning.

'The French are all over to the west of Oporto, sir... they think we're coming by sea. Good news too that the local tripe-eaters here hate the French... Why are they called tripe-eaters? Because when the British fleet is here,

they buy the meat and leave the offal for the locals…
Anyway, these tripe-eaters have had quite enough of the
French stealing and killing. Only yesterday a father was
shot dead by a grenadier just for protecting his daughter
from being raped. The tripe-eaters are hungry for revenge
and happy we are here, ready to drive the French out.

'Yes, Soult is still in the city. This tripe-eater here is
a barber and shaved him only yesterday… The lay of the
land? See that large white building over there, the one with
the zigzagging pathway going up to it. Seminary. Empty,
too, but the French have not realised. The priests and their
pupils have fled. According to our barber friend, there
are four undamaged barges hidden in the rushes bang
opposite here. They just need bailing out. And there's a
ferry downstream which can be easily repaired, that the
French have overlooked.'

'Excellent,' said Wilson, rapidly formulating a plan.
'Would our new comrades be amenable to rowing back
over in the skiff, bailing out the barges and towing them
across? Another party should be detailed to repair the
ferry and row it back here.'

Silva grinned, then talked in a low voice to the huddle
of men.

'Most definitely, sir.'

'Then have them do so, as quickly as possible. Then go
back at once and report in person to Wellesley's staff. Tell
them we have found a crossing. Prearrange some signals.
There is a bridgehead to make.'

Later that morning, Wilson was standing at the prow of

the leading barge as it was rowed across the river by the barber, with de Silva and the local prior who had hurried to join the group. Other locals had turned up and were manning the following barges. Each of the recovered barges had the appearance of a wide ungainly gondola. Each could carry about thirty Redcoats.

As the opposite bank drew nearer, Wilson steadied himself and used his little telescope to scan the trees. Holding his breath all the while, in case a detachment of French were planning to fire on what would be not quite sitting, but certainly slow-moving, ducks. Not a shot. Nothing stirred.

The boat thudded against the bank. Pistol at the ready, with his rifle slung over his shoulder, Wilson with Silva and his own Legionnaires at his back, hared up the zigzag path. At the top, he held up his hand. They paused, waited. He could not quite believe this vantage point was unguarded, had been overlooked, as Marshal Soult had a reputation for not missing the obvious. He was clearly no fool either, despite letting Moore escape from him at Corunna.

The seminary's grounds and terraces did seem completely deserted. Even the front door was unlocked and swung inwards with a mere tap of Wilson's elbow.

It was proving so easy that he half-suspected to find its courtyard full of dragoons or grenadiers. But no. Whoever usually resided here had fled in a hurry and, it seemed, without the French even realising. Wilson was almost overwhelmed with relief. Here was the heaven-sent bridgehead. Here was the key to Oporto.

Within an hour, there were six hundred Redcoats in the building, which was rapidly being converted from a priest's school to a British fortress. Riflemen manned the windows. Others used pickaxes to create loopholes for their guns in the lower walls.

Up on the roof, Wilson and Silva surveyed the land. Out beneath the bright afternoon sky, scurrying across the vineyards and lanes, were blue-uniformed French soldiers.

'Our advance was never going to stay unnoticed forever,' Silva said.

'Oh look, they are bringing up artillery, too,' Wilson signalled. 'Say you're Soult, Silva, what would you do with your artillery?'

'Hit the barges, sir, while our men are still not all across, then pound this building into rubble.'

'Exactly. Order the gates shut. And while you're down there, send word to Wellesley. He'll know what to do about the French cannon.'

'Yes, sir.'

Silva slipped away and, a few minutes later, Wilson smiled when he heard him shouting below in the courtyard. Across on the other side of the river, a mass of red uniforms was lining up ready to board the barges. In front of the convent, on its flat terrace, he could see men dragging cannon, some of them huge, howitzers, the big buggers that fired the shrapnel shells everyone liked on their side, but not on the enemy's. Wellesley was ahead of the game.

Not long after Silva returned, the first French shots

thudded against the facade and jittered the roof. A volley of shots roared back from below. The roof started to shake. Wilson loaded his rifle, rested the barrel between crenelations on the roof's edge and took aim. French infantry was approaching across the flat fields that led up to the seminary. Behind them, gunners were hauling their cannon, looking, Wilson assumed, to secure them on the level ground to fire past the seminary and onto the barges.

He took careful aim. The silver epaulettes of a rather bumptious-looking officer glinted in the sunlight. Wilson's first shot of the day hit the man in the stomach, sent him staggering backwards until he disappeared in the rush of men and the swirling dust. All that rifle practice on the Spanish plain under Silva's watchful eye had not been in vain.

Beside him, Silva gave him the thumbs up, then fired, once, twice. Wilson crept across the roof and looked out over the river, at the barges below, ferrying more men with muskets slung across their shoulders. Once landed, they hurried, ant-like, up the zigzag path.

Wilson located the prearranged lookout on the roof of the convent, across the river. Gave the man the signal, his left arm raised twice, two jabs with his fingers at the sky.

By the time he'd scurried back over to Silva, reloaded his rifle, and picked out another officer coming across the field, a mighty roar sounded from the opposite bank. Cannon balls whooshed passed their heads and, seconds later, smashed into the French artillery before they'd had a chance to properly limber all their cannon. Lucky shots too; they seemed to have killed many of the French artillerymen and obliterated their equipment.

Barrage after barrage followed until the land out there seemed a strip of fire where dead men lay. Smoke hovered and hung until, when it was clear, the French were seen to be retreating. The French had abandoned their one chance to stem the flow of British men across the river. Wilson shot a straggler in the back.

Now it was just a case of holding firm until Wellesley joined them. Oporto would be next to fall to the British. And Soult himself was still in town.

Wilson, still overcome with elation at the success of the action, took a moment to collect his thoughts, thanking God that the musket ball that had come so close in the Praca Nova, Oporto's New Square, had only mildly grazed his cheek and not taken his head off.

He'd found a pail of water in one of the palace's upstairs rooms as he and Silva had gone chamber to chamber looking for any French stragglers, any officers to take as prisoners. Even Soult himself, if Soult had not fled. He washed his face and was relieved to find it merely grimy, no blood.

Last time Wilson had been in Oporto, fresh from England, this white-fronted, red-roofed and, it had to be said, imposing building had belonged to the Bishop who thought he owned the Legion. Since then, it had become the headquarters of Soult, the man who thought he owned Portugal. Wilson wondered idly what had happened to the Bishop.

For the moment, the palace belonged to Wilson, seeing as his men had been first to fight their way up the lanes to occupy it. Soult, though, *damn and blast*, had managed to escape. It certainly was a shame. Capturing him would have been a real triumph. How high would Wilson rise if he captured a Marshal? Wellesley would have to give him a medal if he'd pulled that off. And what would London have to say!

He would just have to make do with tucking into what should have been Soult's luncheon. While he'd been hunting through the upper storeys, Captain Charles had been making friends with the kitchen servants in his usual manner. By the time Wilson came back down, an amazing feast had been laid out on the long table in the main hall: caldo verde soup, hunks of bread, smoked pork sausage, salted cod, and heaps of roasted potatoes. Plenty of wine, too.

He raised his goblet to Captain Charles, sat at his elbow, and to Silva, who sat at his other, and paused, listening, before he took a sip.

'*Viva, viva,*' rang out. He wasn't sure if he could hear it from way off – the whole city was celebrating the rout of the French – or it was just some echo reverberating inside his head as the exertions of the day finally caught up with him.

It had been unbelievable to hear how the people cheered the Redcoats as they cleared each street of the

French. It was fantastic to be feted as liberators. It seemed incredible to Wilson, after Eylau and Friedland, to be on the winning side. At last.

It had not been so pleasant to witness quite so many of the French wounded having their throats cut by the tripe-eaters. The priests had told their flocks that to kill a Frenchman was not a sin, but a step on the pathway to heaven.

He knew he would never forget seeing a crowd of them forcing a dragoon onto a narrow bench; then his blood spreading across the cobbles either side in two red puddles as they sawed him in half. And there were people in Paris and London who said the Cossacks were savages? Come to Spain. Come to Portugal, to Oporto. On this ground, this war was like no other. This war was something else entirely.

Out in the passageway, approaching boot heels clattered, spurs clinked. Wilson looked up and saw his guards step out to block the incomers, then step away saluting. Even though his stiff thighs and shoulders really didn't want him to, he stood up. Wellesley was here, with three aides. Maybe he was looking for Soult, too. Maybe his nose could smell hot food from miles off.

'Ah, Wilson,' Wellesley said as he waited politely for him to move so he could assume his rightful place at the head of the table, then indicating the chair on his right. 'Do sit down. I believe I have you to thank for that scheme of crossing the river?'

'It was just a case of being close to the bank, having a different viewpoint from yours on the convent roof, sir.'

'I agree. Well spotted and well organised.'

'We dealt with them pretty quick.'

'Three hours by my watch. I anticipated a fiercer fight.'

'Wrong-footed at every turn, sir. The unopposed crossing. Your masterful deployment of artillery and shrapnel. Their abandoning of the docks just before we seized them.'

'Yet Soult is still free, but he can't be that far away.'

'We must chase after him before he has a chance to collect his army together in the hills, while it is still in disarray.'

'Exactly, Wilson. We'll hunt him down. We follow tomorrow.' He looked round the table. 'Quite a spread, I see.'

'Yes, sir,' replied Wilson, 'all cooked for the Marshal's luncheon.'

Wellesley made one of his braying laughs. 'I'll tell you something, Wilson, I do wish we knew how Soult took the news when he realised we were crossing the river in those barges. He has quite the reputation for not suffering fools gladly. It's a shame we had no spies in the palace.'

At this, Captain Charles got up and strode across the room, leaving by the door that led to the kitchens.

'Your man indisposed?' Wellesley asked.

'I think we may find that all of Oporto was our spy,' Wilson replied.

As the aides fell upon the dishes spread out over the table and sank the wine as if they had not seen any for years, Wellesley ate two grapes and took a sparrow-like sip of his wine.

When Charles reappeared, he had with him a vast, barrel-shaped and enormously moustachioed man in a striped chef's apron, smeared with flour and some sort of brown sauce.

'General, gentlemen,' Charles said with a flourish of his hands, 'let me introduce you to Maritim. Not only does he make the finest bacalhau in all of Portugal, but he also has procured for Marshal Soult the finest whores in Oporto. I have already taken the liberty of paying him for his tales.'

'If he makes such sensational bacalhau,' Wellesley asked, 'why does he need to double as a whoremaster?'

'There is a war on, sir. Every man is entitled to make as much dosh out of the circumstances as he can,' Wilson replied. 'Silva, please help our new friend, Maritim, out.'

Silva looked a little disgruntled at being asked to leave his sausage half-eaten, but all the same got to his feet, took the fat chef into the corner of the room. The whole table sat in silence with nothing but the sound of whispering for some moments, before Silva returned and stood at Wilson's shoulder, making a point of addressing Wellesley.

'Maritim says that last night the Marshal worked late, longer than usual, writing many letters, many despatches, notes and instructions. He anticipated it would take us at least two days before we found a way across the Douro, and was convinced we'd most probably come by sea, attack the port before we took the town.

'Anyway, despite the late hour, he still has needs and desires and asked Maritim over there, to make a certain arrangement for him. Maritim goes out into the night and returns with Beatriz, known in the local taverns as the Mule, not because of her hardy coat and droopy ears but because she can bear a lot of weight and take a lot of punishment. Maritim takes the great lady up to Soult's chambers.

'This morning, it is her opinion that the Marshal will have to pay double next time, because the tender parts of her body are too sore to touch, and she almost needed crutches to walk.

'She said, earlier, she had been woken up by a knocking on the door that was so loud, but even that hadn't woken the Marshal because his head was buried between her breasts, which she boasted, were quite the largest in Portugal and all its Empire across the waves. She had prodded the Marshal to get him to open his eyes, but all he wanted to do was grab hold of her rear and squeeze it, as if he hadn't squeezed it enough already.

'A man pushed the door open and was shouting into the room, "Monsieur Marshal, the English have taken the seminary."

'The Marshal replied that the man was an absolute dolt. All the boats were at the bottom of the river. The bridge was destroyed. Wellesley was a useless General who had only beaten Indian sepoys and Junot. Any red uniforms near that seminary were probably the Swiss lot having a bathe. Meanwhile, he had his hand somewhere that suggested his mind was on other matters.

'The aide at the door replied that there are rifles firing out of the windows, there are dead men in the fields.

French cannons destroyed. That woke him up with a jolt, the Mule said.

'He shoved her aside, jumped out of bed, hopping around the room, shouted, "*Merde*," as he pulled on his breeches. Once the breeches were on, he'd told the aide to get rid of the Mule and to make sure she was paid. "*Vive l'Empereur*," the Mule said as she was bundled out of the room. In the kitchen, the aide gave her some coins and Maritim here fed her as she was ravenous. She showed him the bites on her breasts. It is believed that the Marshal missed his own breakfast because he had a retreat to arrange.'

Wilson gestured for Silva to sit back down and finish his meal. He'd rather enjoyed the tale, not so much its bawdy details but the flinty look on Wellesley's face, its unflinching, po-faced expression.

'Well,' Wellesley said eventually. 'I suspect I am going to have to offer something of an abridged version in my report to London.'

Wilson noticed both Silva and the aides trying not to laugh. He was well able not to laugh himself, settling back to savour his wine. He really didn't care about Soult's sexual fun and games. He only really cared that the French army did not escape into the hills around Oporto. That so-called II Corps was smashed once and for all, Marshal Soult captured. With his Legion playing the decisive part.

CHAPTER 20

LUGO

JUNE 12TH 1809

The Roman bridge at Lugo was lucky to withstand the hammering of Ney's horse as he thundered across at the head of his men. This miserable, recently bombarded town was the last place he wanted to be. Now, here was Soult, the last person he wanted to see.

He'd been stuck in Orvieto, in Northern Spain, for months, trying to act as policeman in a vast empty territory where the Spanish nobody, so-called General La Romana, wouldn't come out to fight a proper battle. Orvieto. Where no one ever knew what was going on or indeed who was coming. Where the Spanish peasants kept hanging or torturing the couriers and dismembering the spies. Where if you cleared a village out of guerrillas one day, they'd be back in a week and killing his troops again.

This was not the kind of action he was used to. This was no place for a Marshal of France. He had been in this bad mood ever since they had been ordered to Orvieto. His staff, even Fezensac, had learnt to give him a wide berth, only joining him when summoned for terse orders.

He ate alone. Spent his time walking about the camp, playing his flute in the evenings, drilling the men, until they murmured amongst themselves that enough really was enough. Then he received a brief message from Soult of all people, telling him he had retaken Lugo, and summoning him – yes, actually summoning him – to meet him here.

It was a lousy grey day, spitting with rain. Ney used his spurs to speed Concorde onwards. He raised his hand to signal his entourage to pick up the pace, his staff, Fezensac with his Generals, and behind them, the finest of VI Corps' cavalry.

Lugo and its grey towers loomed, as Ney reached the damaged outer wall. Two shabby-looking sentries were suddenly alerted. Jolted awake, they jumped to their feet and saluted: Marshal Ney, the unmistakable Marshal Ney, who must look twice as tall as Soult. Ney noticed the fear in their eyes as he passed, realised how he must look to them, his face flushed with fury, his red hair flaming.

As the members of VI Corps cantered into Lugo's central square, it was obvious the remains of II Corps were in a sorry state. Tattered infantrymen were slumped on the ground, skinny, filthy-faced men with tattered uniforms and flapping soles. There were several dead ones lying on the cobbles, their faces covered by blankets. Their comrades must have thrown them over to protect what was left of their dignity. How tragic to have marched so far, in such circumstances, only to drop dead in some unloved town far from home.

This is what happens when you send a man like Soult to do a proper soldier's job. This is what happens to the men – who were, after all, the heart and soul of the Grand Armée and the Empire and France – when you gave total authority to a greedy commander like Soult.

Looking at these exhausted, played-out men, Ney

asked himself why to God had Napoleon sent Soult and not Ney to hunt down Sir John Moore? If Napoleon had ordered him and the men of VI Corps to take on Moore, none of the English would have been allowed to escape Corunna. Nor return, under their General Wellesley. But then Soult was the political animal Ney could never be, currying favour with the Emperor, exaggerating his successes in every despatch.

Certainly, if VI Corps had been given the vanguard role here, Oporto would still be French, Wellesley would be under the ground with Moore, Portugal would be halfway secure. Half of II Corps would not be dead because he, Ney, would have been concentrating on the war, not looting and whoring and planning to sit on the Portuguese throne.

The Emperor should be told too, that if he had given Soult the task of subjugating Galicia instead of him; let *his* men deal with the guerrillas, the pot-shot takers, the snipers and torturers, the failure would be exactly the same. No Corps in the Grand Armée could win this shadow war in the fields and ditches. No one could have done better than VI Corps in this arena.

Lugo was just south of Corunna. Soult, during his two-hundred-mile ignominious retreat here from Oporto, had lost everything in his hurry to escape. All his wagons, supplies, baggage, artillery, horses and gold. He had even abandoned the wounded who were unable to keep up, the men who were wounded during his aborted effort to hold Oporto. He had left these behind, left them to the Portuguese. To be shot or hanged if they were lucky, or, if they were not, burned, boiled. Dispatched in some way that would have shamed a torturer from the Middle Ages or even the average Cossack. He had a nerve trying to pretend to Ney these hollowed out men had 'taken' this ruined town, adopting a tone that had made it sound like it was some second Austerlitz or Marengo.

Soult sat alone on the plinth of a stone cross in the middle of the square. He must have heard the hooves approach but stayed staring abstractedly up at the sky, not even glancing in their direction.

As Ney was dismounting from Concorde, the tattered soldiers of II Corps did mostly take notice; some at least stood up at something like attention when they saw the Marshal. Tall, ruddy, still martial, and more than anything, here among them. Maybe bringing some hope. They must have noticed too that the cavalrymen and their horses were looking sleek, well fed. VI Corps were properly looked after.

Soult did now stand up and saunter across the square towards Ney, who had Fezensac close beside him, and his Generals and their aides behind. Farther back, though, the VI Corps cavalrymen, as soon as they saw Soult, started to chant.

'*Roi Nicolas, Roi Nicolas. Roi Nicolas.*'

Soult's brows furrowed as he drew nearer, a tell-tale sign he was painfully aware of being mocked but was trying to act nonchalant. As if the men of VI Corps were jeering at someone else. This morning, before they left camp, Ney had clearly ordered them not to do this, 'Nicolas' being some insult that meant 'fool' in the villages of France and that, for obvious reasons, thought Ney, had stuck to Soult since he'd been a boy.

Some of Soult's men were visibly bristling as the chant persisted, forming small, angry-looking groups.

Soult now moved forwards and tried to embrace Ney as if they were brothers in arms, comrades. Ney stepped away and the noise from his men grew louder, more boisterous.

'*Roi Nicolas, Roi Nicolas, Roi Nicolas.*'

Soult opened his mouth to speak, but Ney held up a finger. He feared a full-scale brawl might break out between the two Corps if the chanting continued. He turned to Fezensac.

'Tell our men to pipe down, while I am talking to the King.'

When he turned to Soult again, Soult was speechless with rage. Red blotches appeared on his cheeks. His lips moved but nothing was coming out.

'You've lost an epaulette.'

'It's good to see you, Ney.'

'You look like a Polish scarecrow.'

'I...'

'What do you want?'

'Want?'

'You must want something. You summoned me. For what?'

'My men recently stormed this city. They need—'

'You can lie to yourself, even to the Emperor, but

you are not lying to me. The twelve Spanish brigands garrisoning this rubbish tip of a town saw you coming, ran away before they realised you could have been easily beaten. Your men are in no fit state to fight.'

'The city fell—'

'Not Lugo, the city that fell was Oporto. Your men, Your Majesty, just got hounded out of Portugal by Wellesley. How on earth could you lose everything? How could you lose your artillery? How could—'

'*Roi Nicolas, Roi Nicolas, Roi Nicolas.*'

'Ney, you were not there. Listen, I need artillery, I need boots, I need ammunition and food and wine, and the means to move them. You have plenty.'

'I suggest you go back and get yours from where you left them.'

Soult stood up to his full height. Still a foot shorter than Ney.

'This is an order, Monsieur Marshal.'

'How dare you!'

'I repeat, Monsieur Marshal, an order. Let my aides discuss the details with yours and organise the transfer. While you and I sit down and work out our next move against La Romana.'

Ney clenched his fist into a ball, his temper rising. Then, to calm himself, he tried to think of his hand buried in Ida's hair. But all he could think of was that afternoon at Allenstein. While spending the time chopping logs, in his imagination had been this malicious face, now only a few inches from his. Because this spiteful man had ordered his troops to steal his – Ney's men's – supplies, a chain of events was set in motion. This chain would end in the premature battle at Eylau, where twelve thousand Frenchmen died in the snow for precisely nothing. He forced himself to relax his fingers.

'Let me remind you,' he managed to say, 'you are not my superior officer. I wouldn't even report to you in Hell. You do not give me orders, you haven't even the talent to win against the British. You're no better than the grim reaper to the men you command.'

'Ney, you wouldn't want such talk to find its way back to the Emperor, would you?'

'You're a fucking bastard, Soult. Don't think I don't know it is you who whispers false rumours in his ear.'

'*Roi Nicolas, Roi Nicolas, Roi Nicolas.*'

Soult's shabby men were beginning to creep forward, closer. In his peripheral vision, Ney could see his men doing the same.

'It's an order, Monsieur Marshal,' Soult repeated. 'An order authorised by your Emperor.'

'As I say, Monsieur Marshal, go back to the mountains where you abandoned your guns and your men and your honour. Mine are all in my own safekeeping.'

'Give it a rest, Ney. We all know La Romana is a clown with an army that rides on donkeys, and he's shown your thugs up for what they are for months. Sloggers, sluggers, but incompetent, just like their boss. I have reported all this to the Emperor. Hand over the equipment. You and your Corps have no use for it.'

'*Roi Nicolas, Roi Nicolas, Roi Nicolas.*'

Ney thrust himself forward, looming over Soult, who

shrank and stepped back. His men drawing closer as Ney found the hilt of his sword and began to unsheathe it. Vengeance for the dead of Eylau and Oporto. For the honour of his Corps. For glory and Empire.

Soult's hands twitched, like a man unsure whether he needed to defend himself. He left his sword in its sheath and his hand well away from the hilt. No one willingly sought a duel with Ney. They were certain to lose. Ney was known to be one of the finest swordsmen in the Grande Armée.

A red mist descended over Ney. There was pounding in his ears. The chanting stopped; the square was hushed. Everyone held their breath.

Someone's cupped hand was over his ear and someone's hand was on his sword arm. It was someone saying, 'Conduct unbecoming…' and Ney suddenly came to. No one spoke to him like that. No one. Not Aglaé, not even Napoleon. He was Marshal Ney, Duke of Elchingen. It was Fezensac, though, dear faithful Fezensac. His friend. Fezensac whispered further words of caution and restraint.

In complete silence, Ney remounted Concorde and, leading the rest of his troop, left the square as if on parade, then rode out of the ruined town, recrossing the bridge. They stopped on the far bank to let the horses drink.

Ney beckoned to Fezensac. He leant sideways from Concorde's saddle.

'I have to thank you, Raymond, for your timely intervention just now.'

Fezensac blushed. Ney realised it was the first time ever he had called him by his Christian name.

'You were quite right, of course – Soult has to be allowed to live. Neither of us will be able to forget this, though. How I long to leave this godforsaken place; it is changing all of us for the worse. We need to go back to Paris.'

'I do agree, sir. We seem to achieve nothing here except the loss of unnecessary French lives. The Emperor must come back in person if he doesn't believe the despatches. Just to see the impasse.'

'Don't bank on that. His mind is occupied with marrying a young royal wife and producing an heir. Whatever is happening here is of little consequence. And, of course, he doesn't like to be associated with failure.'

CHAPTER 21

The yacht was a converted four-masted clipper, fresh from the Indian tea runs, according to the lighterman who was rowing Wilson and Charles across the harbour. She stood out, surrounded by tar-coloured Royal Naval vessels. Sleek, white-hulled and built for speed. She, too, was marked out as the only vessel in the harbour to be flying the Blue Ensign, as a privately owned merchant ship. All the others sported the White Ensign, His Majesty's ships. She simply oozed money.

Another chance encounter in a Lisbon street had led to this unannounced visit. Charles had met Adam; they then had adjourned to a wine shop for some tastings. Charles heard – hardly to his surprise, it might be said – that Michael Bruce was actually a guest on the unforgettable yacht he and Wilson had been admiring the evening before. Wilson hadn't hesitated.

'We'll pay him a call then, tomorrow. See how he is.'

As they drew nearer, Wilson could see three figures busy swabbing the decks, or whatever these men did on board. As the lighter nudged the stern, Charles started ahoying. One of the sailors waved. A grim-faced man, dressed rather bizarrely as a Mameluke, appeared.

'Brigadier-General Sir Robert Wilson would like permission to come aboard,' Charles shouted.

'Who?' asked the figure in a strong guttural accent. Hardly a surprise, as Wilson was wearing the green uniform of the Legion, not a red coat.

'Oh, tell him we're selling port, the best in town,' suggested Wilson. 'It's probably the only word he understands.'

A rope ladder was dropped, and the two men clambered aboard. This yacht was huge; the brass shone, the sails were neatly furled, the decks honed teak. Wilson had never seen anything quite like it.

After a few minutes' gazing round, they were ushered below behind the Mameluke into the main cabin. *Quite as opulent as an Egyptian casino*, Wilson thought, having spent some happy hours in one. With ornate chairs and a polished mahogany table. Many empty bottles stood about.

Two men were playing cards, a heap of coins in front of one of them. A slim, tall, red-cheeked man with a sprawling tuft of pale-yellow hair falling forwards across his face and a neat moustache.

He stood up, swaying, looking slightly baffled as they came through the door. Charles stepped forward.

'Brigadier-General Sir Robert Wilson,' he announced.

The other man had his back turned until this moment. He leapt from his chair, spun round. Dropped his pipe on the floor. He looked better fed, tanned and only slightly less well-oiled than the last time they had met. Wilson had to admit he was an extraordinarily handsome young man.

'*Good God*,' he exclaimed, 'I thought you were

still chasing the Frogs. I hope you don't disapprove of gambling; it whiles away the time, don't you know.'

'Bruce, I assume these are friends of yours, not selling port, which is a disappointment, as I fear we're running low.'

'May I introduce Sir Robert Wilson, and his valet, Charles. This, Wilson, is my host, Lord Sligo. He used to fag for me at Eton.'

'Nonsense, I never fagged for anyone. Delighted to meet you, always good to have new company, even Bruce's can wear a bit thin.'

Wilson and Sligo shook hands.

'How ever did you know I would be aboard?' Bruce asked.

'Well, sir,' Charles said. 'I bumped into Adam yesterday; we had a couple of glasses. Didn't he say we had met up?'

'Apparently not. Maybe he thought I should not be reminded of that jug of water in Stockholm. If Sligo doesn't mind, I suggest luncheon. Maybe, Charles, you could find Adam and go on with whatever you were saying yesterday.'

'Luncheon, of course, that would be magnificent,' said Wilson. 'Sligo, I expect you are wondering how I encountered Bruce. Well, I rescued him in Stockholm in November '07, biggest mistake of my life.' He slapped Bruce across the shoulders.

'Yes, he obviously does need looking after, I too had to rescue him from a rather large and irate father who was pummelling our friend's face in Cambridge.'

'Have you not met Sligo before?' Bruce asked, as Wilson drew up a chair. 'He owns half of Ireland, most of the West Indies and this yacht. He's good company, has even been known to enter houses of ill repute, haven't you, Sligo?'

'So, what have you been doing since we last met, Bruce?' Wilson asked. 'It's been months, and you don't seem to be any more sober.'

'I don't intend on sobering up quite yet, Wilson, especially now I'm with Sligo. I've been in Lisbon and around. Then met Sligo, invited to join him. How about you?'

'Only saved Portugal from the French, nearly captured Madrid, nearly beat Marshal Ney on the battlefield.'

'Wow,' exclaimed Sligo. 'Maybe we'd better get the table tidied up so we can have luncheon and allow your friend Wilson to bring us up to date with military affairs.'

'You mean I'm not going to be allowed the chance to win all my money back?' Bruce asked, rather plaintively.

'Later.' Sligo clicked his fingers. A lackey, white though also dressed in an oriental uniform, appeared and received whispered instructions. Other hands cleared the table of detritus and about ten minutes later a scrumptious spread of meats and cheeses, bread and fruit were laid out. Fresh cups of red wine were distributed.

Sligo raised his glass. 'Welcome aboard the "*Piraeus*", Wilson. Now, please explain to us what is going on in the war and your part in it. We have had no news.'

'Thank Christ for that. At least I do know Bonaparte is in Paris and unlikely to turn up,' Bruce said, clapping his hands together.

Wilson picked a couple of grapes from the bunch in front of him, chewed and swallowed another gulp of what could be the best wine he had tasted in Portugal. He smiled at his host.

Then, not leaving one single detail out, he explained how he had secured Wellesley's reputation – who was, of course, now the Duke of Wellington – by not only finding a way to cross the uncrossable Douro River and ferry the army over. But also by holding a strategic point long enough for the British artillery to be brought into action and strike the final blow. He had been the first man into Soult's palace HQ. Without doubt would have been the man to capture Soult if he hadn't, the coward, already taken to the hills, as fast as he could.

The two young men were suitably impressed, especially when he went on to tell how he and his Loyal Lusitanian Legion, of course under his command, were on the brink of capturing Madrid and driving out the fake King Joseph, Bonaparte's brother, don't you know. Wellington then, too cautious, too scaredy-cat, had ordered him back after his battle at Talavera, which, although it had won him a dukedom, was basically a fluke, given that the French had run away for no good reason.

'I'm told Marshal Ney is a fierce bugger,' Sligo said. 'You really attacked him on the field?'

'Lord Sligo,' Wilson asked, 'have you ever been tricked? Thinking you saw something in the distance that, closer to, turned out to be completely different from what you thought you saw?'

'*Sir, you need to see.*' Silva had shaken Wilson awake. This was back in August. The Legion had camped overnight close to the head of Banos Pass, on its way to reuniting with the armies of Wellesley.

Wilson was feeling cheated. Madrid had been unguarded, at one point only fifteen miles away. Capturing the capital, driving out the French, would have been a suitably glorious achievement for the Legion. For Wilson's idea of the Legion. But Wellesley's strict orders had been not to advance. The Legion had stood still until the French found them and drove them hither and thither, until they finished up here.

Wilson could have used a little more sleep. He had been writing letters and despatches long into the night. Silva was insistent, though. Shaking him even harder. Something must be up. Wilson levered himself up and threw on his jacket.

The Banos Pass cut through rocky, craggy escarpments surrounded by brown hills studded with gorse. The Legion was camped on the slope of one of these hills. Wilson stumbled after Silva through the camp, that already smelled of cooking bacon. Campfires glimmered and glowed. Both men kicked up clouds of dust as they went. Looking back over his shoulder, Wilson noticed the hills in the pale light of dawn looked like the desert dunes he had seen in Egypt. War did this to you. Made every new landscape provoke a memory of some other engagement, another march or skirmish.

Silva led him up a bank to the lookout post. They saluted the sentry who had raised the alarm. He pointed at a group of figures on horseback, difficult to see in the cloud of dust that obscured the road through the pass ahead. Ghostly glimpses in the dust and dawn haze.

Both men used their telescopes to study the horsemen.

'What do you see?' Wilson asked.

'Cavalry,' Silva said. 'Maybe ten riders.'

'They're not Soult's men?'

'I think not.'

'An escort then.'

'Protecting a despatch?'

'We'll have to go and ask them.'

For the last few months, the Legion had been capturing the bags of French couriers from Oporto to Toledo. It was hard enough for anyone to know where anyone – friend or foe – was in Spain. Let alone if someone kept seizing your messengers, stealing your orders and intelligence.

After all, the reason the Legion came to be taking this back route down to Talavera, was because they had captured a rider before leaving the outskirts of Madrid. They had found, from the French despatches he carried, the worrying information that Soult was already in position between the Legion and the rest of Wellesley's army.

It crossed Wilson's mind there could well be crucial tactical information in someone's saddlebag down there, that could be used to his advantage. Maybe more news of Soult. A final clash with him would go some way to alleviating his frustration that the Marshal had escaped him in Oporto. Revenge for Sir John Moore. The name, Sir Robert Wilson, would never be forgotten if he pulled *that* off. He'd get a better commission, probably, his chance to really shine on the big stage, get another crack at Napoleon himself.

The men on horseback down below were suddenly waving their arms, their horses making wide and gentle circles as they gesticulated at each other.

'Looks like they've rumbled us,' Wilson exclaimed. 'Damn'.

'Must be the fires. Probably unwise.'

'The men deserve their breakfast, Silva. Let's go capture that despatch, shall we?'

For the moment, Wilson stayed at the observation point. Silva left at a run. The French despatch guards had disappeared. The dust seemed to be settling.

Wilson could see the great cleft of the Banos Pass become visible on either side; a huge 'V' cut into the rock. In the deepest groove, along the narrow road, suddenly appeared, apparently out of nowhere, a mass of men on horseback. Far more than the ten or so guards they had first seen.

It was not a coach bearing letters but a troop of French cavalry wearing their distinctive blue and white uniforms and tall fur busbies. At the head, now trotting straight towards Wilson, was a long-legged man wearing a distinctive plumed bicorne hat, astride a huge black horse.

Wilson couldn't quite believe what he was seeing through his telescope. Again, a memory flashed through his mind. He had seen the black horse before, as the

Russians were withdrawing in the twilight at Eylau. It was *that* horse. And *that* rider was not a second-rate Marshal like Soult. That was Marshal Ney.

Wilson kept his telescope trained on the black horse and its tall rider until he was absolutely certain it was Marshal Ney.

And it *was* Marshal Ney. He could now see his ruddy face and red hair. Marshal Ney was marching away from the south where Wilson knew the bulk of British forces were based. He was probably heading back to Madrid and was no real threat to anyone at that moment. And his army clearly outnumbered the Legion; there must be at least twelve thousand French. The Legion had only two guns, the French no doubt had more than a dozen at the rear. There was no real reason not to be sensible and withdraw tactically, but on the other hand, why not make some sort of stand? To kill or capture Ney would be nearly as satisfying as Bonaparte.

Someone touched his elbow. There was Charles with Pegasus, his Spanish-bred horse, all tacked up ready to mount. Da Silva came back, panting.

'Are we going into action, sir?'

'Take cover,' Wilson shouted in Portuguese to the men who were standing about behind him, waiting to be told what to do. 'Hold your fire until I give the order, then aim for the horses. Limber up the guns and place them at either end of the line of men.'

On the mountainside there was plenty of cover, boulders, scrub and gorse bushes. Wilson mounted Pegasus. He had a far better view from up there. He was pleasantly surprised that his men had taken the orders and were now scattered about on the ground, finding suitable hiding places. Those many hours of training were now paying off; some months ago, they would not have obeyed him without question.

The Legion did have some advantage: they were high above the narrow road, the French were crammed together. Ney slowed down, then called a halt. Obviously wondering just how many men there were hiding above him. With a wave of his hand, he started forwards again with about one hundred of his cavalry.

'Fire,' Silva shouted. Musket and cannon balls rained onto the forward French force. Ney hardly moved, his mount under perfect control despite the noise and the neighing of the nearby wounded horses. The main body of cavalry stood aside as a company of urgently summoned French infantry appeared, along with some ten guns.

Wilson could not help being impressed by the speed all this happened. He had not expected even Marshal Ney to react so quickly.

What followed for hours was an impasse. The men of the Legion were so well hidden and apart from each other, it took a lucky French shot to kill or injure a Portuguese. Wilson stayed sitting on his horse; it was the only way to watch the action. This was his first proper skirmish fought under his sole command, and what an opponent.

Ney too was on his horse, always at the front of his column, seemingly totally unaware of the Legion's bullets as some did find their mark.

Eventually, as Wilson knew would be the case, the

Portuguese ran out of ammunition. Silva made his way to Wilson with the information. There was nothing for it but to order the retreat.

The men, having sat for hours in the sunshine, thirsty and frightened, ran as fast as they could up the mountain, an undisciplined rabble. Once over the top, they disappeared. Even the guns were abandoned with the horses still harnessed.

Wilson could not stay. He had to avoid capture. Someone, somewhere, would have read his book and remember he was a wanted man. He unsheathed his sword and raised it in salute towards Ney. With Silva and Charles, he galloped away, over the top. Out of sight.

'Did they give you another medal?' asked Bruce. 'Wilson collects medals, Sligo. I expect you've noticed the one hanging around his neck. He was awarded that for disobeying orders. Sounds as if he is still doing the same.'

It was most satisfying that these two aristocratic young men were hanging onto his every word and seemed to believe that, somehow, he had made a difference to the Iberian War.

It was still galling that Wellington hadn't believed him. Wilson remembered the shabby hacienda outside Talavera that Wellington was using as a base. The General had brushed his Banos report aside, let it fall from his desk onto the floor.

'I know what you wrote in your report,' he had said, 'but I've heard something different. There was no battle there. At the first sight of Ney's red head, your Legion took fright and ran back over the mountains.'

'Sir, that is not so. We did not run; we retreated when Ney's cavalry broke our lines after my men had done their best. They had run out of ammunition.'

'Yet, you've written this up as a victory? Wilson, I am, I have to say, growing weary of your insubordination and apparent inability to respect the chain of command. You were under strict orders to return here, not engage Marshal Ney or indeed anyone else when you were clearly outnumbered four to one. I should not have to remind you of the necessity of preserving our numbers here, or what exaggerating your achievements can cost our army. What if we really had believed Ney was weakened, what then? We are going to withdraw now, back to Portugal.'

'But sir, why not march towards Madrid, capture it, dethrone Joseph?'

'With Soult and Ney in the way? That would be absolute suicide. From now on, you are to report to General Beresford and follow his orders as if they are the word of the Lord.'

Wilson had nodded, made polite noises. He knew only too well that Beresford was a slow-thinking, overcautious armchair General with no flair, dash or any overall vision. No way would he serve under him. Time to bid a sad farewell to his Legion and return to London.

Bonaparte had just beaten the Austrians at Wagram. A close-run encounter. Shortly before, they themselves had been beaten at Aspern. Rather a repeat of Eylau before Friedland. There were signs that Bonaparte's army was not what it was. However, there really could be an allied victory soon in Eastern Europe. Maybe he could find another diplomatic post nearer the action. Where his efforts were really appreciated. Where Old Nosey was far away.

He did not mention any of this to Sligo and Bruce. They didn't need to know, in any case. These aristocrats and Etonians always stuck together; he was never going to be one of them. The finest sense of camaraderie he had felt was with Platov's Cossacks. Sad but true.

'So, Bruce, I assume you have run out of scandal to create in Lisbon and are looking for further travel?'

'Oh! Forgot to tell you, Wilson, I met this man in Corunna. Boring type, overly involved in the affairs of our time, but could perhaps be useful to a reporter of tall tales like yourself.'

'Why would I need someone like that?'

'Crabb Robinson. Foreign Correspondent for *The Times*. Knows everything. Everybody. Good connections.'

'Well, I ought to look him up when I get back to London.'

'Just remember to mention my name. I'll bet you, Wilson, now you are leaving, that Bonaparte will suddenly appear, sail into Lisbon harbour. So yes, we are, as the saying goes, moving on.'

'You know, you two, you should enlist, buy commissions, serve your King.'

Both young men looked quite appalled.

'We're going to Tangier,' Sligo said. 'Just got to have

the barnacles and weed scraped off the yacht's hull so she will sail even faster. I don't want to be caught by any naval ship, be it British or French, nor, indeed, a pirate. And, before you make any remarks about only travelling for pleasure, I don't know about Bruce, of course, but I fully intend to look at ruins. I dislike this war so much; I would prefer to pretend to live instead in the time of the ancient Greeks and Romans.'

'I have seen what being on the battlefield is really like,' Bruce said. 'I can still hear in my dreams those horses on Corunna beach screaming. I think that is why I find it so difficult to sleep unless I have some female company.'

'That's the best excuse I've ever heard for sleeping with a woman,' Sligo interjected with a laugh. 'I don't believe you think about anything unpleasant, let alone dream about it.'

Bruce dug him in the ribs.

'I can tell you, Wilson, I'm sure you will be pleased to know. I am much more particular who I take to bed these days. I have found female conversation can be just as stimulating as actual poking.'

Wilson raised an eyebrow. There wasn't much he could say. But it did sound as if, at long last, the youth was growing up. He wished the pair of them well on their voyage. As for him, he would hitch a lift on the next Royal Navy ship home. Home to dear Jemima and the children. Hopefully he would not be at home long. Hopefully he would find a way for the war to want him again. Bonaparte was still alive, and Sir Robert Wilson was still not yet the man who had killed him.

CHAPTER 22

The Rock loomed out of the mist. Bruce felt unusually optimistic, as from the deck of the "*Piraeus*", he watched its famous grey silhouette gradually became solid. He had come all this way from home, still felt he was looking for something elusive. He just didn't know exactly what it was. Some sort of purpose? Maybe he would find it here. There was a certain excitement in the speculation.

Tangier was meant to be a restorative holiday, after everything he had experienced in the months before he arrived in Lisbon. No more fighting, no more hunger or cold, no more blood or death, just the life of leisure to which an English gentleman was entitled.

It hadn't worked. The best thing about Tangier was that its streets were refreshingly free of dead soldiers, and no one was doing a 'Wilson', incessantly lecturing him about enlisting in the army to fight Bonaparte – but something was still missing. He could get drunk with his friends in Tangier; so what? He could do that anywhere. He could eat amazing food; so could any fool with a good chef. He had gone out into the desert; it was hot, and the sand found its way everywhere. He had retreated to the yacht to be bored out of his skull.

And then had come the shocking experience the last time he paid for an Arabian tart. He couldn't make out what the problem was – her scent, a mixture of strong body odour and overpowering perfume, maybe – but for the first time in his entire life, he had been unable to perform, although she had tried and tried. Mortified, he hadn't been able to look her in the face, but pushed her, none too gently, out of bed, leaving Adam to find her fee.

Bruce and Sligo sailed into Gibraltar harbour just as dawn was breaking. Sligo had been there before, so almost as soon as the yacht was moored, he sent one of his Mamelukes up to the convent, the Governor's residence, where he was expecting hospitality.

'Exceptional old boy, with any luck we'll be offered bedrooms too – there are plenty; it's a huge mansion. The Governor, Sir Colin Campbell, is an old friend of my Papa. They were at our school together.'

Almost at once, back came the messenger with an invitation.

Come to dinner. About six o'clock. I look forward to welcoming you and your friend. And, of course, you must stay. We have quite a houseful but that is not a problem.

It seemed strange after a week at sea: the ground rolled under Bruce's feet as he walked down the quay, preceded by Sligo's imposing bodyguards, more Mamelukes, dressed in exotic Arabian costumes. Sligo never failed to show off his wealth.

As the carriage drove into the convent courtyard, Bruce could see what Sligo had meant. It was indeed huge, overlooking the sea with verdant gardens and a glimpse of an ornate stone gazebo.

They were shown to their rooms – a certain opulence

about the large bed with its burgundy-coloured damask hangings. All such a welcome change from his yacht's tiny cabin.

After a luxurious, deep, hot bath, Bruce felt a new man in his evening attire. Velvet, black. Snowy cravat, tied in a complicated knot by Adam, tight-fitting breeches. He couldn't stop looking at himself in the mirrored staircase as he descended just after the preliminary dinner gong. The receiving room was equally opulent. Gilt everywhere, even on naked cherubs suspended on the ceiling. Bruce had not felt so at home since leaving London.

Introductions were made and drinks served.

'Back here once again, Sligo?' Sir Colin asked. Hastily adding, 'Not that we are sorry to see you; life is pretty tedious on this damned rock.'

'Bonaparte has certainly done his best to make sure there are few Mediterranean ports left open for us English,' Sligo replied. 'I am planning to go to Greece. So far, Malta is still an option en route, but Sicily is now under his thumb. I know Bruce was hoping to go there, but he is doomed to disappointment.'

Another guest appeared.

'James Stanhope; well, what the dickens are you doing here?' exclaimed Bruce.

The last occasion he'd seen Stanhope, was the dreadful time in Corunna at La Estrella with that rum reporter, Crabb Robinson. Pumping them both for stories. James had survived the fighting there, but in times like these, you couldn't be certain survival was going to last.

'Just arrived here myself; a week ago, to be precise,'

Stanhope replied. 'And dear old Sligo, too. Haven't seen you since Eton. I'm off to join my regiment in Cadiz very shortly. Took the opportunity to escort my sister, courtesy of the Royal Navy. And here she is…'

There was the sigh of smoky silk and the glimpse of rustling red in the doorway.

'Lady Hester Stanhope.'

Always willing to be introduced to an English unmarried lady guest, unusual this far from home, Bruce turned towards her with the usual smile and polite words on his lips. He did a double take. She was not what he had been expecting in the very least.

The figure in the doorway was perfect, statuesque, her dress cut to show her narrow waist, the curve of her enticing breasts, to advantage. Her heavy gold pendant disappeared into her cleavage. Somewhat older than Bruce, he reckoned, but she was handsome – not beautiful in a conventional way, but certainly in a way he could spend delightful hours studying. Her long brown hair was arranged in ringlets, framing her face; her dusky, oriental perfume filled the room.

'Peter – sorry, I mean the Marquis Sligo, but I have known you since you were a babe in arms,' she gushed. Her voice was throaty, melodious, husky. Like hot chocolate.

'I thought the yacht I saw sailing in this morning must be yours. I'm already missing London, it's a real treat to see a familiar face. And who is this dashing friend of yours? I don't recollect meeting him before.'

Her name rang some sort of bell. Bruce introduced himself. 'A school friend of Sligo and James as well. No, we have not met but it is…', he paused. He was going to say, 'a delight to do so now', but this moment was far more than a delight.

She waited, her eyebrows rose slightly.

'Michael Bruce, my Lady, your servant.'

Servant. That would do. A word he never used to a woman, ever.

She held his eyes for perhaps a little longer than strict politeness called for, before holding out her hand for him to kiss. A strange frisson ran through him as he took it, then straightened up to meet her smile. He couldn't take his eyes off her lips, plump and lush. *This lady is worthy of my attention! And she was without doubt a Lady. And how many Ladies had he bedded. Not one.*

The dinner gong summoned.

'Shall we, Hester?' James presented his arm, and they proceeded to the dining room. Bruce trailed at the back of the little group, his thoughts still trying to unravel his disturbing reaction to Lady Hester Stanhope.

Bruce was accustomed to dining in fine surroundings and his hostess had undoubtedly put all her efforts into creating precisely the right ambience. But afterwards he could not recall a single detail about the room, or the no doubt delicious food. Still distracted, he almost let the obsequious butler seat him on the same side of the table as Lady Hester, with Sligo in between the two of them. He would have to talk across his friend, if there was any hope of conversation at all with her. *Unthinkable!*

He pushed past, ignoring the butler's quickly smothered look of outrage and managed to seat himself next to Lady Mary, their hostess. With the intriguing Lady Hester on his other side. She turned out to be an amusing mimic, impersonating the Prince Regent with a strong Irish accent. Or making the King talk like a babbling brook. The other guests thought this hilarious, except for Sligo, who was busy boring Sir Colin with tales of his digs and antiquities.

Bruce had had quite enough of those in Tangier; Sligo seemed to be constantly knee-deep in books and negotiations with guides, leaving Bruce to loaf about, jaded and unfulfilled. And, as he tried to forget, fail to get his money's worth with houris. It did amuse him to notice Lady Hester almost batting her eyelashes at Sligo across the table. No worries there; Sligo ran a mile from any woman he thought might turn out to be a gold-digger. *Which left the field wide open for any other man who might want to move in…*

Suddenly he wanted it to be him. But this time, he felt the affair must be taken one slow step at a time. What they did – if they did it – would be different. Certainly not a quick tumble. Uniquely in his experience, he felt Lady Hester was worth, what did they call it, *courting,* that was it.

It was only a lifetime's practice of social niceties that made him do what he did next. He forced himself to turn his head the other way, ever aware of the divine presence inches next to him, resolved to make polite chat with Lady Mary. This was how Etonians behaved.

'It is so kind of you to have us to stay. This house is truly magnificent.'

They were stock phrases, called up from the memories of a hundred equally dull affairs. 'Have you been here long?'

'Only two years,' she answered, giving him her full attention, with a brilliant smile and a faint flush to her cheeks.

Well, he knew women always found him fascinating. He expected the same effect on the lady placed on his other side.

'Before this we were in Ireland, and I have to say my old bones far prefer the Mediterranean climate! Yes, it is a special place to live, quite large enough for diplomatic entertaining, but one drawback in Gibraltar, it is so difficult to employ the right servants.'

He had already forgotten the first part of her answer, but he pulled an appreciative face to show that he fully understood and sympathised with the tedium of her problem.

'I have some brought over from London,' she went on, and he almost asked, 'Some what?' before realising she was still talking about servants. 'The locals don't like working here; they say I'm too particular, but then I even have to teach them how to lay a table.'

He made a polite gesture with his hands, throwing them up to the ceiling as if to agree that, indeed, the limitations of the natives were simply beyond comprehension to civilised peoples.

The next course was served. Lady Mary turned away to ask something of a liveried lackey.

Just then he remembered where he had heard of Lady

Hester before. That dreadful night in Corunna. *She had been Sir John Moore's betrothed.* What a coincidence. He wondered if he should mention that! Why not?

He turned towards her and lowered his voice.

'Lady Hester, I believe we had a friend in common.'

Her eyes darkened in a perplexed way.

'Pardon, Mr. Bruce, you look too young to have come to the House.'

'The house?'

'I used to be the hostess for my uncle, Mr. Pitt, the late Prime Minister. I am certain you have heard of him.'

The House of Commons! Obviously! He could slap his forehead later, in the privacy of his own room. He decided to continue as if he had not just made himself look an idiot.

'I was actually referring to Sir John Moore.'

To whom you were engaged at the time of his death.

There. He had dropped the bomb on the table. How would she react?

'Oh!' she said, blushing.

James Stanhope leant across from the other side. 'Bruce was with Sir John on the retreat. He was with him almost to the end.'

There was a sudden hush. Even Sligo stopped talking about his plans to visit temples and tombs in Greece. Lady Mary gave her husband a glance, as much as to say, 'For heaven's sake. Do something'.

James already looked as if he was regretting what he had just said.

To Bruce's surprise, Hester started to rummage in her reticule. *What could be in there*, he thought, *that follows naturally from what I just said?* But then Lady Mary put her hand on Hester's arm.

'Mr. Bruce, why don't you take dear Lady Hester for a drive tomorrow morning so she can show you the wondrous sights of our Rock? There is an upmarket coffee shop I could recommend. Going there is an absolute treat. Their honey cakes are to die for.'

Bruce bit back on his astonished instinctive first response, which was to blurt, '*Really?*' It seemed too easy that he might be alone with this fascinating lady, with the permission of his hostess too.

'I'd be honoured,' Bruce said instead. 'I'd like to listen to more of your mimicry – you can practise new voices on me. I'm a good listener, and no way any sort of critic.'

'And what exactly are you then, Mr. Bruce?' asked Hester, in a slightly frosty tone, perhaps insulted by the notion that she might even need a critic. Oh, dear, he hoped he hadn't offended her. He had thought she found him interesting. Handsome. God, he could usually read a woman just by looking.

He opted to turn on the full charm.

'I am Michael Bruce, my Lady. Son of the banker Craufurd Bruce. You will have certainly met him; he arranges money matters for many members of the House of Lords. And, of course, I went to Eton with your brothers, so that does make me a gentleman.' He laughed. 'They probably know me too well. Tell tales of my schooldays.'

'In which case, we should explore the Rock together.' She gave him such an unexpectedly sweet look, Bruce found himself wanting more of her company, purely for her company's sake. If that was all she would allow. *But will she let me see what is in her reticule?* he wondered.

The following morning, the Governor's carriage took them down to the harbour. She was meant to be showing Bruce the Rock, but when Bruce pointed out the yacht waiting securely at its moorings, brass and polished teak gleaming in the sunlight, she asked to be shown around. He was surprised to feel a bit of proprietorial pride as he gave her the tour. It was Sligo's yacht, not his – but Sligo was not with them, so there was only one recipient for her obvious interest.

'You and Sligo and the crew – you never felt cramped?' she asked.

'There are plenty of spare cabins,' he pointed out.

'Room for a sizeable party,' she murmured, but before he could enquire exactly what she might have meant by that, she turned to him with her delightful smile. 'It is mid-morning, and I usually take refreshment at this time. May I introduce you to my favourite coffee shop?'

They strolled down the quayside towards the town, Bruce enjoying her British sense of humour, her amusing updates on London politics and court gossip. She listened to his opinions – such a change for him. She even laughed at his jokes.

Yes, the shop was welcoming. Clean and bright. They moved past the inside tables into the shadiest corner of the garden, surrounded by orange and lemon trees and a riot of pink flowers. No other people, just the place for a tête-à-tête.

Bruce ordered coffee, the local honey cakes Lady Mary had praised, and white port, Hester protesting rather mildly that it was really too early for alcohol. But Bruce was already sliding generous coins ostentatiously from his pouch. Sir Colin had let him know Hester was strapped for cash. It was the real reason she had left the expensive London life to travel.

They started to talk about their lives. Bruce learnt that travelling with her was her doctor, a Dr. Charles Meryon, and Elizabeth, her companion.

'Well, she likes people to think of her like that,' she explained, 'but in actual fact, she's my full-time maid. I took pity on her, you see,' dropping her voice to a whisper, 'she is my cousin, Uncle Pitt's daughter – born out of wedlock – and, now he's dead, there simply isn't any money for her. And I really cannot afford to keep her.'

'That's quite a coincidence,' Bruce replied. 'My manservant, Adam, is in fact my half-brother. My father had a tumble with my sister's French governess. Adam's supposed to be keeping an eye on me and reporting back to Pa, but I have every intention of sending him home as soon as possible. I know I'm completely able to look after myself.'

'It is remarkable how things have changed,' she mused. She saw the query in his face and answered it before he could speak out loud.

'Half the noble peers in the House of Lords are descended from the wrong side of the blanket – and at the time it was fully acknowledged and no one apologised for anything. The results of such immoral liaisons were given titles and estates. Today, everyone knows this happens – you were not shocked when I told you about Elizabeth, and the story of Adam gives me no surprise at all – but no one in the *Ton* speaks of it.'

'Not in Uncle Pitt's London,' he agreed with a smile.

'No. Not in Uncle Pitt's London.' She gazed at the tabletop and seemed to trace a pattern that only she could see there with one finger. 'But we are not now in Uncle Pitt's London, are we, Mr. Bruce? Or can I call you Michael in private? I would prefer to be Hester to you, Lady Hester is just too formal'. He nodded enthusiastically.

'I confess I often felt quite the prisoner in Uncle Pitt's London, the life of an unmarried woman is so restricted,' she continued, 'but now I am away from all that nonsense, I am very eager to explore things that Uncle Pitt would certainly never have approved of.'

She raised her eyes to meet his as she spoke those last words. What he saw there made his heart race and other parts stiffen.

But then she giggled and changed the subject completely.

'I have a wild idea. Why don't we encourage Elizabeth and Adam into a romantic liaison? Even marriage. We might well be rid of both of them! You are without doubt mature enough not to need a wet nurse, and I would certainly welcome the release from my obligation to support her.'

They established a routine for the rest of the week. They met soon after breakfast, then spent the cooler mornings together. They borrowed mounts from the Governor's stables. Bruce discovered she was a born horsewoman who rode astride like a man, wearing an avant-garde design of breeches. Tailored in London, she explained. Racing him, when he considered himself one of the best in the saddle, galloping along the seashore.

This, he thought, was certainly one of those sensations that would not have been countenanced in Uncle Pitt's London. Yet he had a feeling that, while riding horses like a man might be one of the things she had been referring to, it was hardly all she meant. But she never harked back to that conversation, and he was content to let it lie. He was getting closer to her, for now that was what mattered.

On the third morning, they returned to the coffee shop, to what they now called their table on the patio. Fortified once more by two glasses of port, she asked him directly what he had seen at Corunna, now she knew he had really been there. Brother James had confirmed it privately.

'Don't worry. Spare me nothing.'

Bruce did not reply for a moment. He was trying to gather his thoughts. How much detail to give her? Certainly not the image of those terrified horses on the beach or the groaning wounded soldiers. He decided to recount for her a sort of potted history of his time in Spain and Lisbon.

She laughed when he told her Bonaparte had arrived in Madrid, just in time to spoil his social whirl. She was impressed he knew Wellington, even though he was not, in soldiering terms, in the same league as Sir John.

'I was so lucky,' he continued. 'Without the presence of Sir John, I would have either died or been captured, long before I reached safety at Corunna. He never criticised me for putting myself and Adam in danger, though he must have cursed my presence under his breath. He knew my mother and father, you see, so must have felt responsible. He was the bravest man I have ever known. Without Sir John, the war in Spain would have been lost before it had hardly begun.'

Another detail he had remembered from Corunna. A significant one. Now surely was the time to remind her. He leant across the table and took her hand. 'James will have told you his last thoughts were for you. He must have loved you deeply.'

Her eyes were shining with tears. 'Yes, we were to be married. I have only one memento of him.'

With no Lady Mary to stop her this time, Hester opened her reticule. She drew out a man's glove and laid it on the table. It was stained with russet streaks.

Ah… thought Bruce. He understood. He had seen enough of those stains by now to recognise blood. It seemed a strangely macabre memento.

'James brought me this all the way home. You know dearest brother Charles was killed the same night. James has never been the same. He is absolutely terrified of returning to active service with his regiment but cannot face the dishonour of resigning his commission. He would probably be branded a coward. Also, as I keep telling him, he just can't afford to leave the army. Where else would he find paid employment? There is no family fortune left.'

She looked so sad. Bruce held her fingers to his lips. Then, glancing round to make certain they were not observed, he found the courage to put a tentative finger on her cheek, then he kissed her properly – so very lightly, on her lips. *Take that, Uncle Pitt!*

She did not turn away. Seemed to welcome him.

'I can understand why Sir John adored you and why you were in his thoughts on his deathbed. I am beginning to feel the same about you. You are unlike any other woman, so appealing and so adventurous. I cannot think of any other female friend of mine who would dare to explore the world in the middle of a war.'

Hester coloured. 'You must be careful, Michael, I am so much older than you.' *Eleven years older* – he had wormed that out of James. 'You deserve a golden aristocratic girl. You may think age doesn't matter, but it certainly does. Now, take me home, time for luncheon.'

Later on in the week, once again borrowing two horses from the Governor's stables, they found themselves on a headland overlooking the sea. Michael assisted Hester to dismount so they could observe the breathtaking view. She kept hold of his hand. Encouraged, he pulled her towards him. She did not push him away.

'What I would really like to do more than anything in the world right now is to kiss you. May I?' Michael murmured, his lips on her hair.

She turned her head upwards towards him invitingly. At first very gently, his lips just brushing hers, he kissed her, then with more passion. Her lips parted. She tasted so sweet. He eased her lips further apart and deepened the kiss, hungry for more of her. Never had he experienced such a reaction to a simple kiss. She pulled away slowly, smiling. He loved her smile; it lit up her face.

'That was one of those things I mentioned the other day.'

'I was hoping it was.'

'I see why the poets rhapsodise so much about it.' Her expression was thoughtful, and her lips moved slowly from side to side, as though she were savouring a sip of fine wine. 'Yes. It is certainly worth exploring further.'

And if she has never even been kissed, then…

His heart pounded suddenly, like it never had since his first time with the maid at Eton. He felt like a horny schoolboy! He had wondered, but now he knew for sure. He was face to face with his first virgin. Who wanted to explore further. *With him!*

And that made her very vulnerable. He could so easily disappoint her if he moved too fast. Not that any previous bedfellow had ever complained, he reminded himself. How to go about it? Where could he arrange a romantic place where they would be safe from interruptions?

However, there was one problem that had to be dealt with before anything else, and she had been the one to suggest a possible solution.

'This evening, I think it is time for us to put your wild scheme into motion,' he said, leaning on his saddle, letting go her hand. 'We must think of a way to get our two servants—'

He had been about to say, '—out of our hair,' but no.

To play the game properly they had to pretend this was an unselfish action entirely for the servants' benefit. '— together. We have to convince them that they need each other for the purpose of matrimony. We want only the best for them, after all.' *And for us.*

Hester almost grinned, in the most unladylike fashion.

'My dream of an idea. Two birds with one stone so to speak. I know Elizabeth has met Adam in the servants' hall, but it is always difficult for her; she is neither upstairs nor downstairs, but somewhere in-between.'

She thought for a moment.

'I suggest we set up a whist foursome later this evening in the small drawing room. This is, as far as I know, never used after dinner. We could leave them and see what happens. I will lend Elizabeth a suitable frock; she is not unattractive to look at, she has excellent sewing skills and, of course, unlike most of her class, can read and write. Even count.'

Bruce smiled. 'She sounds the perfect mate.'

Bruce had instructed Adam before dinner that he was expected to make up a whist foursome later on, nothing more. Since Salamanca, he had stopped needling Adam as he had in the past, left him more or less to his own devices in Lisbon and Tangier. This suited them both. He did not know exactly what Hester would say to Elizabeth, but he hoped it was rather to the point. Being a poor spinster was not a fun-filled future to look forward to.

The ladies duly arrived together. A few minutes late. Hester had changed from her dinner dress into a floating silky garment, patterned with red roses. Bruce had been sat, waiting, wondering what the evening had in store for him, for a full suspenseful fifteen minutes. The more he thought, imagined, anticipated, the tighter he felt his breeches grow, so he tried to study the wallpaper. Adam had his usual air of being part senior prefect, part footman. Elizabeth seemed nervous, but it was not the first time they had played social card games. Both had made up foursomes for their employers before.

Actually, Bruce thought, *they make an all-right pair. She is as attractive as Hester had remarked, and Adam, although nothing like the ladies' man I am, does have an air about him and is, of course, taller.*

Hester made certain Elizabeth and Adam were partners. After the first rubber, which they won convincingly, they relaxed and were enjoying themselves. Bruce dealt the next hand. Then Hester brushed her forehead against her palm.

'I'm not feeling too healthy, it might be the oysters. I will ask you, Mr. Bruce, to please take me for a stroll round the garden; I need fresh air. I expect you two can think of something you both can engage in.'

Both servants immediately began to push back their chairs, ready to stand. Their master and mistress gently waved them to sit back down again.

'Lady Stanhope, are you quite certain you do not need my presence?' Elizabeth asked. Hester nodded. Bruce simply ignored Adam's enquiring glances. Hester picked up her cloak, which he placed round her shoulders, and they slipped through the French doors onto the lawn.

The garden was lit by a rising full moon, the air was cool and fragrant, and the lamps on the terrace just about showed up a line of trees, a copse or an orchard, in the distance. He took Hester's arm and led her away from the house. Then he kissed her, longingly; he could not help it. But she did not respond as he'd hoped. There was a rustle in the trees. Looking over his shoulder, she screamed.

'There's a man up that tree, he's looking at us.'

Bruce tugged at her shoulder, anxious not to break the mood. 'It's probably an owl.'

'Not with eyes like that!' She dropped her arms and fled headlong into the darkness.

Bruce looked up; there indeed were eyes, reflected in the faint lamplight. Human-like eyes, not those of a bird. When the breeze parted the treetops to let in a little more moonlight for a second, Bruce realised peering down on him was one of Gibraltar's famous apes.

'For whom do you spy?' Bruce asked. 'France or Spain?'

The ape stayed still, keeping his secrets.

Bruce followed Hester through the trees. At first, he could not find her, swearing under his breath at the bloody ape. Had it seriously scared her? Was she still stumbling about in the dark, or would she somehow circle back to the house? Thus ruining all their plans... Well, at least setting them back. Then what? Another whist game, another evil oyster for Hester?

A white ornate gazebo glimmered through the darkness. There was no light other than the moon and stars, but he smelt perfume. Inside was the outline of Hester, sitting on a chaise longue.

'I wasn't really frightened,' she said, with her distinctive throaty laugh. 'I just wanted you to feel the gallant knight. Come and sit beside me and please kiss me some more.'

Bruce needed no encouragement. But instead of her lips, he kissed her breasts. He could feel her nipples harden under the thin material, She pulled away and he stopped. He had never been a man to take a woman unless she wanted him. It was too dark to see her expression as she spoke, but he imagined she was blushing.

'I have to tell you,' she almost whispered. 'It's to be the first time for me. I do have brothers so I have seen a man undressed, but I'm not certain exactly what to expect, so you will have to show me what to do. I so want us to be close. I did change after dinner, put on this simple dress – that red silk is far too constricting – and I left off my corset. I thought that the right thing. Elizabeth was very put out, but I told her I was overheated. I was, but not in that way— I want to experience it all.'

The talking was distracting. He silenced her with a gentle testing kiss. Hers in return was gentle too. She was very exciting to kiss. He teased her lips until she opened them. Tongue to tongue. She made a sort of humming sound. *Thrilling*, thought Bruce. He throbbed inside his breeches, longed to loosen them. But not yet. Not yet.

Her fingers reached up, traced the line of his jaw. Then her arms were entwined round his neck. She stroked his hair. He pulled her onto his knee and so slowly bunched up her silky skirt. She wore nothing underneath. Caressing her thighs, his hand moved up between her legs and he stroked her there with his fingers. She gasped slightly but made no resistance. She was, to his surprise, moist, ready. It was an exciting thought, to be the first. Doubtless she would always remember the romantic gazebo. *And him.*

'I must take off some of my clothes,' he said. He picked her up, so she was standing and placed her cloak on the chaise longue for more comfort, then lowered her back. He undressed. The taste, the feel of her filled his senses. He was more than ready but he knew he must not rush. Many of the tricks he had learnt in Tangier would help him slow down, but that was for his pleasure, not hers. For the first time for a woman, it was important to him that she have pleasure too. In fact, it was *more* important.

He felt her hands on him, the mirror of his caresses a few moments ago, fingertips brushing his thigh and moving upwards. He winced as her fingers made contact.

'Oh!' she exclaimed. 'That will never go— '

'I promise you it will,' he assured her through his teeth, his body screaming *for God's sake get on with it.*

He lay down on top of her. He did not want to cause her any pain, so once again, he used his fingers to feel his way inside. Then he positioned himself and pushed, entering her first with just the tip.

'Oh. It is not so— Oh! That is quite— *Oh, my!*' she exclaimed as he entered her fully. She clasped him to her and squeaked.

He managed to pull away. 'Am I hurting you?'

'No, no, I just feel different, so excited, come here.'

He began to move, thrusting gently and rhythmically. Wave after wave of sensation.

'Mmm...' she breathed. He grinned in the dark. She seemed to be enjoying it too.

'This is remarkable,' she said suddenly, in a conversational tone. 'It really does go all the way in. How extraordinary.'

'Yes,' he groaned.

She fell silent as he continued to move. He could feel himself beginning to peak, but he did not want it to happen too soon. He slowed down, taking longer with each thrust.

'It is the most unusual experience. Not quite like— Hmm. How would you describe it?'

'I wouldn't try,' he almost screamed. 'Please, just—'

He didn't want to say, *Just shut up!*

Deep inside, he felt her relax; it was a new sensation for him too, being wanted for himself, not because he'd paid for it.

There was no further commentary from beneath him, just sighs and gasps as she felt the novel sensations. He knew he had not taken her with him as he finished, but he needn't have worried when she said, still panting, 'That was so lovely. Can we embrace like that again tomorrow night or would that be too soon?'

Bruce hadn't the heart to tell her that he could certainly oblige if they waited just another few minutes. In fact, he was already willing and able. Hard enough. He pressed a kiss onto her forehead.

She pulled down her dress.

'I'm afraid there will be a little blood on it, Hester. Let me clean it.' Bruce pulled up his breeches, reaching in a pocket for his handkerchief.

They sat side by side on the chaise longue. He put his arm round her waist, clasping her tightly.

'You were so clever to find this place where we could be alone,' he told her.

'That was all part of this evening's plan, did you not realise? Not the ape, of course, he gave me the perfect excuse to make sure you followed me here. Yes, I discovered it when walking before you arrived, and thought it would make a perfect love nest. I'm certain it must have been used before, with all those cushions and the daybed. But it won't do for us in the future.'

Bruce felt his heart jolt. Was it to be a single encounter with her? Was she disappointed, then? He was already imagining everything else he could teach her.

'I have yet another wicked plan,' she went on. 'You can show me exactly what I have been missing all these years. I need to be with you in a proper bed, with candles so we can see each other. This is so uncomfortable. We can be together without clothes.' She hesitated, drew a quick breath and glanced sideways at him. 'Or do you think I'm being forward?'

Yes, and I love it!

'No, no, it would be my dream come true, dearest Hester.' He kissed her again, passionately this time.

'I've noticed my room is just down the corridor from yours. Lady Mary sleeps up the other end of the mansion, and Sligo couldn't give a damn. So, you are welcome any time after everyone is abed. I will naturally have to bring Elizabeth into the secret – and you, Adam – but they both know which side their bread is buttered.' She cocked her head slightly. 'Michael, is something wrong?'

He realised he hadn't made any reply. He was simply lost in her. He could spend his whole life worshipping her lips, her breasts, her… She was perfection, mysterious. To have a Lady plan where she might want *him* – in her bedchamber – unprecedented, *thrilling*.

'No, no, it's a fine idea', he assured her quickly. 'The finest I have ever heard. It will be even more exciting for you next time, I give you my word.'

Back in the small parlour, they found Elizabeth and Adam, not playing cards but on the sofa holding hands, their heads close together. When they saw Hester and Bruce, they sprung apart.

'Listen carefully,' Hester said. 'There are to be some new developments concerning myself and Mr. Bruce. What you see will not be told to anyone. No gossiping. Do you both understand?'

They nodded.

'Now, Mr. Bruce and I are going to leave you a little longer, until the candles are burnt down. I am going upstairs. Mr. Bruce will be joining the other gentlemen for cigars and brandy.' She swept out of the room.

Two weeks later, Sligo's yacht left the Rock for Malta. The plan was to sail on to Greece, Constantinople, then possibly Egypt. Any places not under Bonaparte's rule.

Lady Hester's interest in the capacity of the yacht had soon been understood. As well as Sligo, Bruce and the crew, aboard were Hester and Doctor Meryon.

Adam had left for England, escorting Elizabeth back to Falmouth on the packet. Bruce had given him a letter to their father explaining the situation. He was sure he would come up with the dosh, so the couple could marry well, maybe buy a public house to run.

Meryon was Hester's personal physician and acted as her quasi-chaperone. When Hester had first described him as such, Bruce had pictured a withered old cove, the days when he might have needed chaperoning himself long behind him.

In fact, the doctor was only a few years older than Bruce. Even so, it did not take them very long to strike up a hearty mutual dislike, and after that they avoided each other as much as they could in the confines of the yacht.

But for himself, his whole life had changed since he'd arrived in Gibraltar. He had found something with Hester, a state of mind unimaginable to him during all the hours he'd spent sampling the breasts and thighs of other women. It was a feeling that had eluded him during his romps with all the tarts from Stockholm to Madrid, Lisbon to Tangier, where he had finally grown tired of paying for the pleasure.

He no longer needed anyone else. He was in love with Hester. Blissfully in love. A totally unfamiliar emotion.

He did not know if she loved him. She never said so. He was well aware of her financial situation. It was perfectly possible that she would have chosen to come on the yacht, even if they had not become an unofficial couple. Simply because it was cheaper than life on land – *and why not?* he asked himself. Would he have done any different, in her place?

But the fact was, they were on a romantic cruise. Only Sligo's master cabin was really large enough for two – and he had no intention of giving it up – but that barely mattered. The cramped single cabins had space enough, and anyway, they had each other, which was what counted for him. On the first night at sea, as he came to climax and she shattered around him in hers, he knew she was *the* one.

Maybe she felt he wasn't socially important enough for her. Though he certainly had the wealth – he tried to forget that was only thanks to his father. She was the daughter of an Earl, he but the son of a banker – but in the brave new world that would surely follow Napoleon's defeat, was it entirely impossible that she could even one day be his wife?

All that, whatever that was, lay ahead. For now, fate could blow them across this sea wherever it wanted them to go, far away from Bonaparte, far away from war.

CHAPTER 23

The midday sun beat down on the ruins of Almeida and the dusty fields surrounding it. Horses and wagons trundled in and out of the flattened town; the gentle breeze stirred up the dust and rippled the canvas of Masséna's tent. Ney had dust in his hair, dust on his uniform and was rubbing more dust from his eyes the longer he had to stay there. He was on Concorde under the shade of an olive tree, close to the tent. Even the horse was tired of waiting; he was asleep with one hoof resting, tail idly flicking at the flies.

Despite being abruptly summoned by the Marshal, there had been no reception party, just two sentries standing at attention, looking straight ahead. Everyone else was keeping their distance.

Tent: it was more like a city under canvas befitting a sultan. Marshal Masséna was now Commander-in-Chief in the Peninsula. Another Marshal that Ney could not tolerate. He was indolent: interested only in what he could loot. He expected life on campaign to be like life in Paris: food, drink, comfort. And he expected his staff to provide it all, no matter what. Let the men starve; they were of little importance.

More than this, he couldn't care who knew he travelled with another comfort.

Ney knew what he was up to inside, as did everyone

else within earshot. Each time she cooed and giggled, and Masséna made rhythmic grunts, he felt his hand reach for his sword. If Ney were Commander-in-Chief, as he should have been, it wouldn't have mattered who the Marshal was, even Soult, he wouldn't have kept any man waiting.

Masséna's Corps was camped out in the rubble of Almeida. It was only some seven months since Ney had destroyed the town. Wellington must have thought it was so impregnable on its granite plateau that Ney's men would never successfully overrun it. Yes, yes, it was a fluke that a French shell landed on a trail of spilt powder that led to the town's main magazine. The place went up with a concussive blast. The castle, the cathedral, most of the buildings were obliterated. Ney and his staff had looked on in awe, as the debris flew skywards. In that moment they all believed glory was theirs and, at last, victory in the Peninsula seemed possible.

Their elation had been short-lived. Here they were again, back where they were in August, driven from Lisbon in utter disarray.

Ney looked at his fob watch; the bastard had kept him waiting for over an hour. He knew why he was being made to wait. For Masséna, it was a game, reminding him exactly who was in charge. If Masséna didn't know what Ney thought of him and his tactics by now, he was a fool. And whatever he was, Masséna was certainly no fool.

Ney gripped the hilt of his sword. His frustration was rapidly turning into a blinding, burning anger. If only Napoleon had given *him* overall command. He deserved it; he knew the problems they faced, and there were many. After all, he had been in the Godforsaken place for years now.

It was obscene that Masséna had brought this woman with him from Paris. She was even the sister of one of his aide-de-camps. It was even more disgusting that everyone knew about it. Even the Emperor knew. It was insulting that he should be made to wait while the one-eyed buffoon finished up.

Ney stared at the tassels fastening the tent's flaps and the stern, unflinching faces of the guards. Who did they fear more? Masséna or Ney? Who would they rather serve under? Who could bring them glory in Iberia? He was well aware of his own reputation and was certain who they would choose. Not Masséna, the has-been whom Napoleon had pulled unwillingly, so it was said, from retirement.

Give him a fair fight on flat land fit for cavalry. Ney knew he could beat anyone out here, Wellington included. But this was a nebulous war. There was still no end in sight.

Even when he'd managed to go to Paris for a much-needed break, he had been called back straight away. He'd left VI Corps in the hands of his deputy, Marchand.

In Paris, he found Aglaé was extremely agitated by the latest court upheaval. Napoleon was divorcing Josephine and planning to marry the daughter of the Austrian Emperor. Treating their dear friend so abominably. As it turned out, they had hardly any chance to spend relaxed family time together, though he had managed one frenetic afternoon with Ida. Before Napoleon demanded Ney's immediate return to Spain.

Because Marchand had lost Salamanca.

How on earth had he managed to lose Salamanca? Incompetent idiot!

Then he found out Napoleon had given the honour of being the Commander-in-Chief in Spain to Masséna. Masséna, yes, that man was a legend – Genoa, Aspern, Wagram – but he was also a looter and thief on a scale that would make even Soult blush. A parsimonious, ungenerous leader, unable to share with the men that risked their lives for his glory. As well as a brazen boaster of a sexual conquest. That ought to be conducted with some discretion, not rubbed in the face of a fellow Marshal.

Ney didn't know of any other way he could have handled the clash that started as soon as Masséna arrived in the Spanish centre to take command. When VI Corps was, as instructed by the Emperor, besieging the town of Ciudad Rodrigo, Masséna had sent over some engineer of Junot's, with instructions that he should take over proceedings. Ney had no need of this man. Smashing Ciudad Rodrigo would be for the glory of Ney and VI Corps, not Junot and his jumped-up expert.

He sent the man back with a strongly worded letter; maybe, in hindsight, a too-strongly worded letter. This didn't do the trick as Masséna sent the man back again. Ney sent him back yet again so, in the end, Masséna came flying over to Rodrigo and had the audacity to threaten to strip Ney of his command.

He had to admit, he'd been tempted to resign there

and then, get shot of it all, go back to Paris, be with his wife, his boys, Ida, whom he didn't have to parade around in front of armies to prove himself. The war, though, the war won. Loyalty won. Ney still wanted to win the war for Napoleon. With gritted teeth, he submitted to the orders of Marshal Masséna.

After Ciudad Rodrigo fell and Almeida shortly afterwards, Masséna had ordered the march on Lisbon. As an attempt to clear the way, Masséna had launched an attack at Bussaco, about one hundred and forty miles north of Lisbon. The French had arrived there by a circuitous route. Masséna had not listened when Ney told him the roads they intended to use were not fit for artillery. They also had a long unnecessary halt as his mistress had become poorly.

This delay was a godsend to Wellington, who had time to organise his defences and to hide his infantry divisions behind a crest. Ney's men had no conception they were there until it was too late. The attack failed with the loss of over two and a half thousand of his men.

The British retired. Masséna proclaimed a victory. Ney did not agree, but who was he to report to Paris?

They pursued the British towards Lisbon in the wettest autumn anyone could remember. It had been assumed the city would be wide open, but lo and behold, the British had built this impregnable and well-placed secret ring of fortifications around the city.

Ney's men had caught a peasant as they approached a few miles from Lisbon. He had not believed the man when he babbled about new forts, high walls, rocky gun emplacements. *What a tale.* But when Ney made a personal reconnaissance, it all turned out to be true. Wellington had constructed a vast fortified zone guarding the Lisbon Peninsula and, most importantly, the harbour. The British were supplied with everything – food, fodder, arms, ammunition, fresh troops – by the Royal Navy.

Then, even with all communications completely cut off from Spain and Paris by the Portuguese militia and guerrillas, Masséna decided to stay, try to tempt Wellington out. What a calamitous decision that turned out to be.

After a month, it was obvious this wasn't going to happen. The British stayed behind their ring of forts. The men were starving. He had to order the retreat. Then the whole unfed and under-supplied French Armée had to scrabble back to Almeida, some seven months since they left, to sit in the ruins and wait for Masséna to do up his breeches.

As they marched back, he had sent Ney an olive branch, a gift of an ornate and unusual telescope. Ney didn't want it. He knew it had been pilfered from the university. Sent it back with a note explaining how he was no receiver of stolen goods.

Masséna's reply had been the summons to meet him here.

Ney now shifted the top of his sword in and out of his scabbard, unable to contain his towering contempt much longer. He was just about to storm the tent when the flaps parted and out came a Cornet of the Dragoons. This was no Cornet, though. This was Masséna's woman dressed as a Cornet. He recognised her pretty face. He'd been forced to sit next to her at a mess dinner and although she had tried to engage him with small talk, he'd stuck to staring at his plate all evening.

As she tucked her hair into her uniform hat, Masséna swaggered out after her, still buttoning up his trousers; he gave her a playful pat on her bottom to send her on her way.

The men called her Madam X. Dressed up like she was, in uniform, as a soldier, brought back memories of Ida in Boulogne and Eylau, and with them a great wave of resentment at being stuck out here with these incompetents. Ney's face felt hot with rushing blood. He gripped his hilt even tighter to stop his fist from aiming at Masséna's chin.

'This conduct might be condoned in the Tuileries,' he said, breaking the silence, 'but it is not appropriate out here, on serious campaign.'

'Come now, Ney,' Masséna answered, apparently completely unembarrassed, peering up with his one eye. 'We all have our needs, even you.'

'What do you want? I have been waiting here for hours.'

'Calm down, Ney.'

Ney dismounted and vaguely saluted. There were more people gathered now, curious to see how the latest tiff between the two Marshals would end. No one wanted to miss the promised spectacle.

Masséna attempted to lead him away so they could talk well out of earshot of the crowd. Ney stood his ground. He wanted everyone to hear what was said.

'All right, Ney,' Masséna went on. 'I'll cut to the chase. I want you to ready VI Corps. We will make another assault on Lisbon, this time from the south where they won't expect us.'

'Have you forgotten Lisbon is ringed by forts?'

'Then we'll bombard them. Look what you did to this place.'

'That was luck, otherwise I would have been besieging it for months.'

'Luck will smile again. We'll march through Extremadura, then make a swift northward movement... hear me out. This is our last chance to finish Wellington. If he becomes too well established—'

'No.'

'What?'

'You may not have paid any attention to your men since you arrived here, but take a look at my VI Corps. I have never seen my men with such low morale. We're short of numbers in all divisions. Our kit is in tatters. We've no fresh boots, just about enough food to subsist in camp. Guns need repairing. Ammunition is low. Our resupply lines non-existent.

'Wellington can be supplied from the sea. He will lack for nothing. What we all need is time to recuperate after the last disaster. Not be compelled to march again towards Lisbon for your attempt at fame. I have led my men from Ulm to Friedland into *this* shambles, and I will not lead them into another. I'll march them back to Spain, thank you. What you do with your men must be up to you'.

Masséna stood, rising grandly up to his full height,

which still didn't allow him to stare Ney in the eye, only made the point of how much taller Ney was.

'It's an order, Marshal, from your Commander.'

'It's an order VI Corps will ignore until we receive a sensible one.'

'Dear God, man. Just hear yourself. Ney, ready your men.'

'Never.'

'Right, that is it, you pig-headed, impossible, vain, arrogant idiot. You're no longer in command of VI Corps. I'll have you replaced with someone who wants to win this war. Leave right now. You will ride directly to Madrid and wait there until you hear from the Emperor.'

'I'll wait there and watch as you lead your army into disaster. Enjoy the moment you lose yet another battle.'

Ney turned; whatever Masséna was babbling, now became just noise on the breeze. He heaved himself back onto Concorde and spurred him on, not looking back at the opulent tent or the ruined city. He was outraged; it would seem to the men of VI Corps he had abandoned them. The men he had led to such glory for six years, Boulogne, East Prussia, all the way to this indecisive campaign.

He fully expected never to serve again, never to face the enemy on the field, never to risk his own life.

Well, he'd done enough already. He could now retire and live the life of a country gentleman. Let the likes of Masséna and Soult finish the business, if indeed it could be finished. Here, it seemed, a small army was beaten, a large army starved.

In his heart of hearts, Ney thought even Napoleon

would fail. And he certainly wasn't coming back to the Peninsula, he'd be far too busy with his young Empress and the birth of his heir. The Age of War and Glory was petering out, stalled in the dust and the heat and the hate.

PART 4

TRAVELLING EAST

Here we are and there we go… but where?

Lord Byron

CHAPTER 24

The doors into Napoleon's inner sanctum remained resolutely shut. Ney stopped his pacing and looked for the umpteenth time at his pocket watch. He had been waiting for over two hours. It had even crossed his mind that maybe the Emperor had had one of his seizures in there and no one had noticed this time. Ney, it seemed, was trusted to keep knowledge of the Emperor's fits secret, but not to do much more than that these days. He hoped to reverse this opinion today.

The day was hot. The antechamber sweltered. If he closed his eyes, he could be back in Madrid, where he was supposed to be. The heat was like Madrid, anyway, though the new Paris smelled far more pleasant and well kept. As he ran his finger round his sweating collar, he felt sorry for the two huge sentries standing motionless on either side of the door. They were Old Guardsmen, judging by their twirled moustaches, bearskins and prominent *Legion d'honneurs*. They would not be comfortable in this heat.

Though in some ways he also envied them. Command was a hotter place, hellishly so sometimes, and failure could make a bonfire of a hero's glory. For some weeks, he had been preparing himself for the fiery lash of the Emperor's tongue.

He had stayed impatiently in Madrid, kicking his

heels. Daily anticipating a message from the Emperor, ever since he had been relieved of the Command of VI Corps by that arsehole Masséna. Then he heard that Masséna had also been recalled in absolute disgrace, relieved of his command too, and permanently retired.

Considering himself free of a Commanding Officer's orders, Ney had made the decision to return to Paris, confront the Emperor face to face. Tell his side of the story. Report the exact sorry state of affairs in Spain, the poor condition of the French army, the indiscipline in the ranks.

In Paris, the streets hummed and bustled. New monumental buildings and bridges had sprung up on every street or quayside, it seemed. The city's new verve and confidence, so different from the watchful, unhappy mood Ney had experienced during his first visit; when Napoleon had merely been First Consul and Ney a cavalry officer of the Army of the Rhine.

Paris now felt like the capital of the world. And more than ever, Paris seemed to belong to Napoleon.

His first stop had been at the house he leased at vast expense for Ida. She was not there. Her uptight major-domo was evasive, although, as Ney forcefully reminded him, his salary was paid by the Marshal standing in front of him.

'She has gone shopping in Vienna,' was the only information the pompous idiot would divulge.

Furious as well as frustrated – he had been looking forward to sharing a bath with Ida, and other things – he ordered the carriage home. There he was met by his wife, racing down the staircase, clearly on the warpath. He had hardly time to almost drag her into the drawing room, out of earshot of the servants, before she was hammering on his chest with her small fists.

'Michel, do you understand what you have done? What on earth will I tell the boys? You stupid, stupid man. The ignominy! I am the laughingstock of the court. How are we going to live if the Emperor retires you, too, like Masséna? Where will the money come from to afford this house? I will not have the right wardrobe, the right jewels. I will not be able to entertain, host the right sort of parties.'

Ney did manage a little smirk when he thought that would be a small relief.

'And our boys,' she continued. 'Their classmates are bullying them, saying their father is a failure, will no longer be a Marshal. Will we be able to afford to educate them? And how will your affair in Paris be paid for? Yes, I know all about your whore you keep in such splendour just down the road. Go to the Emperor, beg if you must. I am not prepared to be a forgotten country mouse! I will not be... be... *banished!*'

It was her mention of the boys that did it – as well, he had cooled down somewhat on the dusty journey from Madrid. No, he was indifferent to whether Aglaé was in fact banished from the social whirl she loved so much, but he could not condemn his sons too.

Swallowing his pride, feeling he had no option but to do as Aglaé asked, Ney had approached his fellow Marshal, Berthier, the only hand that could be guaranteed to open Napoleon's door. Berthier promised he would try to do what he could to help his old friend.

A few days later, Ney received word that an audience had been granted. Maybe the Emperor had not forgotten Friedland after all. So, here he was, attempting to keep his temper in check. Napoleon was well aware of his presence. Berthier had popped out to tell him so.

He tried to keep optimistic. His military career could surely not be over. He must have another chance to serve France or seek more glory.

The Emperor, according to Berthier, was in a very good mood, ebullient even. Almost his old Consular self at court, he had actually been known to dance. He danced about as well as he rode a horse. This new cheerfulness was, of course, entirely due to the birth of his heir, the little King of Rome, on 20th March, the safe arrival announced by a one-hundred-gun salute. All Paris knew it was a boy, as a girl would have only twenty-one. The master gunner obviously had a sense of humour as there was a pregnant pause after the first twenty-one shots. When the crowd heard the next one, they erupted, throwing their hats in the air, chanting, '*Vive l'Empereur!*'

Finally, the doors parted. Berthier beckoned and stepped aside. The sentries saluted in unison; the only indication that they knew exactly who it was that had been treated with such contempt.

Ney strode in, trying to look confident. He saluted, then stood to attention. The stifling heat was intensified even more by the customary huge fire burning in the Imperial grate. Napoleon was sitting on a throne-like chair, deep in thought, dreamily gazing downwards at the floor. He made no attempt to rise. However, he did appear quite affable, not stony-faced, when he did at last look up.

'Well, Ney, what will I do with you this time? I would not normally tolerate such insubordination. However, I have other intelligence from my spies in Spain concerning Marshal Masséna's ruthless and immoral behaviour, not to mention his failures. I have, as they say, put him out to grass. So, under the circumstances, I have decided to give you a new command.'

Ney just managed to stop himself from smiling. Glory beckoned once again.

'You will depart at once to my Boulogne camp,' Napoleon continued. 'The British may still invade; they are an unpredictable race. They still think they can win. Just because of their navy. All in good time, I intend to teach them a lesson. They have never faced the full might of my army.'

Boulogne? Preparing for invasion? It was as if the last five years hadn't happened. He had come full circle, ended up right back where he began.

'But, Sire...'

Napoleon waved his hand in dismissal, leaving Ney to turn on his heel, wondering if he would ever raise his sword in anger again. This certainly wouldn't placate Aglaé.

Aglaé was out – at the opera, apparently – when he returned home, still trying to come to terms with the Emperor's latest orders. He went to bed, feeling extremely hard done by. Was this the only role he was to be allowed to fulfil now? An inferior drill sergeant? A nothing command? How quickly a glorious reputation could be downgraded.

Out of habit, he fell asleep immediately. A soldier's instinct jerked him awake. Someone else was in the room. He lit the bedside candle. There, to his utter amazement, was Aglaé, shimmering in a sheer silk nightdress, her rose scented perfume filling the room. He tried to remember the last time she had come to him, rather than the other way round. It had been a long time; not since he had last been in Paris when his leave had been overshadowed by the pending divorce of Napoleon and Josephine. He had been a stranger to temptation in Spain. He could at least say he had been faithful to her there.

It was the missionary position; well, with his wife, it always was. They did stay curled up afterwards, again unusual. He slept. She slept.

It was Aglaé who spoke first in the morning.

'I heard where the Emperor has ordered you to go. That dreadful backwater, Boulogne. I never want to set foot there again. Last night's activities were only because I desperately want a daughter.'

She left the room.

Ney lay there in miserable silence, his whole life at its lowest ebb.

CHAPTER 25

Bruce realised, once the wailing from the nearby minaret started, that there was no point in ringing for some more hot coffee. The house servants would be kneeling on their silly little prayer mats. He sat, disconsolate. Hamah was the pits. He knew his mood was daily becoming more and more lethargic and depressed but could see no way out of it.

Flies swarmed round the remains of his breakfast honey cake. He was smoking his lucky meerschaum pipe, which had somehow survived since Stockholm, on the veranda of the rather large, thatched house Hester had forced him to take. Although the rent was exorbitant, no doubt grossly inflated for a European.

'We must keep up appearances for these Arab gentlemen,' she had stated, though Bruce knew there was only one Arab gentleman she wanted to impress – her new acquaintance, the overly wealthy Emir Bashir. An Arabian chief, with crafty eyes and a very long beard.

Yesterday, three horses had arrived accompanied by several grooms, presents from the Emir. Two were magnificent, for the Lady, and the other not so, for the gentleman. *Point taken*, Bruce thought. Travelling with Hester had become a nightmare. Where had the witty, loveable Hester he had met in Gibraltar gone? Lost somewhere in the desert.

Not so long ago, their life together had seemed idyllic. They had voyaged on Sligo's magnificent yacht from Gibraltar to Malta and on to Piraeus harbour, nearest port to Athens. The plan was a Tour of the East – the Greek Islands, then Constantinople, both safely open to British travellers as Bonaparte held no sway east of Sicily. ('Hurrah for His Majesty's Navy,' Hester had murmured sardonically.) The sex with Hester had been extraordinary, especially after he'd taught her what pleased them both. It was all new, exciting, adventurous. Far from Bonaparte, leaving the thunder of cannon, every thought of war, behind.

The only fly in the ointment was the quasi-chaperone, Hester's English physician, Doctor Meryon – though 'chaperone' was a joke; he had frequented the Maltese brothels as enthusiastically as any sailor on leave. Bruce disliked him intensely and the feeling was entirely mutual. Meryon was jealous of his relationship with Hester, not improved by the fact Hester treated Meryon like a rather lowly servant.

As they sailed close to the Piraeus harbour entrance, Hester suddenly shrieked. Standing on the rocks above the seawall stood a completely naked man. Bruce was not sure whether the shriek was because he was naked or because he was clearly about to dive from what looked an insane height.

The man sure enough dived, re-emerged from the

foam a few seconds later, and swam effortlessly towards the yacht, pulling himself forwards with powerful strokes.

'Ahoy there!'

The accent was clearly English and well educated, sufficient for him to be hauled on deck by one of the sailors and hastily covered with a robe.

'Well, isn't this just a thing?' he remarked cheerfully, as he belted the robe around his waist. He took his time doing so, and did not seem remotely put out that one of the onlookers was a woman.

Even Bruce, whose interest in naked men was non-existent, had to admit the fellow was good-looking. The robe that clung to his damp figure outlined a sleek, well-muscled body. The sudden shock of a twisted club foot poking from below the robe's hem, was like a jarring imperfection on a statue, deliberately introduced by the sculptor. His dark hair was plastered by the water to his scalp but was already regaining its natural curls. His grin was at once friendly and mischievous – you could not help liking him.

It was Sligo who recognised him, slapped him vigorously on the back.

'Byron, you old devil! Haven't seen you since that cricket match.' A quick glance back at the others: 'Eton-Harrow, which of course the Etonians won.'

Back to Byron: 'What a coincidence! Meet my friends. Join the party.'

They had all heard of the infamous aristocratic poet who didn't give a fig for convention or what society thought. Reputedly the most handsome man in England.

Though Bruce didn't agree: *wait until I get back to London.* Even so, Bruce was delighted; he was getting rather tired of Sligo's company, all that talk of antiquities. The opinion he had given to Crabb Robinson of Byron's poetry, back in Corunna, had been quite genuine, but Byron himself, it turned out, was something else.

Soon after that, the whole adventure started to sour.

Once in Athens, they couldn't stay with Byron. He was living in a monastery.

'Marvellous,' he said with a wink, 'all those altar boys.' But they still saw him every day. He was amusing company.

Though, not everyone found him so. After a few days, Sligo had told Bruce, with a gesture of distaste, that Byron had made advances to him.

'Didn't even try that at Eton. Must do that at Harrow,' he said. 'Think I'm off home, though. Can't be trusted.'

So, Bruce really should not have been surprised when Byron offered to introduce him to the opium pipe in an Athenian bar. Sligo was gone, Hester had found yet another ruin to go and gape at, and – damn him! – Byron really was excellent, charming company. One thing led to another. It turned out that, while Bruce's interest in other men was previously non-existent, his drug fuelled curiosity won.

He awoke the next morning in a flush of mortification, head and other parts still throbbing. The mortification only increased as every new memory found its way through the opium fumes lingering in his brain. It had not been in the least enjoyable. Then, to his absolute horror, as he performed his morning ablutions, he found he was bleeding from his rear end. There was nothing for it but to take the problem to the despised Doctor Meryon.

'Not the first case I have seen, probably not the last.' There was a cool glint in the man's eye as he delivered his diagnosis, and Bruce could only hope he would not mention the problem in his letters home. Everyone in London would know about the outcome of the Battle for Bruce's Arse.

'It will clear up in a day or two if you do not repeat the same event too often. Next time, you might want to consider the liberal application of olive oil.'

Perhaps he thought Byron had removed a rival for Hester's affections, Bruce said to himself bitterly, as he took his leave, quite certain that it was an activity he would never try again. He would stick to women.

The same morning, when he was feeling so sore, a packet of letters turned up. The usual one from his father that in no way mentioned an end or even a reduction to his allowance, which remained a necessity for Bruce. What with Hester and her expensive travel aspirations to pay for. He did remind Bruce that he needed to be careful as any whiff of scandal could ruin his chances of a future political career. It was pretty obvious that Father did not know the couple's true relationship. A relief: things between Bruce and Hester could continue just as they were.

Then, the very next day, two more letters were delivered. Post was certainly haphazard. One from Father composed several months after the previous one. His tone had become stern, angry even. Some people in London, apparently, had heard that young Michael Bruce was sharing a bed with Lady Hester Stanhope, who looked more like his maiden aunt. Such tittle-tattle could ruin them both. Their supposed affair was the talk of the town. These revelations had been the contents of a poison pen letter – Bruce could only guess that its author was the snake in the grass, Doctor Meryon.

Bruce immediately wrote back, denying all this, insisting he was only interested in Hester's admirable qualities, so rare in a woman: wit, scholarship, perfect travelling companion, and so on. At the back of his mind was always the thought of Father's cash.

The other letter, though, most amusing really, was from Hester's brother, James Stanhope. When he showed it to Hester, she shouted with laughter. James had heard the same gossip. He was horrified, demanding Bruce return to London to fight a duel over the matter of Hester's honour. Should Hester be carrying a bastard baby, it would be to the death.

'On his high horse yet again,' Hester exclaimed, wiping tears from her eyes.

Since Sligo had departed in haste on board his yacht, they had to hire a local caique to continue their journey. To Constantinople, and onwards.

From Constantinople, on the crossing to Alexandria, a Mediterranean storm blew up. Terrifying. Waves taller than the mast raged out of the darkness towards them and dashed them against the north African coast. Everything was lost in the shipwreck apart from Hester's reticule with – thank God – the irreplaceable letters of credit, his precious meerschaum pipe, gold, and, inexplicably, Sir John Moore's blood-stained glove.

Once ashore, the only local clothes available that fitted Hester's tall figure were male. Pantaloons, richly embroidered in gold, silk shirt with a smart striped waistcoat. A sash, into which went a sabre and a pair of pistols, which she did know how to use; in fact, she was probably more proficient than Bruce. Topped off with an embroidered turban worn at a jaunty angle. She professed the outfit to be so very comfortable that it was the last time she ever wore anything else. No more dresses. No more corsets. Bruce, and indeed every other man, especially the important local Arabs she encountered afterwards, were struck by how this unconventional attire really suited her.

Of course, she rode astride everywhere. Unheard of for a woman.

And perhaps that was when the rot set in.

Bruce had always prided himself that his ability to fly in the face of convention was a virtue. After all, he had set out on his travels rather than become a barrister. His experience with Byron, and now travelling with a so unfeminine woman, had demonstrated what he preferred. To be unconventional; while everyone else should fit into the roles he expected them to play. Adjusting to unconventional companions had become more than a little tedious.

Onwards to Cairo, where Bruce was unimpressed

by the Pyramids; as indeed he had been unimpressed by the Acropolis in Athens – maybe the result of a surfeit of lectures from Sligo.

He was finding the endless travelling beginning to pale. The inevitable sand, the shit, the flies, the mosquitoes, the bedbugs. Huge rats. Stifling days, freezing nights. Bandits. The very real fear of the plague. No decent proper food: he dreamt of French sauces, steak and kidney pie. No decent wine. He missed the society of his friends. Even missed his mother. The impossibility of finding a decent bed to play in; Hester grumbled if she was the least bit uncomfortable. And, if he was truthful, he really didn't fancy her anymore, even without the men's clothes.

His mood must have rubbed off on her. It began with criticisms and a certain froideur, but soon she did nothing but complain, as if everything unpleasant was his fault, and treated him with absolute disdain.

After many further dismal miles, staying in dismal accommodation, including sometimes in rickety tents, they had landed up in the Levant, Hamah. Not really a town, more a collection of buildings of tobacco-coloured mud bricks apparently dropped at random into the desert, which could have been anywhere in this godforsaken country.

Here, an incandescent Hester discovered that throughout almost the whole Oriental journey, Meryon had been stealing local artefacts and selling them to fellow travelling Europeans. It wasn't just the deception; he had violated her deepest belief that anything ancient was sacrosanct and should be left where it belonged.

His excuse was that Hester's payments for his medical expertise were simply not enough; he had a family to keep, back home in Brighton. Bruce thought at long last that the doctor would be sent home. He couldn't wait for Hestor to send him packing.

But far from it. Meryon, in the course of his dealings, had traded with one of Emir Bashir's eunuchs. Word had spread of this extraordinary English lady, gorgeously dressed as an Arabian man. Bashir had invited her and Bruce to dine. The Emir was captivated, Hester entranced. Meryon, the author of their new acquaintanceship, just received a sharp scolding and was allowed to stay.

Despite the wind-blown gritty sand, Bruce was still sitting on the veranda. A servant with a packet of letters disturbed his thoughts. One had his father's familiar handwriting and seal. He peeled it off, duly braced for yet another telling off. Paternal remonstrations no longer held any fear for him. He could handle them. After all, how worse could things be?

Well, as it turned out…

His bank was failing, Father had written. There would be no further letters of credit. No more cash of any sort. Bruce was to come home immediately. He was no longer prepared, or indeed able, to fund his son's extravagant travels.

Bruce read the letter again in disbelief. All his life, he

had never had to worry about money; it had always been there. Whatever the expenses, Father had ultimately paid.

His thoughts whirled, as the threatened cloud withdrew slightly to reveal a silver lining. Was this the excuse he had almost been praying for? There was no doubt he would be forced to do as Father demanded, go back to London.

In which case, he would have to finish with Hester. He could offer to marry her, he supposed. Heaven forfend. He wasn't *that* honourable. And, in any event, he certainly couldn't afford to keep her now; *she* wouldn't change her lifestyle the least jot.

Also, he was pretty certain she would not want ever to return to London. Back to the straitened circumstances of an impoverished unconventional woman. Her reputation would precede her. No social doors would be open. She would be shunned by the *Ton*.

And she enjoyed the Orient, revelled in it, even if he no longer did.

He went to his desk, pulled out the current letter of credit. Was there enough left to pay for his journey home? Yes, it did seem so, but not enough to give Hester another penny.

He knocked on her bedroom door and walked in cautiously, Father's letter in his hand. She was still abed, though she looked up as he approached.

She has certainly started to show her age, he thought critically: red prickly heat on her exposed flesh, unattractive sunburnt face. Her hair: could she be going bald?

He presented the letter to her in silence. She gave him

an odd glance, put her spectacles on her nose – which really did make her look like a maiden aunt – and plucked the paper from his hand.

'Well, this is not good news for you, Michael,' she said at last. 'You will have to high-tail it back to Father before he cuts the purse strings completely. You may even be forced to earn a penny or two yourself. Or, of course, you could marry a rich heiress. I will remain here, no question.'

Bruce looked at her in amazement. He had expected a completely different reaction. It wasn't as if he wanted to persuade her to return with him, but he thought he should at least point certain things out to her.

'Aren't you worried about yourself? How are you going to live out here? I know it is nothing like as expensive as Europe, but you will need substantial income to support you and the servants. Let alone feed those three Arab horses.'

Hester stretched, lay back on her pillows. Smiled. 'No need to be at all anxious, dearest Michael. I already have new arrangements in mind. The Emir has made certain suggestions to me; this news has hastened my decision. I will be moving into his palace, but not, I assure you, into his harem. He has christened me "the Queen of the Arabs".'

Bruce fled from the room, chagrined.

He told himself he was at least used to moving on; he would call the servants and start to pack. He had never before been given the heave-ho by any woman. *He always did the dumping.*

But it had happened, and he would have to dwell on it many times in the weeks to come.

Meanwhile, what route to take home? He couldn't return the way they'd come. Spain was now a fighting inferno, Malta rife with plague. War was coming again. He had heard from another European traveller that Bonaparte was threatening Russia. The only safe passage was possibly through Italy, but extreme care would be necessary. He would have to pretend to be French. Fortuitously, his accent was good enough.

But where exactly was Bonaparte? Would he spoil the party as he had so often before? Never mind, there would be plenty of opportunity to enter new bedrooms en route. He needed to experience a much younger woman again. Once more, the ladies of Europe beckoned.

CHAPTER 26

CONSTANTINOPLE

JULY 6TH 1812

Wilson stood, with a delicious minty drink in his hand, on the balcony of his room on the top floor of the British Embassy, overlooking the Bosphorus, high enough to be above the putrid streets. The minarets of St. Sophia and the Blue Mosque spiked upwards against the narrow bustling strait. There was a cooling breeze now. It had been hot, even he had to admit, almost as hot as Spain, when he had ventured into the bazaar earlier on. He had dismissed the Janissaries detailed to shadow him; he felt so safe, they were unnecessary. After so long at sea, he couldn't help noticing the women who swished by, frustratingly wearing yashmaks, although he convinced himself he could tell the pretty ones anyway.

No Englishman ever went out in the midday sun, let alone unescorted, the new British Ambassador, Liston, told him forcefully on his return. Also, there was the constant fear of contracting the plague. Liston was terrified of the plague. Wilson started to list in his head all the things that were more likely to finish a man on active campaign – the enemy's shot, the enemy's sword, thirst, hunger, the cold, the vileness of the air in some countries – but decided this was not the time or place.

Sir Robert Liston had travelled out with him from

England. He was a meek and mild old-fashioned sort of diplomat, of about sixty, absolutely determined to keep his slate clean before his imminent retirement. He was clearly anxious to keep Wilson close at hand in Turkey; he had been horrified to realise who Wilson was, when they first met at the London dockside. Details of Wilson's exploits had preceded him.

Wilson had been languishing in London since he arrived back from Lisbon. Still smarting from the fact he had not been honoured with an English knighthood. They said this was because he had served as a Portuguese officer, not an English one. He suspected this would have been overlooked had he gone to Eton instead of Winchester. After all, he had nearly defeated Marshal Ney at Banos. He would have taken Madrid if Wellington had been less of a scaredy-cat.

While he had been kicking his heels – and in no doubt that this was the right time to publish, hoping to further his chances of serving again in Eastern Europe – he had written a book on the modern Russian Army, full of admiration. Now, that was a patriotic army with heart, an army with gumption.

To make certain the right people read it, he dedicated it to his friend, the Duke of York, the Prince Regent's brother, and Chief of the Army. He'd sent a copy to the Czar. Just to remind him of their previous friendship.

But how could the British government have forgotten Russia was not the only country in Eastern Europe, where he could claim to know all the leading men? Turkey was the other. The Sultan *had* made him a knight there, too, after his exploits in Egypt.

He had frequently bent the ear of Lord Wellesley, Wellington's elder brother, at Brooks's, telling him he was possibly the best-placed Englishman to patch up the never-ending quarrel between Russia and Turkey.

A treaty between them would mean Russia's southern border would be secure and the Czar, if needs be, could concentrate on advancing against the French. The alliance of Tilsit was becoming strained to breaking point. The Polish issue was still a running sore between the former allies. The Ogre had managed to alienate the Czar by marrying an Austrian, not a Russian, princess; even though a Romanov marrying an over-promoted, low-born Corsican like Bonaparte was unthinkable in St. Petersburg.

Wellesley promised an appointment. Unfortunately, he was the laziest Foreign Secretary ever, and there were many diplomatic delays. The government was waiting to see what Napoleon was planning. Eventually, on 6th April, having been promoted to Brigadier-General, Wilson did set sail, together with the endlessly criticising Liston and the ever-faithful Charles.

Whatever Liston may have planned, Wilson had no intention of remaining quietly at the British Embassy as military attaché. His aim all along was to take part in what he saw as the inevitable struggle between Russia and Bonaparte.

Two years ago, the Czar had pulled out of the so-called Continental System, Napoleon's blockade of British ports and the embargo on trading with Britain he imposed on his allies. It was costing Russia too much money. The value of the rouble had plummeted since Tilsit. Napoleon wanted to forcibly remind the Czar of his treaty obligations. The rumours were that both the Czar and Bonaparte were assembling vast armies that would converge on the border between Russia and Prussia.

Wilson could predict a dramatic turn of events, a new war, where he would be in the thick of it. But first he had to see what he could do in Constantinople. Some sort of treaty had already been drawn up by the Turks, but not ratified. Wilson feared the French would press the Turks for better terms than the Russians were prepared to give. Then he discovered the Sultan was in his summer camp, some two hundred miles north in the Balkans.

A passport was required before he could journey on, and he had to wait for this. The Sultan's son and heir had just died, so all public business had been suspended. No passport could be signed. He regarded this as most unreasonable, seeing that at least four of the Sultan's other wives were pregnant; the late prince would shortly be replaced.

Meanwhile, he wasted no time before entering the local social society – parties, banquets, soirées. All stag. Teetotal, but opium offered on every occasion. No balls: no foreign gentleman was allowed even a glimpse of palace ladies. He took care to wear his Turkish decorations and carry his fine Turkish sword, presented to him in Egypt, leaving his Austrian medal with Charles. Liston started to avoid him at such functions. He made no secret of the fact he was jealous that Wilson had much more influence on the local powers that be.

Wilson was, however, getting more and more frustrated and bored. Then, as usual, Charles came up with a diverting idea. He had made friends at a coffee house with one of the Grand Vizier's eunuchs, who had been anxious to practise his French. He had introduced him to Wilson. Apparently, the eunuch could be bribed to smuggle him into the bathhouse of the Sultan's harem. He was curious. What a tale to tell. Even to his wife Jemima. He could describe to her what life was like for the imprisoned ladies.

The bathhouse was magnificent, an enormous mosaic lined pool with rose-tinted marble floor. Opulent sofas piled with cushions and pillows. While he was hiding behind a curtain, which no doubt had been used many times before for the same purpose, about forty of the Sultan's most alluring wives appeared, whispering and giggling. They started to undress. Entering the steaming water in the nude, splashing and shrieking. Despite Wilson feeling very sorry for them, their way of life, chosen for them without consent by their families as it was the highest honour, cloistered like nuns, he found himself titillated. Then they started touching each other in a highly sexual fashion, lying in twos and threes on the sofas. Wilson had never seen such a blatant show of lesbianism. He was disgusted and hurriedly left his hiding place through a secret door.

Later on that evening, much to his surprise, he was invited by Liston and other members of the Embassy to a local bar. Apparently, Liston liked his liquor, though alcohol was not allowed at the Embassy in case it offended the Muslim Sultan. Ladies appeared, fully covered by black robes. As the men plied them with alcohol, as well as drinking plenty themselves, they slowly undressed to show gauzy floating garments, belly dancing. Jewels flashed in navels. Evidently, their favours could be purchased. Wilson, suddenly overcome with thoughts of Jemima, left once more in haste. Still, it did show Liston in a different light. Not quite so pi after all.

In desperation, after a few more days had passed, tired of the slothful bureaucracy, he took himself to the palace, flashed his Turkish medal and came back to the Embassy with two passports, one for him, one for Charles. That very evening came the momentous news that Bonaparte's Grand Armée was concentrating at the River Niemen, the boundary between Prussia and Russia, apparently the largest army the world had ever seen. This was, without doubt, war. *Excellent!*

He would have to negotiate a new treaty urgently now, so his friend the Czar had one less worry. If they hurried, he and Charles could ride to the Sultan's camp, some two hundred miles towards Moscow; it should only take less than four days. Then he fully intended to find the Russian HQ, wherever that might be, so that his undoubted talents for winning could be fully put to use. Maybe link up with his friends from Eylau. Even Platov?

At last, he could scent battle and glory again.

CHAPTER 27

Ney's quartermaster had really done them proud this time. The horses were in luck as well as the officers. Not only was the absent Polish nobleman's mansion quite splendid, but so were the stables. The Count had previously been a leading national influence on horse flesh.

Ney and Fezensac strode slowly across the wide driveway towards the spacious yard. It was more than good to see Fezensac again. Last time, a week or so ago, had been in that village inn in Prussian Gumbinnen, a sort of unofficial officers' mess. They had shared a long overdue drink, elated by the thought they would be serving France again together.

Fezensac had been sent by Berthier – he was his senior aide-de-camp – to check on the state of III Corps, whether they were prepared; as he said jokingly, a rather unnecessary journey, though one he had accepted with alacrity. The Corps forty-four thousand men were spread out in camps and villages throughout the surrounding countryside, every man Ney's, primed and eager for the command to travel east. The delicious smell of baking hung in the air; many baguettes cooking in the ovens, ready to be stuffed in knapsacks.

As they passed, the off-duty soldiers saluted, chatted in German.

'Those Ruskies will run,' Ney overheard. 'They're cowards; they won't attack. We will just chase them and, when we catch them, they will know how the Emperor's army fights, to win.'

The Emperor had given him command of the newly formed III Corps, infantry, cavalry and artillery. Mostly German, which suited Ney, as German was his first language from childhood. There were French veterans too, mostly NCOs, hastily marched from Spain, and men from Portugal, the Balkans and Holland. Ney recognised some of their grizzled, sunburnt faces. The atmosphere was one of seething anticipation. Everyone knew they were soon to advance into Russia. They would scatter the Czar's army close to the border and bring Russia back to the Emperor's way of thinking, a stern reminder of what treaty obligations really mean. Everyone was getting prepared, checking their kit, polishing boots, bayonets and swords, repairing uniforms, assembling backpacks, laughing in good humour. Victory would be easy. Victory was coming.

The tiny figure of Sergeant Bauget, Concorde's trusted groom, was waiting by a spacious loosebox, a few carrots in his hand. He had ridden Concorde from Madrid to Boulogne, then here, nearly into Russia. When he saw Ney, the black horse whickered. Ney stroked his nose and fed him the treat.

Riding Concorde had given Ney his only pleasurable time

in Boulogne, during the long, lonely, bleak winter he had been stationed there. There had been none of the industry, the bustle and patriotic surge of the preparation to invade England as last time he was there in 1806. The force under his command was tiny. Morale was at rock bottom. No one really believed they were ever going to hop over the Channel to take Dover, then London. For one thing, all the specially constructed shallow-bottomed troop carriers were rotting, certainly no longer seaworthy. And the British would not be coming this way either; their limited army was tied up in Spain.

Nothing happened. He wrote reports monthly to the Emperor that never received a reply. Obviously, he was still in disgrace. Aglaé had already told him she would sooner be dead than at Boulogne, she loathed it so much. If she had visited anyway, she would have hated his new shabby, chilly billet even more than the château by the sea, where he had lodged last time. They were to have a baby, though.

No replies from his letters to Ida. He had been trying to put her out of his mind – impossible – or seriously considering whether to cut off her not inconsiderable allowance to get her attention. She would not be able to live in such style without it.

He spent Christmas alone.

Then, late one afternoon in early March, when he was beginning to wonder if he had been completely forgotten by the world, a fine coach pulled into the forecourt. He thought at first it would be bad news from the pregnant, husband-shunning Aglaé. Then he looked closer. He had paid for that coach. He thought his eyes were deceiving him as he watched a lady being helped down. It really was Ida, wearing a dress for a change. Ida… Sex. His heart galloped, rather like a callow youth.

She had been with him three days, and nights. It was early evening. They were tightly locked on the lumpy mattress. He was teasing her, bringing her almost to climax then pulling away. Never fully intent – a soldier could not afford to be – he thought he heard a pounding of hooves outside.

He put it out of his mind – turned his attentions back to her- until he heard the footsteps on the creaky stairs. She heard them too. He felt the immediate tension in her body.

Shortly, there was a discreet knock on the door. Their eyes met, and she nodded, resigned. She knew where even she stood in the scheme of things.

It was his steward with a document pouch. He dismissed the man, closed the door, tore it open. Read it.

Read it again.

She rolled on to her front and pouted up at him, chin resting on her hands.

'Well?'

Slowly, he smiled.

'It seems, *ma chérie*, history really does repeat itself, or maybe you are my good luck charm. It is war again. Silence has been the only response from the Czar. He must be prepared to take a stand, but when or where? Russia is huge, his serf army huge.

'I am back in the Emperor's good books, apparently. He has seen fit to give me another command. III Corps, newly created. He is planning to assemble an enormous number of men. Not only French but Prussian, Austrian, all his allies. Rallying place on the Prussian-Russian border, the Niemen river.'

Ida smiled back and gave him a squeeze. 'That is the best news for you, and for us. But it would happen just as we are together and, I must say, enjoying ourselves. It is only you who can take me to such heights.'

Ney raised his eyebrows. 'I will try to believe that.'

He paused, then went on. 'The men I will be leading, though, are not like last time we went east. Last time we were riding high. Experienced, trained, French troops. And last time we were not supposed to end up in the fucking freezing winter. I just hope this new campaign settles the whole Polish question. Despite what the Czar might think, Poland is France now. We proved that at Friedland.'

'You did prove it all at Friedland, I remember how hard you were afterwards.'

'You know I so want to be part of winning again, I want to lead the charge, but... Napoleon assumes that the Russians will play fair, stay close by their border to take a thrashing. Come to the table to negotiate like last time at Tilsit. I just can't see it. You remember Eylau...'

'How could I forget. I came a long way to fuck you in a woodshed.'

'You,' Ney continued, speaking to her if she were a junior officer, 'are staying in Paris, ready for me when I get back. Advancing east of Tilsit, I don't like it. And, unlike the Emperor, I do not hold the Russian soldiers in contempt. They fight like devils, religious freaks, adore their Czar.'

'Like I do,' Ida said, curling his chest hair in her fingers.

'It's an order, Ida. Stay in Paris. I really mean it. This will all be over in a month or so, or it will get hellishly bogged down, just like last time we campaigned in Prussia.'

'No enticing adventures for me then, no outdoor fucking.' She pouted.

Ney lay back and stared at the ceiling. She gently caressed his chest with her palm. Pinched his nipple. Give him a minute and he'd be ready for more. It wasn't her hand now on his chest but her lips, kissing his navel, swirling her tongue. Sliding downwards. He really ought to get some sleep, but... Tomorrow they would have to leave in her carriage, hasten to Paris; he would take command of III Corps.

He couldn't wait to see the back of Boulogne.

Fezensac's inspection of III Corps could only be described as cursory. He stayed the night afterwards, with Ney, having a riotous evening. Both enjoying each other's company as only old friends can. He rode off early the next morning to report to Berthier.

'See you soon.' He saluted, then raised his hand triumphantly in the air.

Ney smiled, saluted in return. He tried to ignore his misgivings. There was much to do. His Corps must be ready to march tomorrow; it could turn into a logistical nightmare. Watching all the preparations, his heart, it had to be said, swelled with pride. The Emperor had forgiven him, called on his best man, his most loyal man, Marshal Ney of Friedland. He felt as he once had on that day in Notre-Dame, that day when the Emperor promised the world. The road to glory lay ahead once again. Glory beckoned.

FIN

ACKNOWLEDGEMENTS

It is always a surprise to me to read pages and pages of acknowledgements at the end of novels. Non-fiction I can understand! I have only five!

Ashley Stokes. My supreme editor. His patience when he had to help me unravel the mysteries of Track Changes and other computer glitches. (I was, to be honest, not very computer savvy when I started writing this). His passion for correct historical facts, shared by me. (He does have an Oxford degree in History.) And his way with words. I have spent many happy hours with him, deep in the Napoleonic era. As they say, *Glory Beckons* would not have reached the bookshelves without him.

Ben Jeapes. Not just a Beta reader, but he's very good at that! He also copy read the manuscript for the umpteenth time. His input has been insightful, often humorous. At his suggestion, my original overlong novel became two. *Glory Beckons* and *Fleeting Glory*. Another person to urge me on when the ultimate goal of publishing my first book seemed far out of reach.

Anne-Marie Hoppitt. My invaluable young friend who proofread the original manuscript, pointed out many mistakes and put forward fresh ideas. A favourite person, passionate about history.

Major General Julian Thompson. He has been generous enough to endorse *Glory Beckons*. A distinguished military historian and a very old friend, I discussed my rather vague ideas for this book with him many years ago. I have to say his view on Marshal Ney is not as kind as mine. But I will leave it to my readers to decide the calibre of the man!

Troubador. My so-professional publisher. Nothing has been too much trouble. From the original contact, through the cover design, to the actual production, to the finished book.

Thank you all.

HISTORICAL NOTES

Ferdinand de Lesseps

The toddler stuck in snow with his family and rescued by Wilson on his way to Eylau. de Lesseps grew up to develop the Suez Canal, opened to shipping 1869. He was also in charge of transporting the Statue of Liberty, a gift from the French people to the Americans, to New York in 1884.

Lady Hester Stanhope

She became somewhat of a legend in Arabia. She never returned to London, although her letters and memoirs made her famous there as an explorer and archaeologist. Dr. Meryon did stay with her for some time after Bruce left, before retiring to be with his family in Brighton. She died penniless in 1839 near Sidon, in what is now Lebanon. Clutching, it was reported, a single blood-stained glove.

The story continues in

Fleeting Glory

To be published March 2026

Napoleon's Empire is doomed from the moment his army crosses the Niemen, but it takes a long time to die. Between the triumphant advance into Russia and the final decisive victory of Waterloo, alliances continue to form and reform, countries continue to be devastated and hundreds of thousands of men continue to die. Even peace brings its own challenges. Like a dead wasp, Napoleon can still sting.

One thing above all that has not changed is Bonaparte's ability to mess up Bruce's life. Meanwhile, what place is there for a man like Wilson in the new Europe? And will Ney ever be able to separate himself from his Imperial master, or will his loyalty drag him down to his doom?

— YOUR —
RETIREMENT

—YOUR—
RETIREMENT

HOW TO MAKE THE MOST OF IT

Seventh Edition

ROSEMARY BROWN

**KOGAN
PAGE**

First edition 1995
Second edition 1996
Third edition 1997
Fourth edition 1998
Fifth edition 1999
Sixth edition 2000
Seventh edition 2001

Copyright © by Enterprise Dynamics Ltd 1995, 1996, 1997, 1998, 1999, 2000, 2001

Kogan Page Ltd, 120 Pentonville Road, London N1 9JN

British Library Cataloguing in Publication Data
A CIP record for this book is available from the British Library.

ISBN 07494 3738 3

Typeset by Saxon Graphics Ltd, Derby
Printed and bound in Great Britain by Clays Ltd, St Ives plc.